SHERWOOD SMITH

Revenant
EVE

DAW BOOKS, INC.

DONALD A. WOLLHEIM, FOUNDER

375 Hudson Street, New York, NY 10014

ELIZABETH R. WOLLHEIM
SHEILA E. GILBERT
PUBLISHERS

http://www.dawbooks.com

First Printing, November 2012
1 2 3 4 5 6 7 8 9

DAW TRADEMARK REGISTERED
U.S. PAT. AND TM. OFF. AND FOREIGN COUNTRIES
—MARCA REGISTRADA
HECHO EN U.S.A.

PRINTED IN THE U.S.A.

To the friends of Dobrenica

ACKNOWLEDGMENTS

My thanks and gratitude to Koby Itzhak and to two persons who happen to have the same first name (Faye) for help with Jewish lore, to Gregory Feeley for the title, and to Rachel Manija Brown and Hallie O'Donovan for beta reading and support.

ONE

THE JOURNALIST POISED HER PENCIL and looked at me expectantly. "So, Mademoiselle Murray, how does it feel to know that in a month and a half you will become a princess?"

Like living at Disneyland, I wanted to say, but there was a fifty-fifty chance that my interviewer had never heard of it.

In so many ways, Dobrenica was still a century (sometimes more) behind modern times. Madam Waleska, who ran the inn where I'd stayed during my first two visits, had once insisted with genuine horror that I could not possibly be an American because I didn't spit on the floor. That particular rumor dated back to Mrs. Trollope's *Domestic Manners of the Americans*, written in 1832, but to the Dobreni it may as well have been posted on the Internet last week.

Not that you can access the Internet in Dobrenica. You can't. Cell phones don't work, either. Land lines work . . . most of the time.

So here was this question, put to me from Annika, an earnest young woman barely college-age, on assignment for the Dobreni newspaper. A weekly. Judging by her rigorously polite manners, I guessed that this was her first assignment. We sat in a little café in the center of town that was, judging from the architecture, about three hundred years old. Practically new, for Dobrenica.

The editor of the newspaper was probably being modern by sending a female to interview me. I wondered if Annika was the first, possibly the only, female on the staff. But then the newspaper itself had a spotty history, free speech being a relatively new concept. From the days of World War II until relatively recently, Dobrenica had been under German and then Soviet control.

For the Dobreni, the prospective return to monarchy was progress. To me—Los Angeles born and raised—it seemed weird.

And the idea of being a princess made me feel *really* weird.

"First of all, you can call me Kim. It's true my first name is Aurelia— I was named for my grandmother—but it will be relegated to official purposes only. I never use it. To answer your question, what does it feel like?" I practiced my princessy smile. My teeth felt cold, and I had a nasty feeling my smile looked as real as a three-dollar bill. "I've been so busy that I haven't had a chance to figure out how I feel," I said, wondering how diplomacy differed from outright lying. "This is what I can tell you: how wonderful it is to find myself in Dobrenica again, how beautiful everything is."

And I gushed on, praising everything from the royal palace (I was still trying to get my head around the fact that I would actually be living in one) to the historic sites (in Dobrenica, pretty much everything is a historic site), to the shops along St. Ladislas Street, the Rodeo Drive of Dobrenica.

The way Annika slowly relaxed gave me hope that even if my words were boring, they assured her that I was not going to chop her into bits and serve her for breakfast. For her, my imminent rank had historical gravitas, even if it felt like a fairy-tale to me.

When I ran out of things to burble about, Annika's dark gaze narrowed. She squared herself a little on her chair.

I glanced at her small pad of paper, on which she'd written down about five words of my diplomatic burble. *Here come the real questions.*

"There are so many conflicting rumors about how you found your way here from the United States," she said.

I'll bet there are. "I've heard a few."

She flashed me a tentative smile, then pressed her pencil to the paper.

"How did you meet the Statthalter?" Her tone was as neutral as her use of the technically correct title for my fiancé, Marius Alexander Ysvorod, shortly to be officially recognized as Crown Prince of Dobrenica.

He had been unofficially recognized since the bad old Soviet days. He was just a kid when he joined his father in running a kind of shadow government and black market social services. Toward the end of those days the Soviets no longer put much energy into thwarting them, and even permitted elections. When his father's health began to fail, Alec was voted Statthalter, a suitably unmonarchical-sounding title.

As the Soviets began to leave by degrees, the five traditional ruling families began to pick up their ancestral duties—and privileges. Especially the von Mecklundburgs, and in particular the Duchess and her son Tony, Alec's sometimes-friend, sometimes-rival.

"The Statthalter found me by accident," I said. "Or maybe it wasn't so accidental. I was in Vienna, at the Hofburg—the imperial palace. I saw what I thought was someone dressed in eighteenth century clothes, and followed her, but she turned out to be a ghost. Queen Sofia, in fact."

In any other part of the world, the mention of following ghosts would net you, at best, the kind of glance usually reserved for the bug you just discovered in your half-eaten salad. But here? She gave me a cautious nod, and said, "She was a Vasa from Sweden. Very famous in Dobrenica."

"Well, while I was following Queen Sofia's ghost, one of the Statthalter's people saw me and thought I was the Statthalter's fiancé, Ruli von Mecklundburg, who had gone missing." *Kidnapped by Tony, her own brother, in fact.* "So he told the Statthalter, who . . . realized I must be a relation and offered to take me to Dobrenica."

Okay, here I was really stretching things, because the truth is that Alec kidnapped me. And stuck me on a train to Dobrenica, thinking I was Ruli, who must be playing a devious game devised by Tony. Because Tony really likes games.

But I escaped. When Alec caught up with me, the truth hit us both equally hard: I wasn't Ruli, who turned out to be my second cousin in a family I had not known existed.

"I remember some thought she was you, or you were she." Annika's Dobreni had a Russian flavor that made me wonder if she came from one of villages on Devil's Mountain, deep in the heart of von Mecklundburg territory.

"Well, people mistook me for her," I said, not adding that it had been Alec's idea to take advantage of the resemblance, in order to force whoever was holding Ruli out into the open. I'd gone along with it, not because I cared squat for Dobreni politics (at that time) but because I was attracted to him. "It turned out that Ruli was up on Devil's Mountain all along. Duke Tony, er, he was Count Karl-Anton then, was having some trouble with a mercenary captain."

"A Captain Reithermann," Annika said, nodding. "Wanted throughout half of Europe."

Hired by Tony to facilitate his coup d'état. Reithermann also had a rap sheet a yard long in the States.

"The Devil's Mountain people believed that this Reithermann was trying to take over their mines," she said.

It was Tony's plan, I didn't say. *And he wasn't only trying to take over the mines but the entire country, with his mother's help.* I gave Annika that fake smile again. "Not just the mines," I said.

Annika leaned forward. "And so you and Duke Tony fought Reithermann's villains together, with swords? I always hoped *that* rumor was true." The way she said *Duke Tony* was very different from her carefully neutral, respectful mention of the Statthalter. Oh yes, I'd bet anything she came from Devil's Mountain. Tony was extremely popular with the Devil's Mountain people. The wilder he was, the more they seemed to like him.

"I did use my sword," I said slowly. Should I add that we'd been enemies at the time?

My relationship with Tony was complicated, but his plan hadn't worked. Alec had quietly and skillfully outmaneuvered him.

And Tony's own mother had double-crossed him.

So I said, "I used my sword, but at the last moment, before I could get away, I got shot in the shoulder."

"But then you left the country?" she asked.

"Yes. I returned to California before the Statthalter and Ruli got married as planned. It was to bring peace and maybe even the Blessing."

Like the mention of the ghost, the word *Blessing* caused a nod of comprehension. Not every Dobreni believes in ghosts, or magic, but they accept that many around them do. The Blessing is supposed to be magic on a country-wide scale, removing Dobrenica from the world for a time but always contingent on peace among its people. The ability to magically vanish into the magical realm called the Nasdrafus had not happened during the Soviets' hold on the country, some said because of the increased tension and animosities. Now, Dobrenica badly needed its leading families to get along.

She said, "There are some, like Duke Tony, who believe that the days of the Blessing are past. If it ever really happened."

"So much Dobreni history was destroyed during the twentieth century wars that it's hard to know for sure," I said. "But isn't peace something to aim for anyway? I don't just mean the country's leader marrying on September second and maybe creating this magic, which no one seems to think is needed anymore. I mean the kingdom, from the five leading families down to the humblest shepherd, living in peace with one another, whatever their personal beliefs. *That* idea is worth striving for, whether magic exists or not."

She nodded soberly. "I think everybody likes that idea. But whether the Nasdrafus really exists, *that* some are skeptical about."

I'd also been skeptical about the Nasdrafus, the magical realm, but my skepticism had been blasted by the discovery of ghosts, then of vampires, and then of the charms—magic—that kept vampires at bay.

She twirled her pencil. "Do you think the Blessing did not take place because the Statthalter was really in love with you, and Lady Ruli was angry because of it?"

I sighed. "She wasn't angry. She didn't want the marriage any more than he did, but they felt constrained largely for political reasons. It was pretty much in name only. You know, they were married barely three months before the roadside accident that took her away." Not *the accident that killed her*, because that would be a total lie. She hadn't even been in the car. Nor was I going to say *the accident that resulted in her being turned into a vampire*. The von Mecklundburg family didn't want that known.

Annika wrote fast. "The Statthalter was cleared of having driven her off the cliff, though it was his car. And everyone knows he was there."

"He was asleep in the back seat. Nobody likes to say anything, out of respect for the von Mecklundburgs, but the fault lay with an old family connection."

Annika surprised me with a knowing look. "Everyone on Devil's Mountain knows about Jerzy von Mecklundburg. He did not have a good reputation even in my grandmother's day. And so this accident brought you back to Dobrenica?"

Actually, it was Ruli's appearing to me after the accident that got me back to Dobrenica. Thinking she was a ghost, I'd come back to help her, stayed to help Alec, and here I was.

So I said, "Yes," because it was simpler.

After that, the questions were easy stuff: details about the wedding, from the decorations—made up mostly of roses from centuries-old gardens, bred for their vampire-warding properties—to the veil I'd wear, which had been hidden away by my grandmother's governess before the Germans rolled over the border in 1939.

The interview ended on a friendly note. I heaved a sigh of relief as I walked past the new opera house that had been the royal military school four centuries before. I cut across St. Ladislas Street and headed uphill toward Sobieski Square, beyond the Cathedral, whose great bell tower served as a navigational landmark.

It was mid-July. In Los Angeles, taking a stroll in summer's simmering heat and smog wasn't much fun, but here in Dobrenica's mountains the air was warm in the sun, yet cool in the shadows of the old buildings. Each morning I walked to the palace to see Alec, who quite properly bunked there, in order to oversee the reconstruction as well as to keep governmental things going.

Occasionally people waved at me, another thing I'd found difficult to get used to. I was instantly recognizable, and not because tall blondes are so unusual. It was my resemblance to Queen Sofia, whose portrait hung in the royal gallery. She'd brought most of my physical features to the Dsaret family when she'd married the king, and they'd been handed down to her descendants.

My crooked smile, though? The one that I shared with my mom and with Tony, that came from another relative entirely.

TWO

WAITING FOR ME at the triumphal arch was Tania Waleska, middle daughter of the innkeeper who'd been surprised at my disinclination to spit on floors. Tania was now my personal assistant. The idea of having a personal assistant still felt pretentious, but she was such a great help, I understood why people hired them.

"Sorry I'm late," I said. "I thought the interview would be three questions: my gown, the decorations, and where are we going for our honeymoon. She wanted more than that."

"Did they send Annika Kallas?" Tania asked.

"They did."

I should not have been surprised that Tania and Annika knew one another. "Good," she said. "Annika was two years ahead of me in school. She was so very fine a writer. I am glad they hired her. You know she's the first woman writer in Dobrenica to have a byline? Before, articles by women were anonymous."

Before meant in the days before World War II and then another fifty years of official Soviet suppression of the press. During that half a century there'd been some underground papers, but for reasons of safety nobody—regardless of gender—had a byline.

We stepped out from the shadow of the triumphal arch that commemorated some event in 1813. I figured it had to do with Napoleon's second push to the east, but every time I glanced up at it was a reminder that I really needed to dig into the specifics of Dobreni history. Not easy, since immediately following World War II, Stalin had ordered the occupiers to burn the libraries.

"I'm to tell you that your mother and the duke found something while exploring some of the older basements in the Eyrie," Tania said.

I thought of that enormous castle of Tony's, and wondered if they'd unearthed some Crusader-era armor. But no, Tony's family had first "modernized" the castle in the mid-seventeen hundreds. One would assume that, had there been any medieval relics, they would have been found at that point.

"It's a beautifully preserved car that, apparently, one of the German commanders had confiscated during the war. I'm to tell you that it is a Bugatti, and your mother now wants you to ride in it during the wedding procession, if—these are her words—'Milo insists on using the kingmobile.'"

My mom had shown up incognito during the dark days before we found out the truth about Ruli. A haute cuisine pastry-maker and chef, Mom had taken over the von Mecklundburgs' kitchen in order to scope things out.

You'd think that after they found out who she was, Tony's snob of a mother would despise my mom, especially as it turned out they shared the same father, though Mom's birth was not sanctioned by marriage.

Alec's doctor friend Natalie Miller had made one of her typical comments on the situation. "The Duchess von Mecklundburg can't play the snob, because Mom Murray doesn't care any more about being a bastard than she does about duchesses. You can only be snubbed if you're into snobbery, and your mom doesn't give a flying frick. Imperviousness is the best defense."

The amazing thing was that Mom and the Duchess actually got along, in a sort of armed-but-neutral way. The Duchess appreciated five-star French cuisine, and Mom had ruled their kitchen like a red-haired Napoleon. Mom and Tony had become good buddies, being a lot alike.

I laughed. "A Bugatti! It has to be gorgeous."

Tania said, "Their guess is that the commander put it up on blocks then boarded it up before they fled from the Russian advance. He must have hoped he could get back and recover it."

"The surprise is that the Russians never found it. They were pretty good at looting, from everything I've read."

"It was well hidden. The wall had been lightly plastered over, then lumber moved in front of it," Tania said as we walked into the central square facing the palace. "They'd been searching for the other end of one of the old secret passages."

"There are a million of those, I remember. Tania, it sounds like you haven't had any time for your crystal experiments. I know you said you'd help with the wedding stuff, but you don't have to run every errand. We can hire more people."

Tania's smile was brief but real. Tall and long-faced, Tania looked as studious and earnest as she was. I'd hired her to try to run some experiments with the crystals that seem to focus Vrajhus—that is, magic. I could sort of deal with the idea of Vrajhus as a mysterious (and dangerous) power source, but the word *magic* threw me.

Tania said, "I needed a break to think. No matter how careful I am, I still can't reliably reproduce effects. I'm beginning to understand the warnings of the old folks about how unreliable magic can be. As for the wedding, I like the preparations. Your mother makes me laugh—and then she always makes me lunch. Ah, such lunches," she said with a sigh of deep appreciation.

By then we'd crossed half the central square, with its gigantic, mostly obliterated hammer and sickle painted on the patterned brick. From long habit, Tania scuffed her foot as he walked over part of the hammer. The Dobreni had been silently rubbing it out with their feet for three generations.

On the left and right sides of the square stood the imposing buildings of government and finance, including the Council building, now nearly rebuilt after the fire that had gutted it during the vampire fight just after New Year's.

We headed for the main gate to the royal palace, where a cute Vigilzhi guy stood on duty. He saluted, crisp in his blue uniform with the red stripe down his trousers, the gold buttons on his tunic, and the twin falcons on the brass plate at the front of his helmet. The Vigilzhi are the police and army combined. And if Alec gets his way (which he will), women will soon be able to join. The first will be his distant cousin, Baroness Phaedra Danilov, a sharpshooter, a first-rate fencer, and an expert rider.

I gave the guard a grin and a wave, and as soon as we were out of earshot, I said, "You happen to know him? I'm trying to learn the names of the staff."

"Him? That is Chaim Avrameşçu, cousin to my friend Sara."

"Sara Avrameşçu—the rabbi's daughter?"

"Yes. Sara and I studied lens making together, but she went on to work with gems. She has a gift for restoration and faceting. I don't know the two guards at the sentry station."

"I'll find out," I promised, as we entered the main building.

The heavy, wet smell of plaster was evidence that the refurbishing of the royal suite—which hadn't been done for nearly a century—was proceeding as planned.

Tania lifted her hand in a friendly wave and peeled off on an errand of her own as I walked into Alec's outer office.

Alec was alone, as I pretty much showed up at the same time every day. When I walked in, there was that transformative smile that somehow made his eyes seem bluer. I still don't get how that works. He tossed down his fountain pen and came to meet me in the middle of the room for a good-morning kiss.

"How'd the interview go?" he finally asked.

"Not as bad as I dreaded. I didn't have to lie, except about Ruli. For the rest, I just sort of skimmed over the nastier stuff." We sat side by side on the edge of his desk, and I leaned into his warmth as I gave him a fast recap.

I was living in state with my mom at Ysvorod House until the wedding. Just us and the huge staff. It seemed pompous to have this large staff for two people, but (I told myself) that big staff was really there to maintain Alec's family house, not look after me or Mom. Especially as Mom was hardly ever there, spending most of her time with the von Mecklundburgs, who had become her cause. "I'm going to tame them," she said to me.

If anyone could, that would be my mom.

Anyway, my dad had gone back to Los Angeles to shut up our rattle-trap house in Santa Monica, store our cars, and all the other red tape of modern life. My parents had made no decision about moving to Dobrenica, but they did plan to stay for a while. Dad was expected to return by mid-August, so he would be in Dobrenica in plenty of time for the wedding, held on the traditional date for royal weddings: September second, St. Xanpia's Day.

"Heard anything from Paris?" I asked, my mind going from my parents to my grandmother. Gran was sixteen when she gave up being a royal princess in order to run off with the bad boy Count Armandros von Mecklundburg, months before World War II crashed over Europe. She'd ended up a single mom in Los Angeles for the rest of the century, until I went to Europe to search for her roots, and saw Queen Sofia's ghost.

Just after Easter, Gran quietly married Alec's dad Milo, who had been her official intended all those years ago. He'd carried a torch for her ever since.

Gran wasn't much for talking. I don't know if she fell in love with Milo—I can't tell you if "falling in love" means the same when you're nearly ninety and your spouse is even older—but there was no question she respected him, cared for him, and trusted him.

She regretted her past enough to have insisted on a private wedding, with just Alec, me, my folks, and her old governess as her matron of honor. Mina Hajyos was even older than Milo, though still sharp as a tack.

After that, Milo took Gran to Paris.

"Got a call early this morning," Alec answered, as he pulled me up against his side. "They're in Vienna now. Will start back in a few days."

"How is it going? Can you tell?" If anyone was more tight-lipped than my gran, it was Alec's dad Milo.

Alec flashed his smile. "If I am correctly decoding the little I've pried out of Milo, it seems to be going well. He mentioned something about laying ghosts." He played absently with my fingers, turning round and round the Ysvorod family diamond, which he'd had resized for me. I'd insisted he keep the Napoleonic era setting, which I loved for its having been made during a period of history I knew fairly well; he said the ring had been made for one of Queen Sofia's daughters, who married into the Ysvorods.

"That's got to be metaphorical ghosts," I said. "Gran has never seen any real ones."

"Neither has Milo. Metaphorical it is. I think they've investigated all the places your grandmother and Armandros went to. Not what I would have suggested for a wedding trip, but it seems to be the right thing for them."

"Good," I said, eyeing him. I was getting better at decoding his subtle signs. As you'd expect of someone who'd begun taking on governmental duties at age fifteen, Alec was as good as his father at keeping his emotions buttoned up. But I was working on that. "Anything wrong?"

"Nothing is wrong," he said with a quick, rueful smile. "Apologies for seeming distracted. You know how it is."

"Yep. You've got plates spinning, or fires to put out, or whatever you want to call a pack of ongoing hassles. So what now?"

"Kim, how serious was your offer to work?"

"I like work. What do you want me to do?"

"Be a princess and tour."

"That's not work, that's . . ."

"Play-acting?" He took my hands. "Are we going to have The Princess Conversation again? If it's needed, we'll take the time."

"Is there a hint of sarcasm there?" I asked, making a face. "Have I been whining too much?"

"One hundred percent sarcasm-free observation." He kissed me. "You are the only woman I know who was interested in me in spite of the baggage, and not because of it." On the word *baggage* he waved a hand, taking in the palace.

I thought of Cerisette von Mecklundburg, who'd been Ruli's secret rival and my overt one, and not because she loved Alec. She'd been so in love with the idea of herself as a princess that she'd been willing to endure Alec's sense of responsibility if she couldn't get a crown any other way.

I kissed him back. "I appreciate your accepting my ambivalence about the princess issue. But I can't help feeling that it's another Thing for you to deal with, and your life is an endless juggling of Things. So let's skip that discussion and move on. I get it that royal figures are a fiction agreed on by everybody, not just the guys at the top. That we're giving up a certain amount of privacy in living public lives, etcetera. But tours? How's that work?"

"How about I put it another way, then?" he said. "I want you to spy." He gave me a bland smile.

"Spy? On who? When, and where? I don't want to appear ungrateful for my first official offer of work, but you know I'm not very good at lurking."

"Don't want you to lurk. I am hoping you will smile, and look around, encourage people to talk, and listen to them. Especially if you— as a newly minted princess—request a tour of the mines."

"Okay, still trying not to sound like I'm arguing, but aren't you better qualified for mining inspection than I am?"

Alec said, "If I go up there, I will get the official tour. That means everyone will buzz around cleaning things up and decorating, and they will line the streets and salute. I'll get careful speeches. But if you go up there as the new, friendly princess—look around admiringly, get to know people—you will hear all the anecdotes that they keep from me and my father. And among those, you will probably catch references to the mines that I am not supposed to know about."

"So you aren't joking. You really do want me to spy?" I got up from the desk and turned so we stood face to face. He was my perfect guy, from his gorgeous dark hair to his fine-boned face and the body he kept in shape by fencing with the Vigilzhi guards several times a week. But: "*Spying?*"

"Yes." He grinned. "The only reason why those mines are secret is to avoid paying taxes. Understandable, while we were under the control of the Soviets, but now my father thinks it is time for everyone to be contributing equally, just as they have equal shares in the benefits that the taxes bring. However, if you feel uncomfortable—"

"When you put it that way, I don't have a problem," I said. "It becomes a kind of game."

"It is a game," Alec said. "Centuries old."

"So if I discover these secret mines, what's going to happen? It won't be a game if people end up in prison."

"Even if we had a large enough labor pool to be sending miners off to prison," Alec said, "which we don't, they don't see themselves as criminals. To indict them as such wouldn't be playing the game as we Dobreni understand it."

"Is it more like the smugglers versus the excise men of the seventeen hundreds?"

"Exactly. So what will happen is, you'll come back and tell me about anything suspicious. And in a month or two, Dmitros Trasyemova, in his capacity as Jazd Komandant of the Vigilzhi—or one of his captains—will be up there on a training mission, or an inspection, and will happen upon the mine, and Tony—because you know Tony will be behind it—will express surprise and consternation. The miners will express surprise and consternation. There will be an elaborate charade, ending with a conversation between me and Tony—or Tony and the Council—resulting in the safety measures being brought up to date, as there tends to be a somewhat medieval attitude about such things. Until it's too late."

"And half a village's inhabitants are wiped out in an accident. Ugh. I get it."

"So the mine will be officially inspected and registered, the necessary improvements made, the taxes will be collected, and life will go back to normal."

"Or what passes for normal in a country where you have to plant roses to keep the vampires away," I said. "Okay, I'll do it, if only to see Tony squirm. Except that he won't squirm, he'll be all *touché*," I gave

Alec a fencer's salute for a hit, "and go right back to his own brand of ethics. I know your families are ancient. Our families," I corrected, remembering that Gran was the last of the Dsarets, the royal family. "Were the von Mecklundburgs all like him?"

Alec laughed. "I suspect that many of our ancestors would surprise you." He glanced at the elaborate ormolu clock on the other side of the room.

"I know, it's time for the Council meeting," I said. "And talking about von Mecklundburg ethics, I have a meeting with Cerisette to discuss wedding strategy. I figured, get two potentially rough things over with on the same day. But my reward will be lunch with Nat and Beka."

Beka Ridotski was another of Alec's old friends. Daughter of the Prime Minister, she was a teacher at the temple school, and secretly a Salfmatta in training. The Salfmattas and Salfpatras were the ones who studied Vrajhus—magic. Tania was also a trainee.

"I wish I could join you," Alec said. "But this meeting is going to run late."

"Then I'd better scram so you can get to it." I took a step away, then a step back. "Except why do I have this feeling there's something I forgot?"

"Wedding thing? Tania's experiments with crystals? Your family?" Pressed as he always was for time, he did not glance at his clock again. He'd be late if I needed him—what were they going to do, fire the Crown Prince? But he didn't like holding them up unless he had to; it was disrespectful.

"I don't know," I said, grimacing. "Maybe it's just that one-more-thing feeling, like I'll always have one more thing I meant to talk to you about every time we part, even if it's just for a couple of hours."

"Is that because marriage is a lifelong conversation?" he asked, and there he was, taking my hands and kissing me again.

"So what's courtship?" I asked, holding him tight before I let him go.

"The questions," he said.

"That we will spend our lives answering," I said. "I like that. And so, on that note, I'm out the door."

And I was.

I set out into the perfect day, striding back over the hammer and sickle palimpsest, fading symbol of half a century's oppression.

My mood was good in spite of the fact that I was about to face Cerisette von Mecklundburg, Tony's cousin. She'd hated my guts the moment she'd seen me. I'd asked her to organize my wedding anyway, partly in hopes it might somehow lessen her enmity, and partly because I respected her organizational skills. I didn't know the first thing about organizing royal weddings. Growing up an only child, with Mom, Dad, and Gran as my only known relatives, I'd never even done birthday parties, and I didn't want my wedding to be a string of disasters like Queen Victoria's.

When I'd told my mother I was going to ask Cerisette, she whistled and said, "Are you sure? I'm afraid when she's done with you, Queen Victoria's wedding will seem perfect by comparison."

Beka Ridotski had nodded at the same time I did. "Matter of honor," Beka had stated, which put my instinctive reaction into words.

And so far, Cerisette had been an amazing commander in chief, even if she had a tendency to talk to me as if I were the dog's breakfast.

My mood was high as I walked under the triumphal arch again and ducked through a lichen-dotted medieval archway abutting a Renaissance building. Adjacent to that was a half-timbered building with odd walls and juttings, in a secluded corner off the regular path. Somewhere someone was playing a radio or recording of a catchy melody, full of hand drums and cymbals, voices rising and falling in a Caribbean rhythm.

I turned toward the music, trailing my fingers along the wall of the Renaissance building. Only in Dobrenica, I thought: an old-fashioned record playing music from half a world away, in a building constructed five hundred years ago.

I recognized the building, for I'd walked past it several times. Yes, there was the door that had intrigued me ever since I first discovered it, painted so realistically that on first glance it seemed three dimensional, with exquisitely rendered hinges that looked like stylized acanthus blossoms.

The music put me in a good mood, far too good to spoil with Cerisette's antipathy. She could wait two minutes.

I paused to look at the door more closely. Its paint was fresh in spite of the weather-worn corbels and wood all around, the brush work so masterly that the latch looked three-dimensional. It was painted to look like entwined hawthorn, rose, and acanthus, in silver.

So imagine my surprise when my fingers closed on cold metal, the door opened, and I found myself face to face with a strangely familiar teenage girl with honey-colored braids. She wore a bulky homespun sweater and a skirt embroidered with flowers and birds.

Though the door was on the side of a house, the girl stood in bright sunlight, vague colorful shapes shifting about behind her. "Well met, Aurelia Kim," she said, her voice barely audible above the rise in the rhythmic song. Someone had cranked the speakers to the max. "I am Xanpia."

A lot of Dobreni girls were named Xanpia, after the patron saint, or angel, or mythic figure who had saved a group of local kids from marauders millennia ago. Many called that the first Blessing. But the common name didn't explain why she seemed familiar.

"This door," I said, raising my voice. "How does it work?"

"It is a door between." Xanpia held her hands up, palms parallel.

"Between what?"

"Between this space and what you know as the Nasdrafus. It is also," she said, "the door between your past and your future."

THREE

"**WHAT?** Is this some magic thing? No way," I said, backing up. "Uh uh. Nada. Zip! I am getting married in a month and a half, and until then, I do not want *any* magical woo-woo messing up my life. I don't want to be rude, but—"

"It's already happened," Xanpia said. Her smile was entirely sympathetic as the song swelled around us, so close it felt like the singers were just out of sight.

I had it then, where I'd seen her. It was on a cold wintry day at the bee-keeper's house, when the Salfmattas had tested me with their crystals, and I'd looked into the past. It made me sick and dizzy. I'd thought her a ghost.

"You're a ghost? No, don't answer that. I'd rather not know, if I have any choice in the matter. Talk to me after the wedding, if you must haunt me. No, better make it after—"

"There is always a choice," Xanpia said. "But it is between going back to where you have already been, and being unmade."

"*Unmade?*" I repeated, every nerve flashing ice cold. "When you say 'already been,' what do you mean?"

"That you have already been there. Now the time has come for you to go to where you were called."

"I hate time-travel stories," I whined. "So you're saying if I don't go, then I'm going to vanish from history?"

"You and Dobrenica," she said. She tipped her head, and I looked around, half-expecting to see the singers and those playing the instruments. "The ceremony is nearly complete."

She began backing away.

I stepped through the doorway, questions piling up in my head. "Called where? Why? What am I supposed to do?" As I spoke, I recognized the shifting shapes behind her: ghost animals, dancing around the familiar fountain, Xanpia's Fountain—which, technically, was several long blocks away from where I stood now, with a gigantic cathedral in between. The light was as bright as an August noon in Los Angeles. Brighter. And the music rose to a crescendo. "You're *that* Xanpia?" I yelled, running toward her.

She and the fountain were slowly dissolving into sparkles of brilliant light, like sun on water. "You are called to guide the child Aurélie," she said. "But that is only half your task, for those who call you cannot see into their future. I came to tell you the rest: you must bring her here to save Dobrenica."

As the singers gave a last cry on a sustained note and rattled their drums and cymbals, the world around me began to dissolve. "Wait! Wait!" I cried, trying to turn around, to run back. "I have to let . . ."

. . . *Alec know.*

The words fell silently into the white.

FOUR

THAT BRILLIANT LIGHT BROKE into splashes and spangles of sunlight in a deep, cerulean world. Suspended between the blue of sky and water shimmered thin drifts of smoke, or ice, like ribbons, only here was the shape of a hand, and there the hazy outline of an uplifted profile.

Smoke ghosts, Tania Waleska called them.

They hovered above a darker shade of blue, blurred by tones of gray and a dull brown, as if a city had sunk below the surface of the sea.

Where was I? When was I? And how was I going to let Alec know?

Gradually I became aware of uneven juts of land extending into the blue of the ocean, and more across what appeared to be a bay. Close by hulked a monstrous fort built of red brick, an addition of newer brick below, along which were mounted twelve enormous cannon.

Cannon. My first clue to the time, if not the place.

Bobbing on the murky green water under those guns, and above the sunken city, was a pair of dinghies, their sails flapping loose.

In each dinghy a boy sat at bow and stern, with another standing in the middle, balancing precariously. They were all about middle school age, but otherwise, the two boys facing one another could not have been more different. The taller one had the awkward shoulders and bony wrists of puberty. His shock of hair had been bleached the color of corn floss, his freckled face burned a blotchy golden red around a ruddy, much-peeled nose. He wore a loose shirt gaping at the neck, and scruffy trousers that looked handmade.

He scowled down at the boy in the other dinghy, who was thin and light-boned as a reed, brown-skinned, with slanted black eyes under extravagantly winged brows. The hair escaping from his queue curled in tendrils around his face, giving it an elfin look.

His? Those winged brows, the charmingly lopsided grin, sparked a memory: the hunting lodge high on Mount Dsaret in Dobrenica. I was sitting in the breakfast room when I glimpsed that same room in the past, a honeymooning couple: the man blond, the woman with curling black hair, slanted black eyes, and a charmingly crooked smile . . .

The boy in the dinghy not only called to mind that honeymooning princess, he was way too pretty to be a boy. I wondered if this was my charge, Aurélie, dressed in boys' clothing.

The kids looked up. Out on the water beyond the fortress glided tall ships on their slow approach, under full and glorious sail, trying to catch what seemed to be a skittish wind. But I couldn't feel the wind. I couldn't smell the sea. I couldn't hear anything, except maybe the faintest mewling of . . . gulls? Hundreds of them swirled and dove off the coast along with a dozen other types of bird.

I began to assess my own personal details: not only could I not feel anything, but the boys, including the one I suspected was really Aurélie, were totally unaware of me hovering somewhere around them.

The big blond boy and Aurélie were arguing. She gave a tight shrug, then extended a hand toward the water. The big one appeared to reach a decision. When the red-haired boy at the bow of his dinghy gave what was obviously a loud sigh and pointed violently at the water, the big one ripped off his shirt, and with a glance of challenge backward, dove over the side of the dinghy. Within seconds the other five had followed, some shucking clothes, others not. Aurélie dove over fully clothed.

Oh yeah, definitely a girl in disguise.

All I could see were kicking feet in the golden light as the kids swam down and down toward what appeared to be rooftops. *Rooftops?* Waving strands of kelp and the barnacles and growths of sea life blurred the outlines, but it definitely looked like an entire street of houses sunk underwater.

Small splashes flowered around gasping faces as, one by one, the boys reappeared, sometimes throwing things into the dinghies, then diving down again. The big boy stayed visible longest, his pale hair catching the light as he looked around for Aurélie, whose white shirt billowed in the water.

Up on the wall, men swarmed around one of the cannon. In the distance, the schooner foremost of the three ships shivered briefly, its gun ports emitting smoke. The cannon responded, recoiling. *Did I hear a boom, or feel it?*

I tried to look around, but the sea and the sky blended together, the sunlight dazzling me. When I could see again, eddies of smoke were drifting lazily away from the cannon rampart, as below, the dark-haired girl-in-disguise clambered aboard her dinghy.

A distant boom sent seabirds squawking skyward. *I heard that!* Sound was coming, but I still felt nothing, smelled nothing. Aurélie and her two companions hauled themselves into their dinghy, streaming wet, and set their last findings in the bow. Then they turned their hands to raising their sail, as the dinghy rocked on the slowly widening wake from the last of the passing schooners.

The dinghy picked up speed, traveling faster in the light airs than the laden schooners, which dragged long trails of seaweed. All three kids gazed up at the schooners slanting slowly up a long passage that was divided from the sea by a thin peninsula.

The shadowy, wavering underwater city abruptly vanished from underneath the dinghy. The water turned aquamarine, clean except for floating detritus cast overboard from the ships, as the dinghy built up speed.

It soon caught up with the first of the schooners, then slid past them. From the way the sails filled and the schooners leaned and rocked, the wind was rising. The light changed, the westering sun slanting underneath gathering clouds as the dinghy left the schooners far behind.

In the distance, the end of the passage resolved into a forest of masts bobbing on the water, and beyond it, what looked like a handsome city, built mostly of brick.

But the little dinghy wasn't heading there. It curved through green-ish whitecaps into a sheltered cove between enormous limestone cliffs, birds weaving in dizzying patterns far overhead. In this cove a narrow two-master lay at anchor, its handsome lines reminding me of Revolutionary-era privateers.

The dinghy bumped up against a sagging wharf. The kids bound the sail to the mast, then leaped from the dinghy, the tallest one with painter in hand. They secured the craft with practiced speed and ran along the wharf to a path beaten into thick greenery. This led to a low, rambling two-story stone house of Spanish design, with balconied upstairs win-dows framed by wrought iron, windows and doors arched. Surrounding the main house on either side rose small cottages with pitched thatched roofs, wooden planks connecting them over ground that probably turned to mud in the frequent rains. Behind the cottages stretched rows of kitchen garden. I could see the heads of youngsters bobbing among the rows as they tended plants. Beyond the kitchen garden wild growth began: banana, breadfruit, and citrus at the forefront. The Spanish house and the flora made me guess we were somewhere in the Caribbean, and this was a plantation being worked by a variety of people, not just black slaves: As the kids from the dinghy reached the big house, people stilled into a tableau of faces ranging from very dark skinned to golden hued.

Then I found myself inside the house with a rapidity that reminded me of how films are edited—one moment you're outside, a blink, and you're inside. Only it wasn't as neat as a film jump, more like a blur.

Candles and lanterns glowed in the rapidly falling darkness, throw-ing unsteady, ruddy light over a woman seated in a high-backed old chair. "Three ships, you say? But not British?" she asked in French.

Sound was definitely clearer. The woman could have been any age from thirty-five to sixty. It was difficult to make her out in that weak, uneven light, but from what I saw, her fair, freckled skin was sun-lined, her gray-streaked, honey-colored hair a sun-bleached mat untidily pulled back into a braid. She wore a loose shirt and voluminous breeches stuffed into high boots, into which two flintlock pistols had been snugged. The wide belt at her waist supported holsters for two more pistols.

". . . biggest, a ship-rigged polacca, eighteen guns, all carronades," Aurélie said. Her voice was much lower than you'd expect in a kid that size, and a little hoarse—not feminine at all. Maybe I was wrong, and she was a he after all?

A black woman emerged from a doorway, strapping a baldric over her shoulder, with a heavy sword attached. "Whose flags did they fly?" she asked. She had a gorgeous voice, low and husky-rough like a panther's purr.

"Dutch and Swedish."

"Good." The black woman sighed and began to shrug out of the baldric, as the Caucasian sank back into her chair and asked, "So what is amiss with Harry, *ma petite?*"

Ma petite? "Ma" is feminine. So, a girl.

"He turned on me, *Maman!* I did nothing, me." Aurélie answered in English, but she spoke slowly, regularizing verbs as one does who comes to English as a second language. "First he said that I lie, I do not see the ghosts like smoke over the sunken city. I told him what Nanny Hiasinte said, not everyone sees ghosts. Then he said Nanny Hiasinte does devil worship, but the other boys got angry, and George, the artillery sergeant's son, told Harry that next he would slander Papists, and if he did, he could swim back to Fort Charles." So Harry was an equal-opportunity bigot, I thought, first disparaging the Jamaican religious tradition, then taking a whack at the Catholics on the backswing. Typical for the time.

Aurélie went on. "I said we all are agreed against devils, so can we now swim?" Her French accent was strong, the names Harry and Hiasinte spoken without the *h*.

"Stap me!" the blonde said, laughing. "You've a quick wit, Aurélie *chérie.*"

Ah! *Aurélie.* So I was right. Chalk one up for Murray. *I can do this.*

The dark one stepped into the lamp's soft golden glow as she gave Aurélie an approving nod. She was as beautiful as her voice, with long slanted eyes and sculpted bones that would have made Leonardo weep and think of angels. "That was well said. Remember what Nanny Hiasinte teaches about finding the place to agree."

"I tried, Tante Mimba! Then Harry said he must be the leader, because his father is a captain of artillery. So I said, you can be leader, let us dive!"

"Well spoken, *petit chou*."

Tante means "aunt" in French, and I could see a strong resemblance to the girl in her; so Aurélie had a white mom and a black aunt? "You lead by telling him to lead. This is quick wit."

Aurélie's mom cracked a laugh. "So it is."

Aurélie tossed her head back. "But Tante Mimba! *Maman!* Then he said we had to shuck our clothes. I said, we never have before. Why now? He said, you are too fine a gentleman, René? I said like you told me, *Maman*, I cannot take off my shirt for the coral will scratch me again, and the scratch will go bad. The shirt protects me. George said, Are we to argue all day and not find any treasure? So we went into the water. But Harry swam near me, and once he socked me on the arm. I think he wanted another fight."

While Aurélie chattered, the two women exchanged a long look, and *Maman* stretched her hand over a heavy packet tied with narrow ribbon. It lay on a side table with a pair of heavily bound books next to one of the guttering lamps. "It is meant to be," she murmured.

"Nanny said so this morning," Aunt Mimba replied quietly. "The obeah was to be at noon."

Aurélie was not listening as she inventoried the extra hits and kicks Harry had aimed her way, touching her knee and ribs and shoulder as she spoke. She finished in an injured tone, "I think the devils got into Harry, for he was always my friend."

"It's a devil only if nature be devilish, and there are many who will so attest," *Maman* said. "Harry suspects there is something amiss. I thought you would have a year or two more to be a boy, so it is as well that we come to what I—"

She paused as through the window came the sound of high, mellow tooting in a deliberate pattern. "The Abeng," *Maman* breathed, and everyone stilled.

Abeng? Those horns were used both by slave holders and the Maroon guerrillas in *Jamaica!* I was definitely on the other side of the world from Europe. How was I supposed to get this kid to Dobrenica in order to save it?

Aunt Mimba held up three fingers as *Maman* said, "Two smaller ships, night, weather coming. Big one lying outside the cove. Would it be the Swedes? Exploring our cove, maybe?" She shook her head. "I don't like this, Mimba."

"Neither do I." Aunt Mimba slung the baldric back on. "You raise the house and deal with the landing parties, Anne. I'll take the field hands in the canoes. These 'Swedes' are not the only ones who can use the cover of a storm." Her tone dropped to threat on the last words, and she dashed out.

Anne got to her feet and picked up a sword from a sideboard in a shadowy corner. "My sweet, take the small ones and lie up with your weapons. The way we drilled." When the girl began to protest that she was big, now—she could defend herself—her mother flashed up a hand. "Only if they find you. Then strike and run, foot or knee. Just like you did on the ship. You must protect the small ones if I cannot get there at once."

Aurélie sprang away as lightly as a deer, and I found myself bobbing after her into a confusion of shadows as darkness closed in with the building clouds. Lightning flashed. The two ships drifting into the little bay became stark black and white silhouettes.

Well, this really sucked. I had found my charge just in time for her to be attacked by pirates, and I couldn't even pick up a weapon. How was I supposed to protect her?

More lightning. Aurélie crouched with several little kids in the lee of a rotting boat that had been overturned on a pile of mossy rocks. The bluish light revealed their intent faces and their weapons. Aurélie clutched a battered rapier in her left hand. In her right, protected by her body in a desperately dangerous way, she held a flintlock pistol, primed and ready to fire. There was no safety on that thing.

The kids stared out intently. Sand flew, grains glinting in the flare of lightning as a pair of silhouettes charged the kids' hidey-hole, one with a dark-smeared upraised cutlass.

Out came the pistol. Aurélie squinted. *Flash!* Cutlass Guy recoiled, rocking back and forth with both hands clutched over a shattered knee, the cutlass lying in the sand.

The second pirate made a wide swipe with his weapon under the rail of the rotting boat—and met the rapier, which spun out of Aurélie's grip. Then he let out a howl as a small boy stabbed him in the foot with a long knife. Whoosh! Orange flames shot up on one of the ships, lighting the bay. Aurélie led the kids in a low-running stream over the rocks in the other direction. They were partially obscured by the slashing rain.

Pistols flashed and silhouetted figures struggled, some falling. The fighting ended when the pirates fled down the beach to their boats, where they discovered the bottoms smashed. Some swam away. Others vanished into the darkness at either end of the cove.

Once more I heard the Abeng horn's high toot in quick patterns that had to be code, for the kids whooped for joy, then splashed into the house.

A blink, and I was inside. Anne strode in through one of the low arches leading to the farther reaches of the house. She was wrapping a cloth around her arm and grimacing as she said, ". . . are the cottages clear?"

A tall, slender man with black skin and silver hair said, "Three dead, and two ran off into the jungle. We've posted a watch. Was that *Papillon* aflame?"

"Yes, but we took the schooner, and I'm waiting on Mimba. I hope the felucca is ours. We'll get something for that, if Saint-Domingue isn't in flames itself."

"How could pirates find our cove?"

"I overheard talk on the shore, during the fight. It was Ruiz again," Anne said, her breath hissing as she lowered herself into a chair. "Oh, my back."

"Ruiz, *le scélérat!*" Aurélie exclaimed, running up to her mother's knee. "*Maman*, you are hurt!" She gazed in dismay at her mother's bloody forearm.

"Some basilicum powder, if it isn't spoilt, and powder of lead if it is, and I shall be well blooded if fever poisons my veins. It is nothing, child. But bide here, for I mean to talk to you before I retire, in case the fever does come on me."

"I thought the pirate Ruiz was locked up," Aurélie exclaimed.

"So did we all, but he must have escaped in the trouble at Saint-Domingue. This much we learned just now. He took that Swedish tobacco-ship out there, which is how he got past Port Royal."

"But who's in the other ships?"

"His new allies," Anne said, hissing again. "Tie that off, will you, child?"

Aurélie knelt at her mother's chair and swiftly tied the bandage, as she said fretfully, "I thought we were finished with pirates."

"There will always be pirates, it comes to my mind," Anne said. "Where there's gold, there will be pirates to try to take it. I think Ruiz was on *Papillon* when the magazine blew, but enough of his rats got away that they might come back. We'll be ready. 'Tis not to trouble you. Another matter lies before us." She tapped the ribbon-tied paper with her free hand.

"What is that? A letter? Did someone write to you, *Maman?*"

"Indeed yes, a most prodigious letter, which has been waiting in Kingston this half year or more, and I didn't know, or I would've gone into the city earlier. Ah, 'tis prodigious *tidings,* from no less than our great Kittredge relations in England. It seems that news reached them of your Uncle Thomas's death and the destruction of Kittredge Plantation, and we are invited to take ship to England and live with your Uncle William Kittredge."

"Fie! We do not want them."

"Family is one of those treasures it would be foolish to throw away," Anne said slowly. "I'm thinking of sending you."

"Why? I wish to be here with you, and Tante Mimba, and Nanny Hiasinte, and Cousin Fiba. I don't want these strangers, or their England.

I love being René, and having the boat, and exploring the coves and diving into the sunken city."

"I know. I thought you might have these things a while longer." Anne leaned forward, grimacing in the uncertain candlelight, and kissed her daughter smackingly on the forehead. Then her smile vanished. "But as I told you when we first changed you from Aurélie to René, 'tis the way of nature, and one day you must be a girl again. I thought 'twould wait upon our being safely established back here on Jamaica again. But there are legalities tying up the plantation that I hadn't foreseen. And meanwhile, here's this letter with its invitation."

"To take me away from you? That is an evil letter."

"This letter invites me to England as the indigent daughter of James Kittredge. 'Tis kindly meant, child. The Colonial Office received instructions via a land agent to sell the plantation. It seems my cousin William Kittredge is to inherit because my father and brother died without male heirs. I wish I'd gone into Kingston earlier, but 'tis useless to repine. And also," Anne said with heavy irony, "if I can convince Government House that my brother left the plantation to my husband, what confounds a mere daughter of an exiled son might be encompassed by the rich widow of the Marquis de Mascarenhas. That is going to take time. You, at least, can go to safety and certain comfort."

Memory interposed itself. I was sitting in a café with Beka Ridotski, who said, *Have you ever looked at Tony's black eyes and wondered what ancestor is peering back at you? There is some evidence that Aurélie was not the daughter of a Spanish marquis but the illegitimate granddaughter of an exiled Englishman and a runaway slave from the Caribbean.*

"There is no comfort without you, and I do not want safety," Aurélie cried.

"Everyone wants safety." Anne sighed. "As I said, there will always be pirates. However, this discussion must wait upon Mimba's rejoining us, for we all must decide together. Get a meal into you first."

Aurélie shook her head. "Grandmère Marie-Claude will not want me to go to England. She hates the English! She said always, she wished to take me to France."

"*No* one would go to France now," Anne said. "They would cut off your head the moment you stepped on shore, just as they no doubt have done with your Tascher and de Beauharnais relations."

Beauharnais? I wondered. Wasn't that the name of Josephine's first husband?

"What does Nanny Hiasinte say?" Aurélie asked, turning from her mother to her aunt.

There was a step behind them, and Mimba appeared. She laid her baldric on the side table, then straightened up, wincing. "Nanny has said you must come to the mountain. She has made the obeah, and you are to go."

Aurélie sighed. "I will do whatever Nanny says."

Anne said, "I smell pumpkin frying. Go eat."

FIVE

IT MIGHT HAVE BEEN HALF AN HOUR LATER, or half a day. Or even half a week in their time, though for me it felt like seconds later. I can only say for certain that it was daylight, and I bobbed along like a balloon on a string following the three figures as they walked up a narrow trail surrounded by spectacular greenery.

Saving Dobrenica required first getting answers to questions. My hopes were as high as Aurélie's as she skipped and chattered.

White birds darted and dove at the worms washed out by the rain. Aurélie ran among the birds, arms high, as they skirled around her. Then she dashed up the narrow path, the vivid red *poinciana*, the yellow *poui*, and the extraordinary blue *lignum vitae* breaking the patterns of green. Aurélie seemed oblivious to the wild, sumptuous color on either side of her, responding only when vivid tiny shapes hummed and darted close to her—dragonflies, and hummingbirds of an amazing variety.

The two women walked more soberly, Mimba using a gentleman's stick sword as a cane, and Anne holding her bandaged forearm close. The bright morning sun was a lot kinder to Mimba than to Anne, who looked older than she probably was, her freckled skin was so sun-damaged. But the deep lines on either side of her eyes somehow enhanced the intelligence and good humor that I saw in her expression as she trudged slowly up the trail.

My hearing was improving. I could make out the quiet *chuff chuff* of their steps on the trail, the rustle of the greenery, and the hoot and trill of unseen wildlife. The three paid little attention, pausing only when the distinctive high tootle of the Abeng horn sounded ahead or behind them. Someone was signaling as they climbed into the hills above the cove.

"There's the Kindah," Aurélie cried. "We are at Accompong!"

Accompong, I remembered from my college history course, was one of the main Maroon towns in the mountains of Jamaica. So the kids had been diving off of Fort Charles, over the rooftops of the two-thirds of Port Royal that had sunk in a mighty quake in 1692.

We entered a cottage with a steeply slanted thatched roof mostly made of palm fronds, set under a tamarind tree. It was open on three sides. The sun was fast sinking when Aurélie dashed inside, crying, "Nanny! Nanny!"

"Manners," Anne called hoarsely.

Aurélie caught herself up short, and politely greeted everyone she saw, who greeted her in return as they paused in decorating the chamber with bright red silk scarves and fresh flowers.

I looked into faces of varying colors, from Anne's sun-scorched pale to light brown, reddish bronze, and very dark. From the skin colors and bone structures of the people gathered I guessed they were Africans and Spaniards as well as northern Europeans, with youngsters of various genetic mixes.

Most of those faces looked back at Aurélie with love, and some with sadness, though that expression might have been carved in, the silent evidence of the brutal life of slavery: I glimpsed the puckered scars of brands on some, though others' skin had the smoothness of freedom, or else the scars were hidden under the bright clothes.

The center of attention was a very old woman whose lined face was darker even than Mimba's. As Aurélie ran up to kiss her, she smiled and held out gnarled hands.

"Where is the regal?" Aurélie exclaimed. "Is it time for music?"

"You will not play tonight. You will dance, for tonight is yours." The husky old voice was tender, almost reedy.

The chamber filled with life in a fantasia of hues. Scarves, silks, belts, every type of personal decoration enhanced the effect as people and animals crowded in. There was even a snake curling languorously on a silken cushion.

Gradually my perceptions widened as the music began. The regal, ancestor of the organ, began an entrancing melody, given a dancy beat by drums. Threading through the melody strummed a lute and a twelve-stringed harp. The musicians began weaving the people together into harmony via dance. The mesmerizing rhythms, with counterpoint singing, and the explosion of scarlet, molten gold, cobalt, and viridian, fulgent with life, intensified exponentially, until it seethed through me, overwhelming me to the point of pain. I sensed others around me, a shifting, blending luminescence of beings, as Aurélie danced happily among the other children.

Nanny Hiasinte had been sitting in the midst of the celebrants, her eyes closed, as she rocked gently to the rhythms. Now her eyes opened slowly, their expression not vacant, but distant, as if she had been called from a place of equipoise between the past, the now, and the possible future.

She lifted her gaze and focused on me.

I knew she saw me: my nerves prickled though my body was miles and years away. Her voice was low and rough, her French accent singsong, and old-fashioned in the way Anne's English was old-fashioned. "I called upon Ayizan, but you are not one of the *lwa*, the spirits who serve *le bon Dieu*. Your body lives. Your soul is bound to Aurélie by blood, and by magic. You are called to walk in the form of a duppy to guard this child, Aurélie."

"Duppy?" I tried to say—and she heard me.

"You both are called away from your homes. It has been and will be. In French we say *vous-deux*."

You two, I translated into English.

"The future you come from is fog to me," Nanny Hiasinte said. "My understanding is that the future is not bound as is the past, but I called for one from her future in order to secure her survival if I could."

So here was the person who had yanked me out of my life. I could understand her wanting to protect Aurélie by reaching into Aurélie's future, but a month before my wedding, I didn't want to be the one. Anyway, I didn't know anything about kids—I was an only child, and had never even been a babysitter.

But before I could ask her to pick someone else, she went on, her voice thinned to a thread as if this conversation took the strength out of her. "Much can change, but this I know: You have carried the Navaratna necklace with its stones of great power, as will Aurélie."

That caught me totally by surprise. "The what?" I asked. So far, the only famous necklace I'd worn was something Alec had loaned me the night of the masquerade ball, when I was pretending to be Ruli. But he hadn't mentioned any magical powers.

"No one else can see it go from me to her." She closed her eyes.

Another blink and the light of dawn edged the palms and fruit trees and ferns with goldy-green fire. Nanny Hiasinte sat upright in her chair. Before her knelt Aurélie, her head on the old woman's lap. Anne and Mimba stood at either side of the old woman's chair.

"You are called away from here," Nanny said to Aurélie, low and tender. "Your fate lies across the sea. But you will have three things to take with you: our love, a gift, and a guide."

"What guide?" Aurélie asked tearfully, completely hoarse.

"I have bound a duppy to you as your guide. You must learn to listen, and she will speak to you, and you to her."

"I have a duppy of my own?" Aurélie lifted her head.

"She is there to protect you as much as she can, but because she is a duppy, she cannot act in the physical world. So you must listen."

"But I don't want to go away."

Anne knelt down by her daughter. "Child, it is best. Your father died in one sea battle, your brother in another when he was your age. Your sister died in the hurricane when this plantation was ruined, before you were born. When that letter came, my first thought was, if you go, then one of my children might live."

Aurélie wiped teary eyes, and Anne went on. "My father always used to talk about England, how peaceful it is. The ordered virtue of its gardens, which never know the infernal intrusion of pirates or hurricanes. Your life will know prodigious improvement in England. I shall see to that."

Mimba laid her hand on Aurélie's curly head. "Nanny has spoken. What she says, must be."

"I want you to go, too," Aurélie cried to her mother.

Anne winced, and Mimba pulled her to her feet. They started out of the cottage.

Nanny stretched out a gnarled hand toward Aurélie. "Bide a moment, child."

Anne and Mimba withdrew, leaving Aurélie standing with Nanny, and me hovering invisibly nearby.

"You must go, Aurélie. It is to be. But it is not to be for your mother," Nanny said. "Do not make it more painful for her."

Aurélie cried, "My *Maman*, is she in danger? I can feel it, she has the fever."

"The fate of this fever I do not see. I see only that your paths must diverge here. I have called to the *lwa* for aid and guidance, and you have been sent your own duppy to guide you. And now for the gift I promised, which will protect you from harmful spirits and spells."

Aurélie fretted. "I do not want them! Harry says the English call our ways heathen, and devil-worship. He even says bad things about my grandmother Marie-Claude's priests. Why I must go to such a place?"

"There are good and bad among them. Just as there are good and bad among us."

"So these Kittredges are not evil?" Aurélie asked.

"I do not know them. I do not see them. But people who reach so very far to find their family? That is not an evil action," Nanny said.

Aurélie gave a tiny nod.

"Your mother wishes for you to go live among these *Anglais*, and it is natural for a mother to wish her child to know the ways of her people. It might come to pass that the *Anglais* will wish to change your ways, even your name," Nanny said. "Names can be put off and put on, you will find, like the wealthy change their clothes. You are still you, whatever name you wear. Do you comprehend?"

The child ducked her head, then gulped on a sob.

"Then with my gift come three things, as I once heard from my grandmother in Africa."

Aurélie bent her head, listening.

"First, remember that you own yourself. There are many ways to own and be owned, not just on the auction block. Never sell yourself, for a chosen bondage is harder to escape than the chains of the oppressor. I will add, to remind you, that you are connected by blood to the great Boukman, and to Queen Nanny of the Windward Maroons. They are great people."

Aurélie assented with the air of one who knows these facts.

"Second, it might come to pass that your English family will want to baptize you. They will teach you their ways. Take what is good, for that is part of the great Creole. You understand, child?"

"I know what Creole means," Aurélie exclaimed as she knuckled tears from her eyes. "It is like the two kinds of French. There is the kind that I must speak with Grandmère Marie-Claude and the family on Saint-Domingue, and there is the French that *we* speak, that Tante Mimba said is made of words from French and Spanish and Akan and Igbo tongues. I like that French best, for it is quick, and pretty, like the doctor bird."

"You have a quick ear, the ear of the musician, child," Nanny said. "The great Creole unites all faiths as one under *le bon Dieu*." She pronounced the French for "God" with an accent that sounded more like *Bondje*. "But you might have to keep your understanding hidden."

Aurélie bobbed her head, looking troubled. "I know. Grandmère was so very angry when Cousin Fiba talked of praying to *lwa* to help *le bon Dieu* hear us."

"Your third thing is the gift itself. It is a secret thing, to keep hidden. It is very old, older even than our family forced here to these islands. It is older than our family brought to Africa, for it is from a woman who traveled out of far Siam to marry an African prince. And her foremothers were from another part of the world altogether, so you will see."

Nanny opened her hands. She disclosed a worked chain of gold with bright stones set into it at intervals. Aurélie stared, marveling, for each stone was a different color from the next. "It is called the Navaratna."

I stared. I had definitely never seen that necklace before.

Nanny's forefinger touched the center stone. "So it was said in the Sanskrit: this ruby represents the sun. It is your center." She moved on, chanting as she touched each stone. "Red Coral for Mangala, the red star, an emerald for Budah, the green star, son of the moon, a yellow sapphire for Deva-guru, father-star, a diamond for Shukra, the white star, a blue sapphire for Shani, the ring-star, Gomedaka," she touched a ruddy stone that looked like a garnet, "for Rahu, when the moon is on the rise, and a Cat's Eye for Ketu, when the moon is descending." With that, she clasped the necklace around Aurélie's neck, and tucked it inside her shirt, so that it was completely hidden. "There are those who murder and cause strife to steal and sell such stones, but far more powerful are the charms woven into them, with love, and loyalty, and good will. It surrounds you as the stars surround us, sheltering and protecting the good spirits who watch over those who strive to be pure in heart."

Wow, I thought. This Great Creole seemed to have Hindu thought at its base—at least, what I understood of Hindu as the oldest religious tradition in the world: complete freedom of worship that accepts all forms of belief and regards all humans as one family.

"How can I be pure in heart?" Aurélie asked. "What does that mean?"

"It means choosing to do no evil. It is a lifelong struggle," Nanny said. "There are rules that come with this gift. You must never take a life. And you must not eat of any slaughtered creature."

"Creature?"

"You must not eat meat. This is why my obeah is not begun with a sacrifice, though others practice differently. This is why my walls are hung with red to remind us of the lifeblood all creatures share. But I do not spill it."

"Can I eat eggs?"

"You *can* eat anything, but you must *choose* not to eat meat. Eggs are not slaughtered in violence. My grandmother taught me that the hen does not object to the egg being taken, so you may eat of it. You may drink the milk of goat or cow, because she gives it freely."

Aurélie looked confused, then said, "Why is the necklace to come to me, your great-granddaughter, and not to my Tante Mimba, who is your granddaughter?"

"Because it has skipped that generation and chosen you. It is a gift, but it also is a burden, for its protections must stay secret."

Aurélie clutched her thin fingers to her skinny chest. "If, if I don't keep the rules, will it kill me?"

Nanny Hiasinte let out a breath of a laugh, more sad than humorous. "A necklace cannot kill you. It is how you choose to use the power the charms command that will cause good or evil."

"What charms?"

"I will not teach a child powers she does not understand, for that is to put the carving knife into the hands of a baby who only knows how to grasp and to poke. Your work is to listen, to learn through the teaching of dreams and of the wise, to avoid doing harm. If, in the course of time you learn of powerful things, it is to be hoped you will have learnt the wisdom to wield the power well. Always, always, always you must keep it secret. It is too powerful to be taken from you, but demons who see it will do anything to trick you into giving it, and that must never happen, for they will use it to cause more harm in a world already burdened with woe."

A kiss, and Nanny let her go.

Aurélie departed with slow steps, rejoining her mother and aunt at the top of the path.

"As well it's mostly downhill," Mimba said with a worried look at Anne.

The clear morning light revealed that Anne's blotchy face was due less to sunburn than to fever. By the time they reached the cove where the Kittredge plantation's main building was, Mimba was mostly supporting Anne's weight. She sent Aurélie on ahead to alert their cook, who I understood to be their medical practitioner as well.

People gathered around, worrying or offering their own favorite cures as Mimba helped Anne inside and to a bedroom. She flung aside the bed curtains and gently eased Anne onto the lumpy-looking mattress piled high with pillows.

Anne opened her eyes as Aurélie and the other children gathered around, everyone looking worried.

"Shall I send to Kingston for a physician?" Mimba asked.

"What do they know?" Anne said impatiently. "Mumble a lot of Latin over me, then charge a guinea to tell me what anyone but a simpleton should see: It's my arm causing the fever to fire my blood. I just need a thumping good blooding, then a hero's dose of calomel to drive the infection out of my body."

Calomel? I had read about calomel. Its main ingredient was mercury. "Don't do that," I yelled, grabbing frantically at Aurélie, who jumped and looked around wildly.

"*Ma petite?*" Mimba said.

"It is my duppy," Aurélie declared, looking at them, eyes stark with amazement. "I almost heard her."

I tried imagining myself with a tinfoil hat and beamed the thought: *No calomel!*

Mimba shook Aurélie gently. "Use the glass."

". . . and more powder of lead for my arm, to soak up the blood after we clean it—"

NO! I shouted at the girl.

"Augh," Aurélie cried. "You are hurting me, duppy! Go away!"

"The looking glass, Fiba!" Mimba ordered, holding Aurélie against her. Swift footsteps sounded, and something was thrust into Mimba's outheld hand. "Look, *ma petite*. Look into the glass, the way your Papa did."

"Mimba," Anne said wearily. "Remember."

Mimba made a quick gesture. "This is too important." And to the child, "Do you remember your Papa looking into the glass to talk to spirits?"

"No," Aurélie said anxiously.

"You are not at fault if you do not remember. You were only two when he died, *hélas!* So calm yourself. Look. Listen. Tell me when to cease moving the mirror." Mimba was tipping a spotted hand mirror, a heavy thing chased with gaudy baroque gilding. She angled it slowly, and if I were breathing, I would have held my breath the same way Aurélie did as she frowned intently into the age-dimmed reflective surface.

Impatiently I waited as an older woman laid out the things Anne had asked for. Through the open window came the urgent tootling of the Abeng, and again everyone stilled. Then the adults stirred: Not only Mimba but the cluster of people in the doorway.

"More trouble breaking out," came a voice from the door. It was the silver-haired African man I'd first seen the night of the attack.

"There are no slaves on this plantation. Our people know that," Mimba stated.

"But the King's soldiers won't." Anne sighed, stirring restlessly on the bed. "What a time for us to come back to Jamaica."

"All the world is in uprising, it seems," said someone else. I didn't dare look as the old mirror angled closer . . . closer . . .

I gazed into Aurélie's reflected eyes and watched them widen. "There she is. She is *old!* Maybe twenty, or even *more!* Her hair is long, the color of Harry's. She's light-skinned, like *Maman*," Aurélie said doubtfully.

"What Nanny says is true, then," Mimba murmured in a soothing voice. "You are to go to England and be safe. Ayizan sends you an English duppy to watch over you in her land. What does she say?"

"I cannot hear," Aurélie fretted.

How do you speak clearly when you don't have a voice—or a mouth? *No. Calomel.* I tried shaping the words. And in French: *Pas. Le. Calomel.*

"She speaks, but I don't hear," Aurélie said.

Mimba's face joined Aurélie's in the mirror, but her gaze searched, clearly finding nothing besides hers and Aurélie's reflections. She sighed. "My brother was given the Sight, but it was not given to me." And to the girl, "Tell your duppy to speak slowly."

Aurélie commanded in a hoarse squawk, her fright clear, "Speak slowly, duppy!"

I shook my head and mouthed the word *NO*. Another slow shake. *CALOMEL*.

And Aurélie looked up in wonder. "I think she says, no medicine?"

Oh, the joy of first contact!

People looked at one another the way people do when they've just discovered that something they trusted is now suspect.

Fiba, the dark-skinned girl cousin who'd fetched the mirror, said, "Bad spirits must have got into the calomel. Only another spirit would know."

"That is a matter for Nanny. But we must do something now. Aurélie, ask the duppy what we must do."

This was no time to cover two hundred years of medical advances. Especially when no one could hear me, and the only one who could see me was a kid.

And so, with excruciating slowness, I mimed and tried to mouth words. It seemed to take forever, but nobody questioned my instructions once they understood, for they assumed that I had arcane powers, or at least arcane wisdom.

Finally Anne's wound was washed with boiled water cooled just long enough to bear. After that came the toughest one: into the raw wound, which had begun to infect in a sickening way, they poured whiskey. "The soldier's remedy," one of the men had said, as soon as they understood when I'd mimed drinking.

Well, that made sense, if soldiers used it. I could see agreement in the faces.

Poor Anne endured that without benefit of painkillers but soon lay with the wound open to the air. I then said she needed to drink the boiled water. After some discussion of my surprising prescription (leading everyone to agree that it must purify the evil out of the blood from within), they got Anne to drink. When sweat promptly broke out all over her body, and her fever plummeted, they saw the effect.

I'd only meant to keep the poor woman from being poisoned by the grim medical tech prevalent in those days—even if she'd been in London or Philadelphia, the treatment would have included blooding, calomel, and powder of lead. The result that I'd not foreseen was immediate belief, of everybody at the Kittredge Plantation, that Aurélie had a benevolent duppy, even if it came from overseas.

SIX

S O WHERE DO I COME IN? I kept wondering as the days melted together. No one was trying to communicate with me as they went about their daily lives. I thought longingly about Alec, hoping that time had somehow stopped at the moment I left. I missed him, but that was bearable if I could believe that he wasn't tearing his hair out and searching every nook and cranny of Dobrenica looking for me.

Meanwhile, time blurred—it felt like a few minutes later when the news arrived of outbreaks of violence all over the island. It was on a morning so hot that steam rose off the ground outside the windows of Aurélie's thick-walled Spanish house.

The household began speculating, some sure that the Jamaican violence was, in part, a response to the erupting troubles in Saint-Domingue to the east. Anne forced herself to rise and dress, with a fresh determination to send her daughter to safety.

One of Anne and Mimba's workers entered the house, a stoop-shouldered, grizzled white man who still wore his hair in a long sailor's queue. He came to the main room where the children sat in a circle on the floor taking turns reading verses from the Psalms, as Mimba coached them. Mimba said, "Is the carriage repaired, Noah?"

"Repaired, and we even laid on a coat of lacquer. Captain Anne'll look fine as fivepence in Kingston, Guillaume having found a wig to put on as coachman. We used the powder of lead to make it fresh, as Captain Anne said we cannot use it more for the blotting of wounds."

Anne appeared then, walking with care. I almost didn't recognize her, with her hair pulled up under a straw hat decorated with ribbons and silk flowers. She had stuffed herself into a linen gown of cream-colored fabric, with a blue floral pattern copperplate-printed on it. The style was 1790s, the tight bodice coming to a point in front, a lace fichu tucked into the high neck, the long sleeves edged with lace.

"Do I look a proper *marquesa*?" she asked.

"It is the gown that Grandmère gave you," Aurélie cried.

"It is indeed, *ma poule*. I'm off to Government House and thence the shipyard."

She turned around, half-lifting her arms against the pull of the tight sleeves.

"Blast my eyes, how this binds," she exclaimed.

"It looks very fine," Mimba said.

Anne grimaced as Mimba straightened the hat then retied the hat's bow under her chin. Then Anne marched out, the household following to where an old-fashioned open carriage awaited, hitched to a pair of horses, a handsome black man on the box, dressed in a skirted coat with shiny buttons. He wore a George Washington era wig on his head, and on that, a gold-edged tricorne. They looked splendid as they rolled and clattered out.

Mimba turned to Aurélie, and said sternly, "You see? Your *Maman* wears a gown. Now you must accustom yourself to gowns again, or should you like to return to Grandmère Marie-Claude instead?"

"No, no," Aurélie cried.

"Then get ready for practice."

Aurélie's thin fingers flew to her skinny middle where, behind her smock, the Navaratna necklace hung. "Practice? But Nanny told me I must never do evil to another."

Mimba bit her lip, then took Aurélie aside, under a tamarind tree, where they could speak alone. As always, anywhere Aurélie went, I floated after. "You are learning to defend yourself. This is why your *Maman* and I teach you the quick strike, and to run to safety."

"So I am to use my sword? My pistol?"

"To defend yourself, yes." Mimba hunkered down, sighing. Aurélie dropped down next to her with the light, unconscious grace of a child, and waited expectantly. Mimba said, "My grandmother is a great obeah woman. But I have my doubts about that necklace, though she treasures it. Yes, I know you've got it, though only your mother knows I know. I think Nanny treasures it because it came from Africa with *her* grandmother. For I have to ask myself, how good is its protection when your nanny's nanny was captured and brought here to be a slave, and saw half her family die on the ship without being able to do anything to protect them?"

Aurélie clutched the necklace through the thin fabric of her boy's shirt.

Mimba sifted the rich soil through her callused hand, then looked up. "It could be that it only works in the spirit world, and that I know nothing about. To be fair, one could say that I was not chosen so it is not given to me to understand. Perhaps it is because I had to kill or be killed when pirates first attacked, and perhaps because I learnt to take pleasure in killing pirates. They are evil. I have no qualms." She rose. "The only gift I can give you is the ability to defend yourself. It takes skill to disable, so you must be nimble indeed if you do not want to kill. As for your gown, you will put it on after drill and practice your etiquette."

She gave Aurélie a friendly swat and the girl ran off to join the other children.

As time blurred past, I figured out that the people working Kittredge Plantation had been the crews and families of the privateers of which Anne and Mimba were the captains—Anne's inheritance, like the plantation, from her brother Thomas.

The plantation had been abandoned after an especially bad hurricane, and Thomas Kittredge took to sea. But now Anne and Mimba had brought them back to reestablish the plantation. The ex-slaves among them knew the most about farming, the sailors the least.

After pistol and sword drill, Aurélie would put on her gown for the children's tutoring in etiquette. The other kids thought Aurélie much to be pitied for the hot confinement of the gown. But the fact that she was soon to go on a ship caused general envy, even if no one particularly wanted to go to England. I blanked out in the middle of an argument about whether or not it was true that she would freeze to death the moment she set foot on English soil.

Before supper, Aurélie stitched fresh ribbons to the bonnet she must wear as a young lady. And when everyone in the household gathered after supper, they made music and sang.

Aurélie played a regal—the bellows pumped by an enthusiastic six-year-old—as others played the lute or various percussive instruments. The regal was much battered, but here and there was evidence of elaborate baroque decoration. Aurélie showed a lot of talent; she was diligent and smart, but she showed no interest in talking to me in the mirror.

When was I supposed to begin my country-saving? *I want Alec, I want to go home,* I kept thinking, but Xanpia's chilling words about Dobrenica kept me from trying to break whatever spell bound me to that kid.

At last, one day as the sun was setting, Anne walked wearily into the house.

Aurélie leaped up to greet her mother, who looked tired and sweaty. She smiled and kissed her daughter, as Mimba said, "I told you that you rose from your sickbed too soon."

"It was not my wound," Anne said, touching her forearm, which was hidden by her tight sleeve. "It was wearing this devilish gown. Sitting in Government House—trying not to swear—confined as a Bedlamite. It will take a deal of time to contrive with land agents and Government House if my version of my brother's will is to be heeded."

She dropped her reticule, a ribbon-tied paper, and her bonnet onto a side table, and sank into the chair next to it. "I could never go to England, Mimba, I've no longer the way of it. The child must go while she still retains the manners my mother scolded into her. She will have a chance at a better life, but I am too old to leave off my privateer habits. Devil fly away with these clothes. If I do not get out of these stays I shall burst!"

"Is the passage arranged, then?"

"That much is done. I've a letter of credit for the child, and the wife of a warrant officer will look out for her. I paid her a thumping high fee, so I'd better hear a good report when Aurélie writes to us."

Mimba shook her head slowly. "I know that Nanny said it must be, but she also taught us that we shape our futures, our future does not shape us."

Aurélie looked from one to the other, her black eyes so wide that the candle flames reflected in them, points of gold.

Anne said, "I brought comfits for all you children, *ma petite*. In my reticule, there. You and Fiba divide them up."

Aurélie snatched the little bag from the side table, and she and Fiba began dividing the sugar-candies as a cluster of small kids formed a circle on the floor. Everyone was busy clamoring for the one they liked best, and the kids paid no heed to the adults.

Mimba said to Anne, "Your father was sent out of England for no good reason. Do you truly wish to send the child there?"

"The family misliked having a Quaker among them. Aurélie is not a Quaker," Anne said with a wry grin that faded. "I cannot bear to see another of my children die. And Nanny did tell us that Aurélie's future lies overseas. If I balk, will I have another dead child to bury?"

"But *England*. Why not send her back to your mother on Saint-Domingue?"

"Would you?" Anne retorted. "You know my mother and her prejudices. Surely these English will not scold all the time the way she does." Another flash of the wry grin. "My father once told me that the English worship God, honor rank, but worship *and* honor wealth. God put the child here. I can amend His work by seeing to it that the second and third conditions are met."

"By a falsehood? Do you think it will answer?" Mimba lowered her voice. "You think they will not see she's a mulatto?"

Anne grimaced. "Though I've turned my hand to violence, I'm still Quaker enough to hate these terms for their inferences."

"I hate them, too," Mimba retorted. "But they are *legal* terms. If Beauveau catches up with us, he can claim the child."

Beauveau? Who's that? I thought.

"By what law? Has not French law been overthrown at least twice?" Then Anne went on in an even lower voice, and I guessed that Beauveau had to be a French-born landowner on Saint-Domingue. "Aurélie is lighter in skin than Mascarenhas was, and he claimed the pure blood of a hidalgo." Her jaw jutted. "'Twas one motive for my taking his name. But I'll admit my greatest pleasure is thinking of him looking up from Hell as I spend his treasure and claim his noble name, for what he did to Baptiste."

"I, too, hope he burns in eternity for his many murders, my brother among them," Mimba said.

Now I've got it, I thought. Beka had heard wrong: the mysterious runaway slave in Aurélie's background wasn't female; it was her father, a man named Baptiste. He and Anne had been a couple, but after his death Anne co-opted the name of his murderer, a highly born Spanish or Portuguese pirate named Mascarenhas.

Uh oh, I thought, at the very same time Mimba crossed herself and added, "But I fear no good can come of this ruse of yours."

"No one has said aught so far, what with the troubles." Anne patted the ribbon-tied paper. "And with so many churches burnt, more marriage lines than my presumptive ones are gone. How would anyone prove I am not a marquise? With noble rank, I can keep the Kittredge ships, and I can hold this plantation. I will sew this bank draft into oilcloth myself. It is probably the best gift I can give the child, a claim to exalted birth and thirty thousand reasons for the Kittredges not to inquire too closely into it."

Time blurred again, then came a flurry of activity: sewing, packing the trunk, pistol and etiquette practice, good-byes. Aurélie had to wear a gown all day now, which fretted her, for she was constantly reprimanded and reminded how easily muslin shows dirt. My anxiety to get moving, to fulfill my duty to the kid and get back to Dobrenica, fretted *me*.

The day came when Anne, Mimba, and Aurélie climbed into the dinghy, and the entire population of the plantation gathered at the dock to see them off. The sail shook out and caught the breeze as we rocked across the azure water toward Kingston. There lay the frigate that would carry to London the governor's request for reinforcements, along with individuals of sufficient rank, wealth, or importance to demand passage.

Aurélie clung to her mother as they wound through the forest of ships bobbing and rolling to either side, busy with sailors cleaning, caulking, repairing, loading, and unloading. Or lounging about on mastheads, hallooing to passing boats.

As the dinghy neared the formidable ship with its open gun ports, the coldly glinting iron cannon visible within, Aurélie glanced up the huge tumblehome, and tears slipped down her cheeks.

Anne knelt down and took her daughter's shoulders in her hands. "Remember, you go to England as the daughter of the Marquis Alfonso Eduardo de Pacheco y Mascarenhas," she said fiercely. "You are Doña Aurélie de Mascarenhas, *Lady* Aurélie to the English."

Aurélie whimpered. "I thought Papa's name was Baptiste."

A quick exchange of glances over her curly head, then Anne murmured, "That is how he was known in the family. To the world, your father was a Spanish don, that is a grandee, connected to the Portuguese family who were once the Dukes of Aveiro. He had a letter of marque from the Spanish government to cruise against the French."

Aurélie said in confusion, "But your *Maman*, that is, my *grandmère*, she's French. Are the French the enemy, or not? Cousin Fiba said they ended slavery."

"It is all politics, and these days, if the news be half true, the French are their own worst enemy, child," Anne said. "Yes, they did a good thing in declaring an end to slavery, but they are doing many other evil things in the name of liberty, and that's why there's fighting. Remember what I gave you."

Aurélie made a convulsive movement, clapping one arm against her middle. I heard a faint crackle of paper.

"Hssht!" Mimba said. "Do not let anyone know it is there."

They had switched to French, as English voices made themselves heard in the towering masts overhead.

"Wear that oilcloth next to your skin day and night," Anne whispered. "And when you get to England, you give it straight into the hands of your Uncle Kittredge." Anne straightened up as their dinghy drifted alongside the frigate.

Mimba had loosened their sail. Anne left the rudder and caught the rope-chair that sailors threw down. Up went Aurélie's small trunk of belongings, and then it was time for a last kiss and last tearful hug.

Aurélie climbed into the chair, which was boomed up to the deck, and I drifted along behind her, thinking: *Okay, England is definitely happening. England is that much closer to Dobrenica. I can do this.*

SEVEN

THE FIRST VISION I EVER SAW was on a fourth grade field trip to the Mission San Juan Capistrano, when I gazed out the bus window at a girl my own age in Acjachemen dress looking out over the sea. Below her was a row of kiicha huts overshadowed by elderberry trees and lining a stream that tumbled down the rocks from a recent rain. Everything was green—a rarity in what was to become Southern California.

I still wasn't sure if she was a vision or a ghost. If she'd been a vision, that was a brief glimpse of her life. If she was a ghost, earth-bound after a sudden death, then she must have wandered away from the ruins of the mission cathedral after a quake had knocked it down, killing a lot of those gathered inside. Or maybe she had lived a long and happy life, like the second ghost I met: Queen Sofia of Dobrenica, who as a bride traveled to Vienna to make her oath of fealty to Maria Theresia of the Holy Roman Empire. It was there, while I was walking around the grounds of the imperial palace, that I saw her.

The most eerie part of the business is, I know she saw me. She not only saw me, she grinned, and turned in a way that practically begged me to follow her, with the result that I met Alec, and, well, here I was, invisible guide to a kid I couldn't talk to—a kid who was supposed to save Dobrenica.

I have never believed in destiny. But now I wondered if I'd been set up the moment I saw that smile of ghostly Queen Sofia's—maybe before then. If so, why hadn't anyone given me better clues? Like, would it be too much to ask of some ghost to show up a few months ago to intone warningly, *Beware! Read up on Dobreni history, especially the life of Aurélie de Mascarenhas, for you shall be called to great destiny!*

No. I still couldn't get a grip on predestination. Free will was too important to me, and Nanny Hiasinte did say that the future was a fog. That had to mean it could change. But I didn't want it to change, I wanted to get right back to the moment I'd left. Protecting the timeline was going to be my strategy.

That meant thinking ahead on how to be a guide to a kid born two hundred years before me.

There was no guiding at first.

Aurélie was pretty much alone on the man-of-war, ignored by the adults, except for brief, brisk orders from the stout, middle-aged Mrs. Cobb, wife to a warrant officer. Her job aboard ship was to look out for the younger boys. Anne had paid her to add Aurélie to her charges.

Mrs. Cobb's style of looking out was to check Aurélie's head each day for lice and to see to it that she appeared in the gun room for meals. "Mind you keep your distance from them powder monkeys, duckie," she said the first night. "A day out of port and they are always crawling. Bless me, I've never met with worse."

Otherwise, Aurélie was adjured to be a good girl and stay out of everyone's way, and she would probably be invited to Sunday dinner on account of her being a marquis's daughter. In preparation, on Saturday they would air out her Sunday gown.

She was also given a cabin, that is, the tiny closet belonging to the third lieutenant. She had to share it with an older woman, mother to a parson's wife. This woman remained utterly silent except when she wished Aurélie to get out of her way.

The poor kid was soon bored, as no one let her on deck. Subsequently time elided into a confusion of sea and sky and towering sails overhead.

I focused again when Aurélie's emotions spiked into anxiety one morning. Sunday meant divisions, Mrs. Cobb explained. That meant the ship was scoured for inspection, then they stood in the hot sun on deck as the parson led the Sunday service. After that, the captain went on his tour of inspection.

Aurélie's emotions shifted from anxiety to intent when the inspection ended, and the captain gave the midshipmen permission for target practice under the guidance of the oldest of them, a master's mate named Benford, who was around high school age. Aurélie dashed below then soon reappeared, holding her pistol and advancing on the midshipmen.

The boys reacted as if they'd been goosed by cacti as she marched up to them, her muslin hem ruffle flapping around her ankles. She'd kicked off her shoes to get a better grip on the holystoned deck, and took her place in line.

"You must go below," Benford declared, his voice breaking, which caused a flush of embarrassment. The other boys snickered. "You might get injured."

"You make targets. I come to practice, me," Aurélie said in her French-accented English. "I must make sure my aim is ver-ry good."

"Girls don't shoot," squeaked a brat who couldn't have been more than ten. He was lost in a uniform that would have been loose on a boy five years older.

When Aurélie held out her pistol—point properly down—the boys jumped back. "I do."

"Whose is that?"

"It is my own."

"Why do you talk like a froggie?" the littlest one asked.

"Quiet, Fletcher." Benford cuffed the boy on the ear hard enough to send him staggering. "Have you ever shot a pistol, miss?"

Fletcher, who was probably about ten, blinked back tears, but didn't say anything, and Benford turned back to Aurélie.

She said, "*Naturellement*—it is natural that I have shot my pistol. Why else am I here?"

The boys considered this, then one said, "You ever shot at anybody?"

"But yes. Not, what do you call it, a *fortnight* past. We were attacked by Ruiz the pirate, and I shot one in the knee. I hit another with my rapier."

"*You* fought a duel with a *pirate.*" Benford's derision made the others laugh.

Aurélie flushed. "I *shot* him! The other knocked my own rapier out of my fingers. But Benjy knifed his foot, and we ran away before he could pick up his cutlass and try to kill us."

Another brief silence ensued, as far above, the topmen exchanged incomprehensible comments, and the rising breeze toyed with everyone's clothes and hair.

The boys seemed to come to the mutual conclusion that the details in her telling, as well as the matter-of-fact tone, were convincing enough for trial.

Benford said, "Let's have a squint at your shooting, then."

Aurélie brought her pistol up, planted her feet, licked her finger to test the direction of the air, then sighted, all quick enough to make it plain that she was not a complete stranger to the heave of a deck.

The target was a crudely painted man shape on a stained, weather-rotted piece of sailcloth lashed to a grating. A flash—a report—a puff of smoke instantly wafted away on the wind, and the boys looked at the target, already peppered with holes. But they knew whose shots had landed where.

A new hole had appeared, well within the man shape, though to one side. The boys ran down to the target, and Benford stuck his finger in the new hole, as if Aurélie had somehow effected a cheat. But from the way he yanked back his finger, the burned edges were still smoldering from the hot iron ball.

"*You* shot a pirate?" one of the boys asked her, his tone more cautious.

"I told you," she said. "Now I must reload my—"

"I thought this was the quarterdeck of a man-of-war, not a drawing room." The newcomer was the third lieutenant, roughly the same age as

Benford. He and the latter eyed one another like a couple of bristling dogs, making it clear that the real conflict was between them.

Aurélie said, "It is only that the gentlemen wish me to demonstrate my pistol."

"That one is the marquis's daughter, sir," one of the boys said in a significant whisper.

"So I am given to understand," the lieutenant said with heavy sarcasm. After all, it was Aurélie and the parson's mother-in-law who had displaced him from his cabin. "Carry on, gentlemen," the lieutenant said with an air of importance, and he waited.

The others saluted, and he turned away—making it plain that he'd mostly spoken to get that salute from Benford, who as clearly hated being required to give it.

Benford flashed a grim look Aurélie's way, but she was already in retreat, having obviously been around boys long enough to know that when the top dog of any given hierarchy indulges in a spot of legally sanctioned bullying, as soon as he's gone, the next dog down will look for someone else to hassle.

Aurélie did not intend to be the recipient of Benford's bad mood. She dashed down the companionway, dodging around the sailors carrying huge lengths of rolled up canvas, and almost smacked into the oldest of the lieutenants just coming up from the hatch. "I have been seeking you, your ladyship, to convey to you the captain's compliments, and his invitation to dinner."

Aurélie looked frightened as she dropped a curtsey, the pistol hidden in her skirt, which was now dusted with gunpowder.

"One of the marines will fetch you when it is time," the man said, quite kindly. "You've only to look your best."

Mrs. Cobb was waiting for her when she reached the lower deck. Scolding in a constant undertone, much the way she scolded the boys when she supervised their once-weekly bathing on the upper deck, she took Aurélie in hand, exclaiming and blessing herself when she saw the pistol.

She tried to make certain the child was clean from top to toe, forced to call loud directions through the flimsy canvas door because Aurélie would only bathe in private. Perforce I had to remain in the tiny cabin as Aurélie carefully poured hot water into the bowl, and scrubbed herself all over. She put on clean underthings, and carefully tucked the oilcloth-covered letter of credit into her clean chemise. Behind the oil-cloth, the necklace pressed against her skin, its outline completely hidden. Last came the figured muslin gown. She emerged fully dressed.

"What a very fine print," the parson's mother-in-law commented.

"Straight from Paris, that's what the *marquesa* told me when she hired me. Paris to Saint-Domingue," said Mrs. Cobb as she eyed Aurélie critically.

"I am amazed it is not splashed with blood from their dreadful guillotine."

"Heh! The frogs are mad, everyone knows that, and as for that new government, Cobb says worse tales he's never met with."

The gown was patted and twitched into place. Mrs. Cobb's strong hands were respectfully gentle with the fine muslin, edged with green velvet ribbon at the high square neck, along the long sleeves, and along the top of the double ruffle that reached to the tops of Aurélie's slippers.

Last was a broad green velvet ribbon that had been carefully rolled so that the ends still showed a tendency to curl. It was tied high, with a large bow at the back where the V of the inset shoulders met.

"She's brown as a monkey," the parson's mother-in-law declared dispassionately. "No amount of fine French clothing will disguise that."

"That will go off soon's she's back in England's cold," was the cheerful rejoinder, and to Aurélie, "Mind you apply cucumber water every night, and my grandmother always said that bleaching with buttermilk would keep the skin pale as silk."

Aurélie muttered in French, "I do not *wish* to be pale."

The mother-in-law said to Aurélie, "It is rude to speak in heathen tongues before your elders. I trust you were properly baptized, child."

Aurélie's chin lifted. "I was baptized twice. Once by the priests at Saint-Domingue. And by my Nanny Hiasinte the obeah. That I remember, for it was when I turned ten, after we come to Kittredge Plantation."

The old woman hissed. "Hush that heathen talk."

Mrs. Cobb chuckled. "The dons and the frogs are all Popish, ma'am, they cannot help it. Heathens all! Bless me, that fine family she's intended for will beat it out of her quick enough. There you go, lamb! Remember your curtsey for the captain, and let Amos, who is most like to stand at your chair, tie your napkin to keep your gown clean. And you are not to drink wine, even if they offer it. Half-wine at most, and you will do me credit."

When the marine appeared, imposing in his red coat with his belt clay-piped and buttons polished, Aurélie followed close behind him to the doors of the captain's cabin, where the officers were gathered in full uniform, cocked hats under their arms. Off to the side stood the fat, cheerful parson, his wife, and his mother-in-law.

At the sweet *ting-ting!* of the ship's bells, the doors opened, and the guests entered the captain's cabin, which stretched all across the back of the stern, with windows overlooking the ship's wake. Aurélie was escorted to one side of the captain, the parson's wife at his other side.

Aurélie had been taught dainty manners. She quietly avoided the gravy-rich slab of meat put on her plate, confining herself to the potatoes, peas, and what turned out to be the last of the white bread.

For drink, the women were offered citrus juice while the men downed a lot of wine. Big, scarred sailors were on duty as waiters, their manners rough and ready. They kept the wine aflow, as well as demonstrating deft skills at keeping the dishes on the table, a skill much needed. As the meal progressed, the room tilted more sharply, making me glad I wasn't sitting with them. I know I would have been majorly seasick. The parson's mother-in-law put down her silverware, and sat there going pale and green as she kept swallowing.

The captain did not ask if his guests would like to go lie down. He merely observed that the wind was freshening, and issued orders for the officer on watch to clew up the royals and topgallants if he was of a mind.

As before, my awareness of what was passing blurred if Aurélie had no interest, and she clearly had no interest in the conversation, which covered gossip in Kingston, ships and captains at various stations, and rumors about the French Revolution. From the hints I'd garnered so far, I figured the time was somewhere in the middle of the 1790s.

Aurélie brightened when dessert appeared, a suety mass called plum duff, with rum poured over it. Her sailor attendant gave her a hearty helping, with the result her cheeks were quite pink when the captain sat back and decided it was time to pay attention to his guests as individuals.

He turned to Aurélie first. "Now, young lady, how am I to address a marquis's daughter? Are you Lady something, or is it Donna?"

Aurélie said obediently, "I am Doña Aurélie de Mascarenhas. But my mother says, I must be 'Lady' when I am in England."

"Oho, Donna it is," the captain replied. His face was red and shining under his wig, his glass attentively filled every time he took a swallow. "So, tell us about your Papa, young donna. Is he related to the Dukes of Aveiro? I remember there was some kind o' to-do, but that would be in my father's time. Weren't most of 'em put to death?"

"They are the Portuguese connections of the family," Aurélie said. "I do not know them. My father, he died when I was two. He had a letter of marque against France."

"But you speak French, do you not?"

"That's because my Grandmère is French. She came to Saint-Domingue from Martinique when she was small. She told me many stories about her cousins, the Taschers, at Les Trois-Îlets. 'Tis very beautiful, she says."

"Tascher!" one of the lieutenants exclaimed. "Why, isn't that the name of the Creole dasher taken up by one of the Directors in Paris?"

Definitely Josephine—Tascher de la Pagerie was her maiden name.

The captain raised his glass and said deliberately, "We will toast the lady." Ah. A reminder that they ought not to take a lady's name in vain. I knew that wasn't going to last. Poor Josephine was soon to be almost as vilified as her second husband.

The men raised their glasses, but before they could drink, the stern windows filled with blue-white glare, and thunder cracked, loud as cannon, directly overhead. Aurélie jumped, causing laughter among the officers. "It is not pirates," the captain said. "The only battle is betwixt us and the celestial bodies. You will be very glad to live in civilization again, where there are no hurricanes or pirates. For my middies told me that you are quite a fire-eater, young donna. We shall toast our young donna. . . ."

EIGHT

THE ONLY INTERRUPTION to the slow unwinding ribbon of the ship's wake, stitching together the changing sea and sky, was Aurélie's single attempt to climb into the tops. No sooner had she scrambled up to the second level, to the big platform joining the lower part of the mainmast, than the parson's wife let out a faint shriek, pointing.

Alarm telegraphed from officers to sailors, and a sailor's huge, hairy arm wound round Aurélie's skinny waist and plucked her off the masthead. She was indignant and tried exclaiming that she knew very well how to climb aloft, but in her excitement she spoke French, and by the time the sailor holding her had climbed down and set her on the deck, she was surrounded by well-meaning adults who scolded her about danger.

After that, she was confined in morose boredom to the wardroom, which caused time to blur for me until the morning a band of rain cleared off and a sailor called from the heights that Ushant had been sighted.

Aurélie jumped up and rushed up on deck with the other passengers, as the ship's crew began preparing for Portsmouth.

Aurélie was jubilant and nervous by turns, jiggling and jumping around. Mrs. Cobb made her wear her good dress, though poor Aurélie was shivering, her skin goose-bumpy in the brisk air. It had to be cold to a kid who'd only known tropical weather, which ranged from warm to broiling, even during storms. She definitely didn't have any jackets or sweaters or a cloak in her trunk—she'd probably never worn such a garment in her life.

Mrs. Cobb kept Aurélie tightly by her during the chaos of the landing, scanning the crowds that had gathered along the quay. Of course no one was there to meet them. No message could have reached England faster than Aurélie had. Mrs. Cobb took Aurélie to an inn called the Fountain, which was full of naval people, hired a room for both of them, and arranged for a letter to be dispatched.

She would not permit Aurélie to go out exploring but kept her inside and scolded sharply if Aurélie as much as moved. It might have been two or three days later when a tall man arrived, whose riding clothes proclaimed him a gentleman of means. He wore his own ash-brown hair neatly clubbed.

Mrs. Cobb presented the shrinking child to her Uncle Kittredge, dropping a great many hints about the extra care she had taken. She didn't mention the money Anne had paid her but hinted that the care had been entirely Christian charity, with the result that she departed in triumph, clutching several guineas.

Aurélie never looked back, because her entire interest was taken up by the two kids Uncle Kittredge had brought along, who were introduced as Cousin James and Cousin Cassandra.

While their father ordered a repast to refresh them for the return trip, and directed the inn servants to load Aurélie's trunk, James, Cassandra, and Aurélie eyed one another. They reminded me of young puppies as they began cautious questions.

"How old are you?" Cassandra asked.

"I have—*non*. I *am* twelve," Aurélie said. "How many years have you?"

"I will be twelve come Candlemas," Cassandra said.

"Candle-muss? I do not know this," Aurélie said.

Cassandra's blue-gray eyes rounded. "Are you really a heathen? Mama was afraid you would be a heathen. Fancy not knowing Candlemas. It falls on February second."

"Oh, *la Chandeleur!*"

Cassandra wasn't listening. She indicated her brother. "James is fifteen. Our eldest brother, William, is away at school."

"Is this the whole of you?" Aurélie asked.

"Oh, no." Cassandra tossed her head with a self-conscious twitch. She was evidently quite proud of her long curls of a soft shade of light brown. "Diana is the last of us, but she's just a baby of eight. Have you any sisters or brothers?"

"They are dead. I have my *maman* and Tante Mimba, and a prodigious number of cousins—"

"Prodigious!" Cassandra giggled. "Only my grandmother says that. It is odd to hear it from a girl. Is that the way everyone talks in Jamaica?"

James, a typical gawky teen, said rather loftily, "She has been taught the English of our grandparents' day. Papa warned me it might be so; it is entirely to be expected."

They turned to Aurélie, who said, "I lived in Saint-Domingue before coming to Jamaica," Aurélie enunciated carefully.

"So you speak French?" Cassandra began in a self-important voice. "Our governess gives us French lessons, and I am on the fifth lesson in *Adèle et Théodore.*"

I knew that reference! Madame de Genlis's schoolbooks for kids were brand-new at the time.

Cassandra's speech halted when Aurélie clasped her hands in pleasure and spoke in a stream of French, "I have read them. All three volumes, through three times! And *Les Annales,* which I do not like as much."

At the clear incomprehension in Cassandra's and James's faces, she faltered to a stop.

"It sounds . . . different, when you speak it," Cassandra said. "And so very quick."

"You speak quick, too," Aurélie said. "People around me, it is very difficult to understand."

"Well, of course," Cassandra said. "We speak excellent English. Miss Oliver is very careful about our elocution."

James cut in with helpful warning, "What you're hearing from the seamen is the accents of Wapping. I trust you did not learn that, or Miss Oliver will rap it out of you." He smacked one hand down hard on his palm, making Aurélie jump.

Their father reappeared, and both kids resumed company manners. They sat down to a substantial meal, then it was time to leave. James ran ahead to claim a seat on the box, followed by his sister.

Left with her uncle, whose manner had been distant and somber, Aurélie seemed uneasy. But she had made a promise. Turning quickly, she wrestled from beneath her gown the much-battered, grubby oilcloth. "*Maman* said I am to put this into your hands."

Ignoring the waiter who had been attempting to clear the dishes, Uncle Kittredge pulled a pocket knife from his waistcoat and slit the stitching. When he'd read through the paper, the look he turned on Aurélie was speculative, and his voice was two or three notes more friendly as he said, "Thank you. You're a very good girl. We will write to your mother at once to let her know all's been done as she wished, shall we not, niece? But first, let us take you home."

They got into the carriage. His son climbed up to sit beside him, across from the girls, so I heard Uncle Kittredge say in an undertone, "You will be able to tell your mother that you saw many men unpowdered, eh? There are more than I who refused to pay that unconscionable tax."

I didn't understand until later that that comment, mild and minor as it was, was a pretty good indicator of who ruled the roost at Undertree, the Kittredge estate.

The carriage made its way out of the jumble of buildings. England looked to me like movies set in the past, complete to picturesquely rutted roads. I was glad I didn't have to feel the jolts and bumps that the others didn't seem to notice.

Kittredge was anxious to make it into Hampshire before nightfall. Twilight this far north was a long, slow dimming of light in spectacularly beautiful countryside. I know I enjoyed it more than Aurélie did, for as the day waned, she hunched her shoulders up, her hands tight on her arms until her uncle said, "Are you chilled, Niece? Why, it is as balmy as summer!"

Telling her it was balmy didn't make her warmer. She looked back miserably, until he said authoritatively, "Cassandra, give her the carriage rug."

The girl made a noise of protest, reached under the seat, and pulled out a thick furry thing, which Aurélie burrowed into gratefully.

She was asleep when the carriage at last jounced its way up a graveled approach to a sizable square house built in the Palladian style, complete to Augustan gardens at either side, and the farm houses quite banished beyond the wild garden at the back.

Aurélie paid no attention to any of this. She woke, heavy-eyed, when Cassandra shook her. "We're home!"

"Welcome to Undertree," Kittredge said genially.

"We've settled it that you shall have the guest bedchamber near me," Cassandra exclaimed. "Mama said before we came to fetch you that Diana is still to sleep in the nursery, and good riddance. *I* did not get my own bedchamber until I was *ten*. Did you have your own in Jamaica? Of course you did. A marquis's daughter, you must have had fifty rooms all of your very own, and a dozen maidservants, too . . ."

Chattering on, Cassandra led Aurélie, while William Kittredge smiled benignly, and James raced off. Aurélie glanced back doubtfully, to see the carriage vanishing. "My trunk?" she asked.

"The servants will fetch it in," Cassandra said, and turned. "Mama! Cousin Aurelia is here!"

"Aurélie," Aurélie whispered.

Cassandra tossed her hair again as her Papa said, "This is a fine opportunity for you to practice your French," in a meaningful voice, as a woman joined him.

"Awurrr-ray-*lee*," Cassandra said obediently, in the penetrating voice used by girls who are used to being the center of attention and want to make certain they stay there. "Have I said it properly, Cousin? Mama, she talks English like Grandmama, with many French words. It is so very droll!"

"Cassandra, keep your peace."

Aurélie gazed up at her aunt as the woman surveyed her. Philomena Bouldeston Kittredge could have been any age from thirty to fifty, for the lines of habitually suppressed emotion bracketed her mouth and eyes, and lined her forehead. Of medium height and build, she was rigidly corseted under that softly draped gown of heavy rose silk. She had a quantity of light brown hair, pale skin, and pale eyes, as did the small girl clinging to her skirt and squinting at Aurélie.

Aunt Kittredge's mouth tightened, and I thought *uh-oh*.

"Show your cousin the house, Cassandra," Kittredge said.

Cassandra twitched her shoulders importantly and took Aurélie's unresisting hand. They started away, Cassandra beginning in a penetrating voice, "Undertree is actually the old house, built anew at the time of the First George, but then the family wanted a bigger, so they moved into Kent, and Undertree came to my grandfather . . ."

Before I was inexorably pulled after the girls, I saw William Kittredge beckon to his wife and silently show her the rumpled paper that Aurélie had brought all that way. His wife's brows lifted, and her face cleared. "Well," she said on an exhaled breath.

Nice call, Anne, I thought, wishing I could stay with the adults long enough to hear their talk, but I'd learned by now that where Aurélie went, I went.

As the girls walked through the house, Cassandra going on loudly about each piece of furniture and decoration as if Aurélie were blind and deaf, I blurred out—then jolted to awareness at the sound of Aurélie's voice.

"Duppy? Are you here?"

Aurélie gazed into a standing mirror framed by fine wood with grape bunches worked into it. Behind her was a sizable room with a curtained bed against the back wall. Under the window sat an elegant little *escritoire*, gilt and spindle-legged, with tiny drawers worked in. The wallpaper, or what they called "hangings," was stripes of blue ribbon between florets of yellow and pink, barely visible in the light of a branch of candles.

She dodged this way and that, then her eyes widened, and suddenly I was looking out at her face from inside the mirror. "You *are* here," she breathed. "You didn't get lost. There was no looking glass on the ship, and oh, my dreams are so very strange. I have my own looking-glass now, you see. Can you speak?"

"I'm here," I said, ready to launch into my carefully planned explanation about myself and my history.

"I can see your mouth move, I think. Oh, if I had more light!"

"AWR-ray-LEE," came Cassandra's voice from the hallway outside the bedroom. "I'm to summon you to dinner." She flung open the door and walked in. "You do not need to shift your clothes, it is just the family, Mama said. We're to have syllabub with the dressed meat and potatoes."

Aurélie gave me a tiny smile, then turned away, saying to Cassandra, "Pray, Cousin, what is seel-a-boob?"

"Fancy not knowing syllabub! What horrid foods did you eat in Jamaica?" Cassandra went off into gales of shrill giggles as they walked downstairs.

NINE

AURÉLIE SURVIVED HER FIRST DINNER. Everybody was extra polite. That meant the conversation was extra inane, all about the ship and the weather and the captain's dinners to which she, as the highest ranking female, had always been invited.

Afterward, she ran up to her room, where she found the servants in the middle of going through her trunk with the laudable intention of airing and laundering everything, commenting the while. But when the maid saw the pistol, she let out a shriek, and when Aurélie said innocently, "That is only my pistol. There is no ball in it, and no powder—" the maid fled as if it was fully automatic, locked and loaded, and Aurélie was pointing it at her head.

The entire family crowded into Aurélie's room, everyone staring at the pistol. "I need it to fight pirates," Aurélie explained.

Aunt Kittredge said in a determinedly sugary voice, "There are no pirates anywhere in England. Mr. Kittredge, that is, your Uncle Kittredge, will keep it safe."

She gestured for the maid to put the pistol on a tray, which the woman did with great care, as if it would go off if she touched it. The pistol was borne away.

While that went on, another servant prepared a bath. The maids turned to Aurélie expectantly once the steaming hot water was poured.

Aurélie's fingers rose to her chest, where the necklace lay beneath her clothes, and she insisted she could bathe alone.

Aunt Kittredge expressed immediate approval. "Modesty is an excellent quality in a young lady. I will be in to hear your prayers when you are ready for bed. Send Betty to fetch me when you are finished."

"Prayers? *Le rosaire?*" Aurélie asked.

Aunt Kittredge's brows twitched together. "You do know your prayers, do you not? You have not got into any filthy Popish habits, idol worship and the like?"

"I do not know what that is," Aurélie said doubtfully. "I am to say I was baptized when I lived for a time with my Grandmère Marie-Claude—"

"A French Papist, I make no doubt." Aunt Kittredge caught herself up, then said in a determinedly kindly voice, with a false smile, "I am certain she is a very good woman of her sort. But you are in England now, your *grandfather's* family. The sooner you learn proper ways, the better."

"My mother said I would have a better life," Aurélie repeated, her eyes filling with tears.

Aunt Kittredge reached out as if to pat Aurélie on the head, then snatched her hand back. "I will leave you to bathe." On her way out, she said to the maid at the door, "That hair of hers is positively wooly. When she is done, check her for lice. Then fetch me."

There were no lice in her curls, thanks to Mrs. Cobb's vigilance. Before the exhausted kid could sleep she had to stumble through a prayer with Aunt Kittredge correcting her English and her theology every step of the way. Aunt Kittredge instructed Providence on how to run the world, and then lectured the Almighty on how humble and grateful she was. Aurélie dutifully repeated every sentence, though it was clear she comprehended about a tenth of it.

After that, Aurélie was finally left alone, and before she slid into sleep—and I into a dream state—I heard her whispering a prayer in French, a confused jumble of the Latin rosary and a plea for protection of those at home.

*   *   *

The next morning, Aurélie didn't come to the mirror to talk to me. After breakfast, she followed Cassandra up to the schoolroom to be introduced to Miss Oliver, the governess. As the latter got Diana settled, Aurélie was permitted to wander around and look at the books and toys. None of them seemed to catch her interest until she discovered an old and extremely battered spinet that had been shoved into the far corner. She examined it closely, fingering the back as she sought the expected bellows.

But there was no bellows. So she gently pressed the keys, and smiled at the sound. It was tinny compared to a modern piano, but it was not nearly as awful as the reedy squeal and moan of her regal.

She sat down and plucked out a melody, hesitant at first. Miss Oliver, the governess, was a serious woman of about forty. She finished setting Diana to tracing out her letters and came to place written music before Aurélie. On discovering that she'd been taught to read music by her French grandmother, Miss Oliver conducted Aurélie in great state downstairs to the more formal salon, in which resided a fairly new Viennese fortepiano.

Aunt Kittredge appeared from the morning room as Aurélie sat down to the instrument, softly experimenting with its touch and tone. Delighted with the shimmering, ethereal sound, she launched into a French air, causing the adults to exclaim in delight. She did not see Cassandra's jealous pout. Nobody saw it but me.

Aunt Kittredge showered praise on Aurélie for her diligence and taste, finishing with a declaration that Miss Oliver must instantly begin her lessons on the fortepiano.

If Miss Oliver was offered additional pay for getting an extra student added to her workload, I didn't hear it.

For the next few days, Aurélie was the favorite of the parents. They consulted her about favorite dishes. They corrected her English gently, and smiled at her quaint expressions. When they asked if the kids wanted to do something, it was always Aurélie they spoke to.

She was almost never alone, which meant she wasn't thinking about me. I suppose I could have poked her (I didn't know how that worked, as I had no hands) but I knew how much she hated that. And she didn't seem to be ready for my big speech anyway—she was too bewildered by all the changes in her life.

So I waited and watched as everybody tried to adjust to the newcomer. Cassandra, who should have been Aurélie's natural ally, veered between making a pet of Aurélie and bossing her. Cassandra reacted to each sign of her parents' indulgence of Aurélie as if something had been taken away from her.

Aurélie was looking more and more deer-in-the-headlights. She picked at her food, eating so little that at first no one noticed that she lived mainly on bread and cheese, with greens when they were offered. By the end of the week, she looked listless, and admitted to a headache. The Kittredges let her stay with the servants and sleep while they went off to church.

Another day or two brought a startling change in the weather. The glorious autumn colors seemed to change overnight to gray and brown, the world weeping from under a sky the color of iron. Poor Aurélie couldn't get warm, no matter what.

She only came to the mirror once. "Duppy," she said, her eyes brimming with tears, "can you see Jamaica? *Maman* and Tante Mimba? Nanny Hiasinte?"

On each I shook my head. Then I pointed at her, saying, *I see you.*

"You cannot hear Nanny, then? You do not hear the wisdom of the *lwa?*"

I shook my head twice, and began to mouth out my prepared speech about myself, but she turned away on the first word and dropped down onto the hearth, a disconsolate little huddle.

She didn't want to leave the fireside, though the governess believed in vigorous walks each day at noon, unless there was a storm. Aurélie stopped practicing the fortepiano, causing the severe Miss Oliver to mutter about spoilt children, though Aurélie was too miserable to care.

Cassandra loudly went about her lessons, clearly reveling in praise that I suspect she'd been used to getting before Aurélie and her gigantic dowry appeared and used up the lion's share of the adults' positive attention.

Aurélie's headache and listlessness developed into a full-on cold. One morning at breakfast when she couldn't stop coughing, the adults leaped to ply her with remedies—the most common for pretty much any childhood illness being a whopping dose of calomel, which Aurélie refused to take.

"I will not have it," Aurélie whimpered tearfully. "Calomel is evil. My duppy said so—"

"Who is your 'duppy'?" Aunt Kittredge cut in. "Is that what you call your mother, or your medical man? *Had* you a medical man on Kittredge Plantation?"

"My duppy is visible only to me. And to my Nanny Hiasinte," Aurélie corrected herself. "Nanny saw my duppy when she made obeah." And at their looks of puzzlement, "Obeah is magic—"

Aunt Kittredge's face mottled. "*Lady Aurélie de Mascarenhas.* You shall cease your wicked, heathen talk in this house!" she stated, too angry to remember even that big fat dowry.

"My duppy saved *Maman* when she was wounded by pirates," Aurélie declared, her voice wavering.

"Pirates?" James spoke up in the background.

"Where were you?" Cassandra asked. "Did you actually see them, or is this a taradiddle?"

"I fought pirates," Aurélie said to either side. "With my own pistol."

James whistled. His mother turned a killer scowl his way, then said with such saccharine sweetness I'm surprised they didn't all drop dead of diabetes, "*Lady* Aurélie. We have permitted you to remain by the fireside for your health of a Sunday, while we attend divine service, but perhaps we have been too lenient."

Aurélie said, "I am ready to be baptized in your ways. I know it is coming, me."

Before Aunt Kittredge could speak, Uncle Kittredge said quickly, "You are a very good little girl. You know by instinct what is right. Doctor Warren will instruct you in your Collect. We will see to that."

When breakfast was finished, Uncle Kittredge sent the kids to the schoolroom.

James followed, and as soon as the door was shut, he said, "Pirates?"

Aurélie settled herself on the hearth and wearily took up the book they were studying. "The pirates attacked Kittredge Plantation. It was before I entered the ship to come to England."

"Did you really fight them?" James asked.

"Yes."

Cassandra turned on her little sister, who was crouched over a book at the work table. "Go over there to the toy chest," she commanded. "You are not to listen."

Diana pouted. "I will tell Mama if you have secrets from me."

"Go," Cassandra ordered. "And if you tattle, you better check your bed for spiders *every night*. Big, hairy ones. And you will *never* know if you got them all."

Diana ran wailing from the room.

James sighed. "Now she'll peach."

Cassandra tossed her curls. "If she does, I'll say I only warned her about spiders, and ask Mama to keep her in the nursery. We cannot hear over her grizzling."

"Tell us about pirates, Cousin," James asked, leaning forward.

Aurélie did, much as she'd told the midshipmen.

"So you can load and shoot a pistol?" James asked.

Cassandra affected a shudder.

"I am ver-ry good," Aurélie said. "But I must practice, this I know."

James grinned "By thunder, there's scant chance of that. If Mama hears about it—"

Footsteps on the landing outside the schoolroom parted the three. James dashed through the opposite door, and Cassandra took up a book of inspirational quotations as Aunt Kittredge appeared, the governess just behind her.

Everyone was dismissed, and Aurélie put to bed, after a mega-long prayer in which God was told how every religion was straight from the hands of the devil except Aunt Kittredge's, and Aurélie begged forgiveness for harboring any thought but what she was told by her elders.

By Sunday, Aurélie was over the worst of her illness and found herself bundled along with the family to church.

On their return, there was cold food, and for the first time, her aunt noticed her avoidance of meat. "Eat a slice of beef," Aunt Kittredge said. "It is very good and particularly sustaining."

Aurélie shook her head. And when her aunt demanded a reason, she said softly, "I promised my great-grandmother not to eat meat."

"Filthy Papist habits," was her response.

Uncle Kittredge said more mildly, "My understanding is, they only avoid meat of a Friday, and perhaps during Lent."

Aurélie looked down as her aunt chided her with a determined smile, asking her to consider what people will think. Was she setting up to be too fine a lady for the excellence of Undertree beef and pork?

Aurélie said, "Your foods are very good. My favorite is the boiled oats with honey and milk. I like it, oh, much!"

That seemed to mollify Aunt Kittredge, and Aurélie was permitted to retire to the schoolroom. *That woman is going to be trouble*, I thought.

Aurélie sat down at the spinet, a blanket pulled around her. She seemed as depressed by the bleak northern light as by the weather, for though her fever appeared to be gone, she was listless. She touched the keys, clapped her arms to her sides as if to shut out a draft of cold air, then she sat in a small armchair with a book, her feet tucked under her.

James appeared in the schoolroom a bit later. "What did you think of church?" he said in the tone of one inviting complaint.

Aurélie's face cleared. "Oh, the music is very beautiful. It's also interesting, how your church has many things similar to Holy Mass on Saint-Domingue. But Holy Mass is in Latin. Grandmère had her Gallican Missal, and everybody had a book in your church. My religion in Jamaica is not written down, it's taught by speaking, by singing, by dancing. I'm glad that I find a new way to *le bon Dieu* in each country, and do you think that if I am baptized here, too, it will give me extra protection? Three is an important number. This vicar said so, many times."

James twitched a shoulder in a dismissive shrug. "You can ask Charles, my cousin once removed, if we visit him in Yorkshire. It is said of him that he will be a man of brilliant parts, though my brother Will is a fine scholar. They intend Cousin Charles for the law, but he wants to go into the church and will spout off as much as you like about such things at the doff of a hat. Will you tell me more about pirates? How many fights did you see?"

"I think three, though perhaps there were more when I was small. I don't remember. The ones I remember, I sailed with my mother."

"I thought your father was the sea captain?"

"Yes. But he died when I was small."

"Did he gabble the Spanish lingo at you?"

Aurélie gazed into the fire from her accustomed spot on the hearth. "I don't remember any Spanish. I remember *Je t'aime, ma petite*. That is French. He had so deep a voice, very deep. He smelled so good. He had a smile like the north star, so bright in the night sky, crooked-y, with one side curled up. Everybody loved his smile, that much I remember. But after he died I had to go and live with my grandmother, for so very long a time."

"Where was your mother?"

"Sailing with my Uncle Thomas."

"A woman? Sailing? What did she do, mend their sails?"

"No, she is a *ver-ry* good captain. She and Tante Mimba, they taught me to fight with my rapier."

"Were you good at it?" James asked skeptically.

His tone roused Aurélie. "I am good. I can beat some of the boys, and when we first came to Jamaica, I beat Harry one time."

"When the weather warms up, we'll see how good you are," James promised.

It was probably intended as a threat, but Aurélie smiled. "I would like that, oh, much, for I must get the skill to defend myself, Aunt Mimba said. Thank you, Cousin James."

*   *   *

Aurélie avoided the mirror all that winter, so time slid by for me super fast. The only thing that roused her out of her lethargy was her birthday, which, like Cassandra's, was celebrated with a special cake full of currants, and with little gifts—a handmade reticule from Cassandra, and a gold cross from the uncle and aunt. She also roused when she wrote letters to her mother, long badly spelled and blotted passages about how ill she felt, how cold it was, how very much she wanted to go home.

Each Friday, when Cassandra brought to her mother the weekly letter she wrote to her maternal cousin Lucretia, Aurélie also handed off a letter to be sent to Jamaica. She began counting up how many days until she could expect her first answer.

Although Cassandra received regular missives from Cousin Lucretia, when spring showed its first signs, there was still no letter next to Aurélie's plate at breakfast.

Around the time of the first thaw, Aurélie finally started talking to me in the mirror again.

"Do you see me all the time?" she asked.

I brought my head down in a nod.

Her gaze sidled one way, then the other, as her skinny fingers twitched at her high-necked gown, then she whispered, "Even when I am in the bath?"

So she'd hit *that* age. I wanted to laugh, but I was afraid she'd see it. How to explain that all the habitual tasks that we do on autopilot were a blur to me? Keep it simple, I thought.

I mimed sleep, and saw immediate relief in her face. "So you wake up when I talk to you?"

Not quite. Time stopped blurring whenever she was alert or intent about something, but again I opted for the easy answer, and nodded.

So she started talking to me once or twice a day. She paid no attention to my attempts to respond, now that she knew I didn't have telepathic powers or connection with her loved ones on the Spirit Net. She talked for her own comfort, mostly complaining about the never-ending cold and darkness, her confusing dreams, and how tedious were her lessons, mixed up with anxious wonderings about why *Maman* had not written back. *Maman* seldom went into Kingston—there might be hurricanes—the English ship might have gone off course, or had to stop at the other islands.

She also reminisced wistfully about her life in Jamaica, including what she'd learned from Nanny Hiasinte. I gathered that *lwa* and duppies, as supernatural beings, were too strange to be understood. Like adults and their inexplicable behavior, only more so. Maybe that was why she had no apparent interest in me, except as a listener. And until we figured out how to actually talk, I wasn't going to be much use, but I figured it had to come.

My biggest worry was always Alec. I kept telling myself that there had to be a way around this time travel thing—that if I managed to get Aurélie safely to Dobrenica, I'd find myself stepping out of that mysterious door a second after I'd stepped in, in which case Alec would never even know I was gone.

I held hard to that image.

Meanwhile, life went on at Undertree.

Lessons were strictly organized. Aurélie adapted quickly, except for the French lessons. She and Miss Oliver clashed, neither being intelligible to the other. Being a marquis's daughter, Aurélie was exempt from the threat of the ruler, unlike poor, near-sighted little Diana, who often blotted her paper as she crouched over it to write. But the governess was adamant when she declared first that it was unbecoming for girls to correct their betters, second, that Mrs. Kittredge had hired her specifically for the elegance of her French (it was the same French that Aunt Kittredge had been taught) and furthermore, Aurélie's accent was decidedly "colonial." I could have told Miss Oliver that her French, unlike Aurélie's, only slightly resembled anything actually spoken in France, but nobody was asking me!

Aunt Kittredge ended the matter by declaring that Aurélie was excused from French lessons. She was permitted to read any of the French texts in the schoolroom, but she must not interfere with Miss Oliver's teaching of the other girls.

Time whizzed by uneventfully after that.

When the thaw became real, servants threw open the entire house to clean it thoroughly, and the strengthening sun improved Aurélie's spirits and energy. She returned to playing the fortepiano and was far better at it than Cassandra, who had the decided advantage in singing. Aurélie's husky contralto was deemed too low—a clear soprano was the fashion—so it was decided she'd forego singing in favor of playing, which meant the girls no longer shared musical lessons.

One balmy March day, James showed up while Cassandra was downstairs in the salon, having her lesson. He seldom appeared in the schoolroom, being more or less under his father's tutelage. Since he was intended for the army, nobody appeared to be concerned if he actually read any of the books his father occasionally put his way.

Aurélie often sat by the schoolroom window, warming herself by the strengthening sunlight. She was there one day, doing some fine sewing as Diana struggled through conjugating French verbs for Miss Oliver.

James strolled in, obviously bored and looking for distraction. Seeing Aurélie sitting alone in the window seat, he beckoned, a grin flaring in his pimply face. Aurélie put down her sewing and followed him to the other window. "The gallery has warmed up enough to go into without freezing," he whispered. "You said you know the art of the *duello*. Show me."

Her whole demeanor brightened. "Yes." Then clouded. "But these skirts. I can't fight, for I shall tread on my hem. And I couldn't put my René clothes into my trunk. They said I cannot be René in England."

"Be René?"

"I pretended to be a boy, in Jamaica. I was ever so free," she said wistfully.

James pursed his lips, then said, "My old clothes are in trunks in the attic. Let me see if there's something in there you can wear. Just don't let 'em see you, or they'll set up a screech and we'll find ourselves in no end of trouble."

Aurélie fervently agreed, and a short time later, they met in the gallery, a long, high-ceilinged room that doubled as a ballroom if they threw open the back doors to the second parlor, used only for company. As Cassandra and the fortepiano were safely in the front parlor, they could engage with their swords without worrying about discovery.

At first, James seemed somewhat uncomfortable with Aurélie wearing his clothes, even though she was nothing more than a little stick figure in the flapping shirt, waistcoat, and thick breeches. It was the idea more than the actuality that appeared to bother him.

The next problem came when they attempted their first pass. James was used to the art of gentleman's dueling, with its attention to correct position and poise, and its many strictures. Aurélie had been coached to strike hard and fast, using her small size to disable an opponent before she ran.

After some stinging blows from her whip-fast, focused attack, James betrayed surprise, chagrin, and then wary respect. The lesson took an abrupt turn toward the serious, and both got an excellent workout.

He might have asked her out of idleness and boredom, but by the end of half an hour, he'd become as enthusiastic as she was, and when their hour ended, he was a fair way toward treating her like a little brother. Aurélie had found a friend at last.

As the weather brightened into spring, the two met for an hour or so on every day that Cassandra had singing lessons, for she could not always be trusted; if Cassandra thought something improper, she felt it her duty to tattle to their mother.

Their talk ranged widely. Aurélie described life in Jamaica, and James talked about his hope to someday command a regiment. His elder brother Will, at Winchester College, was the bookish one, he explained. The family hoped that Will might one day make his way into Parliament. He usually spent his holidays with friends, in particular one who was the second son of a viscount.

As soon as the weather warmed enough for rambles in the tangled park that stretched up into the wild hills behind the garden, James took Aurélie out for target practice. He sneaked her pistol out of the iron box where it had been locked, so that she might use her own weapon.

She didn't dare go out in her borrowed clothes, for she was too visible from the many windows, but once they were beyond the neat hedgerows, she kirtled up her skirt, baring her thick woolen stockings.

The two shot at rocks set on a fallen tree. James showed her how to load and fire his fowling piece. Just as he respected her wild have-at-you style of fencing, he had been amazed at the quality of her French-made flintlock pistol, small as it was. They traded their weapons back and forth, comparing their range and seeing who could load fastest.

The rest of her time was taken up with lessons and domestic pursuits. Cassandra, encouraged by her mother to correct Aurélie's English, claimed it was a duty, but could not quite hide her obvious enjoyment of implied superiority. Thus, Aurélie seldom had the chance to finish a sentence, with the result that she became quieter around the family, except for James, who told her he found her occasional lapses into French word order or regularized verbs as delightful as her accent.

James had completely taken over as Aurélie's chief confidant, so my careful speech had yet to be heard. I should have expected that, I came to realize. When I was her age, I had zero interest in adults—I never asked strange ones their names, they were always Mr. or Ms. Somebody, or else Teacher, or Doctor, or Police Officer. I was the invisible friend who listened to her and watched over her when she needed me, and that was that.

I knew it would change.

TEN

EACH MORNING AURÉLIE FLUNG OPEN her windows and sucked in lungfuls of fresh air. Sometimes she came to the mirror to tell me the names of blossoms. Once she asked if I knew what was blooming in Jamaica or Saint-Domingue, and when I shook my head, she turned away.

She was happier, and busy: Miss Oliver let the girls go out into the garden in the afternoons if they worked hard in the morning.

The garden was bordered by a ha-ha fence, which partly obscured the home farms down slope and also the wild tangle of woods up the hillside. The girls were not permitted to venture beyond the ha-ha unless accompanied. James and Aurélie had done their shooting well behind the barns. Cassandra would never go beyond the southern hedge, declaring that the stink of the farm made her ill.

Aurélie roamed all over the garden, now that everything was in bloom. She loved the roses most, snuffing in the fragrances that must have reminded her of flowers in the islands.

While cruising along the ha-ha and peering into the wood one day, Aurélie stopped Cassandra, who was describing in detail the latest letter from her cousin Lucretia, and casting sighs about the hundred eternities before the cousins' expected visit.

"What is that music?" Aurélie asked, when Cassandra paused to draw breath.

"What music?" Cassandra said, hands on her hips. "*I* don't hear anything." Her emphasis on the "I" did not admit of the possibility that another's perceptions had merit—one of the less endearing characteristics she'd picked up from her mother.

Aurélie stood poised on her toes, peering into the wild wood, which was dappled with golden light and blue shadows.

Cassandra sighed loudly. "If we must stand about in the sun, you ought at least to fetch your bonnet. Mama does not want you getting all burnt black as a cork again. She said so a thousand times. You are still horridly brown."

I writhed in futile anger not just at Cassandra's thoughtless bigotry, but at how superior she was about it. *It's typical of the time*, I reminded myself. *She's no worse than anyone else.*

But it didn't make me feel any better. As for Aurélie, she ignored Cassandra, staring intently into the wood for half a minute more. The way she stood there peering, head at an angle, made it clear that she heard *something*. Whatever it was didn't reach me.

She followed Cassandra inside, returned to the fortepiano, and warmed up with scales. She worked through her Haydn and Scottish airs. Then she bent over the keys, her brow knit as she tapped out the same pattern of notes, an entrancing bit of melody with two chord changes in it. She kept changing keys, and frowning.

Lessons became more irksome as April spooled away toward May. Only Aurélie seemed unaffected by the first warm spell of the year, though the others looked flushed and damp. Aurélie continued to wear her winter gowns, which were made high to the neck, the sleeves long, though the younger girls had shifted to lighter muslin and cotton prints. Cassandra talked continually of July, when the governess was given a month to visit her home, which meant a month off from school as well as the longed-for visit from her maternal cousins.

This talk of a month's vacation surprised me with its forward-looking generosity, for I remembered the horrible lives of governesses in the Brontes' books and those by Elizabeth Gaskell. But then some things that the kids let fall made it clear that Miss Oliver didn't get paid for the time she was gone. July was the month that various portions of the family often visited others, and Aunt Kittredge didn't feel she was getting her money's worth if some of the governess's pupils were traveling or busy with visiting cousins. So the solution? Don't pay her at all, but send her packing for a month.

On the first of May, the kids were granted a half-holiday. James had planned to go fishing and offered to take the girls along if they brought a hamper of food.

Aunt Kittredge saw them off after issuing scolding reminders to Cassandra and James to watch out for Diana, and, in a determinedly nicer tone, tucking all kinds of "dears" into it, reminding Aurélie to stay out of the sun. "It's in your best interest, as I am certain your dear mother would agree, once we hear from her."

Aurélie bobbed a curtsey, uttering her French-accented thanks, while her gaze kept stealing toward the garden border.

At last they were released, Aurélie and Cassandra carrying the hamper between them.

James led them to the old garden gate. When I say "old," I mean ancient, far older than the house. The stones were covered with moss that didn't quite hide the faint indentations of Celtic knotwork, half-hidden by a tangle of climbing roses whose blood-red hue reminded me of Dobrenica. Sorrow—regret—worry about Alec suffused me, as I watched Diana brush her fingers over the dark green mossy indentations.

"Ugh!" Cassandra slapped her sister's hand away. "You needn't get filthy before we've gone ten paces."

They passed through the gate and walked on. James led them over the top of an old hill, so thick with tangled growth that little sunlight penetrated. The air was cool and still. Diana fretted about branches hitting her face and thistles in her stockings.

"You wanted to come," Cassandra said. "I told you that you should remain in the nursery, like the baby you are."

"I'm not a baby. I cannot see them."

"Of course you can see them. Anybody can. Stop putting on airs to be interesting, or we shan't bring you again."

James ran ahead. A few moments later, his glad shout ended the squabble. "Here!"

He pointed with pride of discovery to a grassy bank under the shade of a willow. "Oh, capital!" Cassandra cried, and took charge of spreading out the cloth and unpacking the hamper. She handed plates to Aurélie to set out, and put Diana in charge of unfolding the cloth wrappings from the food, which short-sighted Diana was able to do.

James put together his fishing rod and tramped off to the stream in search of a good spot to sit.

Aurélie carried James's share of the lunch to him, then rejoined the sisters. For a while, all was quiet as they chose among the cold meats, cheese, bread, and tartlets that had been packed up for them. The food and the cool shade revived them.

After they'd eaten, Cassandra volunteered to repack the hamper before ants could discover it. Aurélie carried the pitcher down to the stream to fill with water, and Diana wandered around from sun splash to shadow, bent over as she examined dainty violet sprigs of bellflower, blush pink dog roses, and yellow iris along the stream bank.

Aurélie kept glancing in one direction as she helped put away the leftover food. When they were done, she said, "Who else shares this wood?"

James, who had pretty much ignored the girls thus far, gave a guffaw. "The fairies!"

Cassandra heaved a loud sigh. "Do not be a simpleton, James. You *know* how angry Mama will be if Diana starts prating of that nonsense again."

James turned his head. "Diana, you are old enough to know that talk of fairies is a taradiddle, are you not?"

Diana tossed her head in a fair assumption of her sister's gesture. "*I* know better than to talk about fairies to Mama."

Cassandra turned a sour look James's way. "Very well. But I don't see why you need mention them at all." She then said to Aurélie, "This is our land. Though sometimes the farm children will come up here. Why, did you hear them? You have very quick ears if you did, for I've heard nothing except birds scolding."

"The singing," Aurélie said. "And a fiddle."

"There's no singing," Cassandra stated. "Or a fiddle. It has to be birds."

"Might I go a little ways down that path, just to see?"

"I want to go with her," Diana said.

"Now look what you've done," Cassandra said crossly to Aurélie. "She'll be pouting about it forever."

James called, "Recollect we've an equally long walk back."

"And I think it's going to rain," Cassandra added, looking around. "The air smells of thunder."

"I was used to walk much longer," Aurélie said. "I don't mind at all."

Cassandra looked up at the treetops and sighed. "If you must. But stay within hearing distance, and be quick about it." She turned fiercely on her sister. "And *you* help me to pack the rug."

"*Bon*," Aurélie said happily and scampered down the path.

All I heard were her steps on the path and the quiet hiss and rustle of her skirts as she pushed past long, tangled grasses and wildflowers. For a time she plunged deeper into the blue-green shadows of the wood, making me wonder if she was going to get herself lost, until splashes of golden sunlight appeared between the tree trunks.

Aurélie slowed when we reached an enormous oak that bordered on a sun dappled dell, the mighty over-arching branches pleached with those of a hawthorn in lacey bloom across the dell to the left; and to the right, the square-cracked, knobby branches of an ancient ash. Sunlight shafted down through those branches onto a circle of tall green grass and wildflowers, about which butterflies dipped and flickered.

Aurélie halted at the verge, gazing in wonder at betony and bluebells, columbine and loosestrife, muskmellow and snapdragon, just to name a few—an impossibility of wildflowers.

Then she said to the empty dell, "Who are you?"

Between one blink and another (not that I had eyes for blinking) there They were.

> *. . . Behold the chariot of the Fairy Queen!*
> *Celestial coursers paw the unyielding air;*
> *Their filmy pennons at her word they furl,*
> *And stop obedient to the reins of light . . .*

Shelley's lines come close to the shock of their glorious appearance, limned in golden shafts. I heard the music at last, an elusive, compelling melody.

Aurélie clapped her hands in delight as the magnificent winged chargers and their airy chariot descended gently from the sky, large as life, ethereally glowing.

The chariot touched down to the grass so lightly that no flowers bent, no grass was crushed. The horses tossed their heads, manes rippling, and sparks flew where they pawed the ground, though not a blade of grass stirred: they were lighter than thistledown.

From the chariot stepped a tall woman whose moonbeam hair flowed in silken rivers to her heels. Her gown floated about her, swirling wisps of smoke and starlight. Next to her, a male who made Tolkien's Legolas look coarse and uncouth by comparison, his clothing as unabashedly tight and revealing as hers, except for honest-to-Romantic Poets ruffled shirt, with lace cuffs to his knuckles. His hair, the color of flame, was almost as long as hers. I swallowed hard and pulled my gaze away with a pop I could practically feel.

"Welcome!" Princess Moonbeam said, lifting her hands in a gesture of benevolent invitation. Her eyes glowed. Really glowed, like gems with sparks of fire in their depths, shifting to different shades as she moved: sapphire, emerald, topaz.

Her skirts flared and settled as from the trees danced a host of figures nearly as beautiful as she. The melody shifted up a half step, then repeated its enthralling pattern, livelier than Pachelbel's *Canon in D*, more captivating than Ravel's *Bolero*. From the shadows emerged the musicians playing on wind instruments of gold, and silver hammers on crystal, ringing the sweet sound of chimes.

The figures were an amazing variety, among them dryads with bark skin and leaves for hair, others more like the moonbeam and flame couple, as they formed in circles and began to dance.

Like a flight of butterflies released, a troupe of little girls appeared, and took hands to ring Aurélie. They danced around her three times, then broke their ring, two girls reaching. She took their hands and joined the circle to dance with them, her husky squawk of a laugh charming among their giggles like tinkling chimes.

Princess Moonbeam walked straight up to me.

"Welcome to our dancing dell. Please join us."

"You mean, you can see me?" I asked.

"See you!" Her laughter was as sweet as the silver hammers on glass. "Why should I not?"

I looked down, and there I was! I stuck out my sandaled foot. There was my chipped toenail polish. Above that, my favorite blue skirt, swinging at my knees. I smoothed my hands down the embroidered linen blouse I'd bought at Madame Celine's exclusive shop in Riev, and suppressed the desire to give a whoop of pleasure.

"Join me," Princess Moonbeam said with another of those inviting gestures, "in refreshment. You must be hungry, so very long separated spirit from flesh."

She indicated a table festooned with fantastic flowers, and set with plate after plate of mouth-watering delicacies, but the first thing on my mind was Alec.

"Very long?" I asked, my pleasure chilling. "How long?"

"Come. Eat and drink. We can discourse at our leisure, whilst the young disport in play."

I looked into her lovely topaz eyes, her joyful smile, and said slowly, "Okay, I'm trying to catch up as fast as I can, here, but one thing I do remember. If you people—beings—are who I think you are, then the food thing might not be a great idea."

"Well spoken." Her laughter was surprised, intimate. "You are quite welcome to partake, but I bow to your caution. It is always wise to step warily when one is in new country."

"Well, this country is not new to me, but this time is. If the past can be new. And this situation. The Kittredge family doesn't seem to know about you. Why are you here?"

She gestured. "This is a traditional dancing dell. The wood is ours and has been, though your folk occasionally come through."

"So you don't interact with the Kittredges?"

"Is that who lives in the barren domicile? They took down the old dwelling, which was filled with charms," she said, "and built that new shell. The people who passed out of life were long our friends. You know the dwelling was once called Undrentide."

"Undrentide? I was told that the house is called Undertree. Or maybe 'Undertree' is the modern form?"

She laughed softly. "*Undrentide* means *midday*. It is always midday here."

She seemed unthreatening enough, and I was thrilled to be *me* again, that is, visible to someone else. "May I get back to my question? How long have I been away from my time? Do you know?"

She spread her pretty hands. "What is time?"

"To you, I have no idea. But my life is governed by the ticking of the clock," I said. "I thought my coming to the past like this meant I'd be restored to the same moment I left. So how long have I been gone? Unless," I added carefully, "this is all some kind of glamour thing, and none of it is real. One of my favorite books when I was growing up was Elizabeth Marie Pope's *Perilous Gard*."

Princess Moonbeam flashed her hand up in the fencer's acknowledgment of a hit. "You are discerning. With your leave, we shall dispense with the glory."

An eye blink—this time I really could blink my eyes—and the guy was now short and round, with a cap of wavy nut-brown hair. He wore homespun clothes of the sort seen on common Western European folk of that period, his manner no longer the dangerous Prince of Air and

Darkness. He took up a fiddle, and joined the musicians now circling the dancing kids.

The music stepped up a chord, minor to major.

Princess Moonbeam was now a small woman maybe in her mid-thirties, wearing a peasant blouse and an aproned skirt. Her hair was a pleasant chestnut, pulled up into a bun. I was the tallest person there, a fact I found oddly steadying.

The dell was an ordinary clearing under the spreading branches of three trees, the picnic table just that, set with doughnuts and jelly tarts and puddings, in the center a bowl of ordinary fruit. The kids dancing with Aurélie were just kids, some with flowers stuck behind their ears, wilting in the warm air. The dryads were gone.

The very ordinariness of the scene was a kind of relief. So *these* were fae, and the dell was obviously one of portals between the Nasdrafus—the world of magic—and the world I'd grown up in. I could deal with this.

"Thank you for your forbearance," my hostess said. "The glamour is traditional. It is expected. But it requires a great deal of effort."

"I appreciate the effort," I said. "I really do. I'll never forget your arrival. But this . . . seems more real."

"And so it ought," she said watching a butterfly alight on a bluebell a few feet away. "Now, to your questions."

"Instead of answering them, can you send me home, just long enough for me to let my loved ones know where I am and what I'm doing?"

She smiled. "It would take me a great deal of effort to send you home. But I can do it."

"Is there some hidden cost? Is that what you're hinting?"

She opened her hands. "Not to me. And you would be returned to your loved ones."

"So there is a cost. To whom?"

"There is no cost in the sense that I believe you mean. Perhaps I should make a demonstration." From a pocket beneath her apron she pulled an oval mirror set in plain wood, and handed it to me.

I looked down, my nerves chilling when I recognized Alec. He sat in my room in Ysvorod House. There was the cream-colored wall with the border of acanthus leaves and laurel painted under the ceiling.

"Is this real? I mean, now?"

"This very moment. Though time does not mean to me what it does to you, I cannot bend it."

Alex sat in one of the armchairs, his head bowed, his profile closed in. I knew that face. It was his Mr. Darcy mask, which he put between him and the world when he was hurting most.

"Why—where—" I gabbled as I tipped the mirror—and nearly dropped it.

She had stretched out a hand as if to stay me, but I turned away, aghast as I stared at my reflection in the mirror. It wasn't the me standing there in the dell, I was in that room with Alec, lying on the bed, my eyes closed.

"I did not think you could see so clearly and with such celerity," she said.

"Alec!" I cried, frantically *reaching* into that glass—

And he jerked upright and looked around wildly, his blue eyes wide.

Then the mirror vanished from my hand.

I drew a deep breath. *Calm! Reasonable. Think.* A temper tantrum would feel great for about ten seconds, but what would it get me? I was not the one wielding magic right and left, here.

"What's the price?" I asked. "Of going home. Or at least getting that mirror back?"

"You may return any time you wish," she answered softly. "I myself will take you where you wish to be."

"How? Before you get to that, you still haven't said what it would cost me."

"There is no cost to you," the fae said. "We only deal in trade."

"As you see, I haven't anything to trade. So if there is a portal here, just point it out. I can go myself. I've dealt with portals before, like last winter, when I had to close one called the Esplumoir."

The world stilled for a heartbeat: no music. No sound. The fae froze, then moved again, first the violin guy, then the children. It was a subtle outward flow, as if they took a step away from me.

One of them spoke, and the girls broke the ring and began picking flowers to weave garlands.

The music shifted to a minor key, the same enthralling melody that imbued me with a sense of urgency, even purpose. *Enthralling*—puts one in thrall.

I tried to shut out the music, to concentrate. *Alec.* I recalled the desperation in his face as he searched that room high and low.

"Do you want to go home?" came the gentle voice.

I glanced down into the woman's eyes, a brown the same shade as my own, and said, "More than anything."

I meant it when I said it. The sight of Alec hurting hurt me so much I longed to be there, to reassure him, and, yes, to get back to my life, which was, at last, the life I wanted.

Yet the moment the words were out I looked Aurélie's way. She stood in the middle of the dell, surrounded by girls, their fingers plaiting pretty garlands. One crowned her with purple knapweed and ivory mallow, lavender loosestrife and wood anemone. No roses.

No roses, but that wasn't a problem. It was the vampires who avoided roses, and that was way, way to the east.

A girl with long, tangled brown hair offered a garland on both palms to Aurélie, waiting for her to take it. There was the deliberation of ritual in the gesture, an intensity that seemed strange for a couple of junior-high aged kids.

Aurélie gazed into the girl's eyes, her fingers slowly moving up from her waist to her collarbones to her neck. Her neck, under which lay the necklace that nobody on this side of the world had seen. That she had promised Nanny Hiasinte she would never relinquish.

"Aurélie?" I crossed the grass.

Aurélie looked up, blinking as if she'd been woken from a daydream. She smiled with her whole face. "Duppy? Are you here?"

Her search reminded me disturbingly of Alec's desperate gaze. I reached instinctively, and touched her shoulder. She gasped. "I see you!"

When I lifted my fingers, her forehead puckered. "Duppy?" Her hands came out, and I closed my fingers over one.

Her hand was warm, the palm slightly rough from all her practice. She smiled up at me. "There you are again. You are real," she said wonderingly. "Like a real person."

"Call me Kim," I said. "And I'm supposed to be your guide. So let me ask you, did they offer you something?" I asked.

"She—the one who looks like Cousin Fiba. She wants to trade me this crown for my necklace."

"Don't," I snapped, unsettled by the fact that I hadn't heard these words. I wondered how trustworthy was this scene of ordinary, bucolic bliss.

Aurélie looked at me in question. "I know I cannot," she said with grave courtesy. "I promised Nanny Hiasinte. But my hands, because of the music, the beautiful music, my hands were moving . . ." She gulped and said angrily, "I will not take it off, even for diamonds and emeralds."

Cousin Fiba? I remembered Fiba, the black girl in Jamaica. "What do you see, Aurélie? Who do they look like to you?"

"The great lady over there, she is more beautiful even than Tante Mimba."

"Her eyes? Her hair? What color are they?"

"Her eyes black as velvet, her hair a puff the color of night, with tiny stars in it. Her skin the color of teak, so beautiful . . ."

Whoa. "We've got to run," I whispered. "We're being—"

Enchanted.

They were gone. A nanosecond later the rain hit us with the force of a hose. Or rather, hit Aurélie. I was invisible again, impervious to the physical shock of the rain, but a deep chill passed through me.

I don't know how long that poor kid stumbled around in the dark, for it was clear that though minutes had passed for us, it had been hours in real time. She was soaked to the skin instantly, and after blundering into trees and gorse and every kind of bush that grew thorns and stickers, she wept inconsolably, sometimes howling, "Save me, Duppy Kim. Save me."

And didn't *that* make me feel extra special.

But I was invisible once again, no matter what I tried. At least I could stay with her, even if I couldn't save her, and I swear those fae must have done their best to put Aurélie in the way of every root to trip over and every prickly bush to run into, until *at last* Aurélie caught sight of a lantern winking between trees.

The lantern was held by one of the farmers. It was soon apparent that the entire population of Undertree had been turned out to search. Aurélie had wandered downhill, as people do when lost, and ended up in the last stretch of woodland beyond the farms.

She was put in a cart and brought back to the house.

Unfortunately, her troubles were far from over.

ELEVEN

THE REPRIMAND STARTED OUT FAIRLY MILD, suitable for a marquis's daughter who came with a thirty thousand pound dowry. Uncle Kittredge stood by, silent and somber as Aunt Kittredge saw to it that Aurélie was wrapped up and fed hot milk. She scolded and questioned alternately. As always, there was a lot of *dear* and *we were nigh dead with worry* interlarded, but it wasn't until she threw a couple zingers at Cassandra and James, promising sharp punishment for their neglect, that Aurélie roused sufficiently to say, "They told me not to go far. And I didn't go far. It was only that the dancing people played their music, oh, it was so like the obeah dances, and they said it was a *kanzo*, just for me—"

"The what?" Aunt Kittredge snapped.

"Obeah dances," Aurélie repeated. "My duppy was there, too. We both saw them—"

"You can be forgiven your wandering off so selfishly," Mrs. Kittredge said, her voice quivering. "We would only put you in your room for a day as a reminder that headstrong, willful girls always end up in difficulties. But when you seek to excuse your behavior with *lies*—"

"I do *not* lie," Aurélie flashed, jumping to her feet. "I *never* tell lies, me. Never!"

Out came Mrs. Kittredge's hand, quick as a striking snake. She slapped Aurélie across the face, knocking her down.

If I could have taken a swing, I would have knocked *her* down.

"Philomena," Uncle Kittredge began.

His wife rounded on him. "Mr. Kittredge! You would countenance this *evil* in your home?" She stood over Aurélie. "Go to your room. You will not take sup nor sip until you admit the truth and humbly beg our pardon."

Aurélie dropped the blanket and fled, me trailing uselessly behind her, leaving the rising voices of the adults, who were arguing about something I couldn't hear. Their voices were punctuated by Cassandra's shrill self-justification, "I *told* her not to speak of taradiddles, and I *also* told her not to go off for long, but *she said . . .*"

Aurélie flung herself on her bed and wept herself into an exhausted slumber. I knew how horrible she was going to feel, waking up in wet clothing, but there was nothing I could do for her until she talked to me.

While she slept, I worried about that vision of Alec. Had time passed after all? Or was that as phony as the Princess Moonbeam/country wife guises? There was no way of knowing. So I tried to reach for him on the mental level. I wasted measureless time without success.

The only way to keep my sanity was to keep my eye on the prize; that is, to help Aurélie, and to remember that the fae were no friends of ours.

Still, it was a relief when she woke bleary-eyed in the morning, having rolled herself up in the bedding. She looked around in a woebegone daze, then tears welled in her eyes and dripped down her face.

Her chest heaved on a sob. "Duppy, where are you?" she croaked.

Here, I shouted with my non-voice, and though I knew she hated it, I tried to touch her on the shoulder. *Here.*

She flinched away from my touch, then slipped off the bed and walked to the mirror, the bedcover still wrapped around her. She peered into the mirror, her eyes swollen. "Duppy Kim?" she said in a small voice. She was using 'duppy' as a courtesy title, like Nanny or Lady.

She stretched a hand out to the mirror, and touched her fingers to the glass. I tried reaching my invisible hand to touch hers.

She jumped, snatched her hand back, then laid her palm flat on the mirror. I laid my invisible hand over hers, and this time it was I who jumped. It felt like the touch of hand to hand, though I did not have an actual hand to be touching with.

In the mirror I could see myself standing behind her in my rumpled linen blouse and blue skirt, my hair hanging down to my hips, uncombed. The light was different on me than on her; I was partly invisible, outlined in a kind of shimmer. It gave me the creeps.

"*M'entendez-vous?*" she asked—*do you hear me?*

"*Je suis ici,*" I said. *I'm here.*

"I hear you, I hear you!" she exclaimed joyfully. "When we touch like this, I hear you!" Her smile became troubled. "Who were those people in the dell? Was that an English obeah? I didn't know there were any of *our* people in England."

"There are some people of color in England," I said, making a guess at what she meant by *our*. "But those ones in the dell weren't people at all, not in the way we mean. They were fae." I used the French word *fée*, though what I was thinking was, *Those beings could be walking mushrooms in their real form, but whatever they are, they sure know how to manipulate humans.*

Aurélie's eyes rounded. "How do you know?"

"By the fact that they showed me two different sets of faces, none of which were the faces you saw. I don't know what they wanted from me. I suspect they wanted to get me away from you, because they were definitely after your necklace."

"Yes." Her hand flew to her collarbones. "They did try to trick me. What do I tell my uncle and aunt? Nanny said my necklace was to be a secret. Perhaps it'll be good enough if I beg pardon for making them worried? You saw. I didn't mean to be gone long. It seemed a little minute, the dancing, and then the girl like Fiba said that I could trade my necklace for a crown, and I was thinking, *How do you know about my necklace?* For nobody has seen it." She made an impatient gesture. "Eh, it's over. I'll *never* go to that place again. Never, never, never! I hate them! But I think I must tell Aunt Kittredge about the dell, and the dancing, even if I say nothing about my necklace."

"I don't think the necklace is the problem. No," I corrected myself, strongly suspecting that Aunt Kittredge was the type to take the necklace away to keep it safe. "The necklace is a part of the problem but only a part. More serious is the subject of the fae."

"They will hurt my cousins and aunt and uncle?"

"I don't believe Aunt Kittredge has ever seen the fae," I said slowly as I tried to think ahead. By modern standards, Aurélie had a rough life, what with the pirates and all. But by the standards of the time, she was better off than a lot of kids because she'd clearly trusted and been loved by the adults in her life, before her great journey. They taught her to the best of their ability—they had hugged and kissed her, and they had lived by the words they taught. Aurélie had brought that trust to her relatives, even if the love was lagging a bit.

I didn't think it right to completely take that trust away, but I owed Aurélie the truth. So I said, trying to pick my way carefully, "I think that if you tell Aunt Kittredge about the fae, she will only say that you're making up lies."

"But I didn't lie. I never lie!" Aurélie's hand rose to her cheek. "She was so *very* angry."

I bit back my opinion of Aunt Kittredge. The kid had to live with her. "She was frightened by your having gone missing. Sometimes when people get badly frightened, and the fright is over, their feelings turn to anger."

"I saw this, once," Aurélie said in a low voice. "Before we left Saint-Domingue. There was nearly a fire on board *L'Étourneau*, and the third mate said Fiba and I were at fault, that we left untended candles. But we took a lamp. That was the rule. *Maman* believed us, though everyone thought we were the last ones in the hold. And later, when the third mate was caught stealing, they knew we didn't lie. But before he was caught, *Maman* knew our words were true."

"That's because she trusted your words rather than what she expected to hear. I think your aunt trusts only what she expects to see and hear, and not your words."

Aurélie leaned against the mirror, her face troubled. "She believes that Nanny is wicked and a heathen, so she does not trust me? But she has never seen Nanny! Never heard her speak. My Nanny is not wicked."

"No. But Aunt Kittredge doesn't know your Nanny, and she only believes those who have her respect. I don't think anybody from Jamaica has her respect."

Aurélie nodded sadly. "I think this is right. So what must I say? I hate to lie. *That* is wicked."

"I don't know what's right here, but I think she'll only believe you if tell her that you walked away and fell asleep in the dell and dreamed about the fae and dancing."

"But that's not true. I was not asleep, and in my dreams, there are many strange people, but never these fae." She scowled down at her hands. "If I say this lie, she will believe me?"

"I think so. Because it will match the world she understands."

"And then she will punish me."

"I think that is going to happen no matter what you say."

"Good." Aurélie's scowl deepened. "I will deserve punishment, for telling lies."

That's what happened. From the second I saw the angry, smug lift to Aunt Kittredge's upper lip, my budding dislike of the woman zapped straight to the red zone, especially when she rubbed in her power over Aurélie by making her kneel and beg pardon before the entire family. I knew she was convinced of right, and that forcing Aurélie to kneel was conventional behavior for the time, but I hated how much angry enjoyment she was getting out of her moral superiority.

Aurélie's head was bowed, and tears of shame dripped onto her hands, but I could see the faces of the family: Uncle Kittredge troubled, clearly wishing himself elsewhere; James equally uncomfortable; Cassandra's chin high like her mother's, though her puckered brow indicated ambivalence, and little Diana squinting solemnly at them all as if trying to bring them into focus.

Aurélie was confined to the schoolroom, forbidden access to the garden for the rest of the month, and made to write out, in her best hand, a book of sermons. The only outside activity permitted was going to and from church.

Aurélie went upstairs to mope with the intensity of the thirteen-year-old who has been wronged. I waited impatiently for her to come to the mirror again. It was finally time to begin communicating—to start the process of making sure both our futures would be secure.

I'd kept amending my long-rehearsed speech over time, except for my opening sentence, one I was fairly sure any girl would love to hear: *How would you like to marry a prince?*

The next day, Miss Oliver saw fit to deliver her own lecture, ending with, "Young ladies must remember that reputation begins in the schoolroom. Mrs. Kittredge will scarcely be able to arrange a suitable marriage if the gentleman hears whispers about fanciful tales and taradiddles, to put it no higher. No gentleman of worth could envision such a woman heading his household."

Cassandra looked quite saintly, knowing the lecture was not aimed at her. Aurélie dropped her head in a submissive posture, but I could see her scowl, and so I thought: Ah-ha, my moment has come.

As was her habit, she touched the mirror when she returned to her bedchamber to dress for dinner. Before she could start in about how unfair it was to be lectured for something she had not done, I gave her my line, "How would you like to marry a prince?"

And waited for the squee, and the "Oooh, tell me what to do!" so I could establish myself as her best bud.

She looked at me in horror. "She wouldn't!"

"Who wouldn't? And, um, wouldn't what?"

"*Maman promised* me I could choose whom I should marry for myself, as she did. She's not going back on her word?"

"No. That is, I don't know any more than you do. I told you, I cannot communicate with anybody but you."

She looked slightly relieved, then wary. "So why would you say such a horrid thing?"

"Horrid?" I repeated, aghast.

"What happens to princesses? They turn into queens." She drew her finger across her neck.

"But not all queens end up on the guillotine," I said, mentally flailing.

"No. The queen of England is married to a madman. The queen of Sweden, her king was assassinated dancing at a ball. The queen of Prussia, her king is ruled by his *maitresse en titre*." Aurélie paused, then said, "I am not precisely certain what that means, but Fiba and I overheard talk about it, and we know it is horrid. Who would want such a life? Not I! I want to go home, and marry a privateer."

I stared at her, my lovingly prepared speech as blown to bits as my expectations. When I was her age, half my classmates had fantasized about somehow getting from Los Angeles to England to marry Prince William; then again, he lived a fairy tale life—the worst battle he'd ever face would be with nosy paparazzi. Princes in Aurélie's time weren't always handsome, smart, or safe. And princesses didn't get to pick whom they would marry. *I should have thought this through.*

Aurélie was still regarding me warily. "Duppy Kim, why did you say that?"

Still flailing wildly, I glanced into the room, and pointed at a schoolbook labeled *The Kings of England.* "I was just thinking about what it might be like for English princesses," I said weakly.

"I pity them," Aurélie said seriously. "Do you think my aunt will try to arrange such a marriage for me, because my father was a marquis? But royalty must marry royalty, is that not true? I should be safe from princes."

"Yes, you should be safe from princes," I agreed in total defeat, as she went away to dress for dinner.

TWELVE

A FTER THAT DISASTER, I decided I had better bide my time and not imagine conversations based on the way girls think now. It wasn't that I had not known about arranged marriages. I'd studied the evolution of marriage in history classes. What I hadn't thought about was how marriage looked to girls of that time.

Meanwhile, Aunt Kittredge announced that the Bouldeston cousins would not be invited this year after all, with a stony glance Aurélie's way. This was also a time when several punishments and reminders for a single misdeed was considered good childrearing by many.

For a few days Cassandra walked about like a thundercloud, for she'd been treasuring up things to show her cousins to impress them. Neither Aurélie nor Diana could speak without being snapped at, the one sharply corrected and the other scolded for being clumsy, slow, and in the way.

Then one morning, Aunt Kittredge said to Cassandra, "Your Aunt Bouldeston writes to invite you to visit Lucretia and Lucasta in July. *You* have earned this treat." Cassandra was instantly restored to good humor.

The following morning found her downstairs singing and Miss Oliver in the front parlor, talking to Aunt Kittredge—which left Aurélie alone in the schoolroom. She was grimly laboring away at her copy-work when Diana approached her, hugging an old book tight against her front.

"Pray look, Cousin. Here is my favorite poem. It is called 'Aire and Angels,'" Diana whispered.

Aurélie said, "Your favorite poem?"

"It was writ by Doctor Donne," Diana said softly, squinting worriedly over her shoulder at the closed door. Whoa—Donne? Diana was not quite ten.

"Great Aunt Edith read it to me when I was small," Diana went on. "His poems are in the book room. Nobody touches the old books, except me." Another quick, squinting look, then Diana whispered, "Great Aunt Edith saw the fairies, you know."

"She did?"

Diana nodded solemnly. "I think I saw them once."

"*You* did?"

"I think so. I think 'twas real, and no mere dream. I was very small. It was raining, and the clouds parted, and there was a rainbow. Over the farm." Diana's arm lifted. "That was pretty. I turned the other way to see if the other end might be closer. There was no rainbow, but a beam of light coming down from betwixt the clouds, just beyond the rose gate. It was there that I saw them. I told everybody, and Mama and Papa scolded me and said it was a dream. Aunt Edith lived with us then. She was very old—she was born in the time of Queen Anne. *She* believed me. She said she saw the fairies many times when she was small, and so did her sister, who married an *earl*."

Diana issued this fact with solemn conviction, as if everyone knew that the word of a countess was to be trusted.

"Why does no one see them now?"

"I don't know," Diana said. "Only that some do. Most do not. Aunt Edith told me stories about the fairies and about magic things. Like how roses have powers against the evil ones."

"Evil ones? *Oanga*?"

"What is that?"

"The bad magic. Some can change from people to beast or bird."

"Shape-changers! I found mention of them once, in one of the books on the top shelf."

Diana scanned the doorway again for lurking parental figures and whispered, "Aunt Edith told me the roses ward the evil ones who drink blood."

"Aunt Kittredge doesn't know that about the roses?"

"No. And she thinks the fairies are taradiddles."

"This word 'taradiddles,' it means lies, does it not?"

"Stories. About things untrue. Aunt Edith said that when her father built the new house, all the old charms inside were done away with."

"Charms," Aurélie breathed. "What's that?"

"A charm can be a carved or painted thing. Your fingers feel odd if you touch it. Aunt Edith said that the charms were to make evil go away. There are two in the stone gate by the roses. It feels like velvet when you touch the cross inside the circle, or the one like a four-petaled flower. I'm trying to find out why. Nobody reads those books on the top shelf but me," Diana confided. "When I turned nine, I set myself a task, to read *all* my aunt's books, but I must confess, I have no end of difficulties with my attempt to learn Greek and Latin. Oh, I know I'm being tedious, and Cassie always says I'm trying to put myself forward if I talk about books, though I assure you, I mean no such thing." She took a deep breath. "*Anyway*, these poems, by Doctor Donne, they're my favorites."

She leaned against the arm of Aurélie's chair and pushed a small, gilt book into her hands. "Will you tell me everything that happened with the fairies?"

Aurélie did, leaving out only the necklace, according to her promise. When she came to the part about seeing me, Diana listened with fast breathing and, at the end, begged to be shown me in the mirror.

I don't know who was more disappointed, the girls or me when Diana couldn't see me, though Aurélie could. Aurélie described my features, touching the mirror as Diana peered so closely that her breath fogged the glass. "I almost saw something. I think. Though maybe it was just the light, slanting through the window." She turned away with resignation. "The fairies didn't sing to me in the garden, or I would have gone with you. And I wouldn't care about the horrid rain, if I could have seen them."

The girls heard the governess's tread on the landing, and Diana scampered out.

———

June was a rainy month, keeping everyone inside. On the first of July, Cassandra set off in the carriage, accompanied by the governess on her unpaid leave. Miss Oliver had to do double duty as guardian on her way, but at least she got to ride post until they reached the Bouldeston estate in Kent.

The long stretch of bad weather confined everyone inside. That, and the fact that Cassandra and her tattling tongue were safely out of reach, inspired James to reappear. He invited Aurélie to take up fencing again.

The rest of the time, she and Diana had the schoolroom to themselves. Diana read ferociously, either seated at the small table bowed over her books, her nose nearly touching the pages, or next to Aurélie, sometimes leaning against her in a way that made me reflect on how affection-starved they both were. Aurélie had come from a loving family. Diana's parents cared for her, but her father was kindly from a proper distance, and Cassandra, like her mother, did not seem inclined toward the warmth of a caress or kiss.

So the two girls sat side by side, Aurélie reading aloud to Diana when the latter's eyes hurt from bending over the page. They read literature, history, theology—everything in the library, talking it over.

Aurélie spent the rest of her free time practicing with James and playing music. She read sheet music downstairs, but upstairs, on the spinet, where no one but Diana could hear, she improvised entrancing melodies. Each time she introduced a new one, it was usually after she'd been sitting in the window seat, making me wonder if the fae were still trying to lure her back to the woods.

August arrived, and with it Cassandra, accompanied by Miss Oliver. Cassandra was full of "Lucretia says." This cousin was held to be an authority on everything fashionable, her expertise based on the Bouldestons going up to London each spring.

Cassandra also had plenty to brag about on her own account. She and Lucretia had delighted and astonished the company by their duets, and Lucretia had taught her the steps to the Passepied and the Cotillion, which "everyone" in Kent of any importance knew how to dance.

Cassandra kept up the *Lucretia says* until the head-on collision with her mother over the necessity for all new gowns, based on the fact that Lucasta, the younger cousin, had overheard Lucretia telling one of their friends that Cassandra's wardrobe was fit only for a dowd.

"If our generosity in sending you to your cousins is going to return a pert, ungrateful fine lady to her home in place of a dutiful daughter, then we shall know not to repeat the experiment," Aunt Kittredge said, touching off a storm of tears, after which Cassandra backed off on the *Lucretia says*, to everyone's relief.

Aurélie continued to chat to me for a minute or two each morning, but it was inevitably about her reading, her letters home, and speculation on what might be going on in Jamaica. When would she hear back? When could she go home?

There was no Dobrenica anywhere in sight and no way to get her there, but at least time whizzed by with the speed of a montage. I reminded myself that I could do this. I had been given a task. I would not believe what I'd seen in the fae's glass, because they'd distorted the truth about everything else. Time was frozen at Alec's end: I held onto that.

As for Aurélie and her future, I decided to wait for her to ask me questions. But so far, she expressed no interest in me or my life, since I couldn't communicate with Jamaica.

September arrived, and James took off with his father for the hunting season. Aurélie's spirits waned with the sun, especially as there still was no letter from her mother. Aurélie still wrote faithfully every week.

After the hunting season was over, James turned up one sleety day, invited Aurélie to take up fencing again, and that became the pattern for the next year. There was even a soundtrack, what with the fae songs Aurélie secretly practiced, shaping them into melodies of her own.

Time blurred.

When they turned fifteen, Aurélie and Cassandra were granted boundaries almost as wide as those given James.

Aurélie and James transferred their practice to one of the old barns when the weather warmed. The boy clothes were kept in the loft, where Aurélie could change in decent privacy, and the fencing and pistol shooting became musket practice. Nor did it end with the warming of spring. She came to the mirror less and less often. James and Diana occupied the most of her time—the one in fighting practice and the other in reading and in talking about magic.

Some nights she had vivid dreams, and those she always told me. Like the time she was a high-born lady with black hair as smooth as silk and skin as pale as paper. The way she described her hair and robe sounded Chinese to me, especially when she got to the detail of her tiny, aching feet. She wore an elaborate headdress and lived in a palace filled with gold. In another dream, she was a great lady as dark as Mimba, living in a house surrounded by flowers, with singing day and night.

I knew the fae were tormenting Aurélie from afar when she stood with her face pressed to the window, tears on her cheeks as she gripped the necklace with her fingers. She'd go downstairs and work fiercely at the fortepiano, trying to capture whatever it was she heard trying to lure her.

She was never satisfied, but the rest of the family praised her according to their personalities: Uncle Kittredge told her she was a good girl and a dab hand at the keyboard; Aunt Kittredge told her that she was a diligent pupil and that perhaps it was time to bring a real music master to train her and Cassandra; James said, "That's a capital tune! Are there any words to it?" And Diana stood listening, her face rapt. Only she knew the truth about the inspiration behind those entrancing melodies.

Aunt Kittredge kept her word, and hired an earnest, vague young man as a music master, who taught both fortepiano and singing. He was a pro, unlike Miss Oliver, who was a jack-of-all-trades, as governesses had to be. Both girls' performances soon showed the benefit.

Then came Cassandra's crowning glory. At last, *at last*, her mother hired a dancing master, who also taught the girls the etiquette of the ballroom. Aunt Kittredge and Miss Oliver sat in the room like a pair of twin dragons on guard as the master solemnly put the girls through their paces. He was probably older than Uncle Kittredge.

The night of the first lesson, Aurélie came to me again, her expression wistful. "This dancing," she said. "It's like wearing stays. It's not the dancing of my home, so free, like water, air, and sky, and when you dance you can be the dragonfly, the doctor bird. Everyone was one, under *le bon Dieu*, at home. Here? You dance in a line, your foot must be so, your hand here, your chin at this angle."

She sighed. "*Maman* said I must come here to learn, so I will learn."

She retired, diligently said her prayers according to Aunt Kittredge's wishes, but then added her own fervent words in French.

Time zipped by at freeway speed.

James was into his late teens, and Aurélie approaching sixteen.

She paid little attention to her looks, except to try to stay neat, but Aunt Kittredge fussed enough for them both. *Stay out of the sun—her brown skin would ruin her chances—could she never keep her hair neat?— her gown was awry—must she gallop about like she was a runaway horse?* At night she had to put glop on her face that was supposed to lighten her skin, and Aunt Kittredge, despairing of the contrast of white fabric (debutantes in those days wore white) even invested in powder, though she despised women who "painted." Most of all, she criticized Aurélie and Diana for not moving like Cassandra, whose prissy, affected airs, modeled partly on her mother's behavior, were extolled as the graceful walk and posture of a true lady.

I felt a little sorry for Cassandra, who, what with the heavy, starchy meals and no exercise other than twirling around the parlor in dance practice or sedately walking fifty yards in the garden, was in her turn criticized by her mother for her increasingly podgy shape. She made up for it by tripping about with her wrists arched, flinging her long honey-colored curls artfully, and talking about her delicate constitution. In contrast, Aurélie, who worked out constantly, moved with the unconscious grace of a wild swan.

Most of my pity was reserved for Diana, whose mother scolded her daily for poking along so head-bent she was bound to grow round-shouldered, and perhaps Diana ought to use the backboard. As for being short-sighted, well, nothing in the house had ever changed position an inch, so there was no need to peer like a mole. Grandmother Kittredge was shortsighted, but *her* spine was as straight as a ramrod: nag, nag, nag.

When Aurélie was not in the schoolroom, Diana lurked in the library as much as she could. Aurélie poured all her free time into music, books, talk with Diana, and practice with James.

James's eighteenth birthday had come and gone, nothing being said about buying him a cornetcy and shipping him off to the army, except vague words about maybe when he turned twenty. He and Aurélie continued their practice. She had gradually grown into James's old clothes, which were shabby from frequent secret washings in the cows' rain barrel.

Then came the day in early January when James showed up at the barn, plainly upset.

Aurélie had been warming up by lunging at the target they'd painted on a post. She turned, smiling a welcome, but her smile vanished when she saw him in the doorway. "James? What is amiss?"

His face flooded with color, which then ebbed as he perched on a barrel. "I—I hardly know what to say. I hate to tell you this. Peaching on my own mother. But I think you should know."

Aurélie set aside her weapon and pressed her hands to her chin. "Oh, is it bad news from Jamaica?"

"That's just it. I—you know, the letter you wrote, and put on the tray for the post? Well, I went back into the book room, for I forgot my—oh, Aurélie, I'd give the world not to be the one to tell you, for it'll overset you. It did me. But my mother didn't see me enter, and, well, the truth of it is, I saw her put your letter into the fire."

"*My* letter?"

A nod.

"Into the fire? Was it misspelt? Was the direction writ incorrectly?" Aurélie asked, her voice higher on each question.

He sighed. "She didn't even open it. She picked it up off the tray, and cast it into the flames without so much as a by-your-leave." He bent his head, struggled, then said, "It was . . . it had the manner of habit. As though she's done it before."

"*All* my letters? Into the fire?" Tears welled and slowly dripped down her cheeks. "So that's why I've had no answer. How can I write to my mother?" she whispered, and made a visible effort to get control. "I *must* write to her. I *will* write. How can I get to the postmaster?"

"I'll ride a letter over," James said immediately, then he looked perplexed. "But I'm puzzled what to do when your mother writes back, for I must give our direction, and you know that Mother sorts the post each morning. I think she reads it all, too, for the seals are always broken."

"Can we have *Maman* direct a letter to one of your friends?"

"I could rely upon my friend Tom Badgerton, say, or George Kidwell, but Aurélie, if post arrives at their houses but directed to you, it'd cause talk all over the neighborhood before you could wink an eye."

Aurélie clasped her thin hands, then flung them apart. "Could I have them addressed to a false name? I could use René!"

"That would cause even more talk," James said. "The letters would still have to be fetched."

Aurélie took a deep, unsteady breath. "Do you think Aunt Kittredge also burned any letters to me?"

James looked away, obviously acutely uncomfortable. "My mother once said that the sooner you understood your home to be here, the happier you would be. And then, you know, a letter might have had bad news and overset you."

"I would have been equal to it," she responded tearfully. "I don't know how they *are*. We girls are not permitted to look at the newspaper, for Aunt Kittredge says it's full of things unfit to be seen, except if you're a man."

"There isn't much about Jamaica in the newspapers, at least so I understand. You know I'm not much one for reading. My father talked about a peace a year or two back. Something about rebellious slaves, and the governor, and the military commander, I forget his name." James now looked resolute. "But I'll begin looking out news, how's that?"

One step, two, and his arms came around her, gently. Awkwardly. The gesture melted the last of her self-control, and she began to weep into his bony shoulder. He tightened his grip. She clung to him.

And though I'd swear he had no designs, and she hadn't shown the least sign of boy-interest, that hug seemed to give him courage and wake her up to some new ideas.

She gave a hiccough. Stepped back a little. Looked up. He leaned down, kissed her eyelids . . . and before either of them took another breath, they were lip-locked like—well, like teenagers.

THIRTEEN

I HAD TOTALLY NOT FORESEEN *that*.

They sprang apart, looking around wildly, then he studied the ox harness hanging on its peg as if his future lay written there, and she pressed her fingers to her lips, horrified. But she wasn't running out the door.

I'll cut out the Romeo and Juliet conversation that ensued. It took them forever to fumble their way through the tangle of *oh-nos*, and *what-ifs*, and though they were both certain that they would be cast into the outer darkness if his parents found out, I was thinking, *Could this be why the parents have been dragging their feet about sending James off to the army? Could it be they never intended letting Aurélie's dowry marry out of the family?* Because when I considered it, they couldn't not know about the hours the two spent side by side shooting in sight of the farm workers, though I was fairly certain they didn't know about the trousers and fencing practice in the barn.

Romeo and Juliet finally remembered the time after interminable professions or love, honor, and fear. Aurélie ran upstairs to the loft to change back into her respectable girl clothes as James stood guard as if expecting a six-headed hydra. Then they slunk out opposite doors of the barn, looking around so guiltily that anyone who saw them would instantly have wondered what was going on.

When Aurélie got back to the house, she came straight to the mirror. "Did you see?" she said breathlessly.

"Yes," I said. "I can't help seeing what you see when you are excited."

"Are we wicked?" she asked with sorrow.

No more wicked than any other normal teenager, I thought, but this was a different age. "Just keep it to kissing," I said. "Any more will cause big trouble."

She blushed deeply and, for the first time, I wondered if anyone had ever given her the Facts of Life talk before she left Jamaica, because Aunt Kittredge certainly hadn't. The girls were scolded if they even mentioned the word *beaux*, and lectured on ladylike behavior and pure thoughts. Aurélie hastened off in embarrassment, and I remembered that my presence made me the perfect deterrent.

A teenage crush wasn't going to hurt anyone, I thought. They'd fall out of their purple passion as fast as they'd fallen into it.

On a bright day some weeks later, Cassandra appeared triumphantly in the schoolroom with two magazines in hand. "Mama subscribed to the *Gallery of Fashion*! We may each order a gown to be made up by Miss Tolbert," she declared, naming the local seamstress. "We are not going to our first assembly looking like a pair of country mice in gowns we made ourselves."

Aurélie took the magazine she was handed, asking, "Is James to attend with us?"

"James?" Cassandra repeated, as if Aurélie had declared that the sky was yellow. "What for? He refuses to learn dancing." She went back to paging through her magazine, without seeing the tell-tale blush under Aurélie's skin. "Just as I thought! The waist rises higher every season. And hair is dressed in Psyche knots, still. When will they give over this taste for everything Grecian?"

Diana had been ignoring them, crouched near-sightedly over a dusty old tome, as usual, but at that last word, she looked up and blinked owl-like. Then she came around and bent over the magazine in Aurélie's hands, before saying dismissively, "Grecian! Those odd gowns are no more Grecian than I am."

"It is printed right there, Miss Pert," Cassandra retorted.

"I can show you things Grecian. There is a book of drawings taken from Greek vases and drinking cups, downstairs in the—"

"Those books are quite wicked," Cassandra cut in. "If Mama knew you were looking at those—"

"They are *classical*," Diana zapped her back.

"Classical studies are not for the gentle sex." Cassandra tossed her head and twitched her shoulders. "Those books are for Will. You had better not be caught looking at them, and I will not sully my eyes with such." She turned her back on her sister, and scowled down at the magazine. "What is more important is this horrid tube shape. Who can look good in this, pray? The drawings make it pretty enough, but these females look every inch of twelve feet tall. That one would make me look like a barrel, unless my stays crack my ribs. I like this one well enough, but Mama would not let me wear pearl gray sarcenet, even without the pelisse of tobine stripes."

"Not until you are married," Diana said, safe on the other side of the room.

"You mind your schoolwork." Cassandra looked up. "What an odd thought, that Diana will turn sixteen in the *nineteenth* century. Eighteen hundred! It sounds so odd." She sighed. "Next year, I am certain I will spoil many papers, writing 'seventeen' without thinking. Look at this gown with the pink rosettes. I do so love pink. It is Cousin Lucretia's favorite color, for Mr. Brummel told her she ought always to wear rose."

Aurélie paged on, her face troubled.

When she got upstairs, she came to me, and we laid our hands together in the mirror. "An evening gown is bare here." She touched her throat and collarbones. The necklace had until now been safely hidden, for the sturdy gowns the girls wore buttoned or laced up to the neck. "Did you see those ball gowns, Duppy Kim? Maybe it is the time to confess the necklace? No one is going to steal it here. It should be safe enough in my trinket box."

I thought of Aunt Kittredge and her sneaky play with the letters. She must have justified her actions with self-assurances about giving Aurélie a good home, and blah, blah, blah—which suggested to me she could just as easily rationalize taking the necklace, claiming it was for Aurélie's own good.

The necklace might be taken away by force, but the dictates of responsibility could be just as effective. "Your aunt will probably insist you surrender it for safekeeping, because it is made of gold with all those precious stones. Nanny Hiasinte did say you were to keep it on you all the time. Why don't you put it around your ankle? Nobody will see it there if you are careful and wear thick stockings."

She nodded slowly. "Then around my ankle it shall go. I'm certain no one will see it there."

Cassandra and Aurélie were ready and waiting when the Kittredge parents appeared for the trip to the assembly. They started out to the carriage, pausing when a shout halted them. His parents and sister were gobsmacked when James showed up in knee breeches, dancing pumps, and a starched cravat between the high collar-lapels of his new coat.

As the carriage bowled along the rutted lanes, Cassandra didn't stop twitting James about his sudden interest in balls—did he even know how to dance? What possessed him? Aurélie sat quietly, her head lowered.

From the glow in faces, and the limpness of starched collars, it was clear that the assembly room was stuffy and overheated. The candlelight didn't quite hide the smoke scorches high on the wainscoting. The chairs set around the perimeter of the room were stiff-backed and uncomfortable, reflecting the more formal styles of the 1740s. But nobody noticed these things, any more than they noticed the odd fit of handmade clothes—that one sleeve was a tad tighter than the other, that added ruffles or lace or brooches didn't completely hide a grease spot.

The girls were proud of their new gowns. This being their first ball, and their first grown-up clothes, they didn't notice that the styling was not great and the stitching not all that much better than their own efforts, and faintly puckered at some of the seams.

But there was no escaping the biggest problem: The high-waisted style was not flattering to Cassandra's body type, whereas it was perfect for tiny Aurélie, who had a figure like a sylph. Her gown wasn't any better made than Cassandra's, but the ivory muslin complemented her slanted black eyes with their thick lashes, her profusion of black ringlets, and her flashing, crooked smile with its dimple in one cheek. Even the powder couldn't diminish her good looks. She wasn't the only powdered girl there; a local redhead, covered with freckles, was thickly plastered with powder, and so was the squire's olive-complected daughter, whose mother was an Italian beauty.

Even more striking was Aurélie's captivating voice, a sultry contralto that contrasted dramatically with the self-conscious, shrill giggles of the other teenage girls. Her French accent had never gone away, adding a stylish air to her speech.

When Uncle Kittredge gave her permission to go out onto the floor with James for the first dance, she moved like a butterfly with completely unconscious grace, her arms shapely because of those daily workouts in the barn. As she and James danced down the line, Aurélie's effect on the young local guys was like a grenade going off in their midst.

I caught the whispers going around the room: "Yes, most unfortunate, that complexion, but I understand it is to be expected of Spaniards, and she *is* connected to a Portuguese duke." "I understand she was sent with a dowry of thirty thousand pounds, and they do not know what she might inherit from the island property when the legalities are settled, for I've heard that the Spanish are proving recalcitrant at their end, as you'd expect of foreigners."

That was the first I'd heard of 'legalities.' Of course Uncle Kittredge would not discuss such things before the girls, which meant I wouldn't hear of them. But it made me wonder what else I wasn't hearing.

Meanwhile, Aurélie floated happily down the line of the dance, a contrast to poor Cassandra, who had ordered the maid to yank her stays unmercifully tight, making her face blotch with red. She sought to make up for it by talking dramatically of her delicacy to her few partners. With the girls she knew from church, she behaved in a languishing, coy manner, giggling at the end of every sentence and batting her fan. *That*, she had not learned from her mother.

Aurélie danced every dance. Cassandra danced four. Aunt Kittredge watched with narrowed eyes.

Over the following week, the invitations came to Aunt Kittredge. Though Aurélie and Cassandra were not officially Out, they were considered old enough for country-house parties. Every single invite made a point of mentioning Lady Aurélie de Mascarenhas.

———

That July, Diana was invited to visit her cousin Alice, whose dad was the baronet, the head of the Kittredge family. Their estate was in Yorkshire. She came home at the end of the month with a subtle alteration in mood.

As soon as they were safely alone, she confided to Aurélie that Cousins Alice and Charles turned out to be interested in the world unseen. "Cousin Charles is supposed to study law, but he intends to go into the church, and he reads *everything*. We have such good talks! He wrote out the Greek alphabet for me, and showed me how to construe. It is ever so much easier when someone just *shows* you."

The girls promptly tackled Latin and Greek.

That December, Sir Henry and Lady Bouldeston arrived with their two daughters for the holidays and to celebrate the close of the eighteenth century. Lucretia and Lucasta Bouldeston looked much like Cassandra—not surprising, as their mothers were sisters, Mrs. Bouldeston having married the second cousin who inherited their estate when their dad died. Lucretia demonstrated a fondness for pink, ruffles, and rosettes, rather showy taste that I could see Philomena did not approve of. But nothing was said . . . overtly.

Lucretia repeatedly lamented how small and delicate she was and in a way that hinted for compliments. After a few of these she glanced at Aurélie, who really was small and dainty (though she would scorn frailty), and also undeniably gorgeous.

Half an hour spent with Lucretia, and I understood who it was Cassandra had been imitating when she was in public, especially around guys. Lucretia was maybe three years older than Cassandra and had gone to London each spring for the social season. Based on this experience, she spoke as the supreme authority about London society, claiming personal acquaintance with every famous person. Cassandra drank in every word.

Lucretia was also an Olympic champion at passive-aggressive social warfare. It took one day for Lucretia to get a hate going. Her speech was full of little compliments for Aurélie that were really complaints, uttered in a lispy voice and ending with a stinger: "It is a thousand pities that she cannot . . ." or "I should perish if an unkind thought were to cross my mind, but I feel it my duty to say . . ." It was all one-way competition, because Aurélie never answered in kind. At first she seemed puzzled, then she just went silent.

For two days, Lucretia and Cassandra linked arms with Aurélie, looking the picture of amity, but as soon as they were out of sight of the adults, they would giggle across Aurélie while making references to secrets, people, and places that Aurélie had never heard of. I don't think Cassandra intended to be mean, but she had met all the people in Kent whom Lucretia discussed, and also, I don't think she could resist the pleasure of being preferred. She sure wasn't at the assemblies.

Lucasta and Diana, being younger sisters, would seem destined to be natural allies, but Lucasta despised Diana for her inky fingers and her books and her total lack of interest in the things that mattered: fashion, romance, and who was secretly in love with whom. Lucasta trailed the older girls, alternately wheedling or serving as dogsbody. Once, after sending her off on an errand, Lucretia warned the other two that she was the worst spy in nature, and to never reveal a secret before her.

Aurélie declared that she did not talk secrets, and Lucretia smothered her with lisped words of eternal admiration and devotion, her tone as false as her smiles.

On the third day of the Bouldeston visit, Aurélie used her pianoforte practice as an excuse to exclude herself when the older girls took over the schoolroom as their personal parlor. This excuse was accepted with obvious relief by Cassandra, who I suspect had been anxious that Lucretia might dump her and suck up to the marquis's daughter.

Aurélie retired to the downstairs parlor to practice her music. It was while she was losing herself in her fae melodies that I overheard Aunt Kittredge and her sister directly outside the parlor door, for they did not trouble to lower their voices.

"...she is really very good," Lady Bouldeston was saying. "You know that my taste has always been superior, Philomena. This is why I hired only the best music masters to my girls. You may rely on my word. You know I never compliment. And in fact, I will observe, to demonstrate my sense of justice, that your niece's complexion is far too brown and though her curls are charming, you must take care that they do not grow as wild as some African savage. And that puts me in mind of a question. Lucasta chanced to observe that Aurélie runs off by herself some mornings."

"Yes. She likes to take walks. I must say, the child is not lazy. I wish my girls were as vigorous, but dear Cassandra suffers with a delicate constitution. We have had to be very careful, and our medical man agrees with our opinion of the case. He says that a mother is always the most reliable judge. Now, Sister, to revert to the previous subject, an idea has come to me this past year. I meant to ask you. I know your husband has a brother at the Admiralty..." They moved out of hearing, and I wondered if the parents were thinking of the Navy instead of the Army for James. The Admiralty was where you'd go to get a son recommended aboard a ship as a midshipman, though James was rather old for that. But money talks, as always.

James slunk in through the back door with a slightly hunted expression, and I wondered if Lucretia had been trying to flirt. These were the days when cousin marriages were common. He offered to turn pages for Aurélie as they stole smiles at one another. Later, they slipped away, met in the barn, and went back to their usual practice of fencing and occasional kisses, glad that the visitors kept everyone else busy so they got more time with one another.

*   *   *

That was Day Three. On the fourth, I became aware of a shadow behind Aurélie that she didn't see. I could sense it—I could almost see it—but it wasn't until Aurélie paused at the barn door and cast a habitual glance behind her that I was also able to turn. I glimpsed Lucasta ducking behind the horse trough. Aurélie's mind was clearly elsewhere, because she didn't react.

I poked Aurélie, who started, then made a face. "Duppy Kim, please do not do that," she whispered, as she sped up the ladder to the loft where she kept her clothes. "There are no mirrors here for us to speak," she muttered as she shed the layers of female clothing.

She was always speedy, but especially now, with her breath clouding in the wintry chill. She shrugged into her outfit and crammed her curls up into a laborer's cap that James had found her.

I poked her hand again. She made an irritable gesture of warding, and kept climbing down, her attention on James, who entered the barn, walked over, and put his arms around her. She reached up for a kiss—

And the barn door opened. There stood Lucasta, looking around with avid interest as she mimed surprise. "Oh, pray, Cousin, I was looking for you to—"

Her mouth fell open. Then the barn door slammed, and Lucasta was gone.

I will draw a curtain over the painful scene that ensued and report only that by the end of the evening, Aurélie was engaged. But still in trouble.

The thing that had upset the adults the most was the breeches.

The thing that upset me was the image of Dobrenica vanishing and along with it, everyone I loved. Me, too.

"That is why you touched me. You warned me, did you not?" Aurélie asked me in the mirror that night, after she'd cried herself out.

"Yes," I said. "I saw her following you. I'm so sorry I couldn't do better than that."

Her chin lifted. "It is I who should be sorry. You warned me. I ought to have found a mirror, or a glass, at once. But I was inattentive. I will never be so again." She sighed. "I find it difficult not to hate Lucasta. Why should she spy on me?"

"I think you should ask why she is angry," I said.

"She is angry? At me? But I have done nothing to her."

"She is angry at the world."

"This is a strange thing you tell me," she responded, tipping her head with a puzzled air. "Well, I shall soon be seventeen. Then only another year and James and I can marry, and my dowry will permit us to live anywhere we like."

Alec—Dobrenica. She trusts me, right? These things streamed through my mind, prompting an instinctive response: "Aurélie, believe me when I say that he's not the right man for you."

Saving Dobrenica came first, but not far behind it was the image I'd glimpsed of her happy honeymoon. And I'd built up a good relationship with Aurélie. She might listen.

But on the other hand, when has anyone ever come well out of the I-hate-to-be-the-one-to-tell-you-but-that-guy-is-totally-wrong-for-you conversation?

Yeah.

Aurélie's eyelids flashed up. Then her chin. "I shall choose for myself. *Maman* promised, and James is my beloved. We have sworn to be true to one another for eternity."

She yanked her hand away from the mirror and didn't come back.

FOURTEEN

BEFORE SHE WENT TO BED, she threw a blanket over the mirror. The next day she replaced it with a holland cover, draping it neatly. The message was clear. She didn't want to talk to me.

Since there wasn't anything I could do except wait, I waited. *I've been here before*, I kept reminding myself. *Somehow I got past this.* I had to keep my eye out for that moment when the past became possible futures, endangering Dobrenica.

I still had no idea what that meant.

And so time blurred on, season following season, each day largely the same pattern. Aurélie's eighteenth birthday came and went. James was still around, but the two were forbidden to interact except with the entire family present. Aurélie was still betrothed, though secretly, and the betrothal didn't stop Aunt Kittredge from lecturing Aurélie about indelicacy and reputation as if she'd been running after every guy in the countryside. The problem was, they showed a distinct tendency to run after *her* whenever they were invited to local parties.

That made poor Cassandra frantic with jealousy, and Aunt Kittredge continued to hector Aurélie about being "fast" even if she sat still. The boys flocked around if she so much as smiled, that charming crooked smile with one side quirked whimsically.

Spring came at last, and still no wedding. Skip all my desperate plans to foul it up, not that I had any magical abilities besides the Power of the Poke. Judging by the holland cover now neatly arranged over the mirror, Aurélie was angry enough to have ignored me thoroughly even if I'd poked her entirely through the ceremony. She was determined to marry James and to prove her loyalty In Spite Of Them All (I was included in the "Them"), and she would Love Him Forever.

The holland cover only got rid of me in her own mind. I think she was so used to talking to me in the mirror that she forgot I was connected to her all the time, not just when she looked in the mirror.

She wasn't the only angry one. Cassandra moped around dramatically when she found out that the family was not going to London for her to be presented to the queen, which was the way the *haut monde* officially launched their girls into society. She pouted for days after Uncle Kittredge and James departed to visit the Horse Guards and see about James's joining the army—I guessed that the naval plan had come to nothing. Cassandra's mood was not helped by her being the recipient of a constant stream of letters from Lucretia, as usual exulting over the Bouldestons' prospective season in London.

Cassandra was furious with envy, but she couldn't bring herself not to read every word. We had to listen as Cassandra read the letters aloud. Lucretia Bouldeston was unsurpassed at wringing maximum drama out of a mere introduction and detecting secret passion in the briefest contact with her partner during a single dance. Cassandra finished each letter wailing that she would *never* see London and she would die an old maid and nobody cared.

Before James left for London, Romeo and Juliet were restricted to longing glances across the dining table, and on the way to church and back. As a consolation (or maybe to get Cassandra out of the house) the girls were taught to drive James's old gig, after which they were permitted to tool sedately to various neighbors to take tea or to attend dance practices, or impromptu dances—although only when the moon was full, and they were accompanied by a sturdy servant armed with an ancient fowling piece that Aurélie could probably have wielded better.

Everyone was getting ready for the social season.

Toward the end of March the girls went off to another tea party, and spent the afternoon eating heavy cake and drinking tea as the select company said the exact same things about the weather, each other's hats, and the new fashions, that they'd said at the last party. When the girls arrived home, they discovered that James and Uncle Kittredge had returned from London.

Aurélie was overjoyed to see James back. But he didn't seem as glad to see her. He appeared uncomfortable and hastily excused himself.

She went upstairs to change for dinner, her expression troubled.

As Aurélie repinned her hair, Diana slipped into her room. "There is something vastly amiss," she whispered.

"What can it be?" Aurélie asked.

"I know not, but I heard Mama and Papa in the book room. Very loud. I detected your name spoken, otherwise I'd scorn to listen at doors. But they sounded so very angry that I felt that I should," she finished frankly.

"Oh, Diana, *pray* tell me what you heard!"

"Nothing to the point." Diana sighed. "Truth to tell, I don't understand how Lucasta could be so adept as such practices. Though my eyesight is poor, there's nothing amiss with my hearing, but I could only make out the occasional word. Pirates? Rebellion. Monalco? Mulatto? Is that even a word?"

"There is a dance called the Monaco," Aurélie said slowly. "A mulatto is a person with one parent who has pale skin and one with dark."

Mulatto? I was thinking. I'd stopped worrying about the fake nobility when that first year had passed without incident, but now that worry came rushing back.

Diana went on, "Well, this much I *can* tell you: Mama is in a bait."

The girls stared at one another in dismay. The entire household walked softly when Philomena Kittredge was in a temper. Meanwhile, I was frantic with curiosity, regret, and most of all, rage at my own helplessness.

Aurélie was subdued when she went down to dinner. To everyone's surprise, they found Philomena smiling broadly, and I saw the girls relax a little. But I didn't. The woman's eyes looked strange in the candle light: Wide, the pupils huge and black. *She's up to something nasty, or I'm an armadillo*, I thought.

"My dears, we are to make a journey," she said with that broad smile. "Now that there is to be peace with France, half of fashionable England is traveling to Paris. Where the Devonshires lead, what is there to do but follow? We would not be thought behindhand."

As soon as the girls had withdrawn upstairs to the schoolroom, Cassandra exulted, "Lucretia is not going. Or I would have heard." She turned Aurélie's way. "Mama hasn't said, but we must be going to Paris to buy fabrics for our introduction to London. And perhaps silks for your trousseau. The French silks are infinitely superior, so I've heard."

"Shall we be presented to Napoleon Bonaparte?" Diana asked, and turned to Aurélie. "I remember when we were small, and someone, I think it was Papa, said that you were related to his wife."

"Aurélie, you must send in your name at the Tuileries," Cassandra declared. "If Madame Bonaparte does remember your family, that would be capital. You could arrange our introduction to the best French society."

"There is no best French society," Diana retorted. "They died on the guillotine."

"There has to be good society. Everyone talks of the beautiful Josephine and her beautiful palaces and clothes. What's the use of that if there's no society to see them?" Cassandra said.

"I hope it's as you say, because that would be one in Lucretia's eye," Diana stated. "At all events, I should like to have a look at the great Bonaparte after all we have heard about him."

"*You* won't see anything at all," Cassandra stated, screwing up her face in a mocking squint.

Diana shrugged. "I will if I obtain a pair of spectacles. And so I shall. I care not a whit that ladies don't wear spectacles. I want to see France in every detail, and no stupid quizzing glass that you have to hold all the time."

"My mother wears spectacles," Uncle Kittredge said a couple hours later, when Diana brought it up.

"That happened after she was safely married," Aunt Kittredge retorted, but she was watching her husband as she said it. There was something going on between them; he seemed to have the advantage, for once, and she submitted. I wondered what had happened, and wished again that I could get away from Aurélie to do some listening on my own.

Then Philomena was back to her usual self as she scowled at Diana. "If you must, then get them. But do not cry out for sympathy to me when no eligible gentleman will offer for you."

Diana shot back, "Cousin Charles likes me the way I am, and he wears spectacles."

"Your cousin Charles is a blockhead, throwing away a good career in law when there is no living set aside for him. You watch, he will end his life in some hamlet, preaching to toothless farmers, chickens, and pigs," her mother said in disgust. "Do not take *him* for a pattern."

Diana looked down, her expression wooden. Uncle Kittredge said nothing, but the next day he drove her into town to the lens-maker.

The first week in April found the family on a packet ship crossing the Channel. This one left Newhaven bound for Dieppe, for, as Cassandra told the other girls, Mama had stated that she did not intend to rub shoulders with every grocer's wife who wished to crowd over to Calais. Papa had been to Dieppe before the Revolution, where he'd stayed at a hostelry he particularly liked. He'd been assured when he arranged the crossing that it was still there and still served only the best people.

The packet set out on the running tide. It was late in the day. They would spent the night crossing and arrive in France in time for breakfast.

Aunt Kittredge went straight to the tiny cabin she was to share with Diana, and stayed there, leaving her husband to hang out with the older men in the wardroom. James remained on deck, at a little distance from Aurélie and his sisters, who listened to Aurélie name the parts of the ship. Diana faced into the brisk wind, her eyes slitted behind her new spectacles, her grin wide. Even shivering, with the wind trying to take her bonnet away and tangling her skirts, she clearly relished every moment and pelted Aurélie with questions.

Gradually James drifted closer and closer. I watched him, trying to figure out why he was keeping so aloof. If he and Aurélie had argued, I would have heard it, surely.

But he didn't talk, and at last, when Aurélie became aware of him, she quite naturally smiled and held out her hand. He flushed to the tips of his ears, his body stiff. He looked down at her with such an expression of mute misery that her smile changed to concern. Diana looked askance at her brother, and I knew something was very wrong.

Then the bell rang for the passengers to assemble for dinner. They crowded into the wardroom, talking and laughing as dishes slid back and forth and lamps swung overhead.

After dinner, the night being fine, the crew strung lanterns along the deck so that passengers could walk about. Aurélie and the younger Kittredges joined other young people on the deck, where they worked through the polite inanities of introductory conversations.

Diana scowled fixedly at the water, then said to Cassandra and Aurélie, "I left my handkerchief in the cabin, and my spectacles are thick with spots of brine." She slipped away.

Sometime later Aurélie became aware of James and Diana standing at the prow, talking earnestly. She made a move to join them, followed by Cassandra. As soon as the brother and sister saw the two girls approaching, they shut up.

For a few seconds everyone looked at everyone else in the swinging lantern light, and I could feel the discomfort radiating off three of them. Only Cassandra seemed oblivious. Aurélie turned to James, appeal plain in her face, but he gazed out to sea as if rescue lay there.

"I'm chilled," Cassandra said finally. "Aurélie, we should retire."

There was only one lantern per cabin, so Aurélie had to go with her. What seemed like a few seconds after they blew out the light Aurélie jerked awake—and so did I. A small hand, just barely discernible in the weak blue moonlight filtering through the open scuttle, slid over her mouth. Aurélie's eyes opened wide.

Diana's profile bent over her, moonlight reflecting briefly off the glass in her spectacles. She tugged on Aurélie's arm.

Aurélie slid noiselessly out of bed and wrestled into her travel gown—like the others, she'd slept in her stays and chemise. She slid her feet into her walking shoes and noiselessly left the cabin. Cassandra slept on undisturbed.

The two girls didn't speak until they were as far forward as they could get, and both shivered in the bleak pre-dawn chill. Diana then took Aurélie's hands. "I want you to know first that I loathe such practices as my cousin Lucasta employs. But I believe I am doing right by you, even if Mama would not agree. James thinks so, as well."

"I don't understand," Aurélie said.

Diana bent her head. "I hate this," she said in a low voice. "But when I thought about it, I knew it would be better if you heard it from me. James thinks so, as well. He—well, I'll leave him to plead his case once we reach France, though Mama and Papa forbade him to speak to you anymore."

"Why? Is it the breeches?"

"No. Here it is. When I went downstairs, or down below, or whatever they call it, to fetch my handkerchief, I heard Mama and Papa arguing in the cabin Mama and I share. Because the walls are just canvas, though they were whispering, I could hear very well, and they were arguing about you. And the things they said—well, James, it turns out, knows all about it. I got it out of him last night. See, Aunt Bouldeston helped Mama to direct a letter to Government House in Jamaica—"

"Then she did *not* burn my letters? She wrote to discover why my mother didn't—"

"Hsst! Listen, for I have much to say, and I don't know how long we will have. She didn't write *to* your mother but *about* her. She had in the last year or two been in want of a way to investigate your father, and . . . and such matters, without anyone knowing what she was about. Not to protect you, but to protect *us*."

Mimba, you were right, I thought, sickened.

"Oh, Aurélie, I do so hate this," Diana whispered, her voice broken. "But, well, it turns out that your father, that is, he was not a marquis, though Alfonso de Mascarenhas really was a descendant of a very illustrious family. But he was disinherited, and though he did have a letter of marque, he turned pirate against Spain and plundered treasure ships for gold. It seems he used to sail into mainly French ports, but also Spanish and Portuguese, and while officials would entertain him, his pirates would attack in secret. He . . . well, there is a very long list of crimes, including the murder of your Uncle Thomas Kittredge."

"But how comes he to—?"

"Listen! Your mother is also a pirate, it seems. Or a privateer, for she took over your uncle's ship, and his letter of marque from our government, which James explained to me last night. A letter of marque means one can attack ships of an enemy government and not be considered a pirate, at least, by one's home government."

"I know that," Aurélie said. "So my mother should be within the laws of Jamaica."

"Except that your mother wears breeches and captains a ship. It's considered scandalous, though it's not *illegal*, James said. That is, there was some question about her owning a ship, but I haven't time for that. She attacked and defeated this pirate Mascarenhas and took his treasure, which was vast. Using that, she came back to reclaim the Kittredge plantation, only she came in company with a lot of runaway slaves, and something called Maroons, or quadroons, or—"

"They are two very different things," Aurélie began.

"Not yet." Diana squeezed her hands. "I will want to know that, and more, but anon. I have to get this out, because you do not yet know the worst of it."

"But if the worst is that this evil marquis is not really my father, well, I am *very* happy."

"He isn't. Your mother took his name along with his treasure, because her real husband—or, that is, they don't know if they were married, or maybe they were married in a Papist ceremony, or some kind of ceremony with the Jamaican witch doctors—"

"*Witch* doctors?" Aurélie began with disgust.

"Oh, *do* be quiet," Diana hissed in an agony. "It's what James said. But yes, that's part of what I'm to tell you—"

"It's good news, because my papa was a wonderful man, that much I know," Aurélie said fiercely.

"It may be, but he was not Spanish any more than he was a marquis, and he was not married to your mother in any English church. In fact, we don't know if it's legal for such a marriage, an African and an English-woman. He was a runaway slave named Baptiste Kofi Beauveau, that is, slaves were given the last name of their owner or his estate, but maybe Kofi was his chosen name? He belonged to an estate called Beauveau. No, *don't* interrupt, I don't know if we can talk again. This name was written on the wanted list, which someone brought from Saint-Domingue to Jamaica. Your father hired on with your Uncle Thomas, the privateer captain. It seems your uncle didn't care where his crew came from, only that they were good at their work, and your father was very smart, and he became the first mate, and then had his own ship in your uncle's fleet. But your father was killed by this marquis in an act of treachery after Mascarenhas lost to him in a sea battle. Your Uncle Thomas was killed, too. Then your mother took over as captain, and they destroyed the marquis and his fleet."

"*Bon,*" Aurélie whispered.

"Aurélie, the worst is this. We are come to France not to go to Paris. That is, *we* may be going to Paris, but *you* are not."

"I'm not?" Aurélie repeated. "Where am I to go?"

"That's just it. We don't know. Mama intends to fling all these things at you tomorrow, when Papa is to take James and Cassie and me on a tour. She will then send you into the streets."

Aurélie stared at Diana in sick horror.

Diana looked down at her tightly clasped hands. "Then, see, when we return to England, Mama can say you ran off. It's our reputation she is thinking of, not yours. She'll not want anyone to know that we had living with us a daughter of a runaway slave, even if her mother was English. Somehow—I don't quite understand how—that makes it worse, for Mama. Though I want you to know that I think it all nonsense, and I will always love you like a sister, Aurélie." Diana's voice wobbled at the end.

Aurélie stared blindly back at her.

Diana gulped and said in a low, fierce voice, "I will *never* forgive Mama for this. James says she claims the privilege, the pleasure, of turning you out into the street because Papa would not do it. It makes me *sick*. I told James that he should marry you anyway, for at least you have your fortune. *Surely* Papa must give it to you, for that was intended once you and James married, was it not? Then you and James can live anywhere you like."

Aurélie was breathing quickly. "Thank you, Diana. Thank you. I will never forget what you have done for me." She was shivering, hands gripping her elbows. "I have to talk to James."

"He was forbidden to talk to you. I will do it. I'll find a way for the two of you to meet tomorrow. How is that?"

Ting-ting! The bell brought sailors swarming up on deck. The darkness was already beginning to gray toward a cloudy dawn.

The girls slipped down below, where Aurélie crept back into her bunk and lay stiff, hands clenched at her sides, silent tears dripping down the sides of her face.

FIFTEEN

A URÉLIE SCARCELY PICKED at the breakfast of weak tea and biscuits they were served. When they disembarked soon after, she walked with her head down. She didn't see the smirking, angry anticipation in her aunt's face, or her uncle's remote expression, the slight betrayal of shame in the tightness of his shoulders. She didn't see the misery in James's face, or Diana's impotent, white-lipped rage. Only Cassandra looked around with interest, unaware.

Aurélie didn't see any of this, but I did.

Soon they were wedged in the carriage together, Cassandra going on about how she hadn't slept a wink for the hideous rolling of the ship, and the terrible excuse for a bed. Aurélie kept her attention on the murky glass as they rolled through the streets of what had been a beautiful town, and would be again, when the ravages of the Revolution were repaired.

When they reached the inn, Kittredge spoke in painstaking French, ordering the disposition of baggage to rooms. Then he gestured to James, Cassandra, and Diana, saying, "We will take a tour of the town, and look at the chateau on the hill, while they settle our things."

Diana whispered to Aurélie, "Meet James at the well at the square we just passed!" She ran after the other two.

"Step inside," Philomena said to Aurélie, and whisked herself into the inn before the spatters of rain could mar her hat.

Aurélie followed, her hands clenched on her skirts as she picked her way to the steps. The innkeeper pointed them to a suite of rooms at the top of the stairs, where male servants were unloading the trunks as a pair of girls lit lamps and the fire in the fireplace.

Aunt Kittredge spoke in a penetrating voice, her French so peculiar that the inn servants just stared at her.

So Aurélie said, "She would like to be alone, and for you to return in a little while."

Faces cleared, and the servants filed out, leaving their work half done. The incident, small as it was, seemed to infuriate Mrs. Kittredge more—or maybe, somewhere deep inside, she knew she was not wholly in the right and needed anger to push her where she wanted to go.

Anyway, the moment the door shut, she let fly.

Poor Aurélie stood there under the diatribe, and her very lack of horror and surprise seemed to enrage her aunt further.

"And so you may take what you can carry, for we will permit you that much, and we never want to see your base-born, half-breed face again. If you dare, you will be driven from the door."

Aurélie stood there a moment longer, as if waiting, until her aunt snapped shrilly, "Did you hear me?"

"I am waiting to hear in what form my dowry is to be furnished to me," Aurélie said with dignity.

Mrs. Kittredge gave a contemptuous laugh. "You mean your pirate ransom? For there is no dowry, not for a blackamoor's by-blow. That money is *ours*, a small portion of what is due us for housing and feeding the likes of you. And for this trespass upon our trust. Right now there is a revolution going on in those islands, the savages rising against their masters. Your mother may be dead, for aught we know. She ceased writing these three years—"

"Because you destroyed my letters," Aurélie flashed.

Mrs. Kittredge flushed, then lifted her chin. "That is as may be. But this is for certain: If your mother ever dares to show her face in England, she will be reported as the pirate's whore that she is."

"So you are robbing me of my dowry? What am I to live on?"

"I lay legitimate claim to what was already ill-gotten gains," was the bitter answer. "No court in England would deny me. As for what you do next, everyone always finds their level. I feel certain, after the way you unbecomingly flaunted yourself all over our neighborhood, you will discover yours on the streets. Now go."

Aurélie walked blindly to the room where the girls were to stay—and found Cassandra's and Diana's trunks before the two beds. Her own had been set against the wall on either side of an old, spotted looking glass.

She knelt and flung it open. "Duppy Kim?" she whispered.

"I'm here," I said.

She swayed with relief, and with her eyes tightly closed and tears leaking from them, she whispered, "I don't know what to do. I can't think."

The creak of floorboards outside the room caused her to recoil. She dug through her trunk until she found her little trinket box. From it she pulled her few nice pieces, like the gold cross she'd been given for her thirteenth birthday. "At least you're with me still," she said, then hurried to Cassandra's trunk. Her expression tightened as she sifted deftly through until she found Cassandra's little mirror.

She slipped this into the pocket of her traveling pelisse and then returned to her own trunk. Here she dug feverishly through her clothes, as if seeking a gown and accoutrements small enough to roll up. Her hands shook, and she had to give up.

She tied her bonnet on more firmly, opened the door, and sure enough, there was Philomena standing in the doorway of the room opposite. Waiting for tears? Begging? Recriminations? To make certain Aurélie left only with her clothes?

Aurélie walked past her without so much as a glance.

I admired her guts, but cascading in my mind were the ramifications of an eighteen-year-old girl being totally alone and friendless in the tumbled country of France at a time when the government had been changing every year or two for over a decade.

My first taste of Napoleonic history had come from Annemarie Selinko's *Désirée*, when I was twelve. I'd found it so glamorous and romantic—

this story of a shopkeeper's daughter who was engaged to Napoleon, married a general, and found herself Queen of Sweden—that I'd later traced the history of all these people in college. It turned out that Selinko had glossed a lot, but the result was, I had a reasonably good memory of the main players and key events of this period.

For example, I was pretty certain that Napoleon had just (or was about to) restore the authority of the Catholic Church, but I had no idea if that restoration would have propagated out this far. So taking sanctuary in a church or convent might not, in fact, be a safe refuge. He'd reorganized France into the prefecture in 1800, but I don't remember reading that it was all that reliable in its early days.

And here I was, restored to guardianship again and no power to actually do anything.

But at least we're on the right subcontinent, I thought. *We've just got to get her east. Somehow.*

Aurélie headed into the wind and marched down the street. She crossed a muddy square with tough grass coming up between ruined flagstones, and stopped by a well, her cloak pulled around her.

She pulled the mirror from her pocket, worked her glove off, then touched the glass. I put my 'hand' over hers, and she breathed a sigh of relief. "You must see that you were very wrong, that James and Diana are loyal and true."

"I'd be glad to be wrong," I said to comfort her, and added, "If you want to elope, you needn't wait weeks for banns to be posted or to find an English divine." The fact that Diana alone had done all the communicating worried me, but I didn't tell her. "All you have to do is go to the prefecture for a civil ceremony. It should be simple enough."

Her worried expression eased slightly. "Thank you, Duppy Kim. This is good advice."

All right, I was out of the doghouse. I had to make sure I didn't lose her again.

A man rode by, giving her a long glance. She looked at the ground, and hurriedly tucked the mirror away.

Rain began to spatter but, at least, never turned into a downpour. She stood there. And stood there. I don't know how long it was, but the light was fading when she spied a furtive figure bent into the rising breeze.

This figure scurried along the closing shop fronts then darted to her, revealing mud-splashed knit stockings and caked walking shoes. Once again, it was Diana.

And it was time for the final blow.

"I hope someday you can forgive James," Diana said quickly. "He feels wretched. I know he does. But he can't . . ." She shook her head, her bonnet turned the other way. Then she sniffed and gulped.

"I see," Aurélie said. "It's the dowry, isn't it?"

"And they will not buy his commission if he—well. They think I'm bathing for supper. I have to get back. Listen, Aurélie, James and I settled it between us. You are to have these things. We're agreed it might be safer if you go about as a boy than as a girl." She thrust the bundle into Auré-lie's arms, leaned up to kiss her, and said, "I love you always. You are a true sister. I will pray for you every night. And I will also ask God to give Mama a calenture for cruelty." Then she darted away, muffling a sob.

Aurélie watched her until she was out of sight up the twisted lane, and she wept, too. When she was done, she gave a shuddering sigh, and pulled out the mirror again, peering at it in the dimming light. "Duppy Kim, is this why you turned against James?" She frowned. "Did you know this was to be?"

"I did not," I said, feeling my way. I couldn't lose her again! "Remember the obeah ceremony, when you were twelve, and Nanny Hiasinte bound me to you?"

She wiped her eyes on her sleeve, then nodded. "I've not forgotten."

"Do you remember her saying that the future was a fog to her?"

"I don't remember that."

"She said it to me. And it's true. Your future is a fog to me, too. I don't see your path, except in very small glimpses. But in those glimpses, I never saw James."

She nodded slowly. "I remember Nanny Hiasinte saying many times that the *lwa* would show different futures, and that we choose where to go when we come to crossroads."

Relief flooded through me.

"You didn't see James on my path. You only said he was wrong for me," she said with quiet dignity. I could sense that resentment remained.

"I apologize," I said. "I went about it all wrong."

"And I didn't afford you the opportunity to explain it better," she said, wiping her eyes again. "Forgive me, Duppy Kim?"

"I'm just glad you're talking to me again. I can't help you if we don't talk."

"Do you see my path now?"

"No," I had to admit, and braced for her to retort, *Then what use are you?* I probably would have, but she gave a slow sigh.

"It helps to think of my peril as a crossroads. It also helps that you are with me in spirit again."

"I was with you all along," I said. "I just couldn't talk to you."

She nodded again. "That was my error. But I must go onward if I cannot go back. I'll seek an inn that isn't so fine. No. First I'd better become René, as Diana suggested. We've always been warned about the dangers of girls alone, and I can see from the stares I've received that it is so." She peered around the store fronts in the darkening gloom. Most were shuttered for the night.

She slipped into the narrow space between two buildings, grimacing, then breathing through her mouth. From the looks of things I was really glad my nose didn't work, as the glories of plumbing had not quite reached this area. The walls and ground in that alley had been used as an open-air restroom.

She picked her way carefully, found an old, broken cart, and climbed onto that. Then she unwrapped the bundle that Diana had given her and disclosed James's second-best beaver, a shirt, waistcoat, breeches, stockings, and James's dancing shoes. When she unfolded the shirt, she found two unexpected treasures, her pistol and James's coin purse. Aurélie checked the pistol. It was unloaded, so she laid it gently aside.

Then, with many desperate glances around, she wrestled out of her clothes and into James's. The pants were nankeen breeches, rather than buckskin, and though on James they buttoned just below his knees, on her, they hung to just below her calves. His long stockings went under, thoroughly hiding her slender, feminine ankles and the double-looped necklace with its glittering stones.

The trinkets went into the purse with the coins. She tucked the purse into a waistcoat pocket, and into the other pocket, where guys usually tucked their timepiece, went the little mirror. The pistol got stuffed inside her waistcoat. She wrapped the neck cloth around her throat, pulling it well up under her chin, tied it in a plain knot, and tucked the ends into the waistcoat, fussing over it to hide her slight figure, which was already well hidden by the voluminous shirt and the thick waistcoat.

Diana had even included James's black hair tie. Aurélie pulled out her hairpins and cast them into the muck, then clawed her hair back and clubbed it with the tie. What emerged was a handsome boy's face. She didn't look all that much older than she had at twelve.

She rolled up her clothes and shoes, and set them on the cart. "I hope they will be found by someone in need," she said softly into the mirror. "I am ready, am I not?"

"Not yet," I said. "Try the hat on."

It was too large—it slid to her nose.

"The clothes will pass, I believe," I said. "In France, mobs still hang persons who look too aristocratic. James's clothes are so large that they look shabby, but that hat, even though it also is too large, is too clean, too obviously the hat of an English gentleman. I think you should knock it against the cart. Dent it. Get it well smeared with dust."

She whacked the beaver against the grubby rail of the cart, rubbed it around, then clapped it on her head. "Is that sufficient?" she asked the mirror.

"That's better," I said, and she tucked the mirror back into her waistcoat.

Then she climbed carefully to the ground, for the pumps threatened to fall off her feet. She cast a last, longing look at her own shoes. But she couldn't wear the pointy-toed female walking slippers. So she reopened her bundle, pulled out her stockings, wadded each up, and thrust them into the toes of James's shoes. The way she walked reminded me of a kid with her first pair of swim flippers as she proceeded carefully into the square.

The shine on the shoes was soon obscured by muck.

She headed toward noise and lights of the town center, and its rows of taverns with people coming and going. All around were mostly French voices, with a smattering of English and Dutch. Everyone used the informal *tu* with one another, instead of the polite, formal *vous* for 'you.' This, Miss Oliver had told them in hushed, disapproving tones, was a result of the Revolution. It was strange to actually hear it in practice, so strong was my habit and training. Aurélie proceeded slowly, watching everything. Rain spattered now and then, ruining the clean look of her clothes.

Furtive figures slunk here and there, and from the open doors of taverns erupted loud noise: laughter, shouts, bellows and, in a couple of places, music. Tipsy customers roared songs and stamped and clapped.

Most people who wanted to be safe were probably home, locked in tight, and here she was, a kid alone. My strategies for the future had shrunk to one anxious worry: Keeping her alive through a single night, though I had no physical form or powers.

"First, I must eat," she whispered with her hand closed over the mirror, as if I couldn't hear her any other way. "Then I must find a safe bed. Then tomorrow, back to the quay. I shall find a ship to take me back to Jamaica."

SIXTEEN

S HE MIGHT HAVE BEEN BETTER OFF at a nicer inn—except a nice inn probably would have turned her away. She picked a total dump that advertised a bed and supper for two for a *decime*.

Her first mistake was taking out the coin purse to pay. By the light of the single guttering lamp in the common room, I saw the quick grin on the innkeeper's grizzled, greasy face. I knew there was going to be trouble. I poked her, but she was too wary to pull out the mirror and be seen talking to me.

The innkeeper acted pleasant enough as he set a bowl of fish soup before her and a hunk of bread. She sat down to the meal, and her second mistake was her manners. She delicately picked off the bits of mold, and broke off pieces of the hard bread, which she determinedly chewed. She was too hungry to notice the innkeeper whispering to a hard-faced woman with a filthy apron and a hulking guy of about twenty who looked like their son.

Aurélie finished the bread. She picked through the soup, which swam with grease, until she found a few scraps of cabbage. She left the rest, then stood up.

"My soup not good enough for ye?" the woman asked in an angry voice, as the other few customers looked up. They were no more than vague, shadowy shapes in that dim light.

"It is fine," Aurélie lied. "I am very tired, is all."

"Then come this way, your majesty," the innkeeper said.

The others burst into a loud guffaw at this witticism, and I thought, *This is so not going to end well.* I railed against my own helplessness and tried futilely to reach for any idea.

The innkeeper picked up a candle, lit it at the lamp, and led the way upstairs to one of the two rooms. It had two items of furniture: A bed on the floor and a slop bucket in the corner. The bed already had two men asleep in it.

The innkeeper walked over and kicked the nearest of the men, who was snoring in a drunken stupor. "Make space, citizen, make space," he ordered. "You didn't pay for two places."

In the light of the wavering candle, the customer rolled blearily, and as he shifted, several insectoid shapes crawled out of his dirty cravat into the hair behind his ear.

Aurélie leaped back. "He is crawling with lice!"

The innkeeper gave a crack of laughter. "So will you, citizen. So will you."

"I'll not sleep there," she said. And then came her third mistake, "I'll pay for my food, but I want my *decime* back. I cannot sleep here."

"He wants his *decime* back, he does, because my bed isn't good enough for his aristocratic hide," the innkeeper roared.

Angry voices down below responded in language that Aurélie hadn't heard since her days in Saint-Domingue's harbor.

"Keep it, then. I will go elsewhere," she said, backing down the stairs.

Mrs. Innkeeper stood there, a cleaver gripped in her fist, and her hulking son with a cudgel.

"I'm thinking you will go to the prefecture," the innkeeper said menacingly, following her down. "You and your clean hands and your risto tastes. You're either one of *them*, escaped justice, or you're a thief. Either way, it seems to me my duty as a patriot and a citizen is to report your thieving, aristocrat carcass."

Aurélie's lips tightened, and she reached for the pistol—which she'd tucked securely into her waistcoat.

"He's going for a knife," the missus shrilled, and the innkeeper kicked Aurélie down the last two stairs, causing her to fall with a splat.

The missus thrust an efficient hand into the waistcoat pocket and pulled out the coin purse. She let out a laugh when she encountered the trinkets. Aurélie rolled blurrily to her feet, having managed to fish out the pistol, which she leveled desperately.

The three fell back.

"You got one shot," the innkeeper snarled. "And then whoever you don't shoot will be on you."

Aurélie didn't answer, but backed to the door. They followed, but at a respectful distance. She got to the door, stepped through . . . and ran.

The rain was coming down too hard for them to chase her, or maybe they figured she wasn't worth pursuing as they'd gotten her money. At any rate, she lumbered in those awful shoes down the narrow street and dodged desperately between houses until she stumbled on a hen house, into which she crept.

She cried herself to sleep.

When I say that was the highlight of the next few days, you can imagine how rotten things got.

She still had the mirror, so we arranged a system that next morning: If I poked her once, it was a reminder that I was with her. She seemed to need that. But if I poked her twice, it meant I thought she was in danger, and she was to run and hide as soon as she could find a place to hide in.

She made her way to the harbor, her plan to stow away on board a ship to Jamaica. I told her I didn't think it was a good idea, but she put the mirror back, and I knew she wasn't going to listen. I couldn't blame her for the longing to go home.

After two anxious days of lurking about, she discovered that first, ships did not go to Jamaica from Dieppe, and second, it was impossible to sneak onto them. And even if she could have managed it, the roughness of the sailors hanging around the wharfs frightened her. Though she was still pretty clueless about the facts of life, it didn't take much imagination to guess that nothing good would come of those sailors discovering she was a girl.

That wasn't the only threat. While she lurked around barnacled pilings and noisome, fly-swarmed corners, she was eyed in no friendly way by some of the ragged, miserable homeless kids whose parents had either died in the revolution or else left them for whatever reason. They made it real clear that interlopers could expect no mercy if they tried begging in their territory.

The only thing I could think to suggest was, "Watch how they get food when they aren't begging."

She did, after a morning's begging in a place where the orphans didn't hang out. Her attempts earned her cuffs, kicks, curses, and threats from the shopkeepers. So she followed some of the smaller orphans and discovered a few of them lurking behind the dockside taverns and inns. When the scrapings of meals were tossed to the pigs, the kids would scramble into the sties, picking out whatever didn't get immediately immersed into the disgusting black mud.

After a day or so of watching, she got in first and managed to snag some old potatoes and a stale bit of bread.

How to get her out of there before she either got murdered or died of some disease? The horrid problem of the poor confronted her—too many desperate people competing for scant pickings. But if she tried the nicer part of town, she'd be chased away, or worse, dragged to the prefecture. Where she would no doubt be searched, the necklace and her gender discovered, and thence to a short, sharp end.

Barns turned out to be guarded by dogs, but hen houses, too small for adults, worked as shelters, and she could usually find a raw egg to suck. She cried herself to sleep every night, waking each day to the quest to survive.

"You've got to find a way to earn money," I said to her one night, when she took out the mirror for the comfort of my useless company. The mirror and the necklace were the only things she'd managed to save. I'd tried to talk her into selling the mirror, but so far, she wouldn't. She knew it wouldn't bring much anyway.

"How can I earn money?" she asked. "The only thing I know well is how to play the fortepiano. Would anyone hire me as a governess? Where do I go to get hired?"

"I don't know much more than you do about that. But here's another idea. Remember that first night, before you went to that horrible inn? You passed by some places where I heard music. Try going back there. See who is playing, and if they are friendly, ask how they got the work."

"Oh, what a very good idea," she said. "But first I must eat. My head swims every time I stand up."

A sudden noise silenced her. People crashed through the yard—thieves or drunks or who knows what. The bangs and crashes and screams of someone getting strangled set the chickens clucking, and somewhere a dog let out a hoarse howl, then yapped. More dogs barked, pigs grunted, and the scream cut off short.

Gradually silence fell, and all living things settled back into torpor.

As soon as the sun was up, Aurélie felt around for eggs and found one. She cracked it open and slurped it out of her filthy hands. The rest of the day was entirely taken up in hiding, cruising pig yards, and scavenging for anything she could eat.

When the sun sank, and the taverns opened to nighttime entertainment, she made her way back to the center of Dieppe and the row of shops, taverns, and pubs.

Rain fell, hard. "At least I will get clean," she said, teeth chattering.

The taverns all seemed to be full, the voices mostly male, loud and rough. From one came ragged singing and from another the tail end of a French folk tune played on a violin, nearly smothered by a roar of laughter.

Aurélie paused, uncertain. The fiddle player started up again—and this time, I recognized the melody, an Eastern European Jewish folksong.

I wasn't aware that I'd poked her until Aurélie jolted. She backed up onto a porch, lurked behind a stack of old baskets, and pulled out the mirror. "Duppy Kim? What is it?"

"I'm curious about that melody from the other side of Europe being played in the north of France," I said. "Why don't you go into that tavern? The fiddler is good, and at least you will be out of the rain."

"Very well," she said, and tucked the mirror back into her waistcoat pocket. "I shall go in here."

SEVENTEEN

⟡

SHE DUCKED UNDER ELBOWS and dodged the rowdies busy whooping it up. Even in the lamplight she was as grungy as any of them. At least no one was going to accuse her of being an aristocrat anymore.

In the corner near the fireplace, surrounded by a thickening crowd, three musicians played. Aurélie worked her way into the press, her attention on the tall black-haired guy with the fiddle. His eyes were closed, his face pale and mournful as a romantic poet. He seemed to be in his mid-twenties, his coat patched and threadbare.

Seated on a three-legged stool next to him, another equally skinny guy in shabby laborer's clothing played an hautbois, a kind of oboe, as one foot jerked up and down. His face was lowered, greasy hair the color of cookie dough escaping under a shapeless worker's cap. His much-patched boot had a tambourine tied to it by twine, and when it hit the floor, it clashed with a percussive beat. The guy had the toe of his boot thrust through a bit of frayed rope that was attached to the bellows. As he thumped his foot up and down, he not only played the tambourine, he pumped the bellows for the regal.

Hopping on her toes, Aurélie spotted the regal, played by a third guy. He was ruddy-faced from the heat and probably from the tall mug sitting on the floor, next to the barrel on which he'd propped the regal. His playing didn't always keep the beat set by the tambourine or the fiddle, creating a ragged effect that caused the audience to rock with laughter.

The fiddler lowered his bow and began to sing, joined by the regal player. They both had very fine voices, the fiddler tenor to baritone in range, the regal player baritone to bass. The audience's mood shifted as the duo belted out words about equality, brotherhood, and the blood of martyrs, but just as the audience got into the song, the regal player faltered, scowled, and let out a stream of curses.

The mood was lost. The audience broke into laughter and cat calls. A few rinds of cheese and bits of food were tossed at the players. Things were about to turn nasty, but then the hautbois player set down his instrument and took up an odd-looking pipe-like instrument that came to two parallel points—a *sheng*! How had one of those managed to get all the way from China to Western Europe? Theft, loot, trade, who knew?

The fiddler joined his voice to the reedy melody. The two were far better as a duo. The audience began once again to be pulled in by the song, as the regal player signaled for more of whatever was in his cup. The other two gave him the hairy eyeball, and I wondered if Regal Guy was drinking up their profits.

Aurélie was staring at that regal.

The song finished, and Hautbois Guy started up another song on his *sheng*. The regal player put down his mug, said something in a rude undertone, and Hautbois Guy stopped, set aside the *sheng*, and took up his first instrument. Fiddle Guy lifted his bow.

Regal Guy crashed his fingers on the keys, Hautbois Guy started pumping, but not quick enough for the regal player, who stopped and cursed his fellow musicians. They started again, and this time the trio got through the simple melody of the "Hymn of 9 Thermidor," a Revolutionary song commemorating the downfall of Robespierre. Most of the audience joined in, roaring out the chorus, *Il ne fut brisé que par toi / Il ne fut brisé que par toi!*

The audience showed their approval by tossing a few low-denomination *assignats* and *centimes* into the upside down cap in front of Fiddle Guy's left foot. The musicians then swung into the bouncy tune called "Ça ira" which eventually came over to the Yankee side of the Atlantic as "It's Okay."

This time the entire inn joined the song. They sang so loud that their noise drowned out the missed notes and jagged timing of the regal player, who swayed on his stool. None of the audience seemed to notice his bad playing—except Aurélie, who watched intently from between an enormous man wearing a grocer's apron and a Revolutionary veteran in a threadbare uniform, who leaned on a stick. When the song ended, Regal Guy swallowed down the last of his wine, then got up abruptly, fumbling at the buttons of his breeches as he shoved his way drunkenly through the crowd.

The other two struck up a rollicking melody on fiddle and hautbois, "La Carmagnole," which Aurélie had played back in Jamaica. It was a popular dance melody, adapted like many popular songs into a typically bloodthirsty Revolutionary tune.

Aurélie looked from the regal to the hat with its coins to the players, then she eased around the veteran and approached the regal.

The two musicians glanced her way, exhibiting only a mild, distracted surprise. The dark-haired one with the striking face seemed to be staring right at me, but I knew it had to be a trick of his gaze, for nobody else had seen me. Sure enough, he returned his attention to his fiddle.

Aurélie put her hands on the keys. Some of the audience laughed to see this sprig pop out of nowhere, but Hautbois Guy obligingly began to pump.

Aurélie played, hesitantly at first, rapidly gaining assurance. The regal was old and wheezy, its inner workings clunking, but she stayed squarely on the beat. At the end of the song, the audience gave a genial shout of approval for the "boy" who gave them a cheeky grin. This time, it was she who launched into another French air.

The two musicians joined right in. She kept a steady beat, and on the second verse the fiddle player began to curl out riffs and experimental arpeggios. People began to clap and stamp, and things were swinging along nicely . . .

And then Regal Guy reappeared. He howled a curse, made a fist, and tried to knock Aurélie off the stool.

She ducked under the blow and whirled away, but the tip of her extra-long shoe got caught in the twine attached to the bellows, and she hit the floor with a splat. Her hat came loose. She nipped it up and clapped it onto her head, raising a howl of laughter.

The regal player, instead of reclaiming his stool, decided to go after her. Aurélie rolled to her feet, one hand to her hat, the other yanking her pistol free.

Regal Guy staggered back. Half the audience did as well. Some of them exclaimed in her favor, others in Regal Guy's favor, as the unloaded pistol wavered in her trembling fingers.

Then Fiddle Guy put bow to instrument and played a complicated cadenza that caught attention. "Leave the boy alone," he said into the moment of relative quiet, his French marked by a faintly guttural accent. "At least he can play, Jules. You have only been playing at playing."

Laughter and a shout of approval went up.

Jules responded by shouting threats at Aurélie.

"Run, boy!" several shouted.

Aurélie's chin came out. Her gaze flicked revealingly to that hat with the coins. She wanted the share of the take that she'd earned. Even a few centimes would buy her a stale bun.

The audience began shouting advice: "Stand up to him, little bant-ling!" "Shoot him, and let's have some music!" "A fight, a fight!" Then a nasal teen voice cat-called mockingly, "Afraid to pull the trigger?" as a butcher's apprentice hefted a squashy vegetable on his palm, ready for throwing. From the bulging pocket in his apron, he'd obviously come prepared for his own style of entertainment.

Aurélie glanced around, then turned the pistol upside down and shook it. Of course no ball rolled out of the barrel. A gust of laughter rose. This was better entertainment than mere music.

Sympathy promptly swung back her way—for the moment. Jules threw his mug at her. He was too drunk to aim. She dodged easily and flipped up the back of her hand in the age old gesture of repudiation, used by the boys at Port Royal.

Maddened by the resultant laughter, Jules charged her; a tactical error, because the entire inn howled him down as a coward. He lurched toward Aurélie, who leaned to avoid his swinging fists. She reversed the pistol the way Anne had taught her and whacked the side of his knee. Jules hit the floor, bellowing curses.

At that point customers shifted as a force of nature thrust violently through, and there was the innkeeper, a massive man of about fifty, with two brawny sons or nephews flanking him. Efficiently, and with no gentleness, they took hold of various parts of Jules, hauled him up, and made for the door. The guy shouted in inarticulate rage as customers pelted him with their recreational garbage.

Aurélie thrust her pistol back into her breeches, straightened her hat, then looked up at the two musicians. Hautbois Guy apparently did not notice. The cap covering his greasy, tangled hair was the only thing visible as he twiddled with the reed on his instrument. But Fiddle Guy flicked his bow in a magnanimous gesture toward the regal. "Permit me to introduce myself," he said. "You may call me Mord."

"Mord?" Aurélie repeated doubtfully. "'Bites'?"

"'Murder' in German and Lithuanian," Mord said with an air of mockery. "A very good name for an ex-soldier with no pay. And my companion is Jaska."

"Yas-ka?" Aurélie repeated.

The bow wrote in the air, J-A-S-K-A. "Jaska. And you, bantling?"

"René," Aurélie said firmly as she sat down at the regal.

The crowd roared approval, and so began an evening of music.

There was very little talk, no more than an exchange of songs, or chords, between pieces. Aurélie, long accustomed to playing accompaniment to Cassandra's singing, already knew how to match tempo, and so the three soon found a mutual rhythm that permitted both hautbois and fiddle to take off on flights of embellishment, which were generally hailed with appreciation.

When at last the crowd began thinning as people went home, they played the "Marseilles" as their last piece. Aurélie stood up uncertainly, and Mord said, "Will you share our meal, Citizen René?"

"Yes," Aurélie said, with heartfelt conviction.

The innkeeper heaped three plates from the last of the night's menu, extracted from the hat some coins for the broken mug, then left them to eat.

Aurélie took a stool next to Mord. She avoided whatever meat was swimming in its sauce, in favor of small potatoes, and oh glory, she practically inhaled the apple compote with cheese crumbled over it.

For a time, nobody spoke. Three mugs of something frosty appeared. Aurélie took a gulp of hers, then coughed, her eyes watering. Before anyone could say anything, she took another determined gulp, and only betrayed a gasp. Her face was flushed when she finished the ale, but at least she'd downed it on a full stomach, which lessened the effect.

At any rate, she was steady enough when Mord counted out a portion of the take and gravely offered it to her. As she tucked it into her waistcoat pocket, he said, "You know that Jules will be waiting outside to crack your skull."

"Jules?" Aurélie asked.

"Our late and unlamented third," Mord said. "We have had ill luck with finding a third. He's our—what, Jaska?—our sixth in as many months?"

Jaska shrugged as he pulled a knife from one pocket, a piece of reed cane from another, and resumed the painstaking process of carving it.

Mord said, "Considering our success this night, I think we owe it to you to see you to safety. Where's your house?"

"Haven't one," she said, and at two muted looks of surprise, she flushed and added, "I want to find a ship to Jamaica."

Mord gave her a sad smile. "As well seek a journey to Mars. You'll find no ship sailing to Jamaica from this side of the Channel, and only warships going to Saint-Domingue, which, last I heard, was still claiming independence under Toussaint L'Ouverture."

"I have heard that name," she exclaimed, then clipped her lips shut.

"Rumor has it that he was a slave before he became a military man. He is now leading a revolt for freedom."

"Do the warships go to his aid, or against him?"

"Rumor is unclear. In any case, you would have to make your way to the harbor at Brest, or Toulon, to volunteer."

Aurélie lifted her chin. She was a little soused, or she would never have talked as much as she did. "I will not go on a warship if they fight for slavery. It is evil."

"Agreed," Mord said. "Agreed. For all forms of slavery, including serfdom."

Jaska ducked his head in a nod and returned to carving. Mord said, "You are a little young, but from the bravado with which you pointed your piece, it is to be hoped you know how to load and fire a pistol?"

"I do," she said.

Jaska put away his reed and knife, and led the way back to the corner where their instruments lay. They packed up quickly, Mord putting the regal in its leather case. Jaska shrugged his arms through the straps so that the thing hung against his back. Last, Jaska plucked a tattered, ragged-hemmed cloak from the corner, disclosing their own weapons: A cavalry sword, a rapier, two pistols, a powder horn, and a bag of shot suspended from a walking stick, long enough to double as a quarterstaff.

With a quizzical air, Mord offered the rapier hilt on to Aurélie, who took it in hand. She checked the balance with a couple of expert swipes. Mord's brows twitched up as he grabbed the cavalry sword, leaving the walking stick to Jaska.

The three moved out, the two men ahead of Aurélie. She held the rapier nervously, her gaze intent.

As expected, Jules was lurking well out of the cone of light from the inn door. He had four other toughs at his back. All drunk, or maybe they were just rotten fighters. The five rushed at Aurélie and her two new companions.

The fight was over in about ten seconds flat, as Jaska and Mord neatly whacked, tripped, and thumped them in a practiced display of divide and conquer. Aurélie got in a good lick when she stuck her sword between the legs of an attacker who tripped and fell with a splash into the nasty murk in the street.

Jules lay groaning a few paces away. Mord stood over him with one scruffy boot on Jules's chest. He rained a few *centimes* onto the man, and a few badly crumpled *assignats*. "Your share. I wish you luck getting value for the paper," Mord said cheerfully. "The journey should inspire you to reflect upon the principles of virtue. In trade, we shall take the regal. Which is more than fair, as I am reasonably certain you looted it during your excesses in La Vendée. But musical instruments must be played and, if possible, played well, or life becomes more absurd than it already is. Farewell, Citizen."

Mord wiped the mud off his sword with the hem of his cloak, sheathed it, hefted his violin case more securely over his shoulder, and started off, Jaska following, limping badly. Neither said a word to Aurélie, who hesitated, then dashed after them, their sword still in her hand.

By then she was yawning almost continually, stumbling with exhaustion. She followed them into the misting rain, looking neither right nor left, but trusting to the two as they skipped down a couple of alleys, crossed a churchyard, and then entered the church's barn.

There were no animals, as the church had long ago been looted. The guys climbed to the loft, where a few remnants of stale, limp straw still lay about. Jaska gathered them in the weak light from a candle stub that Mord lit from his tinder box.

"Palatial quarters," Mord said with satisfaction. "Rain, do your worst. You are still with us, young René? Musicians should stay together. We shall be snug here."

"We and the fleas," Jaska said in a low murmur. He had an accent, too.

Aurélie looked from one to the other and down at the warped boards of the hayloft. She set the sword down, yawning, lay down, curled up . . .

EIGHTEEN

"... NEUFCHATEL?"

"No. That's where Jules will come looking if he finds himself a gang. Let us make for Yvetot. We can hear as much there."

"Better, perhaps. We'll move up the Seine. It's bound to serve as a conduit for talk as well."

Aurélie's eyes popped open to the sounds of the men's soft voices. The light was weak, watery blue. She turned her head. Mord sat cross-legged on the floorboards, scraping the beard from his sharp chin with his knife. He looked romantically dangerous, with his startlingly pale skin, his long dark hair loose on his shoulders, and a baldric across his chest for the cavalry sabre.

When he noticed Aurélie, he said, "Awake?" He held out the powder horn. "You may use some of ours if you are not planning to rob us."

Aurélie's voice, which was normally husky, sounded even more hoarse. "I am not."

"Well, then."

Jaska pulled out his knife, but instead of attending to the stubble on his chin, which, like his hair, was the color of cookie dough, he pulled out his unfinished reed to work on. Aurélie loaded her pistol.

Though both guys kept their hands busy, I got the feeling they were watching obliquely, and I think Aurélie was aware of that covert scrutiny, too. Her cheeks showed dull red as she quickly loaded her pistol, then looked about. A broken leather strap hung from a beam overhead, probably once attached to a cow's halter to keep her still for milking. She took aim and shot.

The strap gyrated wildly, and when it slowed, a hole was visible along one edge.

"That pistol throws right," Mord observed.

"Yes. And I pulled too far left for balance," Aurélie said as she placed the hot pistol inside her mashed hat.

"Nonetheless, a fine shot. I believe I have an extra cross belt somewhere here." Mord dug through his shapeless haversack. Out came a shirt even dirtier than the one he was wearing, another capped powder horn, a clinking bag of pistol balls, a second knife, and then a rolled item that turned out to be the cross belt. "Observe! Frogged for the pistol." He pointed out the loops.

Aurélie wrestled her way into the thing, which was ridiculously large. The pistol hung down to her thigh. She yanked on the buckles until she got the belt fitting more or less across her front. James's overlarge shirt and waistcoat thoroughly smothered her contours, rendering her shape indistinguishable.

Mord had expertly rolled the greatcoat he'd slept under and affixed it to the back of his cross belt in the efficient manner of European soldiers. Below that went the haversack. "We are about to depart, Citizen René," he said as he checked his pistol a last time, then slung it into the side frogs. "You can either come along or stay here and sleep. You may keep the regal." He pointed at where it lay. "But I suggest leaving the area, as Jules will be seeking retribution as well as our earnings."

Aurélie sat up and swallowed painfully. It was clear from her wince that she had a pounding headache, but she said, "I am ready."

She hefted the regal, her feet planted wide. I couldn't tell how heavy it was, but anyone who has ever carried a heavy backpack knows that a long hike under a lot of weight can get pretty grim.

Before she could wrestle it over her skinny shoulders, Jaska nipped it from her fingers and slung it over his own back, then pulled on his own cross belt, all without speaking.

Mord had a *sabretache*—a pouch, usually part of a cavalryman's uniform—connected to his cross belt, the front defaced by fire, the edges of what had been a regimental coat of arms, blackened. He slung the cavalry sword from the dangling slings.

Mord picked up his violin case and followed Jaska around to the back wall of the barn, free fingers working the front flaps of their trousers. Aurélie's steps faltered when she realized what they were doing. She backtracked hastily and scooted across the barnyard to the scruffy hedgerow, where she could hastily relieve herself without any witnesses. When she was done, she scampered out to meet the two on the road, twitching her clothing straight.

They didn't give her a second glance as they set out at a brisk pace under clearing skies, splashing along the muddy, rutted road. Jaska still walked with a limp, using the stick to balance against a stiff knee.

Time blurred. When I jolted into awareness, I discovered Aurélie lagging behind at a painful shuffle, the mud in the lane sucking at her shoes. Every step made her wince. Those past few days, she'd mostly spent lurking and hiding; she hadn't had to walk all that far in James's shoes.

When Mord and Jaska stopped at a well in a deserted circle of burnt-out farmhouses, she sat down on a fence stump and pulled off the shoes, her breath hissing between her teeth. Mord worked at the well as Jaska went off exploring.

The shoes had rubbed blisters into her ankles right through the stockings. Her mouth tightened into a pale line as she stuffed the stockings into her pockets, and flung away the shoes as hard as she could. She made certain the edges of her breeches covered the necklace, applied handfuls of mud to her feet and ankles, then stepped carefully onto the muddy ground.

A few steps later Jaska limped into view, the shoes in either hand. "You steal these, René?" He shrugged, not waiting for her to answer. "A good soldier learns never to waste good footgear. These can be remade by a cobbler."

Jaska's French, unlike Mord's, was educated, what the Parisian upper class would call pure. A few years ago, that accent could have won him a free trip to the guillotine—and probably still could, if he was a Royalist deserter. He seemed to remember that, for he looked around quickly with a frown. Though Fouché's spies were nowhere to be seen, he thrust Aurélie's shoes at her and walked back to the lane.

She silently took the shoes and off they set.

Occasionally she winced at rocks, but the lane was muddy, which protected her feet somewhat. They made one more stop for water at a clear-running stream. Again, Aurélie availed herself of the bushes. "Oh, Duppy Kim, I am so very hungry," she whispered when she was done, but said nothing to the guys when she rejoined them.

If they were testing her, they must have decided she'd passed, because midday found them in a tiny village, no more than a scanty circle of slant-roofed cottages around a tiny church. They entered a small, dilapidated inn. The woman who owned it scowled when two tall young men ducked under the doorway, but her expression changed to smiles when Mord held open a grimy hand, disclosing coinage.

Within a short time the three of them sat at a rough-hewn bench in the inn yard, facing a big plate of stale bread and *canard a l'orange*, with a lot more cabbage than duck. To wash it all down they had pear cider.

Aurélie sent occasional considering glances at her silent companions as they wolfed down their meal. When she was done, she surreptitiously slipped to the dog the bits of duck.

So far the guys had been decent enough, but they looked like a couple of rough articles. From the way they fought, my guess was deserters, or else their unit had been disbanded after the Peace of Amiens.

Mord drank the last of his cider, wiped his sleeve across his mouth, and picked up his violin case. That was the signal to get moving again. They walked out of the tiny village down a lane, with spring growth on either side. Jaska presently dug a hand into his pocket—Aurélie's head turned sharply, a flash of fear widening her eyes—but then her lips parted when his grimy fingers emerged with a jaw harp, and he began to play a tune with a quick, catchy melody.

The sky began clouding up midway through the afternoon. They wound their way up a hill. The wind strengthened, sending spurts of rain into their faces as they looked out over the land at farmers busy in the fields or climbing all over the thatched roofs of longhouses. The farmers worked in teams, beating the lifted thatching, stripping the roofs of winter moss, and repairing. Sheep and cows wandered meadows fuzzy with new growth.

I hoped the sight of those cows meant relative quiet, after all the trouble of the latter years of the Revolution. For the millionth time I wished I could have known that this was going to happen to me. I could have prepared. I had to rely on memory; I knew that the farther away you got from Paris, the less governmental control over the provinces.

Napoleon was just beginning to change all that, but so far, his reorganization was little in evidence.

"Here's a sizable village," Mord said as they spotted rooftops clustered around a central spire. "We will try to earn our meal, as these coins won't last long. Citizen René, you were very useful yesterday. As long as you continue to attract the stray *centime*, why, you may stay with us, share and share alike. Is that fair?"

"Yes," Aurélie said. Her fingers were stuck in her armpits to keep them warm.

Aurélie followed them as they tried first one inn, were turned away, then a tavern. The owner said, "Let's hear you first, citizens. If you draw custom, there will be a meal in it and anything you can earn. But if you turn away custom, I'll throw you out into the road." He flexed brawny arms roughly the size of beer casks.

Aurélie watched as the two set things up. They were fast from long habit. Several local urchins wandered in to watch, a couple of them holding rotten vegetables in hopes of fun. Mord pulled out his violin. "I have to tune it."

He drew the bow across the strings, drawing a whining note that dwindled to a groan. A couple of smaller kids snickered. Then he made the violin mew like a cat, and bounced the bow over the strings like a yappy dog. More laughter, and a few more kids crowded in.

"Show us a horse," someone said.

Mord's bow drew out a fair enough whinny.

"A cow!"

That was easy. He drew the mournful note out, making them laugh, as the crowd grew bigger. His nimble fingers twitched the pegs until he got it tuned, then he sang a patter song about a series of revolutionary animals who called one another 'citizen,' but the song was clearly far older than the Revolution.

Jaska set up the regal for Aurélie, and included his twine-to-boot pump arrangement. He fitted a new reed into his hautbois, and on a nod from Mord, they swung into "Ça ira," which drew more of an audience.

The hat remained barren of coins, but at least the rotten vegetables stayed in aprons and pockets. Then they launched into a Breton melody that I recognized from modern folk music, "Tri Martolod."

Aurélie did not know it, but she picked up the main chords very fast, which permitted Mord to riff improvisation as a counterpoint to the melody played by Jaska.

They were joined by an old man's thready voice, the words Breton. He was hastily drowned out by some young people singing a new set of verses in French, a revolutionary adaptation, as quick, defensive looks went round. When no one emerged from the woodwork to arrest the old man, a couple of teens took hands and danced around the benches and tables.

That prompted people to clear a space, and the trio went straight into a refrain. The audience began stamping and twirling and clapping, skirts flashing, faces red with effort, dust rising in the humid air. Aurélie played unerringly.

After a range of dancy folk tunes, Mord offered the Eastern European one that had first caught my attention. After that, Jaska answered with a Russian folk piece, and Mord countered with a Polish tune, then Aurélie plunged into one of her fae pieces, flushing with pride at the audience's stamping and clapping.

The few coins they earned were all *centimes* with a few *decimes*—no *livres*, which were only about the equivalent of a dime or quarter. It was plain from the patched clothing and their listeners' lack of shoes that nobody had much money to give. The tavern keeper showed his approval by the generous meal waiting when at long last the evening drew to a close.

After they'd eaten, he said, "You can sleep in the cow byre. And if you are going to Yvetot, be sure to stop at my cousin's inn . . ." He gave them directions.

As they went through the kitchen to the back, Mord looked less mournful than usual. Once they were in the byre, he said to Aurélie, "A recommendation, you will find, is sometimes better than gold coins. We'll have a place to go in Yvetot, and we're less likely to find trouble with the prefecture."

Jaska found an empty bucket and turned it upside down. He reached into his haversack for last night's candle stub. Aurélie had been yawning continuously. She swept together a pile of chaff to sleep on and curled up. The candlelight gleamed in her eyes as she watched Jaska pull from his pocket a small book.

The gilt lettering flashed briefly in the weak light, *La Monadologie*.

"Leibniz?" Aurélie asked sleepily, then closed her eyes. She didn't see the surprised look Jaska sent her way, but I did, for my own surprise kept my focus 'awake' for a few moments, as I had not expected a scruffy bum of a deserter to be reading a German mathematician-philosopher from the previous century.

NINETEEN

LIGHT FLARED. Noise. The tavern keeper appeared, a lantern swinging from one hand and in the other, a loaf of hot bread and a wedge of cheese that looked mouth-watering even to me, without a mouth.

No doubt he wanted to be sure they didn't make off with his belongings, but the fellows accepted his friendly, "okay, move on" hint as business-as-usual. Aurélie slipped away while they were eating, then returned to take her share.

They set out in the direction of Yvetot under clear skies and balmy air. Aurélie began walking with interest in the early flowers, but she was soon wincing as if her feet hurt. She persisted in going barefoot, the shoes tucked through either side of her cross belt.

After a time, Jaska flashed her a quick look. "So you went to school?"

"No."

"You had a tutor, then."

Aurélie ducked her head and mumbled something about cousins, muffling the second syllable, which in French differentiated between male cousins and female.

Mord squinted at Aurélie as if she'd grown an extra ear. "What is that, bantling? You and a cousin read Leibniz? A pair of prodigies, are you?"

"No. Aurélie scowled at the muddy path. "We merely wished to discover . . ."

"What?"

"How magic works." She looked up, her expression mutinous.

"Sa-sa," Mord exclaimed, the fencer's acknowledgement of a hit.

He sent a mocking glance at Jaska, whose expression was bland. "What inspired this direction of study, René?" Jaska asked.

Aurélie visibly struggled, then said, "If I say, you must promise not to laugh."

Mord placed a hand at his heart, his eyes smiling, his mouth mock-solemn. Jaska gestured with his walking stick. "Say on."

"A few years ago. When we were small—" She glared. "You promised not to laugh."

"It was only at the idea of your being smaller than you are now. My pardon." Jaska made an airy gesture better suited to a palace drawing room than a muddy road.

Mord's brow wrinkled as if he were trying to bring Aurélie into focus. "What age are you, ten?"

"Old enough," Aurélie said, her husky voice dropping a note lower— she was clearly regretting having said that much. But she pushed on. "We saw the fae. We wanted to know why some people see the fae, and some don't." She glowered in challenge.

Mord flung up the back of his hand. "Tchah! Do not waste your time, is my advice. Where is the supernatural of whatever type or degree when your home is invaded?" His tone sharpened. "Did you hear that noise?"

They looked right and left, but the lane was thick on either side with leafing greenery.

Jaska said, "So what did you find in Leibniz about magic?"

"Nothing about magic. But we thought, between the Law of Continuity and that of Plenitude—"

A woman screamed. Jaska stilled, head lifted.

"Came from that way," Mord said in a form of German. No, it was Yiddish.

The two took off through the trees, Aurélie toiling determinedly behind them.

The scream was followed by raucous laughter. Mord and Jaska faltered, then shot off to the right. The noises were closer, no longer echoing through the trees.

The two burst into a cleared space before the husk of a burned cottage. Nearby a cow bellowed in distress; her calf lay dead a few paces away, hacked up with a sword. Trampling an overgrown kitchen garden were five or six youngish men in tattered remnants of the revolutionary uniform. They shoved a teenage girl between them as she wept and made futile efforts to defend herself. One of her hands was sticky with blood.

A man slapped her then grabbed at her bodice, half-ripping it. From the state of her clothes, they'd been playing this game for a while.

The bodice tore, causing another roar of laughter that nearly smothered the hum of Jaska's walking stick.

Crunch! The stick thudded into the side of the nearest of the men. The rest of them whirled, grabbing for weapons. They froze when they saw Mord with two pistols leveled at them, and Aurélie next to him, her pistol in both hands, aimed at the leader's head.

"Giles, get up!" One of the men roared, kicking the one who'd fallen.

Giles only groaned.

The leader said, "That leaves five of us against two. Three shots, if the brat knows how to shoot."

"He's the best shot of us all," Mord said.

The girl they'd been tormenting had fallen into the cabbage row, cradling her cut hand against her half-bared breast.

Everyone was still, except for the cow, who went to her dead calf, sniffing the little creature, then raising her head and lowing.

The first move was by one of the gang. He brought a pistol out of his ragged coat.

Mord shot him.

The man staggered back, screeching on a high note with his hands pressed to his ribs.

Jaska advanced, the stick whirling.

The gang turned and bolted, one bending down to grab the dead calf before joining his fellows.

The girl looked up in fear.

"I shall shoot the next rascal who touches you," Aurélie said fiercely, taking up a stance next to her. "You are safe."

"There might be more of them," Jaska said. "Let's get back to the road."

Mord made a rude sign. "They know we are armed, and they can see there's nothing much to steal." But he kept the other pistol at the ready as Aurélie helped the girl rise. With shaking hands, the girl did her best to straighten her bodice. She went to the cow and tried to soothe her.

"Is this your home?" Aurélie asked.

The girl shook her head. Making soft noises, she tugged at the rope around the cow's neck, until the animal began to lumber. The girl then turned her face to Aurélie. "I stopped here with my cow and calf. I spied the garden and thought to gather some vegetables. Those wolves were foraging." She sent a look of loathing after the men. "They killed my calf."

Her chest heaved on a sob, and she looked down as she walked. "I will stay by your side," Aurélie said. "I have a sword."

I don't know how long the four walked. Time blurred until they were sitting inside a storage shed of some kind. Roof tiles were stacked against one end and bales of cotton at the other.

They built a fire in the middle of the hard-packed dirt floor as rain pelted on the roof overhead. They sat around the fire, Jaska feeding it twigs one by one, and Mord toasting bread over it, stuck on the end of his sword. Aurélie was slowly rubbing her grimy feet, her wide eyes gazing at the fire. The girl sat like a statue, the light picking highlights from her tousled brown braid.

The cow let out a long moo, and the girl jumped up. "I must milk her."

That seemed to stir everyone. First a pail must be found, and that meant a search, which meant lighting the candle stub, which had about an inch of wax left.

A bit of time passed, and then they were sharing the warm milk and hunks of the bread, which—judging from the way they chewed—were so stale that toasting didn't improve it much. Aurélie dunked hers in the milk and sucked on it.

The business of milking the cow and eating seemed to rouse the rescuee, who, other than mumbling her name ("Charlotte") hadn't spoken at all. She'd walked like a zombie until roused by the cow's need.

Aurélie said, "Charlotte, where are you from?"

The girl whispered back, "My village was near Cailly."

"What happened?"

The girl drew up her knees under her chin and clasped her arms tightly around her legs. She gazed into the flames as she said, "I know I was born somewhere north of Rouen, but I never knew that place. I was given to the convent when I was very small. How I loved the convent! I had charge of the chickens, and very proud I was if I could bring a full basket of eggs to Sister Benedict."

Charlotte had taken the question in the widest possible sense. Though she'd been silent all day, now she wanted, or maybe needed, to uncork. Under cover of her low, fervent voice, Mord addressed Jaska in German. "How did we end up here with a train?"

". . . and I had turned nine. You must understand that they gave us a saint's day as our own, and we could count it as our birthday . . ."

"Ah, Mordechai, would you have left either of them?"

". . . but it was in the Year Three. Year Three!" Charlotte's voice thickened with loathing. "I spit upon their 'years' and their Fructidor and their ten-day weeks. Reason! Was it Reason that brought them to murder the nuns, who never harmed a living being? Who gave homes to their unwanted children, and nursed the sick, and laid out the dead? There was no one to lay *them* out, I can promise you, after . . ."

Jaska was checking his pistol. "No. But we were agreed we were not to draw attention."

". . . then Sister Margareta tipped over the butter churn and pushed me into it, and they did not think to look inside with the butter spilled all around . . ."

"We haven't drawn any attention," Mord said. "Any significant attention."

". . . crawled out to find the convent on fire, and everywhere the sisters lay dead, their robes in disarray, so I covered them as I could . . ."

"Significant. Yes, that I grant you. But those *crapauds* are out there."

". . . ran into the woods after I heard terrible noises from the sanctuary, and I do not remember anything else, but running and running . . ."

"I know," Mord said. "We've our weapons. We can set up a defensive barrier if you like, but they did not look like the sort to mount a well-planned assault."

". . . called upon my Saint Catherine, my patron saint, over and over, and she guided my steps near to Cailly . . ."

"Mord! You're not going outside." Jaska looked askance, then started up.

". . . very old, and they needed a girl to help them, for the mob had killed their daughter, and—"

"Stay." Mord raised a hand. "Stay here. It's merely that I wish to sleep tonight." He shrugged into his greatcoat.

"—by the time I was twelve, I could do all the indoors work . . ."

"Sleep, is it?" Jaska cracked a laugh. "Nothing to do with the sun setting?"

". . . when Grandmother Agnes died while I was out planting seeds . . ."

"And here you are, your Friday-meal meatless, *mon ami!* Spare your breath! I know it is perforce. We are faithful apostates, you and I. Off I go to clear the perimeter, and to argue Talmud with the ghosts." Mord picked up his cavalry sword and his pistols.

Charlotte stiffened, looking up in fright as Mord passed her close enough for his greatcoat to brush against her shoulder. She shrank away, fists under her chin, but he did not look down as he paused near the doorway, letting his eyes adjust to the darkness beyond the shed.

Charlotte turned back to Aurélie. "There was nothing to stay for, with them both dead. After the burial, I heard from the cutler's wife that there is a new convent all the way north. She said that there is a nun who is secretly gathering women to start a convent far away from Paris and all its devils. She said they will take any women, not merely daughters of the noblesse or the bourgeoisie, but I am thinking, it will be easier for Sister Mary Magdalen Postel to take me if I bring my own cow and calf.

And I can prove my worth, for I am a very good worker. Work is good," she murmured in a low, fervent tone.

"I hope you may find her," Aurélie whispered back.

"If you were a girl, I would say to come with me," Charlotte responded.

Aurélie's quick smile was more lopsided than usual as she began pulling handfuls of cotton from the huge wicker baskets and patting them down into a nest. "You rest. I will guard you."

"You are but a child," Charlotte murmured.

"One with a pistol. And a very fierce temper," Aurélie said sorrowfully. "It is not right to kill, and I wanted to, oh, much. Now I think I understand what my Tante Mimba said to me once, long ago. Oh, don't mind me. You rest. You're safe."

Charlotte curled up on the puffy cotton, her head resting near Aurélie's knee. She gazed up at Aurélie in puzzlement. "Your French, it's foreign. But very pretty. Are you from the Languedoc, then? You're very brown. I hear the people are brown, in the south."

"I come from the islands. Do I have an accent, then? To myself, I sound ordinary."

Charlotte whispered, "I like the way you speak. Do not grow into one of those wicked men, René."

"I will not," Aurélie said with a husky laugh. And then more seriously, "I'll try not to be wicked."

Charlotte squeezed her eyes closed, her mouth twisting. Tears sparked between her lashes and dripped down her face as she cried noiselessly, except for the quick gulping breaths of suppressed sobs.

Aurélie touched her head gently. Charlotte stiffened, her eyes widening in fear, but then she smiled, and laid her head on Aurélie's leg. Aurélie stroked Charlotte's hair gently, slowly, until the tears ceased, and the broken breathing eased into slumber.

For an immeasurable time there was no sound but the rhythmic munching of the cow. A distant clang caused both Aurélie and Jaska to freeze, hands touching their weapons. A shot cracked, then silence.

After a time, Jaska turned a page. He glanced up, found Aurélie looking at him, and said in a soft voice, "You were talking about Leibniz's laws." He lifted his book, a different one. "Have you read the *Tractatus Theologico-Politicus* or the *Opera Posthuma*?"

"No," Aurélie whispered, and glanced down at Charlotte, whose breathing stayed deep and even, her face relaxed. "I thought we had everything by Leibniz, but I see I'm wrong."

"Those were written by Benedictus Spinoza. Some say that Leibniz was influenced by him."

"How's that?" Aurélie asked.

Jaska began to read a passage, but Aurélie raised her hand. "My Latin is that of a beginner," she admitted.

Jaska's brows lifted, but he began translating.

I don't know how long they sat there talking philosophy in low voices, as Charlotte slept and the cow munched. Could have been five minutes or five hours. Mord reappeared, grinning in the firelight. "They won't stop running until they reach Dieppe," he said. "I believe we can sleep."

"As well." Jaska almost smiled. "Look here, this candle is shortly to be mere memory." It was guttering in a waxen ring about the thickness of a quarter.

He nipped it out, and they slept.

TWENTY

THE NEXT MORNING THEY WOKE and brushed the cotton off themselves. Aurélie looked tired and muttered to me, "I had very bad dreams."

Nothing marred the rest of their journey to Yvetot.

When they reached the city, which was busy with repairs after revolutionary depredations, they stopped in a central square built around a well.

Mord turned to Aurélie. "We all have tasks. If you wish to rejoin us, let's meet here at this well when the bells strike—"

A glance up at the cathedral tower, and he gave a short sigh, no doubt remembering that the bells had been melted down to be turned into cannon ten years ago. "At three, which would put the sun approximately there." He pointed up at the sky. Then he turned away, before anyone could answer.

Aurélie stared at him in surprise, then looked around. Charlotte had already started with her cow in the direction of the cathedral, which was bracketed by scaffolding as artisans repaired and rebuilt the defaced stonework.

Aurélie stared after Charlotte, then fingered the mirror out of her pocket. She peered down into a sliver of it, her thumb pressed to the glass, and whispered, "Duppy Kim, she thinks I'm a young man. She doesn't trust men. James was not evil. Do you think he didn't love me the way I loved him? I will *not* cry over him tonight. I am more grieved for Charlotte."

She pushed the mirror back into her pocket without waiting for my answer and ran off in search of a cobbler's shop. When she spotted the sign, she paused long enough to pull on her filthy stockings again, hiding the necklace. Then she marched inside and put the shoes on the counter.

"Well, well, young fighting cock," a grizzled cobbler said to her, with a laughing glance at her pistol and sword. "I trust you took these fine shoes off a damned aristo and before his feet were cold! Excellent leather. I can cut them down in a trice, and if you give me the scraps, I'll shave that much off the price, *hein*?"

"Done," Aurélie said.

"Then place your foot here, that I may take its measure."

The cobbler continued to gab about the scarcity of jobs building the First Consul's little boats for the invasion of England. I recalled that Napoleon had put together a couple of invasion plans, then abandoned them. This seemed to be the first one.

The cobbler confidently predicted another, and wouldn't it be fun to serve out those aristo-loving *roasbiffs* in England, now that they'd done for aristos in France. He made it clear he'd taken part in at least some of the mob action of the Revolution, and thought he'd done a fine thing thereby. Yvetot, he felt sure, would prosper now that the evil d'Albon family was gone.

He promised to have the shoes ready in two hours.

"Next, my clothes," Aurélie said aloud, when she reached the street, barefoot again. "I do not think Jaska and Mord are evil. And I very much like making music, but I don't want to carry that regal all the way to Paris. And I don't know how many people would listen if I played alone. I wish I could sing!"

She paused to look around the market crowd then glanced skyward. "There's enough time for one more errand, I think. Duppy, I don't dare to take the mirror out, but if you think I should go on alone, then you must poke my hand. I tell you honestly I'm a little afraid of traveling alone. Being a boy will not stop a gang like those ones yesterday, if they think I have anything they want."

And when I didn't poke her—though I wasn't sure about anything—she gave her little nod, the corner of her mouth lifted in a slight smile, and she said, "Then I shall find me a needle and thread, and mend these breeches so that I can stop holding them up."

This was the land of cotton, here in the north of France—cotton and excellent cheeses. Aurélie clearly enjoyed copying the local dialect as closely as she could as she bargained for not only a sturdy little sewing kit, but a goodly length of cloth, from which, she told the draper, she would make a shirt and a few neck cloths.

"You sound like a southerner, I'm thinking," the woman said. "Come up here to join the flotilla? Well, that's over, though you might have better luck at Le Havre, I hear. My advice? Go for a soldier. My youngest went to Egypt, and though he ended up a prisoner of the English *dammits*, he said there's loot for the taking, if you survive . . ." *Dammits* seemed as popular as *roasbiffs* as pejoratives for the English.

Aurélie completed her purchases, which used up nearly all her coinage. She returned for the shoes, which were now sturdy and snugly fit her feet.

Properly shod, she looked around carefully, then used the trellis on the side of a building to climb nimbly to the roof, where she wedged herself between the chimney and the overlapping roof slats. Here, she could look below at the square, specifically the well next to the ruined shrine, where the two would meet her—or not.

She said, "I don't want anyone to see me sewing and say I sew like a girl. I think it's better to be René as long as I can."

She pulled off her breeches and set to work tailoring them. Years of needlework made her fast. She cut some fabric and made secret pockets inside the waistband. Before she put away the mirror she touched it to make certain I was still around. When she saw me, she smiled, stored the mirror in one of her new pockets, put on the breeches, which were still loose, but no longer falling off. She climbed down again, the sword catching on the trellis slates and the grape vine, and the pistol banging against her leg.

She dropped the last of her *centimes* into the hands of a street vendor selling fresh bread and then sat down on a bench to eat as she watched the crowd cross and recross the town square. Presently, "Ah! Here is Mord! I must go."

When Mord saw her, he squinted to make certain it was her, then laughed. "And so I win our wager. Jaska thought you'd run off."

"No."

"I sense that whatever you have been doing did not include a bath."

"Nor did you," Aurélie retorted.

"True," Mord said, flicking dust from the grime on his shirtsleeve. "In true republican fashion, I'm carrying half the soil of *la belle* France on my person. Well, then, here we are, a trio again. Musically, that's a benefit. Let us join Jaska, who discovered us a friendly hostelry. They promised a small room if we bring in the custom, and it's the barn if not. Almost always it ends up being the barn, but I've discovered there are fewer lice that way. To business. Whose music have you been playing? Most of your airs I recognize, but not all."

"Some are mine."

"Ah, a prodigy is among us!"

Mord led the way down a narrow, winding alley, to another, smaller square with a rambling inn, its swinging sign designating it *La Republique.*

Mord ducked through the doorway. The hour being early for custom, the common room was largely empty, crowded with plain wooden tables and benches. Jaska sat on a stool against a wall, his brows lifting when he saw Aurélie with Mord.

He said only, "They want republican songs here. Shall we work a few up?"

It was the barn for them, which was a big relief for Aurélie.

They departed the next day. The traffic along the river was reasonably heavy. They were attacked twice within as many days. The first was more of a standoff, as they rounded a corner to find themselves facing a gang of young guys, mostly carrying sharpened farm equipment, except for one ancient gun (an arquebus) and a rusty Renaissance-era sword.

Our three had their pistols up in heartbeats.

For a few seconds nothing happened, except for flies buzzing around both sides—the last bath for all combatants having been some time in the past. Then the gang's leader, who was probably all of sixteen, said, "You've five shots. There are twelve of us."

"Who's first?" Mord responded.

The three at the rear of the gang edged away, then two more, and when the leader looked back, cursing violently at his disintegrating force, Mord took careful aim and shot the arquebus out of its wielder's hand.

The ambushers bolted, the arquebus guy having dropped his powder and shot, along with his ruined weapon.

Mord picked it up. "You know what this means?"

"Target practice," Jaska said. "Let's find a clearing."

Aurélie smiled sadly and murmured in English, "Oh, it reminds me of James."

She acquitted herself well.

The second encounter might have been related, or might not, but it occurred the next day as the sunlight was fading, and the trio crossed a vineyard. They passed under a stone archway into what had been a village below a walled medieval manor—how jagged rubble on the hilltop above—and a gang closed in from either side.

Mord, Jaska, and Aurélie looked around the small circle of buildings for aid, but shutters slammed. They were alone except for a few chickens and a dog who barked excitedly from a distance.

No time to grab pistols. The guys were on them in seconds.

Out came the swords.

Aurélie did exactly what she'd been taught: Let the adults take the brunt of the attack, for they were used to fighting side by side. She took on stragglers who tried to flank them, one fast strike in knee or elbow, sending them staggering back. I don't think the attackers were used to trained defenders, for they fled in disorder, limping and clutching at wounded limbs.

That night Aurélie had nightmares.

There were no more attacks. They were eyed from time to time, but that was it. Either word had spread, or else nobody wanted to mess with two tall, well-armed men who walked like veterans, even if one had a slight hitch in his giddyap. Aurélie mimicked their manner, looking like a pint-sized badass with her cross belt, her pistol and sword.

And so they began to talk, subjects branching from Spinoza to Descartes, and from Descartes in general to the specific in comparing linguistic implications of *Je pense, donc je suis* and *Cogito ego sum*.

"*Sum, suis,*" Aurélie said. "*Cogito* is not much like *penser*, but it is like the English 'cogitate.'"

"So you know English?" Jaska asked, as he peered down the road, always on the watch.

"Yes." Aurélie conscientiously peered around, hand on her pistol. "And our own language, in Jamaica. You can call it the Creole, a word that means many things. Will you read the Latin aloud? It has a fine sound when you do. We did not know how to read aloud. We were not always certain how the words should be pronounced."

"This is New Latin," Jaska warned her, flashing his rare smile at the puffy white clouds overhead. "I don't think anyone really knows what Classical Latin sounded like, though the graybeards all seem to think they have the right of it."

"New or old, it's the same to me," Aurélie said cheerfully.

Jaska pulled the Spinoza from a deep pocket and began to read as they walked along. He stopped to translate sentence by sentence, then initiated her in the intricacies of Latin grammar as Aurélie listened closely.

Mord walked largely in silence until he couldn't resist correcting Jaska once or twice, after which they argued declensions the same way they argued points of philosophy, with the easygoing back-and-forth of long habit.

It was exactly the same way that Aurélie had argued with Diana, and to a lesser extent with James. She clearly found the mode and tone of the interchange comfortable as they marched through a series of Placenames-*sur-Seine*. Twice they caught a wagon ride, but mostly they walked, for there were no horses to be had unless you were rich, the army having requisitioned every quadruped it could buy or bully out of the citizenry.

Every so often either Mord or Jaska would separate off when they reached a village or passed a hill. In fact, if a road branched near a hill, they inevitably chose the climb.

A few days later, Mord cast Jaska a glance, then took off up a narrow path to a rocky hillock, atop which sat the mossy remains of a medieval keep.

Jaska was playing his jaw harp again, so Aurélie used the opportunity to make a pit stop. When she was done, she nipped her mirror out. "We seem to toil up every hill, even if the road goes around most sensibly. Why can this be?" She peered under her hand against the strong spring sunlight, but the thick foliage hid Mord from view.

I got an idea. "Climb the tree?"

She flashed her merry, crooked grin. "Capital! Why didn't I think of that?"

A minute later, she peered out from a sturdy treetop, mirror clasped in one hand. Mord stood in the lee of a fallen stone wall, one foot propped on the wall, his elbow on his knee to steady the field glass in his hand. He was gazing at a distant light, glimmering in the hazy sunlight. No, that was not the glimmer of nature, it was winking in a pattern. "He's watching the semaphore," I said.

"Semaphore?" she repeated, and then gave a short nod. "I recollect! James explained how they use it to flash news by light across great distances. It is very, very fast, so much faster than a galloper, but you must have hills and the codes." She cast a doubtful look over her shoulder. "Do you think Mord and Jaska are . . . are *spies*?"

I considered that. Spies in these strange days, with rapid change in the French government ringing outward, sometimes violently, could hardly be defined so simply as 'bad' or 'good.' Meanwhile, I knew the broad outlines of what was to come, even if I didn't know all the regional details. Yet she was waiting for me to answer, so I said, "Perhaps the question is better put, are they dangerous to you? So far they have been civil."

"Yes," Aurélie agreed with an emphatic nod. "And I do like playing music. And learning Latin. But it must end, for they think me a boy." I could tell from her tone that she didn't want it to end. She liked traveling with them, and who could blame her, after the horror of her initial experience in Dieppe?

So I didn't say anything. I didn't want to risk losing her trust again, especially as I still had to get her to Dobrenica. And how were we supposed to save the country? No clue.

She put the mirror away and slipped back down to the road.

Mord rejoined them a short time later, saying nothing as Jaska went right on with the Latin lesson. But as they approached another village, and Aurélie wandered a little ways off to peer at some lovely deep red climbing roses at the side of a cottage, Mord looked around. Again, he seemed to stare right at me before he said in German, "Something's going on. I counted ten signals in three minutes."

Jaska's answer was in French as he pointed out the sign of a local inn. "Shall we try this place? I don't like the looks of the sky."

The thunder held off for a few days, then crashed over them in a spectacular storm late one afternoon. The trio got a gig at a prosperous inn directly on the riverside, where it caught some of the Seine traffic. Everything started well, if you didn't count Mord's silence all day. They had developed a standard list of tunes, including some of Aurélie's fae songs. But as the daylight faded beyond the low-pressing clouds, Mord, who left the singing to Jaska, began drinking heavily. He'd never done that before.

Aurélie's gaze followed the journey of pale liquid from glass to lip, over and over. Mord played with his eyes closed, his profile severe; as usual, some of the young women in the gathering watched him, though he seldom responded past a quick smile and a flippant answer. The light was low enough to mask the grime and shabby, patched clothes. He made a romantic contrast against the fire, his sharp-etched, mournful face so pale, framed by his tangled dark hair.

Jaska, too, was watching Mord, but his expression was wary.

Finally Mord set the cup down with exquisite care, as if its placement was a matter of cosmic importance, then he stood up, grabbed his violin and bow, and left.

Jaska gave Aurélie a rueful smile, and the two of them launched into a popular dance tune. Promptly the young paired up and began romping their way through the *Monaco*.

It seemed that Aurélie and Jaska would cover Mord's inexplicable absence, but then the innkeeper's wife said during the lull after a dance, "*Alors*, citizens! You must see this. I have never witnessed the like!"

Jaska cursed under his breath as many of the customers ran to the windows, then threw them open. Rain dripped from the eaves, but the storm had lifted, leaving a sky full of racing dark clouds. In the west, the sun rested on a bluff, the sky above like melted gold shading upwards to the cobalt blue of sunset, departing ragged purple clouds edged with fire.

Silhouetted against that golden sun was a tall, straight figure. Seen in silhouette, Mord was the very picture of romance, even to the drips from his wet hair that caught the light before they fell in diamond sparkles all around him. Birds dipped and dove, swirled and circled around him, blackbirds and starlings, skylarks and jackdaws.

That was nothing to the sound.

How to describe that music? The fiddler had vanished, replaced by a violin master. The closest music to the passion, the joy and grief expressed in those complicated, soaring flights is Ernest Bloch's *Nigun in the Baal Shem Suite*. Though it wouldn't be written for a couple of centuries, the comparison is eerily appropriate.

Since pretty much the entire audience stood at the windows, Jaska and Aurélie remained with them. For a time they stood in silence.

"Why does he do that?" Aurélie finally asked. "If the rain comes back, it will ruin his violin."

"Then he will clean and revarnish it. Tonight is the fifteenth of Nissan, which the Jews call Pesach," Jaska murmured.

Aurélie said, "He is Jewish? I thought they had beards."

"He shaved his off."

"And they don't eat the same meats."

"He makes a point of partaking in *treif* every day he can get it."

"I don't understand."

"He's an apostate. Though some Fridays at sunset, if he's been drinking enough, I find him outside with his Siddur in hand—even though he cannot see it to read—disputing the wisdom of the Baal Shem Tov with his father's ghost."

"His father's ghost?"

"He says he sees them all around. He says there's one following you." Aurélie flushed but didn't answer as Jaska went on, "I've never seen any ghosts, so it all may merely be the effect of drink." Jaska shook his head. "He's angry, that's all."

"All?" Aurélie's crooked smile was tentative. "My Nanny Hiasinte once said that anger eats the soul. Why is he angry?"

"You know what happened at Praga? To Berek Joselewicz?" Jaska's voice dropped a note, roughening. "To the Great Kosciusko?"

Okay, Praga was vaguely familiar, and Kosciusko I recognized at once. But that still didn't explain the connection, like if Mord had been fighting with or against the famous general.

On each name Aurélie gave a tiny shake of her head, her eyes wide.

Jaska's mouth was bitter as he looked down, sighed, and picked up his hautbois. He began playing very softly, one of the madrigals from *Lagrime di San Pietro*.

There was no more conversation. Aurélie seemed lost in reverie as I thought, *So Mord does see me*. That made three people, including Nanny Hiasinte. Four, if you counted that fae, but I wasn't sure they could be termed people. The weird thing was that Mord was the second to see me without the aid of the mirror, Nanny Hiasinte being the first.

Mord returned when the light was gone, and again he seemed to look right at me. As he set bow to chin, his movement was tracked by Aurélie's thoughtful gaze. He ignored exclamations and questions. Jaska pumped the regal, and Mord played the first few measures of the lively dance *Les Deux Coqs.* The other two joined in, and the moment passed.

But it wasn't forgotten. Why is it that a guy has only to reveal depths of emotional pain to rivet the interest of every romantic girl around?

Because Aurélie was romantic, of course. And because he was striking in appearance, and so kind, and musical, and mercurial . . . Aurélie had got over James, but she was in the process of shifting all that tender interest onto Mord the mystery man, who couldn't possibly be Dobrenican royalty.

TWENTY-ONE

MORD BEHAVED AS IF that sunset on the bluff had never happened, and somehow this total shutout only increased Aurélie's interest. She didn't pester him with questions, but her manner toward him became tentative, almost tender.

This raised another hideous question: What if they'd be happy together? Had I any right to interfere? But the horribleness of balancing my life and future against the possible happiness of a couple right now was mitigated by the fact that Mord clearly thought she was a boy and showed no interest in her except as a fellow musician.

This made it easier to try to interfere without seeming to interfere. I poked her one evening when she was alone, coming back from a visit to the outhouse.

She took out the mirror at once. "Duppy Kim?"

"You're forgetting to be René," I warned her. "Do you want them to guess that you aren't a boy?"

A deep blush gave her away. "Mord doesn't see me. He's short-sighted like Diana, though not in the same way, for he can see at a distance, but she cannot. And Jaska never looks my way, did you notice? He looks at the road for danger, or at the sky for storms, or at his books or musical instruments. But he never looks at me, even when we talk."

"Do you want to tell them that you are a girl?"

"Should I?"

There were so many things I could say, but I had to think ahead to the questions that would follow. "They've been good companions, but I believe they are both army deserters. Maybe not from the same army. And deserters don't have the best reputation for behavior with women. It might be safest not to tell them. Especially since you plan to part when you reach Paris."

She sighed, her expression wistful. But she didn't disagree.

A few more days on the road brought them near Paris.

Aurélie withdrew, her troubled emotional state bothering me enough to attribute to it a growing sense of unease. I certainly felt it.

The last day, when they reached the outskirts of Paris, this before-the-thunderstorm feeling coalesced into the deep bone chill you find in caves underground.

Maybe it was the ghosts. Except for those floating above the sunken portion of Port Royal in Jamaica, I hadn't seen any until now. The closer we got to Paris, the more of them I saw, some bright and glittery, reflecting a quality of light different from the hazy spring sunlight. Others were vaporous as wisps of smoke.

The traffic increased steadily, as did the number of buildings, many undergoing repair, renovation, or rip-down-begin-again construction.

During the last couple of days the trio continued to play for their supper, but the guys' conduct had altered. Instead of one of them vanishing to hilltops to watch for signals, they engaged customers in talk about Paris news.

And there was plenty of it, most concerning the Concordat of Easter, and its *Te Deum* in the Notre Dame cathedral, which had not heard the Mass echo in its vaults for several years. Napoleon had shown up in all his glory—liveried servants, trumpets—and the churches were to officially reopen. "Everything like the old days of the kings, except no king," said a man with joiner's tools at his belt.

"*Pardieu!*" An older man spat upon the floor. "He will be king yet. 18th Brumaire, it was the Directors and the Council of Five Hundred thrown off their curule chairs, red robes and all. Next it'll be *Your Majesty*, you watch."

"Not even the Luxembourg Palace was good enough," the innkeeper's wife observed sarcastically, strong arms akimbo, and I wondered if she had numbered among the roaming female gangs during the Terror who had lynched people who didn't look properly *sans-culottes*. "He's moved into the Tuileries!"

"Peace, daughter. If he so desires to be king, let him. At least we can walk the streets again and not fear being dragged off by the mob if we forget and say *pardieu*," an oldster said with a meaningful look at Citizeness Innkeeper. The other elderly people in the common room laughed, then the old man went on with the expansive tone of the person who knows the audience is on his side, "If he wishes, the Corsican can call himself High Mandarin, or Grand Turk, if we may be done with Madame la Guillotine, and Frenchman fighting Frenchman."

"Yes! A drink to that!"

Mord struck up *La Marseilles*, which ended the discussion.

The next day we reached the inner city. When the road veered off the bend in the Seine and headed south toward the heart of Paris, it broadened into a boulevard ever more crowded with both the living and the dead.

I had never before encountered so many ghosts for so sustained a time. The chill came from a specific direction, but as usual I could not look around, being bound to Aurélie, who seemed unaware of any change in atmosphere.

The three walked in silence for a long time, until Mord abruptly said, "I shall see if the lens maker is still there." He touched his eyes, then turned an absent smile Aurélie's way. "To be denied reading one more hour than necessary is to be denied life. Fare you well, Citizen René." He walked off without a backward glance.

That left the other two alone, Aurélie gazing wistfully after Mord. Jaska fidgeted with his walking stick, looked all around, and then at last faced Aurélie. "Do you know what you want to do, now that we're here? I've been in Paris before. I can point you in the right direction."

Her chin came up. "I'm going to seek news of my homeland from a connection who assuredly might know."

Jaska said, "Where lives this person?"

"From the news we overheard, she is now at the Tuileries," Aurélie said.

Jaska's brows twitched upward. "Of course! You mean the wife of the First Consul, who I understand came from one of the islands." He pointed. "That street, last I heard, was called the Rue du Mont Blanc. I don't know for certain if you'll suffer a fate most sanguinary if you use the wrong name anymore, but to be safest, just keep due south. That should lead you straight to the Tuileries."

"I thank you." Aurélie straightened her shoulders. "Should I relinquish to you your sword? The regal is yours as well."

"Keep the sword," Jaska said. "You might need . . ." He frowned at the ground, and for the first time, snatched off the shapeless cap that he had been wearing night and day. Under it his hair was flat and grimy, but even so the color was noticeably paler than the rest of his unkempt locks. He ran his hands through his hair in a gesture of tension, then looked at Aurélie , his smile rueful, almost sweet. "You are as game a youngster as ever lived, but . . . *sacré nom!* If you run into trouble, go to the Swedish embassy. I don't know if Madame de Staël is still in Paris, but if she is, she will surely help you, especially if you give her my name."

He crammed the cap back on and marched off, leaving me wondering if I should try to get Aurélie to seek Madame de Staël. From what I knew of her history, she was outspoken and unafraid of consequences, but she'd also been capricious and got herself into hot water, especially with Napoleon. And even if Madame could arrange to send Aurélie to Dobrenica, what then? Send her to the palace so the crown prince could take one look and fall in love? It sounded ridiculous even to me, and *I* knew what the future was supposed to bring! Sort of.

Argh!

"Duppy Kim?"

Aurélie looked around, fumbled for her mirror, then shook her head.

"It's not good to talk to you here. I don't feel safe. But I know what I'm going to do."

She began to run. All of Paris seemed to be undergoing repairs and renovation. The ghosts thickened exponentially, and I knew we had to be near the Place de la Concorde, where the guillotine still stood. The chill that wreathed the area like invisible fog reminded me of the bone chill I felt in the proximity of vampires. Only this was vast, deep, and somehow *aware*.

My mind swarmed with questions, but foremost was the wish that Aurélie avoid walking anywhere near the guillotine. I didn't want that memory imprinted on my retinas.

Aurélie reached the broad Place du Carrousel, the square before the Tuileries palace, which was a long building with a central dome like a mansard roof pulled inward and rounded. The square was crowded mainly with men in flashy military uniforms: Gold braid, dolmans, clanking swords, glossy high boots with tassels swinging. They were too busy with one another to pay the least heed to a grubby urchin darting among them.

No one stopped Aurélie until she reached the entrance. There, a couple of guards stood duty dressed in brand new green and gold livery. One was about her age, the other stooped, his face lined with cynicism.

"No entry for the likes of you," the older one said.

"I am here to visit a relation of mine," Aurélie declared. "Marie-Rose Josèphe Tascher de la Pagerie, who is now Citizen Bonaparte."

The older one gave a crack of laughter. "Citizen! That's Madame to you, brat. Get along—unless you've a letter of introduction under those rags?" He burst into loud laughter.

The younger one said more kindly, "I suggest you visit one of the public baths. There are three, the Vigier, the Tivoli, or the Albert. If you return properly dressed—"

"I can do that," Aurélie said.

"—with your papers—"

"Papers?" Aurélie repeated in dismay.

The first one laughed again, nearly muffling the sound of a female voice floating from somewhere above. But not quite.

Both footmen looked up. So did Aurélie. A window was open on the second story, a girl leaning out. "I said, who's there? Alphonse? Who is that boy? I know that accent."

The younger one called up, "Madame, it is an urchin who claims relation to Madame Bonaparte."

"Send him inside. I will be there directly," the female said, and vanished.

The young one began to open the door, but the old one pointed at Aurélie. "Hold hard, Monsieur Firebrand. You'll not be going in there with any pistol."

In answer Aurélie snatched her pistol from her grubby belt and shook it. "I have no powder or shot," she said with dignity, causing a guffaw from a number of uniformed idlers who'd gathered to see what the fuss was.

The first one scowled and let her pass. "Go in. You heard Madame Hortense. But don't touch anything! The days of looting are gone, so you remember that, or the *mouchards* will be on you faster even than me." He spat on the ground.

Aurélie slipped inside a large vaulted entry hall and looked around with her mouth open.

This was her introduction to Josephine's taste. She gazed in astonishment (and I'll get to what she saw in a moment) and I was trying to see as much as I could within my usual limitations. Though I'd visited Paris before I met Alec, all that was left of the Tuileries in my time was the garden.

Aurélie recollected herself when she heard the swift hiss-hiss of slippers. A slim figure descended the last of a grand stairway. She seemed to be floating, an effect caused partly by her draperies but also by the rolling, toes-out little steps she took. We were seeing the results of Josephine's courtly training, gained when her first husband sent her to a convent on Martinique.

As her daughter Hortense approached Aurélie, I thought about the irony of Josephine's being trained so far away to mimic *la vraie Parisienne*, the true Parisian woman, when she was now the leader of fashion here—in Paris, in France, and soon enough in the Western world.

Hortense stopped, and for a moment the girls regarded one another. They were the same age almost exactly, Hortense a little taller, her honey-colored hair and blue eyes much the same shade as Cassandra's. But there the resemblance ended.

"You are from Martinique?" Hortense said.

"Saint-Domingue," Aurélie said. "And Jamaica."

"Jamaica is English." Hortense looked askance.

"My mother's family is English. But my mother's mother is connected to the Taschers of La Pagerie. I had hoped to find out news of the islands. I want to go home, if I can."

"I can only tell you that there is much trouble there. In all the islands, English, French, Spanish." Hortense shrugged a little. "The slaves have revolted."

"Good," Aurélie said fiercely.

Hortense betrayed surprise, then stepped closer. "You look like an urchin. And, forgive me, you smell like one. But you don't speak like one."

Aurélie said, "I am Aurélie de Mascar—well. I'm a girl, and I hate living this lie. If you've no news, then I must go." Her voice, husky and low at the best of times, went breathy.

Hortense gave a trill of laughter and clasped her hands together. "I dressed as a boy once. When I was small. It was when we left Martinique. There was fire, and *Maman* ran with me onto a ship, and we had no clothes. She had to make a gown out of sailcloth, and they dressed me as a cabin boy."

Aurélie said with heartfelt sympathy, "It must have been terrible."

Hortense flushed. "It was fun for me, though perhaps not so much for *Maman*. But that's of no importance. If you cannot take ship, what will you do?"

Go to the Swedish embassy, I shouted mentally, poking at her. I was thinking they might be able to send her east.

Aurélie recoiled, and shook her head. "Not now, Duppy Kim," she whispered in English. "I must think."

Hortense's eyes were huge. "Did you say 'duppy'?"

Aurélie flushed. "And if I did?"

Hortense took a deep breath. "My mother will want to meet you. I know it. Will you stay a bit?"

Aurélie looked down at herself. "But I'm not at all *comme il faut.*"

"That's easily repaired," Hortense said. "Come into my mother's suite. They're at Malmaison just now. Things could not be more perfect. And here I began the day so sad . . ."

She led Aurélie into the adjoining salon. Aurélie's steps faltered as she gazed around at the furnishings freshly covered with blue-violet taffeta and embroidered with golden honeysuckle. Dominating the room was a gold-framed portrait of St. Cecelia. "It's so beautiful," Aurélie exclaimed.

"Oh, you ought to see Malmaison. Here, Bonaparte would not permit her new furnishings. She could only refurbish the old. *Maman* hates this place," Hortense said as she led Aurélie into the next salon, even larger than the first, done in yellow and brown satin with red highlights. The mirrors on the walls were draped, the porphyry side tables supported Sèvres vases and rose granite decorations embellished with bronze.

"She says the ghosts linger, and though she does not see them, she feels them. Her bedroom is through there. That was the room used by the Committee of Public Safety. She says she can feel the grip of death in that room, all those lives they ordered to be ended. Out there, on a table—now gone—in the entry, that is where Robespierre himself lay bleeding while they decided his fate. He shot himself in the jaw, you know. Then they carried him out to the guillotine."

"I'm glad he's gone," Aurélie said as they entered the bedroom.

"Oh, he's not the worst of them." Hortense paused and looked around with a frightened face, her hands clasped tightly under her chin, as if she expected spies to leap out from behind the blue and white, gold-fringed coverings. Then she caught herself. "But Bonaparte can stop him."

"Stop who?"

"Fouché. He has his spies, his *mouchards*, everywhere."

Mouche is the word for fly. Aurélie grimaced as Hortense leaned toward her. "He even pays *Maman*, who always has debts. She tells him little things about life here and pretends to be his friend. She says it's foolish to turn your back on a snake, just because you don't like venom."

Hortense opened a door.

"This was Marie Antoinette's bedroom, and *Maman* says she knows her sad ghost is lurking. Here's the wardrobe." They passed the great mahogany bed in its alcove and entered a dressing room filled with mirrors as well as shelves and trunks, the hangings simple blue and white muslin.

"Look through the clothing while I summon the servants." Hortense flitted away, leaving Aurélie staring at an enormous room full of trunks and shelves holding every color of fabric. The number of hats alone seemed to stun her. She stood there unmoving.

When Hortense returned, she let out a peal of laughter. "I see that I'm going to have to take you in hand! There's nothing I like better. Now, you must choose one of these pretty muslins. We have ever so many, but Bonaparte hates to see us in them. Everything must be French silks and velvets, he decreed, but you're a young girl, not married, am I correct? *You* can wear muslin. And it's a shame for these not to be seen."

As she spoke Hortense pulled out one gown after another, while shaking her head or pursing up her mouth. The flimsier gowns of the Directoire were instantly discarded, the older tunics modeled on Greek figures, everything diaphanous.

Hortense settled on a pretty gown with tiny puff sleeves. "And if we need to pin up the hem, why, it's still very much in fashion to drape and hold it in place with cameos. Come, the bath should be ready by now." She pointed to the adjoining chamber.

A short time later, Aurélie stood straight in the gown, her skin glowing clean as Hortense fussed happily with her wet hair. "It will dry in kiss curls—oh, you are so beautiful, Aurélie! I am charmed, and envious, all at once. *Maman* is going to love you. I think I have an idea, but . . . who did you say you were?"

Aurélie stared down, her face reflected her inward struggle, then she said, "My mother sent me here with the name de Mascarenhas and a dowry, she said to help me. And it did, but the name, it's not truly mine, and the dowry, my English relations kept."

"If that is not just like the English," Hortense exclaimed. "Though I must confess I very much liked the Duchess of Devonshire. We've met some very fine English, but those newspapers! The horrid things they say about *Maman*. And that *mechant* Lord Morpeth, who would not permit his wife to be presented to her—" Hortense gave a little shrug and threw up her hands. "What is a name? Bonaparte changed his. He changed my mother's! Did you know she was always Rose, until she met him? Keep your fine name, for these days it's Madame this and that, instead of Citizeness, and some whisper it will soon be Her Majesty. I wish I could see your duppy!"

Aurélie ran to the mirror and touched it. I laid my hand over hers. "There she is, do you see?" Aurélie cried.

Hortense gazed into the mirror. For a moment her eyes met mine, but then she frowned and shook her head. "For a heartbeat, I saw a woman, but there was another woman, like smoke, or steam, and many men. It makes me dizzy." She pressed her hands to her eyes, then turned away.

Aurélie looked around quickly. She spun too fast, but I thought I saw shifting shadows in the corners, the shape of an inclined head here, a silhouetted arm there. A lifted wing, or wings, smoky and blurred.

These were not like any of the ghosts I had experienced so far, so I didn't know what to make of them. It was clear to me that Aurélie didn't see them as she walked away from the mirror, examining the gown with its embroidered bunches of grapes.

Hortense dropped her hands and regarded Aurélie in satisfaction. "Yes, you simply must come to Malmaison. We'll go today. I was so unhappy that I refused to go with them, for they've been arguing. Mr. Charles James Fox wishes to visit, you see, and Bonaparte won't permit him to present his wife. I don't know if it's spite because of Lord Morpeth, or what, but he and *Maman* argued and argued, and . . ." Hortense gave that little shrug. "I was feeling ill this morning and begged to be left behind. But we may order up a carriage."

Hortense pulled a pair of shoes from a shelf. "These are mine. I think I only wore them once. See if they fit."

Aurélie slid her feet into the slippers, careful to keep her ankle from showing. "They fit well enough."

"Then it's perfect. You shall be, how do they say it there? Donna Aurélie de Mascarenhas, and that'll be good enough. Bonaparte will never trouble himself beyond that, not for a mere girl. And if you come among us, no doubt he will soon marry you off to one of his generals, and then you'll have another name altogether."

"I don't want to be married," Aurélie said quickly.

"What has that to do with anything?" Hortense said with a sad smile, and some bitterness. She lifted her shoulders. "It is the way of the world. Unless you're wealthy, how is a woman to live unless she marries? I can promise that *Maman*, at least, will try to find you a *good* man, not just a powerful one." At Aurélie's doubtful look, Hortense colored, her hand stealing over her still-flat midriff. "It was Bonaparte who wanted me married to his brother, but he seldom takes a hand in the marriages of *Maman*'s ladies, unless, well. Are you a maiden still?"

It was Aurélie's turn to color. "That, I do not know."

"How can this be?" Hortense asked in amazement. "I think one would know *that*."

Aurélie blushed. "I remember Tante Mina and my mother tried to tell me some things when I was young, thinking it better for me to know, but it was boring and confusing, and I had no interest. It seemed one of many warnings about dangers, especially from men. My aunt in England told us nothing. She scolded terribly when my cousin asked once why married people go on honeymoons. But then." Aurélie sucked in a determined breath and took me as well as Hortense by surprise. "I was traveling with two men recently. And because my—how do you say here?—'Aunt Rose' has not visited—"

"We call it 'the English,'" Hortense said with a grin.

"There's been no sign. I heard my Cousin Fiba say once that if Aunt Rose doesn't come, then a baby will, and so I ask myself, am I with child?"

Whoa! She'd never given a hint of any such thoughts to *me*. So much for our new level of trust, I was thinking, as Hortense said, "How long since your last?"

"I don't remember, but more than a month."

"Courses can be late for many reasons. You were dressed as a boy, so I take it your companions thought you were one. That suggests to me that you couldn't have done anything with them, or they would certainly know you were a girl!"

"Done what?"

"How did you sleep? Did any clothing come off?"

"Never! I was very careful. Not once, except when I sewed my trousers, and I did that while hiding on a rooftop. We shared barns and haystacks, and horse stalls, though, and so, if proximity does the business, well . . . I do remember that *Maman* said, 'Never be alone with a man.'"

"You cannot get with child by sharing a barn with a man, or even two men! You have to share a lot more than that." Hortense let out a peal of laughter. "I think we shall have to have a talk in the carriage, which I will order this very moment. And then we'll talk about other things, like, are you musical? *Maman* loves music almost as much as she loves flowers. Don't be afraid. You'll love *Maman*, I promise you. Everyone does." She sighed, then amended, "Almost everyone. But as *Maman* says, the Bonapartes are laws unto themselves."

TWENTY-TWO

"OH, DEAR HORTENSE, how very clever you are," Josephine said, as Aurélie lifted her hands from the beautiful new fortepiano recently delivered from Vienna. She had played a French air, causing Josephine to exclaim with delight. "You've brought us a treasure. My dear child, I trust you will remain with us? Did Hortense tell you that Bonaparte and I are forming a theater group here at Malmaison? We both of us are passionate about the arts."

"Thank you, Madame. I would be happy to serve you," Aurélie said. She had reverted to the formal *vous*, though Josephine used the familiar *tu*.

"You say you cannot sing? It is a tragedy, with such musical talent."

"My voice was deemed too low, and I never learnt."

"La, child, your voice is most ravishing, like a panther's growl. Not that I have heard a panther or even so much as seen one. But your voice is most singular, and very, very charming. You shall see, the gentlemen will be transported. *Bon!* Bonaparte is impatient for us to move to Saint-Cloud, but everything smells of paint, and there is that incessant sound, hammer, hammer, hammer. We are getting up a play. That will please him enormously, for he is working night and day on his educational plan. It is to be the most singular, everyone to benefit. *Voyons!* Hortense says that you arrived in only the clothes you stood in. How very romantical! Let us see what we can contrive, until we can get my seamstress to attend you. So very clever a woman."

Josephine rose and led the way out, her movements so fluid she seemed to float. She was as graceful and light as the false Princess Moonbeam, but this was no illusion. Josephine looked what she was, a woman of almost forty years, but the shape of her head, the way she carried herself, embodied style.

Aurélie followed like someone in a dream. Josephine personally chose a room for her, then wafted away, leaving Hortense to lead Aurélie around the chateau.

Not that it was large (though larger than it is today); by far the most extensive portion was the garden, constantly undergoing change. It was spring, and it was abundantly clear that Josephine loved flowers as much as she did exquisite furnishings and clothing, if not more. The garden was a sea of color, not a weed in sight.

"And there you have it," Hortense finished. She looked around, then said in a lower voice, "When we are alone with *Maman*, we can talk about your duppy and consult her if she appears. Is she still here?"

"I must touch hands with her in a mirror to see, but she has followed me all the way from Accompong," Aurélie said. "I believe she is with me still."

"*Bon!* Bonaparte hates it when *Maman* talks about obeah, or miracles, or anything such. He does not believe in any of the things we do. Did you know that our Nanny Euphémie predicted that *Maman* would be married twice, and that the second husband would be covered in glory and would raise her above a queen? *Maman* sleeps in the rooms of Marie Antoinette, as you have seen. But Madame Villeneuve, the fortune teller, foretold that she would only wear a crown for a little while. *Maman* will be anxious to consult your duppy to clarify the future."

"I will show Madame my duppy, if it pleases her," Aurélie said slowly. "But I must warn you, she said that she has no powers in the spirit world or this. And she can only talk to me when we touch in the mirror."

"That is more than I have ever heard," Hortense said. "Though I remember many who saw *lwa* after we danced on the hills. But I was so very small!" She shrugged. "In any case, if your duppy cannot foretell the future, or prescribe magical cures, then she can wait. The future, and cures, are what *Maman* most wishes, you see. But you are still very welcome for your musical talents, I hasten to assure you. *Maman* likes to be surrounded by pretty people, and she cherishes those from the islands."

"Thank you." Aurélie dropped a little curtsey, and Hortense acknowledged it with a self-conscious smile "If I may, I have two questions for you," Aurélie said, as they walked back toward the house. "If one wished to speak to someone. At an embassy, say. How would one go about it? I had a . . . a musical friend, a violinist, whose well-being I would like to be assured of."

Hortense laughed. "Nothing easier! The world comes to us. You will see. Which embassy?"

"Swedish."

"Ah, I haven't personal acquaintance with anyone there, since the Baron de Staël von Holstein was called back. And Bonaparte hates his wife with such a passion, you cannot conceive!"

"I do not wish to raise difficulties," Aurélie said quickly. "My second question is the more important. I wish to write to my mother in Jamaica."

"Of course you do," Hortense said with ready sympathy. "I can ask Monsieur Talleyrand when next we see him, or if he comes to us first, you can ask him yourself. He is the foreign minister. He regularly dispatches letters all over the world, and he is everything of the most kind."

"Thank you," Aurélie said.

Josephine did not summon Aurélie in order to consult her future with me, which was an intense relief because the irony, of course, was that I knew the broad outlines of her future quite well. But my instinct at this point was to keep that to myself. I couldn't see it doing any good, but I could definitely see it doing harm, specifically to the stream of history. I'd read a lot about Josephine during college, and though I vaguely recollected those prophesies—and how she constantly consulted people who claimed occult knowledge—not once had I seen reference to a duppy that fitted my description.

Aurélie's room had its own *salle de bain* off it, and a chambermaid to see to her things. This girl, who was younger than Aurélie by two or three years, introduced herself as Marie as she set about putting away the things that Josephine had given her new lady in waiting. ". . . and so," Marie said, "Mama told us that we must never use our names again or they would chop off our heads! My brother Paul became Liberté, my sister Jeanne became Floréal, and I was Messidor. *Mess-i-dor!* It means *harvest*, I am told, and *mordieu, how* the others teased me. I am so very, very glad to be Marie again, though it is so common."

When at last she left, Aurélie flew to the mirror and smacked her hand against it. "Duppy Kim! Are you there?"

"Here I am."

She drew a deep breath. "I see you. I was a little afraid that you would vanish, now that I am safe."

So, there we were. She expected to be done with me, but I knew she hadn't yet come near the future that was true to my timeline—my existence.

So far, I'd operated on instinct, and look at the mistakes I'd managed to make. Though I'd spent all this time bound to her, I was not inside her head.

Spending time around someone doesn't grant complete knowledge, that much I knew to be true. My sporadic listening at Aurélie's shoulder wasn't a fraction of the real time I'd spent with my grandmother, talking to her, listening to her, sharing days with her . . . but until the summer her cold turned into pneumonia and then a coma, we had known absolutely nothing about Dobrenica.

Then there was the "future" question.

Here, I could only go by my own convictions. Like, if someone told me they were from the future, I'd ask first when I was supposed to die, and if they told me that I would one day die in France, I would take the next plane out and avoid France like the plague.

This was my understanding of the Heisenberg Principle: knowledge of the future was almost certain to affect it.

In that case, I should not tell her I was from the future.

So what could I work on? Our relationship. "Hortense gave you good advice, but you could have asked me, and I would have told you that you were not with child."

She gazed at me in surprise. "Oh, of course! You are a *duppy*, not a *lwa*. That means you do have a body, do you not? I am so used to thinking of you living in the spirit world, I did not think to ask you about matters of the body."

"Yes, I have a body."

"Where?"

"I'm not exactly sure," I said, remembering that false door—and the fae vision of me lying on my bed. "But it is very far from here."

"Do you have a name besides Kim?"

"My full name is Aurelia Kim Murray."

"We share a name!"

"Yes. But I am usually called Kim."

"How did you come to be a duppy?"

"I was called by your Nanny Hiasinte." Who, I realized in that moment, had not told Aurélie that I was from the future. All right, then.

"Because you can do nothing in the physical world, I did not think to ask you."

"I am still learning what I can and cannot do. And things are changing rapidly."

"How? Are you gaining powers?"

I said carefully, "I have somewhat more knowledge of things. Like, in the carriage ride on the way to Malmaison, when Hortense told you the things that some of the Paris fortune tellers predicted for Josephine. I know that some of them are lies."

"Oh! Should I tell Hortense, or Madame herself?" Aurélie looked intimidated at that idea.

Pitfalls again! "I think that might get you into trouble. Remember, there is no way to *prove* these predictions wrong, and saying 'my duppy tells me' will probably cause these others to point out that their spirit guides are telling them something else."

"Are you saying that their spirit guides are wrong?"

"Or that they might be only pretending to have spirit guides. But I can't prove that, either. One thing I do know, if you accuse them of being false, you are certain to cause resentment in these people, and I don't think Madame Josephine is going to stop doing what she is doing. I can warn *you*, I hope. In turn, you can help me by sharing the things that you worry about. Like when you thought you were with child."

"I understand." She flashed her crooked smile. "And it is not as if you could tell anyone my secret thoughts."

Someone had taken Marivaux's unfinished novel *Le Paysan Parvenu, The Unfortunate Peasant*, and turned it into a play. Marivaux had been popular in Louis XV's time for his romantic comedies. Hortense was composing music to embellish this play, but when she heard Aurélie's songs, she demanded her aid. Aurélie threw herself happily into rehearsals.

When they weren't working, the ladies had free time. Josephine had yet to be constrained to follow the elaborate imperial court ritual that Napoleon would love so much.

Aurélie used her free time to wander through Malmaison. At first she was drawn back to the enormous gallery full of the paintings that Napoleon had shipped back from his various wars, especially from the Italian masters. I noticed she avoided the grand rooms designed to look like royal war camp tents. Napoleon hadn't spent all that much time there, but his presence seemed to be stamped all over. No one went there except to clean and dust.

Aurélie did venture into those rooms once. She tiptoed in as if Napoleon could hear her all the way from Paris or Saint-Cloud and have her arrested. She pored intently over the enormous map lying on a table then murmured, "I do not see Praga."

I touched her hand from long habit, though there was no mirror around. "It might be the name of a village."

She jerked upright, eyes wide. "I heard you."

She ran to her room and shut the door. After a quick experiment we discovered that she still couldn't see me without a mirror, but she could now hear me if I touched her and spoke.

I suspect that, somehow, I'd learned to focus my mind better, but Aurélie now regarded me as gaining in abilities. Though it made me feel like a fraud, I didn't deny it, because we still had to get to Dobrenica. And save it. Though I had no more idea why or how than I had at the outset, I felt certain I should use what little advantage I had.

Time blurred by again.

One morning Aurélie woke to find the household rushing around frenetically cleaning, dusting, and twitching things just so. She went to Josephine's rooms, expecting the usual leisurely, pleasant breakfast over which the women conversed informally about all manner of subjects. But Josephine was not there, and instead of the usual carefully planned and beautifully presented meal, there was only a tray of last night's bread, some fruit, and slices of meat.

Aurélie grabbed a peach and a piece of bread and went out in search of news. When she found Josephine's most trusted maid carrying a great pot of fresh flowers, she said, "Is something amiss?"

"*He* is due." Agatha peered over the blue and pink stalks that had been fitted among pure white roses. "Get dressed. Silk!" Then she flitted away, leaving Aurélie standing there apprehensively.

Josephine wore her soft muslins by preference, but when the enormous military cavalcade clattered and swept into the courtyard before the house, Josephine, her daughter, and all the ladies wore silk gowns, Josephine's with a velvet train that had to be gathered up in one arm when she walked.

A short but sharp thunderstorm must have halted or slowed Napoleon on the road, because it was late when the outriders finally arrived. Word zapped through the mansion, *Le voilà—he's here.*

The women gathered in the entry hall, still and nervous. Even Josephine betrayed nerves in the restless way she smoothed her skirt and tucked back a tendril of curly dark hair from her brow.

A rumble of boots, and in clattered a group of officers, gold braid swinging, swords jingling in their *sabretache* harnesses, the spurs on their boots ringing on the marble floor like discordant chimes. With them was a file of the Consular Guard, tall, immaculate, martial-looking, though I knew they were a few years from developing into Napoleon's formidably elite Guard Impériale.

At first I wondered if the sentient chill I sensed was caused by Napoleon, because alone of all the people there, I knew what he was. I knew what he was going to do. The energy blowback from Napoleon's entrance was so strong it was nearly physical in my non-physical existence. But it was not the terrifying, brooding lour I'd detected on our way to the Tuileries.

The women curtseyed, their manner slightly self-conscious, underscoring how new this behavior was, like using the formal *vous* again.

Napoleon was skinny in those days, his hair a flapping tangle on his shoulders. It was so strange to see the much-caricatured face, instantly recognizable, as he flushed like a boy and marched up to Josephine to kiss her soundly.

He was dressed in the blue and white of the *chasseurs* of the guard. He turned, holding Josephine against him so that she lost hold of her train, and greeted Hortense with a forced-sounding laugh. Or maybe he was used to shouting to be heard. "How's the belly, Hortense? Nothing visible yet, but you are still healthy? Sick of a morning?" and when she assented, "That is a very good sign. Larrey tells me that it means you will carry it through."

He turned to his wife. "Ah. Josephine, when will you carry ours?" He did not wait for an answer but gestured toward the hall. "What have you got for us? That ride is more damnable every time we come out here. Saint-Cloud will be finished in summer, and it needs you to put your finishing touches on it. There will be no place finer in the world. Our grandchildren will be proud of it."

She responded with the words he wanted to hear, and as the clock chimed six, she led him and the officers to the splendid meal awaiting, as Aurélie and the troupe moved to the new theatre for one last rehearsal.

The sharp voices and nerves reminded me of my own days on stage during high school and college, dancing in the ballet chorus. Only I had never danced before a collection of generals who would leave mayhem across an entire continent as they followed their soon-to-be emperor.

The play went off without a hitch, but the quick glances out at the audience made it clear how aware they were of Napoleon talking almost non-stop. Occasionally he beat time on his knee to the bouncier tunes, and he laughed aloud at a couple of the jokes with double-meanings.

At the end, he said, "Very well done! Very! This is what we need in Paris, and what we shall get."

When Josephine said something too low to be heard, he exclaimed, "Bah! Of course I am busy, but these things must be done! Legitimacy." He began to pace back and forth, while the players and the audience remained standing, according to his new rules of etiquette. "That is what Talleyrand told me when I returned from Italy, and he is right. A government rests on its legitimacy. I do not have the tombs of St. Denis and Versailles to give me legitimacy, as your friends at the Faubourg St. Germain are the first to point out."

Josephine raised her hands as if to protest, but he went on. "No! The Revolution cleared all that away, bad as well as good. We will keep only the good. French theater restores legitimacy when people go home smiling. No more historical plays that stir the blood to trouble. No more tragedy, no more destructive ideas. That leads directly to suffusions of blood and the guillotine, did we not see? That means we must exert ourselves. We must oversee the plays. Especially now, eh, Junot?"

A bow from the young general whose curly hair did not completely hide hideous scars on his scalp. I looked away, remembering what head trauma would do to him after another ten years of bloody war for Napoleon—madness and suicide.

"I must oversee everything," Napoleon stated. "Everything! I am giving my faithful Junot a Municipal Guard, half in red with green facings, half the other way. They will not be recruited from every loiterer on the street, they must be veterans of campaigns! Men of good standing! They must read and write! Josephine, you will never again have to fear infernal machines blowing up your horses on your way to the theater, eh? Eh?"

"Thank you, Bonaparte," she said softly.

If that was a hint to lower his voice, he didn't hear it. "Legitimacy! Theater. Monuments to peace and prosperity, and my name on every one. And a new civil code, and my poor army, oh, where can I get enough horses to mount my cavalry? But that is not your concern. Women know nothing of the army. They *should* know nothing of the army. Josephine, you shall lead the fashion, and everyone will follow. As for those despicable newspapers, if they care not for the legitimacy and security and order of our government, then they may serve France as sentries at the frontier, for I shall shut them all down. But you must do your part. I can do nothing about these damned English newspapers and their calumnies about you and our women, but if these English flocking here now see your elegance, and grace, they will go home and talk of nothing else, and we shall see the last of *that*. Legitimacy! This is how it begins."

The players were stiff with exhaustion, some subtly shifting from foot to foot, as they'd been on their feet all day rehearsing.

He seemed to become aware of them. "Well done! I am pleased with your troupe, Madame. Hortense, did you arrange the music? Of course you did."

"It was partly me, sir," she said. "And partly by Mademoiselle de Mascarenhas, who has lately joined our household. She is a connection through the Taschers." Hortense indicated Aurélie, who curtseyed.

Napoleon stepped up to her. "This little thing? How old are you, ten, twelve? And you write music?" He took hold of Aurélie's chin. "You are a pretty little thing and talented, but you are very dusky. Did one of your noble ancestors tumble with a slave? One of my best generals came out of a nobleman and a slave, a fine officer, but a fool to criticize me. No lack of courage, though, I will say this for Dumas. Heh! When you get a year or two older, we'll find you a good husband among my generals. They could use a good dose of noble blood, even if it's got a dusky tang." He gave a laugh and let go her chin at last, and though tears had gathered along her eyelids, she did not let them fall as he passed on by to compliment and lecture the rest of the company by turns.

TWENTY-THREE

L ATER IN HER ROOM, Aurélie said, "I did not expect to find him so handsome. James told us the London papers described him as small and ugly, like a toad." She touched her chin, which still showed a dull red mark. "He is very loud, and he pinches."

Napoleon stayed one more day, holding military court in his wing of Malmaison, with officers clanking and rattling around like gaudily dressed worker bees. But promptly at six the officers were sent off, and he dined with the family and a few of the women. Afterward, he, the family, and the ladies-in-waiting played a lot of games like *tric-trac* and *reversis.*

He left the following morning, bearing Josephine back to Paris. The place seemed empty without them and their personal attendants. Aurélie and the theater company were left behind to rehearse for a formal reception to be held the next week in the Tuileries. Hortense selected the music and then she, too, departed for Paris.

The day arrived. Madame Bonaparte's important ladies were to attend the opera, which included the prettiest of the theater troupe, Aurélie among them. They were transported back to Paris in comfortable carriages, guarded by uniformed outriders. They chattered with anticipation, for the troupe were to make music at the gala reception after the opera. Everyone who was important in Paris would be there.

When they reached the Tuileries, Aurélie dressed in the gown that Josephine had personally picked out for her: white of the finest muslin with golden embroidery down the front in scrolled laurel leaves, tied high with embroidered gold ribbon. Her hair was bound up with gold ribbon in the French version of Grecian style. The outfit looked fantastic against her warm brown skin.

She stood in her little room, smiling at the mirror. "I think of myself as Aurélie de Mascarenhas," she said to me. "I don't even know for certain my real last name, for I do not think of myself as a Kittredge, but I do not believe my father wanted to be called after the one who regarded him as a mere slave, this Beauveau."

I nodded in sympathy, inwardly thinking, *I hope before long—somehow—your new last name will be Dsaret.*

"And in dreams—some dreams, when Mordechai plays his violin—I'm René." She touched her collarbones. "My question is this. Do you think it is safe to bring out my necklace, just once? It's beautiful, and it's a *necklace*, it ought to be seen! In my dreams, many times, the women wear it, and I'd love to wear it to the opera. To do so somehow brings *Maman*, Tante Mimba, and Nanny Hiasinte closer to me."

"Everybody will be wearing jewels, and you'll be surrounded by the Consular guard," I said. "You should be safe."

As soon as I said the words, I thought about those fae, but they, too, were far from here. And though I'd seen plenty of ghosts, I didn't think revenants would have any interest in jewels, magical or not.

Aurélie beamed with pleasure as she clasped the necklace around her neck and turned this way and that to admire it.

Seen in the bright candle light, it was undoubtedly ancient. The gold was smooth from countless generations of women wearing it then handing it down, so the carvings had become faint and difficult to make out. Set against the classical lines of the gown, it was the perfect touch. She fingered it, whispering, "I wish you could see me now, Nanny," but broke off when a footman out in the hall shouted for everyone to get to the coaches.

Only Josephine's and Hortense's carriages were pulled by six horses, although the carriages with the lesser ladies were just as fast, and the distance was not much more than a stone's throw. They reached the Théâtre des Arts, an enormous building lit up as well as they could be in those days.

The vast space was packed.

The Bonapartes sat in the Consular box, which was royal in everything but name. All eyes turned up that way almost as often as they took in the stage below.

Napoleon was the center of attention, of course, Josephine at his side, dressed in white velvet with a green overskirt, trimmed with golden embroidery set with emeralds. A headdress very like a princess's coronet threaded through her soft dark curls.

A military accolade brought everyone to their feet, and Napoleon smiled broadly left and right, his eyes wide, his whole being radiating pleasure at the volume of nearly three thousand people cheering.

As soon as he sat down, the opera began, and the audience's attention shifted to the stage. The ladies-in-waiting sat elbow to elbow in little gilt chairs behind the Bonapartes—Napoleon; his thin, intense brother Lucien (who I knew would be in exile within two years, disgusted with his brother's imperial ambitions); Hortense; and Josephine on one side of Napoleon, while on his other side, obvious in their dislike of Josephine, two of Napoleon's sisters. They whispered incessantly, the younger one leaning out with her fan up to make absolutely sure that Josephine saw that she was excluded.

Behind the ladies in waiting stood a number of Napoleon's officers, and guards surrounded them all. Napoleon wasn't watching the stage as much as he was the box seats. From time to time he beckoned to his aide-de-camp, who would bring one or another officer forward to converse with him.

I was distracted by a figure who strolled in, solitary and grave. At first I took it to be a woman, but that perfect face could also have been male. He—she—ignored the aide-de-camp, who did not appear to see anything amiss. The being had deep-set eyes, fine-boned pale features, and long black hair worn loose so that it blended into the filmy black cape draped over the shoulders. The clothing was like vapor, the same ivory shade as the being's skin. I thought, this has to be a woman.

She reached Napoleon's side and glanced down at him with a faint smile, but he was busy whispering to a tall, severe-looking man who bent to listen, then withdrew without looking at anyone else.

The woman turned her head. Eyes the color of topaz reflected the light from the crystal chandelier. She smiled dreamily my way. Her eyes reflected a brief, startling crimson glow, the way cats' or dogs' eyes will sometimes do if the light is right. Then with deliberate steps, she somehow mounted the low balcony without bending.

The black cape lifted into wings, vaporous and shadowy, creating a multiplicity effect, as if she had not two wings, but six.

For a heartbeat she stood there, black hair flying in no wind that I could feel, her gown shimmering, framed by the astounding tower of black wings. Then the wings came down all at once, lifting her upward toward the chandelier . . . the hundred tongues of flame glowed through her, then she shot skyward and vanished into the shadows obscuring the ceiling.

In ones and twos, other winged beings shot upward from all around us, but no one seemed to see them.

I looked at Aurélie to see if she, at least, had noticed, to discover her bent a little forward, gazing at the boxes on the other side of the theatre.

He was instantly recognizable: tall and blond, his cleft chin shorn of whiskers, Jaska was dressed in a fine brown velvet coat cut high and tailored sharply back, his cravat almost up to his chin.

And he was staring across the sea of faces into the Consular box, not at the mysterious winged beings, or the soon-to-be emperor, his beautiful wife, his generals or their ladies, but at one petite young lady dressed all in white and gold.

TWENTY-FOUR

———————

WHEN THE OPERA WAS OVER, Aurélie and the lesser ladies were whisked to the Tuileries to ready themselves for the gala, while Napoleon and his entourage made their stately way to a waiting carriage—royal in every way except for coats of arms on the doors, though the drivers and footmen all wore the new green and gold livery.

As soon as they reached the Tuileries, the servants zoomed around putting the finishing touches on things. The homely lanterns were removed when all the chandeliers were lighted at the last possible moment, so the candles would be tall. Someone went around on a last check of the flowers to make sure none were wilted, a little girl following with a flat basket full of blossoms to replace the rejects. Food and drink were brought out, fresh and ready.

And the musicians all took their places.

Aurélie had been assigned to one of the salons away from the Gallery of Diana, which was the main reception room and contained the professional orchestra from the opera, also whisked away to perform yet again.

The farther salons all had at least a trio stationed in them, the idea being that guests would hear music no matter where they wandered in that long string of rooms.

Aurélie was playing on a beautiful Pascal Taskin harpsichord that someone had managed to save from the revolutionary mobs. Later, I overheard Marie say that the Versailles servants and their counterparts in Paris had melted away when the troubles began, knowing that no one would defend them, though the poor Swiss Guards had stayed to the end, ripped apart by the murderous horde. Many of the escaping servants had saved what they could, including musicians who dismantled the better instruments to hide in barrels and boxes until the troubles were over. Throughout Paris these treasures were slowly making a reappearance.

Playing with Aurélie were two other young women, one with a cello, and the other on a clarinet.

In the distance trumpets blared. "They're here," hissed a maid, scurrying with her tray, the dishes rattling.

Aurélie settled on her stool, exchanging excited, frightened glances with her trio, none of whom was any older than she. Then came the noise of arrivals, and the pretty room filled with people in fashionable new clothes, talking and laughing as the many candles gave off waves of heat that I could see in flushed faces, busy fans, and wilting flowers, even if I couldn't feel it.

The trio at first played nervously. They smoothed it out, playing beautifully, though they could have been banging away on washboard, kazoo, and cowbell for all the attention guests paid them.

But they played womanfully on, and when Napoleon marched through with a comet tail of hangers-on and petitioners, they gained a nod of approval from him.

It was later, probably about three a.m., when Hortense appeared, leading a tall, handsome young man with blond hair neatly pulled back, and light brown eyes.

Jaska.

"Aurélie, this envoy wished to be introduced to the player of such charming music. Monsieur Dsaret, may I present Mademoiselle Aurélie de Mascarenhas? Monsieur Dsaret is from, what was it? Poland, via the Swedish legate?"

Dsaret?

He's the guy, I shrieked, though I didn't dare touch Aurélie. *Jaska is the guy!*

"It is close enough." Jaska spread his hands.

"You said you are also a musician?" Hortense asked him.

"I play a little," he said modestly, as I was thinking, *It's him! It's him! Light brown eyes, blond hair . . . Dsaret! Why isn't he telling them he's crown prince of Dobrenica?*

Because maybe he wasn't?

They chattered a little about music, then Hortense said to the trio, "You may take a little time for refreshments."

This was generous, since they'd been told they were expected to play until dawn. The cellist and clarinetist walked away. Hortense caught sight of another guest and left the two alone.

"I had to see if it was really you," Jaska said.

Aurélie ducked her head. "I hope you will forgive me for the deception."

Jaska raised a hand. "I comprehend that we were honored with a Chevalier d'Eon when I assumed a disguise of necessity."

"You guessed?" She flushed with embarrassment.

"I was not so sure at first." He glanced to the side, then said in a low voice, "When I was young. My sister and I . . ." He trailed off.

Aurélie didn't prompt him for more. "Does Mord know? About me?" She looked past him and asked, "Where is he? Is he in Paris, or did he return to Poland?"

His face smoothed into polite reserve. "Mord never guessed. You must remember he has difficulty seeing things close by without his spectacles. Do you wish me to be the bearer of a message to him?"

Aurélie fingered her necklace, then quickly dropped her hands. "Oh, no. I—I merely miss his violin playing." She seemed to feel how inadequate that sounded and blushed again.

Jaska's expression cooled from polite to inscrutable as he bowed. "I will convey your words. *Au revoir,* Mademoiselle." He walked off, leaving me face-palming metaphorically, since I didn't have face or palm. For the first time, Jaska had mentioned his family, but Aurélie (quite naturally, if you're crushing on someone else) galloped right past.

My soaring hopes smashed, leaving me depressed and even desolate.

Alec seemed farther away than ever, his very existence threatened by my inability to *act*.

———

Aurélie was awakened a few hours after she went to sleep.

I came out of the blur, determined to do *something*. Whether or not Jaska Dsaret was Aurélie's future prince, at least he was from the right family. It's progress, I told myself firmly. I had to make certain the two met again.

Hortense stood there as Aurélie blinked at the window in the mid-morning light. Hortense was still in her gala gown, though somewhat rumpled.

"Have you been to bed at all?" Aurélie asked, sitting up.

"I am going now. Listen, I promised I would find a way to introduce you to Talleyrand, which has puzzled me exceedingly. I hoped to bring him to you last night, but he was in the Gallery, surrounded in a positive crush. I could not get him away, or you, without causing a deal of talk. It will probably always be that way at galas, for your duties will keep you in one place, and Bonaparte often keeps Talleyrand at his side."

Aurélie got out of bed, and Hortense followed her to her little *salle de bain*, still talking. "And I cannot take you to his house, which is a shame, as he gives the very best parties in Paris. Bonaparte has taken against Madame Grand, Talleyrand's hostess."

Aurélie paused in washing her face and blinked in surprise.

Hortense sighed. "It is vexatious. Bonaparte now wants all his prin-ciple leaders married, you see, but he does not approve of Talleyrand marrying Madame Grand. But however, I think mother will have her way there, for she is always tender-hearted."

"I do not understand."

"*Alors!*" Hortense waved her hands. "That is not what I came to say. The important thing is, Talleyrand comes to Bonaparte every morning, that is, morning as he sees it, midday at least. You must catch him on the way in." As Aurélie brought her hands up in apprehension at the idea of trying to corner one of the most famous men in France, Hortense said, "He is very polite. Even if he refuses, you will not know it, I assure you. And he may agree to send your letter. He can be very kind, even when it is not required. Especially to a pretty woman. But it is best to catch him coming or going, or you will be kept waiting forever. If you were to volunteer to take Fortuné II into the square for his morning walk, you could watch for Talleyrand while the dog is about his affairs." And she gave a quick description of the famous minister.

As she did, Aurélie hung up her towel and turned around. She had not taken off the necklace. It glittered above the neck of her nightdress, and Hortense paused, then looked closely. "Where did you get that? It looks very old. You already have a suitor?"

Aurélie flushed and said with dignity, "I do not seek a husband."

Hortense laughed as she flitted away.

Aurélie dressed quickly, then hunted up Agatha Rible, Josephine's personal maid, who was delighted to find a volunteer to help walk the dogs. Fortuné I had been Josephine's favorite of her many adopted strays.

"Where is his ribbon?" the woman said. "Here! Green again. *Pardieu!* How strange life is. During the early days, green meant liberty, but then it was declared the color of aristocrats, and no one dared use it. Then, when Barras ruled France and Madame Tallien and our dear Madame ruled society, I do not remember why, but it must always be a green ribbon for one's dog, as the ladies walked about in their damped muslins. Then that fashion passed, and here we are again, green is fashionable again, and still yet for a different reason. It is the First Consul's favorite color, but the clothes, ah, everyone is respectable, now that life is less uncertain. There." The woman straightened up, regarding the little dog with satisfaction.

Fortuné was small, with silky hair brushed every day. His collar was studded with real gemstones. He wagged his tail tentatively as Aurélie took the ribbon in hand, and then, understanding that he was to be let out of the small room where he was kept out of Bonaparte's way, he trotted happily, ears flopping.

Servants, guards, ministers and secretaries alike smiled as Aurélie and the dog passed.

Aurélie ventured into the enormous Place du Carrousel, which was dotted with the leavings of all the carriage horses of the night before, as well as the horses of the officers going in and out of the Hôtel de Longueville on the opposite side.

The dog sniffed happily at every speck as Aurélie searched among the crowd of military figures. There was no "older man, still quite handsome, dressed perfectly in the old fashioned style, his hair light."

She walked the dog toward the river and along the new quay. She paused at the railing and looked down at the pretty gravel walk lined with flowers and shrubs leading to the colorful bathing machines. The busy washerwomen out on the water called to one another and laughed as they worked.

Aurélie turned back, tugging the dog away from a flock of birds pecking at a pile of garbage. From the crowd came a thin cry, "Aw-ray-LEE!"

She turned. There was Diana Kittredge pelting toward us, one hand pressing her spectacles on her nose, the other keeping her bonnet on.

"Diana?" Aurélie exclaimed as Diana drew up, grinning.

Diana was breathless. "I have been walking up and down for an age, hoping you might come out. I did not dare to inquire." Diana glanced back at the Place du Carrousel, then laughed. "Oh, Aurélie, you look *beautiful*. You have no *conception* how furious Mama is! Serves her out, too. She was so *smug*, you should have heard her, all the way down the road from Dieppe. What happened? I have been *so* very worried!"

"I found a safe passage to Paris, after a time," Aurélie said, with Olympian understatement. She obviously didn't want to upset Diana. "How did you know I was here?"

"Papa took Cassie to the opera last night, as James went to another theater with a party of young gentlemen."

"But you did not go?"

"Mama declared I ought not, as there might be something *warm* in it. So I took great care to read Mary Wollstonecraft instead, though

Mama is not to know. They had the most abominable seats, in fact, they were still standing about in the crowd, unable to reach them, when Napoleon Bonaparte and all his party arrived, and Cassie said you could have knocked them down with a feather when they saw *you.*"

"I did not see them," Aurélie said.

Diana swept on, unhearing. "Oh, it is so very good to see you, and to know that it truly was you, and that you are well. I am so happy." Diana blinked tears away as she tucked a straying lock of brown hair back into her bonnet. Her tightly buttoned spencer jacket looked out of place among the simpler empire-waisted gowns the French wore, and she was flushed both from running and the warm air.

The two girls stared at one another mistily, neither speaking, as if they were so full of possible subjects they couldn't choose which one to begin.

"It is wonderful to see you, too," Aurélie said finally, and blinked away her own tears. "How . . . how do you find Paris?"

I wondered if she had meant to ask about James, and changed her mind, as they stood in the middle of the quay, oblivious to the breakneck pace of carriages, hired chairs, tourists and loungers, the tangle of street-sellers hawking their wares . . . and oblivious to a pair of tall, drifting figures with long black wings that looked like rippling cloaks.

"Strange—beautiful—ugly, all by turns. Oh, Aurélie, to think you were in the box with *him!* Everyone talks about Bonaparte. They do not know whether he is a monster or the greatest man in France. Building going on everywhere by his order, and Providence knows, they need it."

Diana looked around, completely missing the winged beings, who both smiled our way as they passed. "I always heard how beautiful Paris is, but I find much of it sadly shabby," Diana said, as chill permeated me, soft and indefinable as vapor. "These buildings remind me of molting birds. All scarred! The chambermaid told me that's where the revolutionaries knocked the fleur-de-lis off, and other noble coats of arms, during the dreadful days when she said the street quite *ran* with blood so it got into the river, and the stink! Only I don't know how it could stink worse than it does now. James said that the older parts of London are quite as bad, but that is neither here nor there. I was most disappointed that I could not find out the important buildings. Everything is changing so much, they all say."

"Which buildings?" Aurélie inquired.

Diana waved her arms. "The ones where the important women, the ones cognizant of making history, stood up. I know about the Champs de Mars, where everyone laid down their titles, but that place was made horrid by a massacre. Where exactly did Olympe de Gouges deliver her Declaration of the Rights of Woman and the Female Citizen? Where did Madame Roland work on the treasury? No one can tell me. No one seems to want to talk about them at all. At least tell me you have seen their ghosts?"

Aurélie said, "I am sorry, Diana. I have not seen any ghosts. I only see my duppy."

"There are ghosts all over," I said. "I can't say for certain who they are."

Aurélie repeated my words.

"Oh, I seem doomed never to see anything." Diana let out a sharp sigh. "I shall *not* repine. It is enough to know they are there." She clapped her hands to the sides of her bonnet. "Why have my wits flown away? I have more to tell you, and I must do it before Mama *sweeps* us back to England. She desires our departure *today*, if she can contrive it."

"Why?"

Diana grinned. "That is the best part, and you have no *notion* how much I hoped to see you—and it would really be you—so I could tell you. Because I don't know how I would get a letter to you else, without Mama seeing it, and then, would they even deliver to Paris? Anyway, it was at breakfast this morning. The English legate's lady has relations also staying at the Hotel Penthievre, and so we English all ate together, or I assure you we should not have had such fine company."

Diana made a face, as from the Garden of the Tuileries drifted tall, winged figures. They were joined in their slow motion drift by a flock of them from the Place de la Revolution.

"I have not met any English ladies," Aurélie said.

"But Lady Whitworth knows of *you*. At least, she turned to Mama, after they were talking of the opera. Some gentleman was saying that you were said to be the most beautiful of the new ladies-in-waiting, and then the legate's wife said, 'She is the daughter of a Portuguese marquis, I am told. Mrs. Kittredge, is this not the same name I remember your sister Bouldeston inquiring about at the Admiralty? If so, you have managed to do very well by her.' Mama was near to choking!" Diana laughed.

Aurélie blushed, looking down.

"But don't you *see*, Aurélie? Mama could not slander you without exposing herself, after that! So she could only say something about how she believed that you were related to the Taschers of Martinique. You know, 'believed,' like she didn't believe it at all. I suspect Lady Whitworth does not like Aunt Bouldeston, because her tone was like *that*, you know, a smile, but cutting, when she said, 'Whatever else they say about Josephine Bonaparte—and they say plenty, as you no doubt have heard—she is apparently generous to her ladies. With those looks, even with the touch of the tar brush, which I understand is to be expected of Spaniards, that girl could catch herself a general or a duke at the least. I hope you may do as well for *your* girls.'"

"Oh, Diana."

"Yes, that about the tar brush was nasty, but for all of me, that fling about 'your girls' was a capital hit! Though I felt a little sorry for Cassie, who had already endured a scolding for making eyes at the legate's secretary whose family is nothing. I am so very glad I know whom I shall marry."

Diana bent down to ruffle the dog's fur, still talking. "Afterward, when we were alone, Mama raged and stamped, and Papa said it was her own fault. James agreed! Cassie and I fled, but I heard Mama shrieking that she would leave this benighted city today, if it was the last thing she did, and he must order a carriage, and she would pay our respects to the proper people and make our excuses."

"I will never understand why she hated me so much."

"Papa said that Mama fears the rules about rank and place will change. We will wake up one day, and it will be the Revolution, only in

England. Mama is afraid of losing everything she has." Diana bent once again to pet Fortuné. "But I don't think I can forgive her for being hateful. What a pretty little dog. Yours?"

"Madame Josephine's."

My attention was divided between the girls and the winged beings, who prowled around us in a circle of soft, floating shadow.

"Fancy! I shall have to tell Cassie to tell Lucretia in her letter that I petted Madame Bonaparte's dog. It will put Cassie into a good humor again. Aurélie, I had better go, for I have been walking about this age, and I do not want Mama raving at *me* next. But I wanted to tell you that, if I could, and to say, after I turn eighteen, do write to me, care of Charles Kittredge, who is now serving as curate at the parsonage in Winkton Grange, in Yorkshire's East Riding. I mean, you could write to him now, of course, and he would save the letters, but remember that Mama reads all *our* letters. So he could not send me anything from you."

"I understand," Aurélie said, tearing up again.

Diana took a short, decisive breath. "I didn't tell anyone this, even you, for it wasn't entirely my secret to tell, but as soon as I turn eighteen, Cousin Charles and I have made a pact to marry, even if I have to run away. I quite like the idea of helping the poor, if that is where he is to remain. We are agreed that we would not like to spend our lives looking across the breakfast table at someone you haven't a particle of affection for, just because he, or she, is rich. For you know, my aunt and uncle expect him to marry an heiress, at least, if he must be a clergyman. As for me, no rich man would have me, Mama says. But I don't care a fig!"

"I agree," Aurélie said fervently, and the two girls regarded one another with teary smiles. Diana was nothing out of the ordinary, with her countrified clothes and her spectacles, but Aurélie's voice carried the tremor of conviction when she said, "To me you are beautiful, as beautiful as my Tante Mimba, who was the most beautiful woman I ever knew."

"Even more beautiful than Josephine?"

"Even so. Though she is beautiful, too."

Diana laughed heartily, then wiped her eyes on her gloved hand. It came away with smudges from the ubiquitous chimney smoke, which she tried to scrub off against her skirt. "Oh bother," she muttered, then sighed. "Parsonage, Winkton Grange, Yorkshire. *Remember*, Aurélie! And I hope you *do* marry a general, if he is kind as well as brilliant."

Aurélie was laughing and crying as she shook her head. They hugged one another, then Diana ran off along the riverside to return to her hotel, brushing right past two of the winged things as she dodged a fast-moving cabriolet pulled by two horses.

"Let's get away," I said.

"What is it?" Aurélie whispered.

"I take it you do not see these tall people with the black cloaks? Which I think are wings."

"Wings? Oh, I missed Talleyrand—see there."

Aurélie pointed to the main entrance to the Tuileries, where a tall, well-dressed gentleman was at that moment being let inside by attentive footmen. She sighed, then said, "What wings?"

"Since you don't see them, I'll wait until I either see more, or know more," I said. "I don't know if they're bad or good, but they certainly are persistent."

"I will have to come out again tomorrow," Aurélie replied, yawning. "Oh, how can they keep such hours?"

TWENTY-FIVE

A URÉLIE HAD TAKEN A GREAT DEAL of time over her letter to her mother, writing and then destroying half a quire of expensive paper until she finally settled on short and general. She talked out loud to me the entire time she was writing, finally deciding that until she had an address, and a reasonably safe way to send the letter, generalities were best, save a single line that she had never seen any of her mother's letters. She did not know how many eyes would be seeing what she wrote before it reached Jamaica, so she gave no details beyond that.

It took her several days to meet Talleyrand. I suspect it worked only because he was curious about the pretty girl and he knew whose dog she walked. When she saw his carriage, she started toward it, her manner determined. His face was visible behind the glass as he glanced out, saw her, and rapped on the roof of his carriage, which pulled up near where Aurélie stood.

She peered in at the window, saw the weary, lined face, and her lips parted.

"Did you wish to speak, Mademoiselle?"

"Sir, Madame Hortense tells me that you are the one to ask: Could you get a letter to my mother? I left her in Jamaica nearly seven years ago."

Talleyrand lifted his brows. "Jamaica? Why have you not addressed your concern to the English legation?"

Aurélie blushed. "I do not know anyone there. And Madame Hortense said that you can do anything."

He laughed softly. "Ah, if only that were true! But my abilities, such as they are, can probably compass a letter to your mother. I will be speaking later today to the English concerning the arrival of their ambassador. Surely one of the secretaries can be obliged to include your letter in the diplomatic pouch." And he held out his hand.

Aurélie surrendered the now-wrinkled, sealed paper that she had been carrying for days. On the outside she had written *Anne Kittredge, daughter of James Kittredge, deceased, at Kittredge Plantation, Jamaica.* She had been afraid to put anything about 'Mascarenhas' on it after the way Aunt Kittredge had reacted.

"And that is that," she said to me as she hurried away to Josephine's suite. "He was very nice, but oh, very daunting!"

But she was not done with Talleyrand. A few days later, Napoleon held a select dinner and a private ball at the Tuileries, at which he told everyone how pleased France would be that he had given orders to commence building a new theater, smaller than the Théâtre des Arts, which still had revolutionary connotations. He was thinking of changing its name.

The assembly cheered, of course, and then he signaled for the dancing to begin.

Talleyrand sat at one end of the long table in the Gallery of Diana, Aurélie at the far end, seated next to a young general whose fate I was glad I couldn't remember. When they weren't playing music, Josephine's lesser ladies were expected to smile, look pretty, and dance with all the military men.

There was no conversation between the greats and those at the far end, but Talleyrand must have spotted her, because late in the evening, after Aurélie was dismissed to the salon to perform, a messenger appeared and discreetly whispered to Aurélie that she was summoned.

With him he brought another musician, who slid onto the bench in Aurélie's place.

She looked nonplussed and a little frightened as lightning flared in the long windows.

Aurélie found herself before Talleyrand, who was ensconced deep in an armchair beside a fire, wine glinting with ruby highlights in a crystal glass at his side.

On the other side of the room, in a shadowy corner, a tall, severe-faced man played piquet with a burly fellow in a plain coat, watched by a third.

"Come hither," Talleyrand said, beckoning to Aurélie. "Do sit down. You needn't stand. I have no royal aspirations." He pointed to a footstool beside his chair.

Aurélie perched somewhat nervously and rubbed her hands up her arms. They were covered with goose flesh, though she was scarcely five paces from a roaring fire.

"One of my aides who is more sensitive than most finds you interesting," he said in English.

Aurélie's hand stole toward her collarbones, where the necklace lay under the neck of her gown. Then she jerked her hands down to her lap.

Talleyrand appeared to notice nothing amiss, though his gaze was steady and acute. "Mine own interest is inspired by the appearance of so young a lady coupled with mention of Jamaica, I must confess. What is your story, Mademoiselle?"

"It is very boring, sir," she replied. "There was much fighting there, and so my mother sent me to relations in England. They came over to France because of the Peace, and . . . here I am."

"And here you are. Yet you did not apply to Lord Whitworth's office. He will be officially introduced as ambassador very soon, did you know that? Nor did these relations, on your behalf. A Mister Kittredge and his family, I apprehend? They departed Paris five days ago. Perhaps they are now arriving at Calais. Yet, as we established, here you are."

"I am also related to Madame Bonaparte, though more distantly," Aurélie said, as I looked beyond her into the gloom. The chill deepened.

"And so you chose to seek your fortune through Madame? It was a shrewd move for one so young. Especially if one considers your having calculated this move from the relative distance of England, where news about our French progress makes, ah, none-too-savory reading in the daily newspapers, I collect."

Aurélie blushed. "In truth, my aunt did not want me," she said in a low voice.

"And why should a blood relation take against so very beautiful and engaging a young lady?"

I touched Aurélie's hand. "Tell him as little as possible," I whispered, though even the great Talleyrand could not hear me.

Aurélie sighed. "I think, perhaps, in part, my dark skin, and, well, she did not like my French relations."

"I see I tread upon delicate ground here. My apologies," Talleyrand said, as the shadows shifted in that far corner where the men played piquet. "My questions are prompted by the most idle curiosity on my part, merely to pass the time. In truth, the current topic of conversation among those who, like me, choose not to dance, interests me little. I care not whether the dragoons' green uniforms ought to be sky-blue or stay green though it conflicts with the dark of the *chasseurs à cheval*. I understand that clothes make the man to a certain extent—I sympathize, I really do, and I am convinced that a well-uniformed squadron is intimidating as well as full of pride—but I wonder if our friends understand that the most gallant uniform will not stop a bullet? Ah, do not heed the ruminations of an old man. Instead, in payment for my intrusive nature, and because we converse to pass an hour, I will grant you leave to ask me any question you wish."

Aurélie pursed her lips, then said softly, "Can you tell me the importance of Praga?"

Talleyrand sat up a little and regarded her with his head slightly tipped, as though to bring her into focus. He flicked a look at his waiting manservant, who went away, closing the door soundlessly. Then he said, "A very unexpected question. And yet it comes, ah, shall we say, not as a complete surprise."

"Why is that?" she asked. The shadows had stilled, and I could make out the edges of those figures, tall, slender, the outline of wings. Were there really three on a side, or were those shadows? The whole was indistinct, as if seen through smoke.

"You will tell me," Talleyrand drawled, "but after I elucidate. Praga is a section of Warsaw, which sustained a particularly sanguinary battle in seventeen ninety-four—three years, you must understand, after Poland's remarkable and entirely bloodless revolution. So far, Poland is the only polity of significance to achieve such a thing, but alas, not all its nobles accepted the new constitution, benign as it was. The disaffected invited Catherine of Russia to send a force in, ostensibly to restore the ancient rights of the noble class. The result is that the state of Poland has effectively vanished, divided between Russia, Austria, and Prussia."

The door opened, and the servant reappeared with Jaska.

Once again Jaska was beautifully dressed, his face inscrutable when he saw the two by the fireside. He never glanced at the card players or the numerous shadows gathered around them.

At first, Aurélie didn't see him, and I dared not distract her. I had the weirdest feeling that Talleyrand might see me or sense me, though from anything I'd ever read he had no interest in magic or the occult. He had thrown off his priestly vows as soon as he could, during the Revolution. But he, unlike Fouché, had never advocated the destruction of churches or the wholesale slaughter of nuns and priests.

"Ah, now I understand, I think," Aurélie exclaimed in French.

"Understand what, child?" Talleyrand asked, switching back to that language.

"Why the mention of Praga should be so hurtful to some people," she said.

The corner behind the card players had become so dark the walls seemed to vanish and the room to open into a vast, cold space. The result left me with a weirdly vertiginous sense.

"That would depend upon the people, do you not think?" Talleyrand responded. "The Russians, I am certain, consider it a glorious triumph.

But is that not the nature of glory, that it is seen so only by the victor? Do we see glory in loss? Ah, you will no doubt retort on me with Thermopylae. Perhaps Praga will serve as a rallying cry for the Poles, as Thermopylae did for the Spartans. What say you?" He lifted his head and addressed Jaska.

"I say that the Poles only seek to reestablish their borders and their constitution," Jaska said. "But the First Consul is well aware of our wishes, as we make known when he honors us with an audience. There is no secret about that. Mademoiselle. We meet again, it seems, not by accident." He bowed, his glance toward Talleyrand wary.

Aurélie shot to her feet, curtseyed belatedly, and said, "I do not know if I should be glad to see you again or not."

"Monsieur Dsaret, I gather, is 'some people'?" Talleyrand asked.

Aurélie blushed, but said steadily, "We met on the road to Paris. We three played music together."

"Three? You two and . . . the mysterious courier who was last seen riding to Berville to visit General Kosciusko?"

"Mord is the finest violinist I have ever heard," Aurélie exclaimed with fervor.

"Mord? Is this his name? How refreshingly brief. I trust Monsieur Mord will favor us with a concerto on his return to Paris." Talleyrand looked pointedly at Jaska. "Thank you, Monsieur. We will not keep you from enjoying the festivities."

Jaska said with a slight lift to his voice, almost a challenge, "I will escort Mademoiselle back to the salon, where I believe she is expected to play to us."

Talleyrand smiled and lifted his hand in benediction. "I trust we shall meet again, Mademoiselle."

Aurélie glanced from one to the other, curtseyed to Talleyrand, then went to the door. It was not quite shut when Talleyrand said, "Do you see, Fouché? A light hand is always best in these matters . . ."

Click. The door closed.

Fouché! The Butcher of Lyon, who had more than 1,900 citizens slaughtered, probably the most sinister figure of the past fifteen years of violence. There were parts of history that I wish I could scrub from my brain, and he lay behind several of them.

Jaska looked down at Aurélie and murmured, *"Putat sunt explor-atores."*

She translated softly as they walked away, " 'He thinks we are . . .?' "

"Spies." He regarded her with cool politesse. "You would be wise to be circumspect for a time."

He was silent until they reached the salon. Voices rose and fell above the clarinet and flute playing a Haydn duet. She put her hand out, and he stilled. "I am so very sorry."

"I was already being watched," he said, with a brief, rueful smile. "I believe that the gentleman was honoring me with a warning."

"I am sorry about Praga," she said. "I think I understand a little, what you were trying to tell me that day."

He passed a hand over his face, then dropped it. "I was luckier than most. I lived and only came away with a shattered knee." He brushed his hand against the stiff leg.

"No one is lucky with such memories," she whispered, "or dreams. I know one is grateful to be alive, but gratitude can be a burden, too." She curtseyed again and slipped inside before he could respond.

Alone later in her room, she touched the mirror so she could see me before exclaiming in a choked whisper, "He thinks I am a spy! Monsieur Talleyrand was so very nice to me, yet he thinks I am a *spy*."

"He thought you were a spy," I said. "I don't think he still does, or he would have had the Kittredges arrested. I agree with Jaska, that he was issuing a warning."

"How?" she asked. "To whom?"

"To you both. Talleyrand mentioned the Kittredges to let you know that they were not arrested. That means either he doesn't suspect you, or he does, but there are *mouchards* watching you. He was also warning Jaska because he was watching how the two of you interacted when Jaska was brought by the messenger."

Aurélie said, "But he did not have him arrested."

"That's because he might not believe that Jaska is an enemy spy. There are all kinds of spies. As for the *mouchards*, they not only listen to French people, but they also spy on all the foreigners touring through France right now."

"Oh, Duppy Kim, I would feel terrible if by my actions I got Mord arrested."

"If Jaska isn't sending a message to him right now—or going himself—then I'm a . . . well, never mind, but that reminds me. Aurélie, I saw more of those winged beings in that room. There were so many of them I couldn't see faces, just shifting shadows. I got the feeling there were hundreds of them."

"But that room was so small." She ran her hands up her arms. "And so very cold. I could not feel the fire at all, yet there it was, almost in reach."

"I think the cold was from those winged people."

"I thought angels were made of fire and light," she said.

"I doubt that they're angels," I said and then shrugged. "But then I don't know anything about angels."

Aurélie accepted this and turned around. "I'm so glad that you are still a secret, except for Hortense and Madame. I'll be more careful when I talk to you. Let the *mouchards* spy on me! They will get a fine concert for their pains. I will be a very good lady-in-waiting until I hear back from my mother, and she tells me how to get home."

Or I get you to Dobrenica, I thought. Which at least had to be safer than Paris.

Then I remembered Xanpia's warning about its destruction.

Alec! I yelled, but not so Aurélie could hear. I was getting scared that nobody would hear me ever again.

TWENTY-SIX

HE REST OF THAT YEAR SPED BY FOR AURÉLIE, as she bounced between Malmaison, the Tuileries, and Saint-Cloud, so it sped for me, too, but with a relentless escalation of emotional tension. I had only to see Napoleon kiss Josephine or a romantic play by the Comédie-Française, to hit me with the thought of Alec still sitting at my bedside—which reminded me of Xanpia's warning. And then I'd fret about how to act when I had no power to act. I couldn't even pick up a feather, much less a sword!

Part of the pressure was my awareness of the inexorable unfolding of history. My knowledge of this period, incomplete as it was, could only be a powder keg. I didn't intend to let anyone sit on it but me.

At first I was relieved when events unfolded as I remembered: in the summer Bonaparte was elected Consul for life; at the same time, he became infatuated with the fifteen-year-old actress Mademoiselle George, who I knew would go on to fame and fortune, a collector of crowned lovers. Then the birth of Hortense's first child.

Because the number of newspapers went from over a dozen to basically just the *Moniteur*, which was all Bonaparte all the time, actual news was difficult to come by. All Aurélie heard among Josephine's ladies was rumor and, of course, innuendo when Napoleon's sisters were feeling extra mean toward the woman they considered an interloper.

I knew what was coming.

"Now we have this Madame Campan," Aurélie told me early in March, after the caravan of coaches rattled back to Saint-Cloud. There never seemed to be any reason for the various shifts between the palaces; only Napoleon's whim. When he was with us, everyone moved fast. When he sent Josephine, there was a more leisurely pace.

Aurélie was tired, not only from the all-nighters but also from lack of sleep due to worsening dreams, and the tediousness of the increasingly elaborate ritual. "I understand Madame Campan was once a lady-in-waiting to Marie Antoinette, but oh, it is so boring. She tells us where to stand, how deep to curtsey, how many steps forward and backward. Nobody can remember all the rules, and—" She slipped into English, "—the First Consul's sisters squabble so about who is to go first, and who last."

I thought, *That's only going to get worse, especially after they start collecting crowns.*

"Imagine walking backward! But apparently the sky will fall if we turn our back on the first consul or Madame Jos—Bonaparte. We cannot presume to address her as Madame Josephine anymore, though that is what she asked us to call her. The sad thing is, I can see she doesn't like any of these changes. The more like a royal court we become, the more afraid she is."

"You didn't sleep well last night. You kept tossing and muttering."

"Another of those dreams." She shook her head. "If only I recognized people or events, I would take some comfort. But these are always of strangers, in strange places. Last night," another fierce yawn, "the people were brown, like me, but their eyes were round, their hair black but very straight. Many wore marks of red here." She touched the middle of her forehead. "*Tilaka.* Their clothes were very beautiful, somewhat like the toga of the Roman and yet not. Bright colors, and oh, the palaces . . ." Her hands swooped, shaping the distinctive archways and domes of Akbari architecture early in the Mughal period.

"India?" I asked, wondering how she could dream about a place I knew she had never visited.

"I know not." She yawned so hard her eyes watered. "Even the language is strange, yet I always know what the words mean. *Tilaka.*" She made as if scooping something with her forefinger, then touched her forehead. "*Bindi*, for a wedding. But there was fighting, ghosts and sky chariots and things with eyes like fire."

"Mademoiselle! It is time," came a call from the outer room, and Marie raced in to hurry Aurélie along.

As Aurélie carefully walked downstairs in her new gown (all the ladies were dressed in green and white velvet with gold trim for this fete) I thought about Nero's bread and circuses, and wondered if he, too, had been trying to impose legitimacy, or at least order, from the top down.

Someday I was going to have to study Roman history, I thought uneasily, as we entered the long gallery, and there were the winged beings. They floated like vapor, only shadowy, I noted as I watched them cluster around Napoleon. The only other person who attracted so many was Fouché. When we showed up, however, they would widen their circle and float around us, the wings rising and falling with dreamy rhythm.

Once in a while a couple of them glided close. I recognized them—the androgynous creature from that night at the opera, with the long night-black hair; and a tall male with half-shut sleepy eyes of so light a gray they looked silver, his hair the color of pewter. His smile reminded me of Tony at his most mocking and untrustworthy. Yet it was not without humor, as if he was very well aware of my distrust, and he would be patient. There was no anger, no affront.

Why were there so many around Napoleon and Fouché? The two seemed completely oblivious.

Aurélie took her place in the grand *salle*. Today she was not playing music, she was there to dance with the zillions of military guys swarming around; to smile and add beauty to the backdrop.

The atmosphere was sharp with anticipation. Though arriving in state with her four chief ladies-in-waiting, it was Josephine who drew the eye. A slender, graceful figure in a deceptively simple gown of pure white, ornamented only by the thin band of lamé trim around the hem, the gold band binding the high waist, the black cameo ornaments holding together the filmy cap sleeves. Around her neck she wore a serpent necklace, and her hair spilled out of a gold band that bound it up Greek-style. The effect so charmed Napoleon that he rushed forward impulsively and led her to the mirror. He admired her from all angles as he pressed kisses on her.

She flushed and made the courtly beckon that Madame Campan had taught her. Napoleon kissed her again as the officers raised their swords with a scraping and ring of metal. They shouted in approval, Napoleon beamed with equal approval, then he signaled imperiously.

The musicians, instruments poised for the past fifteen minutes, launched into the first piece. The wives of the officers and the titled ladies were led out first for the quadrille and gavotte, and then the waltz, which had been introduced in the Year Six—1798—at a ball Talleyrand had given for Josephine. It was already popular, though the visiting English would find it scandalous, and it would be nearly another ten years before it was introduced in London by ladies of rank sufficient enough to provide an excuse for adopting this dangerously enticing dance.

Aurélie had her usual swarm of partners, and as she twirled around the ballroom floor, I got a chance to look around the room. Not only were there more of those winged beings than I had ever seen, but the officers seemed rowdier, more intense.

I witnessed at least three incidences of *sabrage*. Opening a champagne bottle with a sabre may have been swashbuckling, but it was definitely not courtly behavior. Yet Napoleon did nothing to halt them, even when a bottle broke all over the newly laid parquet. His treasured officers in their sexy uniforms were not savages in his eyes. That opprobrium was reserved for the civilians who criticized him.

Raucous behavior was not limited to the wild Hussars, with their mustachios and *cadenettes*. One of the younger generals whipped out his sabre and expertly snapped the neck of a bottle of champagne, causing a roar of approval as he filled the champagne glasses held up to him. He poured with an air, sabre still gripped in the other hand.

As dance after dance formed its patterns then dissolved to form another, I caught snatches of speech—"Malta," "England"—and nasty adjectives coupled to "Whitworth." The British ambassador had been feted to his face but sneered at behind his back. If history stayed true, he was shortly to get the sneers up close and personal, from Napoleon himself in one of his soon-to-be famous rants.

It was very late when a uniform different from all the others emerged from the relaxed, half-drunk crowd and approached Aurélie.

It was Jaska.

The room was filled with gaudy uniforms. But for those who knew lapels, facings, ribbons, and orders, there was an especial resonance in the challenge, the poignancy, of his wearing the dress of Poland's National Cavalry: the crimson square-topped *czapka*, a tailored blue jacket with gold epaulettes and red lapels, and a white cross belt. His trousers were red to match the lapels, with six buttons pulling the pants legs tight to the ankle over his cavalry boots with their jutting spurs. At his left hung his curved sabre, and in his right hand he carried a tasseled walking stick, which he used to ease his limp.

The Polish National Cavalry had been disbanded after Poland was partitioned, but the reputation of the Polish soldiery was evidenced in the way the officers parted with respect as he walked to Aurélie. Then he made a short bow, epaulettes glittering in the light of a zillion candles.

"Mademoiselle, I have been entrusted with a letter to deliver into your hands. It was passed to the French fleet by the British in November."

"November?" she asked, as she took the letter. Then she looked down, and said, "Oh."

It had taken that long for the letter to make its way to Paris, and thence to Fouché's *mouchards* to read before being resealed. She looked up again. "I have so many questions."

"Those are perhaps better put to the foreign office," he said kindly. Then, his faint smile vanishing, "We have almost four thousand families to apprise of the deaths of the Polish soldiers sent to the islands. I am one of those honored with this task." He bowed again.

"Thank you," she said, rising to curtsey deeply. "Farewell."

He bowed again. She watched him until he vanished in the crowd, then she clutched the letter to her heart, her eyes closed.

The nearest ladies began whispering, "Open it!" "Read it!" "Oh, Mademoiselle Prude hath a secret lover!"

Joseph Bonaparte, not far off, was looking her way, his gaze speculative. But Joseph's wife Julie, who alone of the Bonaparte family was never unkind to Josephine (or to anyone), sat down next to Aurélie in a rustle of silk. "You go read your letter in privacy, little one. If Madame Bonaparte looks for you, I will tell her I sent you away. I know she will understand. Then wash your face and come back and smile, for remember: You are alive even if your lover was snatched up to Heaven. There are many here who would rejoice in the chance to take his place." She smiled and patted Aurélie's hand.

Aurélie managed a curtsey and thanks, then fled down the halls, past the rigid Consular Guards, and upstairs, away from the brilliantly lit state rooms. She ducked into Josephine's pretty anteroom, which had a fire roaring and lamps lit, sank down onto the hearth, ignoring her velvet gown, and tore the crumpled, water-stained letter open.

Anne's handwriting was a headlong dash, complete to the old-fashioned *f* for *s*, even when she wrote in badly spelled, mostly phonetic French, interspersed with equally idiosyncratic English.

My very dear Daughter:

We lost hope of ever receiving a letter, but as my Cousin Kittredge writ yearly for three years, to assure us you were happy and busy, we Councell'd Ourselves to be Content with having achiev'd our Primry Resolve. After that, Events kept us from seeing letters at all for a vast deal of Time.

I am seated here in a side-chamber at Gov't House, with borrowed Pen and Ink, as I dare not wait upon my own Convenience, but must seize this Opportunity, for the diplomatic pouch goes out on the tide.

The secretary who is to carry it is at this moment at sup, and kindly said he would include my letter if I am expeditious.

We understand that there is Peace between our two Nations, England and France, but you would not know that for the Fighting we have seen in both Jamaica and St-Domingue, which is now in changing of Name to Hayti, at least at the West end. Heaven only knows if anyone, white or black, will survive to speak old Name or New.

I am confound'd to know what to write. It is not for want of words. Instead, it is for their very Prolixity. You will have better News than we get, for the papers from London are at least two months out of date before we see them, and the French even longer. Instead, I will confine myself to news of those you know.

She went on to name people in Aurélie's life. The list of those who'd died, been wounded, or nobody had word of was depressingly long.

At the end, Anne wrote:

It is our way of thinking that this Island does not want our kind, black or white, for we are Interlopers here, even though many were constrain'd against their Will. But the Land does its best to rid itself of us all by Pestilence, Earthquake, Hurricane, and Drought. And that is beside the monstrous effect of Warfare.

We think of sailing for the Colony at New Orleans, which is said to be salubrious and peaceful. But we stay'd because of Nanny, who would not come off her mountain, in part because of you.

Here is the Particular article of the business. Your Aunt Kittredge writ again, after the long Silence, almost the same time you did to say that you had run off to France in Consequence of the Peace, taking your dowry with you against their Better Judgment. Yet the Secretary here informs me that she hath occasion'd, through her sister's Connection to the First Lord of the Admiralty, Inquiries into me and my Marriage Lines, without troubling to write to me directly. There seems a vast deal here unexplain'd.

Nanny will not leave Accompong until she knows you have listen'd to your good guide. She instructed me to write that, and only that. You ask if you should come to us, but I put it to you most reluctantly that it is nigh impossible, given the state of Affairs here, and our not knowing if we are to take ship for the colony in the New World. Do what Nanny says, and know that our love and Prayers go with you.

(signed) Anne Kittredge de Mascarenhas, your loving Mother

Aurélie read it through twice, then got up and flitted to one of the many mirrors Josephine had in her rooms. When she could see me, she said, "It appears to me she expected it to be read by others."

"I believe so, too," I said, thinking, *It would help if you gave me some guidance here, Nanny Hiasinte, if you are listening.*

"The part that puzzles me is Nanny—" Women's voices echoed down the marble hall. Aurélie glanced at the windows. "Dawn is not far off. I must not be found here."

But she had only taken a few steps in the other direction (the rooms being laid out in strings, with doors at either side) when one voice rose. It was Agatha Rible, Josephine's chief maid. "Have you seen Mademoiselle de Mascarenhas?"

"I am here," Aurélie called, as she stuffed the letter down the front of her gown.

In came Josephine, tears dripping down her wan cheeks. She looked back and said, "To bed—all of you. It is late. Get some sleep." To Agatha, who stood inside the doorway, hands pressed against one another, she said in a tender tone, "Please, my dear Agatha, brew me an infusion of orange leaves. My head aches so."

Agatha scurried away, her steps noiseless, and Josephine beckoned Aurélie into her bedchamber, an enormous room with a canopied bed.

Josephine rushed around the chamber in a frenzy, blowing out all the candles so that it was only lit by the fire, reducing the light to a dim, ruddy glow that cast gigantic shadows on the velvet canopy.

She dropped onto the bed and pressed her hands to her forehead. "Why do the Bonapartes so enjoy being cruel?" She dropped her hands. "I thought that marrying Hortense to one of them would please them— that Bonaparte would adopt darling little Napoleon-Charles—but nothing I do is right. Nothing. Hortense once said that even if I could become pregnant, they would only spread lies about the father."

Aurélie wisely stayed silent.

Josephine turned her head on the pillow, her dark eyes reflecting the flames as she regarded Aurélie. "I know Bonaparte is going to claim the crown of France. All the changes, the court etiquette when once we were so free. He wants to be called Napoleon, when he has been Bonaparte these ten years. I went to his chamber myself, the other night. Before we married, I could sit on his lap, and wind my fingers in his hair, and talk to him like a little girl—he liked that. He would give me anything I wanted. I asked him to give up the idea of a crown, and he only smiled, and nodded, and I knew I had lost."

She squeezed her eyes closed. Tears gathered and tracked down her cheeks. "I am so afraid, Aurélie. Madame Fortuna swore to me on her mother's grave that my life would be long and illustrious if I followed her instructions to the letter, and I have. It is the same with Monsieur Herne, the Seer. I pay them well. They instruct me according to what the stars say. Yet I cannot but help remember what Madame Villeneuve said: that I would only wear a crown for a short time. And when I was a girl, the nanny. . . ." Her voice suspended. She gave a sob, then gripped Auré-lie's wrist. "You must do something for me, Aurélie. Say you will do it. I can trust so few—and I cannot send Hortense. You know how she is situated."

"What is it, Madame? If I can, I will do anything for you," Aurélie murmured.

"I know. You are a dear girl. And not a spy—ridiculous. I do not believe anything they say. Listen. Bonaparte will not permit me to ride down to Aix-en-Provence, where Mary Magdalene's grotto is at Sainte-Baume. It is said that women find healing there. He says if I go, the world will know the reason, and laugh at us. But he loves me, I know he does." She sat up. "Joseph. Caroline. The Bonapartes all press him and press him to divorce me. Divorce! It would scarcely take that. Do you know the truth about our marriage?"

Aurélie said, "No, Madame."

Josephine smiled as she pulled a handkerchief from under the pillow and carefully blotted tears from her eyes. "I shall never forget how long he kept me waiting that night! It was a civil ceremony, of course, for in those days, you could only hear Mass in secret. It was at the Hôtel de Mondragon, which was once so very beautiful, but after the Revolution made it over into a district office, it was dismal and filthy. There was a single candle sitting in a tin sconce, throwing light on the marble fireplace and the broken chairs alike."

Her eyes half closed, and she spoke dreamily. "I wore white muslin, of course. And a tri-color sash. My only jewel was a medallion Bonaparte gave me, inscribed 'To Destiny.' Barras was there. He hates me now. He blames me for 18th Brumaire, though I . . . but we were friends then, and he was to be witness. But Bonaparte was so late! The registrar went off to bed, leaving the ceremony to an underling who had no civil powers. The man hobbled about the room on his wooden leg, *thump-tap, thump-tap.* Then Bonaparte came at last, and oh, my dear, I lied about my age, and he lied about his, and even his address was false, for he listed it as the town hall, though at that time he was living in the rue des Capucines. Barras had gone by then, and all we had was his aide to witness, but he was underage. And later that night, my darling little Fortuné—the first one—bit Bonaparte, oh, so jealous, it was like an omen, I sometimes think!"

She fluttered a hand through the air. "La! I stray from my point. This marriage certificate, full of lies, issued under a government no longer existing, could be so easily set aside even if he were not First Consul. Ffft! Like blowing out a candle. And yet he doesn't. Is that not evidence that he loves me still?"

"I believe he does, Madame," Aurélie said. "Did he not kiss you and admire you before everybody tonight?"

"Yes." Josephine's smile vanished. "But *they* say it's because he is dallying with yet a new actress. I can scarcely blame these women, he is so fascinating. Georgina is vastly younger even than you, a pretty girl, so full of life."

She sat up restlessly. "Aurélie, what he wants is an heir. My womb was injured beyond the repair of the best physicians. It happened when a balcony fell at Plombières that summer, in the Year Six. Did Hortense tell you what her girl said about miraculous cures?"

"I have not spoken to Madame Hortense but a handful of words this month," Aurélie said.

"You know it is due to the grippe," Josephine said. "It has been exceptionally virulent this winter, and she is so afraid for the child. She scarcely wants to poke her head out their door. And then she is positively surrounded by spies. Her own husband, it is said, the worst of them. Louis is so glum and so strange! But it is useless to repine. She reminded me that you speak regularly to a spirit. Please, Aurélie. Will you consult this ghost for me? We are alone. Not even Agatha is here. Dear Agatha, who is a good Catholic, does not like the consultation of spirits. I will be a good anything, as long as they can help me."

Aurélie said to the air, "Duppy Kim, will you help Madame?"

The safest thing was to keep silent, partly because I knew what was coming, and because my own name had not come down through history as one of Josephine's many seers. I wanted to give her something to hang onto because I didn't want to see her suffer, but I did not dare be too specific. "Tell her . . ." I began.

Aurélie started across the room to the framed mirror.

Josephine got up and followed. "Is she *here?*" She looked around wildly.

Aurélie laid her hand to the mirror. "There," she said, pointing at me with her free hand. "But so far, it seems only I can see her."

"Kim, a very odd name," Josephine said. "Was she a slave? I recollect they had some very odd names."

"I do not know."

"Give her this message," I said, avoiding the question about my identity. "Tell her that I know this to be truth: that whatever happens, Napoleon Bonaparte will always love her, to the end of his life. Tell her that when he dies, it is her name that will be on his lips. Tell her it is true—tell her *it is written*. But that is all I will say."

No need to add that it was written in my history books.

Aurélie related my words exactly as spoken. Josephine let out a long sigh, then said, "Will he divorce me, Kim Duppy?"

I remained silent. Let her have a few years of relative happiness before the Austrian princess is brought to Paris to replace her.

"I do not hear her," Aurélie admitted.

Josephine sighed. "Aren't they always like that? They speak, then they disappear most inconveniently. But Bonaparte loves me. He will always love me. That gives me hope. I can endure anything, if I have hope."

She peered into the mirror, touched the soft lines at her chin, then turned away. "I know what *he* wants more than anything is a son. Hortense told me that her maid Marie-Alexandrine told her of a cousin who lives in a small convent in Vienna, who in secret practices magic. Marie-Alexandrine promised they care nothing for political divisions. Aurélie, will you go to them and ask? I will give them anything, *anything*, if they can tell me how to conceive a child. I am not yet too old—not if we act at once."

Aurélie drew in a breath, and said, "I will."

"Bless you! I knew you were as loyal as you are discreet. Oh, I hear Agatha. Say nothing! In the inner chamber, there, you will find a *rouleau* of the old *louis d'or*. Everyone accepts gold! That ought to get you there and back. But before you leave, you must request of Bonaparte the necessary papers to get you through the frontier."

"But if he is not to know the reason for my journey? What am I to tell him?"

"That you have family, that you must see to the estate of your betrothed. Everyone witnessed your receiving a letter." Her smile flickered, rueful and sweet, and she made a shooing motion with her hands. "Go!"

Aurélie darted into the inner chamber, picked up a little purse full of coins, then kept on going through the farther chambers.

Aurélie passed through Hortense's bedchamber, which was dark and empty, and lifted her hand to the hall door, when the door was pushed open from the other side by an impatient hand.

Aurélie fell back and stared up at Napoleon.

TWENTY-SEVEN

HE WAS CARRYING A TAPER. At his side walked a man unsettlingly like Jaska, except for the dark wings curving at his shoulders, the quiet step.

Neither Napoleon nor Aurélie saw him.

Napoleon and Aurélie stared at each other for a second—Bonaparte and a pretty girl—and I had a feeling of what would come next as he said, "Mademoiselle, an unexpected encounter."

The winged figure whispered, *He is here for diversion. There is no danger.* I was the only one who heard.

"Madame sent me—sends me—on an errand," Aurélie began disjointedly. "I had a question to put to you, sir."

She can have anything she wants, the shadow wing said conversationally, hands open.

Napoleon gave Aurélie a top to toe scan, and smiled. "What can I offer you, Mademoiselle? Or do I mistake, and it is you who has something to offer to me?"

His tone was playful and insinuating both. She stared, aghast, her eyes enormous.

"I do not know what to say," Aurélie said breathlessly, her pulse ticking in her throat.

Encourage her. What can be easier than shared passion?

I tried to shut out the soft whisper. This could go bad so easily. The most powerful man in France, maybe the world, was in reality a total geek. Napoleon knew what to do on the battlefield because he knew every inch of the terrain, and he'd work out in his head every possible combination of actions and reactions. Socially, unless everyone was on cue, he was hopeless.

"What is this reticence?" Napoleon asked. "Do you have a price?" His tone was still playful, because after all, price was no object to him, and he took a lot of pleasure in knowing it.

What is her ambition?

"Sir, you mistake. I am not that kind."

Napoleon laughed, and I remembered reading that he liked a little show of reluctance. "Every woman has her price."

"Not I."

What is yours?

Go away, I yelled in my mind at Winged Jaska. I did not want distraction.

So be it. I do not understand your objection to love, but I honor it. We will speak again.

This is not love, I began to say, but the candle flickered and streamed. Winged Jaska was gone. "Oh, so high. What is your ambition?" Napoleon asked. "A crown? I could give you a crown. Two!"

"What should I say?" Aurélie asked, her voice high with stress.

He thought she was talking to him, but I knew she addressed me.

Anything but *Yes* was going to be wrong. I had to give her something that would save face for them both. "Remind him that crowns fall off as easily as they are put on. But be polite, because he will not like being turned down."

Aurélie turned her wide gaze to Napoleon. "Crowns," she said earnestly, "I have learned in my short life are dangerous things. I do not want one. I want nothing, sir, only to get by, if I may."

His smile hardened, and he backed up a step. "A good answer," he replied, tone belying the smile. Talleyrand might have been able to coach him in what to say, but he was caught in a potentially ridiculous situation and didn't know his cue.

Aurélie gave him a deep curtsey. "I must go."

"Your question, mademoiselle?"

"Question?" she repeated.

He took a step into the room, as outside, the heavy tread of a guard on duty passed by. "You said you had a question for me?" He was on the edge of irritation now, his lips thinning.

Aurélie made a hasty curtsey and said, "I—I will ask Monsieur Constant, or one of the secretaries, in the morning. I should not trouble you so late, sir." She fled.

When she reached her room she shut the door and stood with her back to it, shivering with reaction. "I *can't* ask him for travel papers," she said. "Not now, not after that. Everyone says he turns very angry if some-one says no."

That was certainly true to everything I'd read. Napoleon held grudges for years, and even as emperor he enjoyed petty revenge.

"I dare not even approach Monsieur Constant," she added, naming Napoleon's chief valet. "I'm afraid he'll ask why Madame Bonaparte sends me, and I promised to secrecy to Madame." She began to pace. "Vienna! I have the money, but a woman alone . . . How can I . . ." She paused, staring down into the fire. "I know whom to go to."

She glanced at the window, which showed the blue of darkness. Without pausing to light a candle, she eased out of her room and flitted down the hall to the state stairway, ghostly gray, the friezes a blur of mythological shapes on the wall. Lights bobbed here and there, small circles of gold as servants picked up stray glasses, bottles, other detritus, and cleaned the parquet.

Aurélie dodged around them and picked up a lamp someone had left on one of the porphyry sideboards set between pilasters. She halted when she reached the small storage chamber off the cold, empty theater, where the costumes and extra musical instruments were kept.

She rummaged through those, careful not to disturb the neat piles, and pulled out a shirt, trousers, waistcoat, coat.

"It is René who must ride with the subaltern carrying the Daily Orders," she said to me as she dressed with feverish speed.

It took a couple of tries, but from among the costumes she found a number of clothes that fit and took them all. Then a man's scarf, gloves, a *chapeau-bras*—Napoleon required the old courtly headgear now, and someone had unearthed hats from Louis XVI's day. Last, a greatcoat.

Back upstairs, she changed swiftly, then flung the rest of the male clothes, her music case, her old pistol, and the sewing kit into her satchel. The purse went into her waistcoat. She pulled the hat low on her head and crept outside, looking everywhere at once until she reached the sweep between the stable and the road, where she stood shivering and hopping up and down to keep warm.

The officer carrying the Orders of the Day was already gone, but she was not the only one waiting. Servants and soldiers alike were constantly sent into Paris on various errands, and she just had to wait for whoever was driving a wagon, or if she were lucky, a cabriolet.

Two officers came out of Napoleon's wing. A cabriolet was standing with a groom at the harnesses. One of the grooms gestured an invitation, and the two young ensigns and Aurélie hopped onto the back to ride as they could fit themselves. Aurélie perched on the sword case.

The ground was iron hard, so even though the road was still being worked on, they zipped along, and the eastern horizon was just beginning to shade from light blue to peach when they emerged from the frost-tipped wooded area of the Bois de Boulogne, and there were the smoky chimneys of Paris, Montmartre rising in the distance, where the day's bread was daily ground.

Finally they reached the snarl of narrow streets and high, narrow houses of the inner *arrondissiments*. The last of the up-all-night stragglers were dispersing in their rumpled finery as, elsewhere, servants and market folk and storekeepers began to stir.

When the cabriolet drew up before the garrison at the Hôtel de

Longueville, Aurélie hopped down. She chose a guard she did not recognize, and with her scarf well pulled up and her hat low, approached him. "I've a message for Baron von Lagerbielke, the Swedish Ambassador."

The guard gave her directions. She walked until she was out of his sight, looked around the Place du Carrousel, then said, " Duppy Kim, you know what I want to do. If it is wrong, tell me now."

"I think it's a very good idea," I said, hiding my frantic enthusiasm. *Yes! Find Jaska!* "But hurry. He might already be gone."

"He could not depart on a moonless night," she said, but she began to walk fast, careful where the grunge in the streets had frozen into oily ice. She crossed the Jardin des Plantes, where already the old women were out, their rolled pastries of flour and honey still steaming hot as they cried, *"Plaisir! Plaisir!"*

Aurélie paused long enough to dig into her waistcoat. She gave an especially ragged old woman a golden *louis*. The woman blinked closely at it, then sighed. "Oh, for the old days. We did not know how good we had it." She kissed the coin before making change in *livres*, half of which Aurélie thrust back at the surprised woman. Then she took her pastry and devoured it as she ran.

The sun had begun slicing milky-thin shafts between houses when she arrived at the impressive house that had probably once belonged to an aristocrat. The pediment showed signs of repair, and the Swedish flag flew.

Aurélie glanced up the stairs at the doorway, her breath clouding. Soberly dressed civilians and gaudy attachés and subalterns, punctuated here and there by a peacocky hussar, were already coming and going, early as it was.

"Message for Monsieur Dsaret," she said over and over, as she elbowed her way into the busy ground floor apartments. Here, young officers in Swedish, Polish, and even Russian uniforms came and went. Most ignored her until someone pointed up the stairs. She stared in dismay at the crowded stairwell, then elbowed her way up, until she stumbled into an antechamber.

Jaska, still in his Polish cavalry uniform, stood talking to a couple of epauletted officers in Swedish blue. They looked at Aurélie, took in her sober civilian garb, and turned away. Then Jaska did a double-take, his eyes wide.

Aurélie said, "I carry a message."

Jaska beckoned curtly, drew her down a narrow hall past a fellow with lots of gold braid chatting with a horse chasseur in green, and into a vast chamber done up in white and gold. The morning light picked up the colors in a mural high on the wall, depicting the martial Greek gods.

"Where are we?" Aurélie asked apprehensively.

"This is the ambassador's office. He is at breakfast. Mademoiselle—"

"I am once again René," she said, with a sad attempt at a smile.

Jaska was clearly as exhausted as she. "Why are you here?" he asked quietly.

"Will you take me with you?" she asked.

He stilled, his expression difficult to interpret. Not quite angry but almost. "How did you know I was going anywhere?"

"You said you had to deliver those messages to Poland, and I thought, is not Vienna on the way? We traveled so well before. It was safe," she finished wistfully.

He looked away, then back. "Why do you go to Vienna?"

"Madame Josephine sends me to the Sisters of the Piarists in that city. It is a personal mission," Aurélie said hastily when he brought a hand up.

Jaska's lips parted when he heard the word "Piarists." He took a turn about the room, frowned down at the empty fireplace, then turned back. "First, if you are sent on a mission by Madame Bonaparte, where is your escort? Your passport?"

"It is a secret mission, a personal one for Madame. It is *not* military."

Jaska's eyebrows shot upward. Then he took another turn around the room.

She regarded him worriedly. "You brought my mother's letter in so friendly a manner. And we traveled so well last year . . ." She faltered. It was clear she was puzzled why she had to defend herself, to explain the obvious, when they'd had such a good understanding the spring before.

But it was just as clear that nothing was obvious to him. He said rather painstakingly, "The Baron sent me to deliver certain ones to Saint-Cloud, including the one for you, which arrived in the same diplomatic pouch." He took another turn, gazing sightlessly at the marble fireplace, the tall windows, the Neoclassical frieze above the door, the brass sconces sculpted like laurel wreaths, but I would have bet anything he didn't see any of it. "In short," he said, "I am not certain of my duty at this moment."

"The ambassador has given you other orders, then?" Aurélie asked.

"I am not under his command," Jaska admitted. "I am here as a courtesy. An aide, in certain matters I am not at liberty to discuss."

Aurélie said, "We determined that you were some kind of spy, you and Monsieur Mord." Their formal clothing seemed to require them to return to formal titles as well as the formal *vous*.

"A spy? *You* took *me* for a spy?" He laughed, not a fun laugh. More bitter. Reluctant. Then: " 'We'?"

"Yes. Duppy Kim?"

"Tell him," I said, touching her hand.

She brought her chin down. "The easiest explanation is to say that Duppy Kim is the ghost whom Monsieur Mord saw. Well, she is there, only she is not, strictly speaking, a ghost, but a duppy."

"A what?"

"A duppy. In the Creole, there are many terms that do not easily translate into French."

Jaska said, "I thought you followed the Gallican heresy? I feel certain you mentioned the Gallican Bible once, when we talked Latin translation."

"Heresy?" Aurélie repeated. "My grandmother was so very—"

"Strictly speaking, Gallicanism was declared a heresy, though in most regards their practice is the same as other Catholics. But they differ in—" He shook his head, stared at her, then shut his eyes. "Forgive me. My thoughts are disordered by too many questions and too little sleep. No sleep, events not permitting that luxury. Back to your ghost. It speaks to you?"

"She. Speaks to me."

He sighed. "I used to think Mord's ghosts were a result of his drinking. He never talked about such things before Praga, but we were merely acquaintances, then. Surviving the battle made us brethren. I don't suppose it is possible you could cause this ghost to materialize?"

"Nobody except my Nanny and me has been able to truly see her," Aurélie said, walking to a sideboard where a heavy silver tray sat.

"And Mord," Jaska reminded her.

"And Mord." She reddened. "But we can try." She examined the polished tray. "This will do, as we haven't a mirror." She held it up. I laid my hand over hers—and Jaska recoiled.

Aurélie dropped the tray with a crash. "What is wrong?" Then her eyes widened. "You saw her?"

Jaska said slowly, "I saw a . . . a vaporous form. A young woman with fair hair, and on her blouse, she has embroidered the amaranth pattern that is distinctive in my homeland."

"Poland?" Aurélie asked.

He looked away again, then frowned at the door. "The ambassador will finish his breakfast any moment, and we must not be found loitering here. Your ghost took me by surprise. It changes matters. May change matters. Ah, I hardly know what I say. First, a question. Where is your ghost from? Why does it wear that pattern?"

"I don't know what pattern this is that you see. But maybe I see something different. It was that way when we met the fae, when I was small. She saw different faces than I. As for her origin, I don't know that, either. Once I thought England, but her accent is different, and she hasn't said."

The expression I was seeing on Jaska's tired face? I recognized it now. It was distrust.

Talk, Nanny had said.

"Tell him that Bonaparte is about to declare war on England," I said.

"He is?" Aurélie exclaimed, peering intently into the silver tray.

"Who is what?" Jaska said, bewildered.

"Kim. My duppy." Aurélie hefted the tray. "She was speaking to you. She wants me to tell you that Bonaparte is about to declare war on England."

Jaska's gaze narrowed, and he stilled. "How does she know that? Can she walk through walls and listen to private councils?"

"Tell him that Bonaparte is going to pick a fight with Lord Whitworth over Malta and use that as his excuse to go to war. And if that happens . . ." I hesitated, furious and anxious. What knowledge would be safe to tell, and what might damage the timeline? *Why* hadn't Nanny Hiasinte given me rules for being a good duppy?

Jaska was listening, so I tried to dredge up details from my college reading. "But the first attack will not be northward. Within a year or two Bonaparte will betray the Treaty of Lunéville, and strike to the east, into the Austrian empire."

Aurélie repeated my words.

Jaska rapped his knuckles lightly on the desk. Then he looked up sharply. "If you still wish to ride to Vienna, then I will accompany you. Come. I'm going to leave you in the kitchen, if you don't object. You may eat a good breakfast while I arrange things."

Not two hours later, a pair of plainly dressed young men rode sedately down the eastern road, the tall blond riding like a hussar, the smaller one with the curly black hair under his hat rocking unsteadily on his horse, fingers death-gripping the reins.

"We'll stay at a walk," Jaska had said when he had helped her mount. "You'll learn as we go."

She kept her teeth gritted as they crossed a bridge newly cleared of ancient buildings. Presently she said, "Are we not supposed to go on the east road?"

"With your leave, we shall first head south," he said. "To a farm in Berville, near Fontainebleau."

TWENTY-EIGHT

—⟡—

THE SUN WAS SINKING beyond leaden skies when they rode into the farmyard, weary on the backs of drooping horses. A gangling boy ran out, followed by a subaltern in shabby Polish uniform. Seeing those plain dark coats, the subaltern almost turned away, then exclaimed, "I know these horses." He peered up. "Is that you, Colonel Dsaret? Why are you out of uniform?"

"I am on a civilian mission," Jaska replied. "Is the General here? We did not miss him, I trust?"

"No, no, he is here. Come inside!"

The farmhouse was old and rambling, with a thatched roof, none of the deep-set windows quite square. But inside the rustic parlor a fire roared and three children played some sort of game, watched from the table by a thin middle-aged man whose scarred face and gnarled hands betrayed long years of soldiering.

He looked up. Long, loose gray hair streaked with brown fell back from his face as he smiled. He was handsome in that distinctively eastern European way, with the Slavic cheekbones and the dashing smile. The years didn't vanish—he was too scarred for that—but the charisma radiated from his sudden and heartfelt smile as he exclaimed, "It is young Dsaret! Why, this is good time. Or would be, if my expected guests were here."

"I hoped we might arrive first," Jaska said.

"So you knew, then? Ah! Come, who is this?"

"A young musician by the name of René Baptiste. We are riding for Vienna. I had word that Mordechai was expected back and hoped to meet him here."

"Lady Vera-Diana Kwilecka was expected yesterday. We all are anxious for news from the fatherland." Kosciusko turned his head. "Madame Zeltner! Is there room for two more at table?"

"Of course there is, General." A middle-aged woman spoke from the kitchen doorway, with the whole-face smile of love. "The children may eat in here. It's warmer for them. I really think it is going to snow again, and here we were, talking about the kitchen garden . . ." She vanished with a flash of skirts.

"Sit down, sit down. What is the latest in Paris?"

"The news from Saint-Domingue worsens with each dispatch," Jaska began.

"That I have heard." General Kosciusko raised a hand, his brow contracting. "Five thousand of us, he sent, not to spread freedom, but to take away the freedom of the black peoples enslaved on those islands. You know those were the secret orders? We received coded confirmation that I do *not* believe Fouché never saw. It was hidden in the list of dead, among the Polish names."

Jaska shot a questioning glance at Aurélie, which surprised me, though she seemed too tired to notice. "Perhaps we can discuss those things later."

"Very well! I would rather think of better things. Did you know my friend Jefferson is now president in the American republic? I could say that word forever, *republic, republic.* Washington stepped down, just as we knew he would. *He* would not make himself a king," Kosciusko said with meaning, then sighed. "I trust the next generation will raise more like Washington and Jefferson. Neither of them had sons. Like me! I told Jefferson in my last letter, it is not enough to found a military school— though he has, at West Point. And he used my model. Education for all, that is the key to unlock the future we want. Including the slaves, once they are freed. I am going to give him all my American money for just that purpose." He tapped the table with a gnarled finger. "Ah, here is supper! And none too soon. Citizen René Baptiste, you look as if you might fall asleep in your soup. And such good soup, too, ha ha! You both look tired. You shall have the guest room at the top of the stairs."

When the meal was over, Madame Zeltner bundled her children off to bed, and the general sent Aurélie and Jaska up to the room they were expected to share as two young men.

They got inside and stood there staring at the straw-stuffed bed, which took up most of the space in the tiny room. There was a corner fireplace made of age-blackened stone, a pile of wood, clothes pegs on the wall, and a three-legged stool. Jaska was doing his best impression of a stone statue.

Aurélie said, "Why is it that we could sleep all together in barns and byres without a thought, but now I feel very awkward?"

"I'll sleep on the floor," Jaska offered, his manner easing fractionally. "It's no worse than bivouac on the march. Warmer, in fact."

"You may have the bed," she stated. "Your past two days were far more wretched than mine. I don't mind the floor. Sometimes in Jamaica, I slept on the floor, for the tile was cooler in summer."

"But there are two of you, the ghost and yourself."

"Ah, she feels nothing. Isn't that so, Duppy Kim?" And when I said, "Not a thing," she threw her hands wide. "Hear?"

"I didn't hear anything, but I'll accept it as truth. We'll break straws, how's that?" he asked, smiling.

For answer she hung her hat on a peg, kicked off her thin costume shoes, and pulled one of the thick woolen blankets off the bed. She wrapped it around herself, and lay down before the fireplace, curled in a cocoon. Her eyes reflected the firelight. They misted over, and I wondered if she was thinking about poor Josephine and the life she'd left behind. Or maybe she was thinking about the fact that the easy friendship of last year was gone, and this new Jaska didn't trust her, and she didn't know why.

Jaska hung his jacket neatly on the peg next to hers, his hat over it, then pulled off his boots and set them below. He reached into the pocket of the jacket, pulled out an elegant pistol much like her own, and slid it under the pillow. Then he lay down fully clothed, and the last thing I saw before Aurélie blurred into sleep was him staring upward at the ceiling.

———

In the morning, everyone's breath was visible, and I judged that the ground had frozen hard sometime during the night.

Aurélie woke first, but the slight sounds of her stirring brought Jaska alert, hand to his pistol. Then he relaxed when he saw Aurélie standing there with her coat in her arms. The fire had gone out during the night. In the bleak blue light they pulled on coats and shoes, then walked quietly downstairs to discover General Kosciusko struggling with pieces of wood at the fire. Jaska sprang to help.

In the Zeltner household, everyone worked. After breakfast, the General spent the greater part of the morning tutoring the children, his educational method (as he explained later) to follow the interests of his pupils so that he might explain things they wished to learn. He requested 'René,' as a musician, to take the day's music lesson afterward, and so she was there to hear what he taught.

It was inevitable that his own worldview would influence his teaching. He was a staunch Physiocrat—one of those who followed the ideal that working land was the true source of wealth—and Thomas Jefferson was mentioned frequently, the General sometimes interrupting himself to go hunt up this or that letter to read from.

I think Aurélie was more amazed at how little those kids seemed to care that their tutor was one of the most famous generals of the day. Their interests bounced around in typical kid fashion, and names like General Washington and Prince Adam Czartoryski, Empress Catherine and the Prince of Wales, brought no reaction, even when mentioned in the context of direct quotation from face to face conversations.

Nor did the general seem to expect any interest in himself. If they showed interest in a subject, he hailed their questions with praise.

Eventually, the kids were relinquished to Aurélie's charge, to perform their fingering exercises on the fine spinet—a surprise in that old farmhouse—donated by one of the general's admirers. The general didn't stay to supervise. Aurélie had never taught before and assumed a bit of Miss Oliver's manner, but tempered with the general's fondness for approbation. She sounded more natural as the hour progressed.

At length the kids were either free to run around out in the cold air or to help in the kitchen, and Aurélie was called to join Jaska and the general at the table that served as the common gathering place.

The general smiled at Aurélie and said gently, "You play very well. From where do you come?"

"Jamaica, Saint-Domingue, then England," she said. "Then France."

The general waited, as the fire snapped, and from the kitchen came the low voices of Madame and her cook and the clink of dishes being stacked. *This is a set-up*, I thought. *He's questioning her. Jaska asked him to.*

But when Aurélie offered no more information, the general gave her his friendly smile and said, "Here we sit, and dinner is not yet ready. You have heard my method of education. Have you questions for me?"

It was the same method of gathering information that Talleyrand had used.

"Yes. Did Monsieur Mord come to visit you, then?"

"He did."

"But then he left?"

"Ah, I sent him away."

"Why?" Aurélie asked. "Surely you could not suspect him of being a spy, as they did in Paris."

"No, no." The general took up a carving knife and a piece of wood, from which he was carving a toy horse. "The very opposite. No one has a truer heart, unless it is my friend, Colonel Dsaret here, or, oh . . . so many very good friends. And Mordechai is among them. Do you know his history?"

"I know nothing about him," Aurélie said.

The general turned to Jaska. "You permit?"

Jaska nodded. "You are better at explaining than I."

Kosciusko sliced a thin curl of wood as he said, "My dear young Dsaret here was sent to Poland to learn military ways from me, and so he did, but he also learned much more, it is fair to say. Is it not?"

"Much more," Jaska said.

"I appointed Jaska my liaison to Colonel Joselewicz, who raised the first Jewish brigade in history. At his side, acting as aide, was our republican friend, a Frenchman, come to Poland with the Declaration of the Rights of Man in hand. Do you know Hippolyte Vauban? He was born 'de Vauban' but he laid aside the 'de' at the Champs de Mars in seventeen ninety."

The general paused, and when Aurélie shook her head, he went on. "You must realize that not everyone favored the idea of a Jewish brigade, not just from without the Jewish community but also from within. So it is with new ideas. Like the republic! Mordechai was one of the first to join the dragoons, though his grandfather was against it. A good man, Rabbi Elizier ben Isaac, a holy man. His reasons for caution were understandable, for he grew up hearing his own grandfather's stories of the terrible pogroms of the last century. And Mordechai's own father, Aaron ben Elizier, another good and honorable man, though he, too, disagreed."

Jaska's head was bowed, his empty hands dangling between his knees, but the set of his shoulders revealed tension.

The General paused to shake curls of wood from the toy, then worked his thumb over the rough muzzle. "Mord's father felt that no good could come of Mord joining the regiment. He said that a Jew who takes up arms is begging for a Christian to take the sword away, and punish his entire family for his temerity."

"Mord believed in the cause of freedom," Jaska said, looking up. "Not only for the Jews, but for the serfs. We first became friends over our agreement that the *corvée* is another word for slavery. So we all fought for Poland's constitution, and its freedom."

"I was on the way to Russia as a prisoner, unconscious, when Generals Suvorov and Fersen attacked Praga, on the east of Warsaw," the general said.

Jaska spoke, staring into the fire. "The brigade died all around us, heroic to the last," he said low-voiced. "Only a handful left, most wounded. I was knocked unconscious, Hippolyte defending me until he, too, was wounded and left to die. I woke to discover my knee shattered. Hippolyte had lost an eye and a good section of scalp. Mord's squadron was all dead, and he, too, was unconscious and presumed dead. When we came to, we had been looted of everything, even our coats and boots. Mord, the most whole of us, helped us off the field. It took us all day to thread our way among the corpses, and when we got to his village, all the civilians—mostly the old, the women and children—were dead. Every-one."

"The Cossacks had been given permission to chase and kill," the General said.

"We stood there looking down at his betrothed, who had died in the doorway of her house, trying to protect her grandmother, who was also dead." He stared absently at the curled wood shavings on the table under the general's patiently working fingers, and began absently to scrape them into a neat pile. "Mord said, 'The only things moving are the ghosts and demons.'"

"And now we come to where I sent our friend Mord." The General opened his hand; the carving knife pointed one way, the little wooden horse's face another. "But first, you must understand that many lose their faith in war. I myself attempted the sin of self-murder not once, but twice, the second time by starvation when the Empress Catherine sent men to get the names of my allies from me. There are some who shed the faith of their fathers like old clothes, and never look back. Did you know that Minister Fouché was once a monk? It is said that he took the great-est pleasure in ordering the executions of ecclesiastics. Not just the bish-ops and so forth, some of whom were reputed to be steeped in sin, but the simple nuns and monks who did nothing but care for the sick and the poor."

"After the slaughter at Praga, Mord had me to take care of," Jaska said. "I believe it was the only thing that kept him alive." Jaska scraped the wood shavings into his hand and tossed them into the fire, where they flared briefly. "After that, our goal was the reunification of Poland and the restoration of the Constitution. The three of us stayed together, bound by our experiences and the cause of freedom. Hippolyte left us for another mission, and Mord and I were sent on a mission to ascertain Bonaparte's intentions, and then to report what we found to the general, here. We were gathering information in the north of France when we met you, Citizen." Jaska nodded at Aurélie.

Kosciusko smiled at her. "He reported to me as ordered, but then there was no goal, for I still cannot get Bonaparte to honor his promises to arm my Poles for the freeing of our homeland. I was afraid, in his anger, Mord would do something desperate. So I sent him with a message to a holy *zaddik*—you know this word? I do not know how to translate it other than holy man, a follower of the Baal Shem Tov, who was a mystic, one in favor of the simple folk, of heartfelt prayer rather than the minutiae of law and custom. A man of miracles, it is said. And the same is said of his descendant, Rabbi Nachman. Mordechai needs a miracle, thought I, and so I sent him to this young holy man with a request for news of my Jewish friends. I heard nothing for months, until two weeks ago. Mordechai is riding as guard for a visitor I expect to arrive at any time. And now you know a little of his history."

Silence fell. I suspect that the two men were waiting for Aurélie to disclose her mission, or talk about herself, but she stayed quiet, her expression troubled.

The General began to carve again, gouging the tool into the wood to fashion an ear. "So melancholy a subject, the war. Let us banish it with music, since, from the sounds, our dinner is still in preparation. Citizen René Baptiste, will you and my former aide-de-camp favor us with a tune?"

Aurélie agreed at once and ran upstairs to pull her music case from her satchel. When she came down, Jaska was fitting together not his old hautbois, but a beautiful clarinet. His careful fingers, his little smile of pride, betrayed his feelings before he played a note.

He'd been good with the hautbois, but on a clarinet, he was (at least to my ears) an orchestra-grade artist.

Aurélie, very much on her mettle, began hesitantly, then plunged boldly into a Bach piece, as Jaska tapped the floor lightly, then came in on counterpoint, the notes clear and sweet.

The music acted like a beacon, and before long the entire house had accumulated, from the kids to the servants. Jaska and Aurélie played three more French airs, then Jaska trilled the opening notes of one of Aurélie's fae pieces. She flushed with pride and dashed off an arpeggio. They launched into the piece, which was one of my favorites.

The older kids began dancing about, the General beating time with his hand on the table.

They'd just settled into the chorus when, high as a nightingale's call, a violin echoed the main line, then soared up and up in a complexity of notes.

Everyone froze.

The sound, coming from nowhere and yet everywhere at once, was like the fae had arrived in secret. Only better, because they could only mirror emotion, but the violin brought it straight from the heart.

The door opened, and there was Mord, looking like an ancient prophet with his long hair, his short, silky beard and mustache, violin under his chin, a host of travel-worn people at his shoulder.

TWENTY-NINE

THE FIRST DAY, everything was great.

The second day was proof that you can't cram a lot of strangers into a small house and not see signs of strain.

For one thing, there was not enough room in the barn for the farm animals and all the horses, even with Lady Vera-Diana's carriage left out in the weather. As for the ladies, I don't think I was the only one noticing that Lady Vera-Diana and Madame Zeltner both, though exceedingly polite to one another, each wanted the general's attention. The Poles wanted to talk politics, and the rest of the family was trying to live around the visitors. The kids got louder, and the adults got more polite, the smiles more fixed.

When Jaska came alongside the spinet after Aurélie tutored a lead-fingered little kid, he said softly, "When you're finished, Mordechai and I request the favor of your opinion."

As soon as she slogged out into the muddy yard, Aurélie found the two awaiting her in the cold air, Mord looking at the ground, his hands loose. His new beard curled softly, emphasizing the fine bones of his face. He had a new hat, low in the brim, that shadowed his eyes, and he wore a long, shabby black coat over his clothing.

He glanced sideways at Aurélie, then away very quickly.

Jaska said, "We are ready to leave for Vienna. But there is a question to be settled first."

"Which is?" she said.

"We might have to walk most of the way," Jaska said. "It's ten times the distance from Dieppe to Paris. We can take mounts, but if we encounter any French, especially if you are correct that Bonaparte is shortly to declare war, the French military will at best offer to buy, and more than likely requisition our mounts. The animals deserve better than a battlefield. I'm thinking that if we continue to travel as musicians, we have a better chance of passing undisturbed if we walk. Musicians never have any money, thieves have no use for musical instruments, and if we look sufficiently armed, we should dissuade the lout looking to pass the time by thrashing strangers."

"I will need better shoes," Aurélie said. "These are from the theater. They won't hold out more than a day."

"We will stop at the first cobbler we come to."

"How will we afford that?" Mord asked.

"We have means," Jaska said at the same moment that Aurélie tapped her waistcoat pocket. She spoke: "Madame Josephine gave me plenty of money."

Mord looked up, his brows lifting. "We serve Bonaparte's wife?"

"It is a personal errand," Aurélie stated. "It has nothing to do with the military."

Jaska started toward the house. "We will leave in the morning."

And so they did.

They could hire two rooms at decent inns. Jaska saw to it that he and Mord were always next door to Aurélie. Thus, she told me, she felt perfectly safe.

With her own room she was able to bathe and to wash out her shirts, stockings, and underthings before she slept, and dry them at the fire at night.

The trio offered music wherever they stopped. Some of the better inns even had a keyboard of some sort in the common area.

The first few days of their journey were under snowy conditions. Their progress was slow at first. Toward the end of each day, Jaska leaned more heavily on his walking stick (from which he'd removed the dashing military tassel) and Aurélie winced as she broke in her new shoes. All that week, France's landscape was blanketed with white, cross-hatched and stippled each day a little more by the carriage tracks and foot or hoof prints of regular life.

Mord was mostly silent. He would take out his spectacles when it was time to play, and rehearsed whenever Jaska suggested it. He memorized all the new music Jaska had brought, so he could play without having to read.

He had always been good, but something had changed. There was an urgency to his interpretations of the pieces, the volume sometimes flamboyant, sometimes diminishing to a murmur, the tempo speeding up and then slowing to a lingering poignancy. Sometimes he would go off into solos of his own, leaving the others to accompany as they could. And early in the mornings, if Aurélie came downstairs in time, we sometimes saw him walking off a little distance to play to rustling evergreens, or a trickling brook.

When they set out, Mord took care to position himself so that Jaska always walked in the middle. It was so casually done that they had fallen into the habit before Aurélie became aware of it.

Jaska tried to make conversation, asking easy questions—never about politics, the Bonapartes, or Paris, but of reading, childhood, families. To the latter, Aurélie returned evasive answers, and he was not exactly forthcoming, either, so I still didn't know how he related to the Dsarets.

Mord didn't talk at all.

One night, Aurélie said to me, "What have I done to Mord? He will not talk to me. He barely looks at me."

"I suspect it's because he knows you are a girl inside those clothes."

"But nothing has changed!"

"Everything has changed. Here." I touched my head, since she could see me in the tiny shaving mirror set on a stand. "I believe that in his culture, unmarried women and men do not mix. It's not respectful."

"But he is apostate, I thought."

"I know of people who have no belief in God, but who celebrate their religion as a cultural tradition," I said. "Those things are not always easy to define."

"Nor the perception of God." Aurélie crossed her arms. "I came to hate the word 'Providence,' because it was Aunt Kittredge's God, the one who gave things to people who acted like her because they were supposedly good and let others starve or die because they deserved it. That's not *le bon Dieu*. Enough of her. We shall never see one another again. I think I see, now, why Mord calls me Citizen René, or sometimes Monsieur Baptiste. He is more comfortable if he can *pretend* I am a boy."

"I think that's correct. And as long as you both maintain the pretence, then he can be comfortable."

"But with Jaska, it's different. He knows I'm a girl, and the pretence is also different. He never says 'he' about me, though he calls me René. There are little things . . . I cannot explain them all. But I know he knows who I am. And he's very respectful." She was silent for a time, then smiled. "I like it." Her smile vanished. "What I don't like are questions about my origins. I don't want to lie about who I am, and yet I don't want to tell him that I'm the daughter of a slave."

"But he talked about how he believes in freedom for all."

"Yes," she said, her gaze uncertain. "But I can *never* forget the horrid things my aunt said. I don't think I could bear it if he heard the truth, and I saw that same disgust in his face, though I am the same person I always was! When Aunt Kittredge thought I was a marquise's daughter, my aunt was good enough to me, but though I had not changed, her idea of me changed." She clapped her hands. "Like that. No, I can't bear thinking of it."

"We all want to be accepted as we are," I said. "Including Jaska."

Aurélie brought her chin down in a slow, thoughtful nod. "'Tis just."

"So talk to him about other things."

That next morning, Jaska gave up the questions entirely. As soon as they hit the road he pulled a thick little book from his pocket and began reading aloud from Fielding's *Tom Jones*.

Within half a page, Aurélie clapped her hand over her mouth, trying not to laugh.

When Jaska looked her way, she begged his pardon.

"Was it the text or how I said it?" he asked. "I'm teaching myself this language. I was trading lessons with the English courier last fall, and as I don't want to lose what I learned, I'm puzzling out meanings by virtue of this dictionary, but it doesn't tell me pronunciation." He plunged his hand into another pocket, and there was a very battered copy of Johnson's dictionary. "*Peste!*" he exclaimed. " 'Through.' Is this said *thruff*, or *throw? Throff?*"

Aurélie tried not to laugh as she corrected him.

"*Threw?*" he exclaimed, a hand raised in protest. "Why is *through* said *threw*, but *though* is *thoh?* All one does is remove the R. But if one then removes the H, the word becomes *tuff.* So why is the first one not *thruff?* And this one." He coughed. "Is *c-o-u-g-h* said *coo* or *cow?*"

Aurélie muffled a snicker.

Jaska waved the book. "If *gh* is to be *f,* then is not *ghost* properly pronounced *fost?*"

Aurélie smiled as she gave him the correct pronunciation.

Mord pulled his spectacles from his pocket and regarded Jaska to see if he was kidding. A quick, sideways look at Aurélie, then he snatched off the glasses as if he'd been burned. "It appears that this language was fashioned by a madman. I like that," he added thoughtfully as he folded his spectacles again and slid them inside his coat.

Jaska grinned. "Have you read this book, René?"

"My cousin and I were taking turns reading it aloud as we sewed, the winter before we left for France. But we only got as far as London before my aunt took it away and scolded us mightily, saying it was written only for men."

Jaska looked surprised. "Is that English custom, then?"

"It depends upon the household. Another female cousin had read it."

"Will you help me learn these words?" he asked.

"In trade, will you teach me German? I know you know it. I remember you and Mord speaking it once or twice, on our journey to Paris. The nuns

I am to visit will probably speak Latin, and everyone says French is universal, but I would prefer to speak the language of the country I am in."

"Agreed. How is this? Mornings, we spend in English, and afternoons in German. I have in my haversack two fine novels, one by Goethe and one by Richter. Do you have a preference?"

"Not if it's *The Sorrows of Young Werther*," she said. "It sounds horrid. Madame Bonaparte told us that it's the First Consul's favorite book, so I do not want to read it. Is the other one amusing? I like comical novels."

"I've only the first volume of *Titan*, which is quite new. It was given me by a courier from Prussia, but he had none of the rest of it. We might find other volumes where we are going. In the meantime, I assure you, there will be plenty to discuss. And to laugh over, for Richter loves a good joke."

"And I discover in myself a desire to learn a language where one cannot tell by spelling if one is hacking with a cold or warbling like a dove," Mord observed. "I foresee endless amusement."

So that's what happened.

On the first Friday night, Mord vanished before the sun set. He returned well after dark without saying where he had been. The next morning, they found him standing in the common room, head bowed.

"My knee pains me," Jaska said. "Let us not travel today."

Mord turned a smile his way, then vanished outside again. To Aurélie's quizzical expression, Jaska replied, "I think when he goes off to play in that solitary manner that he's making *Hitbodedut*, that is, devotions. And last night, when he vanished coincided with the start of the Sabbath. But if he does not wish to tell us that he is making devotions, our part, I believe, is to pretend we don't notice."

After that, they halted for the Sabbath by mutual accord. And Jaska needed the rest. He never complained, but the difference between his stiff gait of a Friday and the freer walk when they pushed forward again was apparent.

Eventually they crossed from Lunéville to the forested, hilly territory west of Strasbourg. The secluded timberland seemed to bring darkness earlier, and they sought shelter earlier, especially when the thick woods echoed with the howl of wolves. They often practiced shooting as they walked, which kept their weapons in shape and also scared off lurking predators.

Aurélie told me that she hated the loudness of the noise, the stink of burnt metal and powder, but she was determined to so refine her aim that she could wound the hand raised to strike her or hit the knee bent to lunge without destroying the attacker's life—even the life of someone bent on evil.

"There are too many deaths in my dreams," she said to me one night, when cleaning her pistol and reloading it before she went to sleep.

Early stops meant rehearsals, to which the locals listened with interest. By now they were a musical trio of professional quality, but even so, the listeners almost invariably leaned by increments toward Mord, whose playing continued to achieve extraordinary range and power. But he never seemed satisfied.

Aurélie began having nightmares again. I'd thought those had ended when we arrived in Paris. Jaska looked with concern at her heavy eyes on those mornings, but when he asked why she didn't sleep, she only said, "Nightmares."

The day before we reached Strasbourg, she took everyone by surprise. "I have a new song," she said, as she sat down to the village's single fortepiano. "It is called 'Miyyah fi Miyyah.'" She worked it out with determined fingers, as Jaska picked up the melody on his flute. And to me, in English, she murmured, "It came in last night's dream. The woman in the dream was Spanish. If I have to have nightmares, then at least they can give me music."

She turned away, yawning so hard that her eyes watered. She did not see the long, thoughtful look that Jaska gave her.

Strasbourg revealed the familiar depredations of the Revolution, the oddest, the gigantic Phrygian cap still covering the spire of the vandalized cathedral. On either side, French mixed with German voices. When she heard the latter, Aurélie lifted her face with a delight I recognized. It's cool when the indecipherable patterns of a foreign language begin to make sense.

That night, having located an inn with a resident spinet, they offered to play. After an early dinner, they were going about setting up their instruments—reeds, tuning, Aurélie getting the touch of the spinet— when a loud clattering outside the inn caused an abrupt drop in voices and a tense shift of attention to the door.

In strode a captain and two attendant guards, muskets at the ready. The captain unrolled a piece of paper and read, "By order of the first consul, war has been officially declared against the British for their refusal to obey the terms of the Treaty of Amiens. All English are to be arrested. If you see any of the following, you are to report them immediately to the local prefecture."

He then read out names and descriptions of persons suspected of being spies against the Republic of France. Most of them were men, and then:

"Going by the name of Aurélie de Mascarenhas, female approximately sixteen to twenty years of age, petite, black eyes and hair, Mediterranean complexion, dressed as a court lady."

THIRTY

THE CAPTAIN ROLLED UP HIS PAPER, turned with a self-important air, and walked out followed by his guards, who had scrutinized the adult males in hopes of nabbing a spy and gaining a promotion. They'd looked right past the young boy hunched on the stool at the spinet, hat jammed low on 'his' head.

As soon as they were safely gone, the innkeeper said mournfully, "My dear fellow citizens, I have little respect for the *roasbiffs*, but even an English spy would know that England lies to the north and not to the east?"

This heavy-handed joke at the expense of the English received appreciative chuckles as a round of wine was served out to re-establish the proper festive atmosphere, and the innkeeper gestured impatiently for the musicians to play.

Aurélie's hands trembled, causing a false note or two. But she flexed and shook her fingers, then pounded the keys until she recaptured the rhythm.

The next morning, she waited until they were well away from the inn, and exclaimed, "They think I am a spy!"

"Yes," Jaska said, his expression wary. "This should not be a surprise."

"But it *is*. I remember Minister Talleyrand warning us, but that was months ago. I have never done anything to warrant accusation."

Mord kept broody silence as Jaska said mildly, "Apparently Madame

Bonaparte said nothing about your departure so, effectively, you vanished the day after receiving a letter from the islands. That must have raised suspicion, if no other of your actions did."

"That letter came to my hands *months* after it was written. Surely the *mouchards* read it many times first. A child could see that the seal had been broken and reheated."

"All true," he said. "But it could have been in a code. Such things often are."

"A letter from my mother?"

"How are they to know that?" Jaska asked. "It was conveyed through English diplomatic channels, and if there is now a state of war . . ." He sobered. "As you predicted."

"Kim predicted it. My duppy."

"That is true, I am corrected," Jaska said. "Perhaps we ought to get well away from the city before we discuss this subject any further?"

Aurélie looked around with startled eyes at the shoppers and travelers on the busy street. She bit her lip and said nothing more.

Later in the day they reached the outskirts of the city and started up the road, but the subject of Aurélie as a spy was not revived.

Nor was it during the following days. Aurélie never introduced it. I think, from the wary way she regarded Jaska if he began a question, that she was dreading interrogation about her origins.

After a long tramp spent translating the second volume of *Titan* and practicing German, they traded the serried vineyards of Charlemagne's empire for the Hapsburgs': the many castles with their carvings of angels and heraldic devices, the Gothic spires and reaching arches, jutted upward from beyond the increasingly rough hills. Late in the day, lamplight shone through stained-glass windows in martial or saintly scenes, beckoning gemstones for the tired traveler.

Mord commented one day that the news about the war declaration had probably gone to French forces via semaphore within a day but had taken longer to spread to ordinary people, and then make its way into the empire. They could tell when the empire had heard because the signs

of military preparations were evident in the increased patrols, the many
soldiers marching hither and yon in towns and villages.

They jigged north from Kiel to ancient Baden in order to avoid a climb,
then cut south of fortified Stuttgart and down into Württemberg, where
the duke would shortly make himself a king.

Those winged beings showed up again, drifting like vaporous clouds
along roads, through trees in dark forests, over the heights of the many
castles. It was the end of March, and spring had loosened the last of the
snow underfoot in the deeper valleys. The world was full of the trickle,
tinkle, gurgle, and rush of water as winter snow melted, added to inter-
mittently by rain.

The weather was as vile as the roads, but sometimes a wagon stopped
to give them a ride. By now Jaska and Aurélie were chattering regularly
about reading in their new languages. Sometimes (usually when least
expected) Mord would put in a word or two. During the early days, while
they were still in French territory, Mord, the ferocious warrior and
moody musical genius, revealed a lamentable taste for puns; the worse
they were, the more he would shake with silent laughter. But as they
reached deeper into the Austrian empire, his whimsical moments were
replaced by a wary—even bitter—silence.

They'd finished reading *Tom Jones*, the reading lengthened by much
discussion of Fielding's opinionated, frequently funny introductions to
the various subsections. Their next morning book, found in a narrow
printshop on a street that looked unchanged since the 1400s, was *Or-
lando Furioso*.

"I do not know Italian," Aurélie said.

"Tchah," Jaska scoffed. "It's the next thing to Latin. I promise, you
will like this one, and why not learn yet another tongue?"

They pulled discussion of that into their ongoing talk about *Titan*,
once they located volume three. There was no personal talk. It was all
wider subjects: chivalry, romanticism, republicanism, extreme philoso-
phies of any kind, what they meant in human terms, and what I would
call political terms: the responsibilities of kingship and power.

Mord either stayed silent, or sometimes he'd interject a trenchant quote in Yiddish, German, Polish, French, and once, in Latin: "*Qui male agit odit lucem,*" he said on a day when a cold wind rushed and roared through the new leaves. *He who is evil despises light.*

Aurélie had told me, when we were alone in her room, that she didn't recognize many of his quotes. He didn't offer translations, and she hesitated to ask, given their odd relationship. So this time, as they tramped downhill in a misting rain, she said with mild triumph, "That is from the Bible, John 3:10."

"The Christian Bible," Mord said. "But as it happens, I was thinking of Camille Desmoulins."

Aurélie frowned, and then got it. She bent her head to hide her grimace. "Ça ira," she whispered under her breath.

"We played it often enough," Mord rejoined. "Did you not listen to the words, Citizen René?"

"I didn't always understand them," she admitted. "But enough to know that in spite of the cheerful tune, it is a very cruel song. Marie—a chambermaid—told me about the lamppost at the corner of the Place de la Grève. Where the crowd would hang people without so much as a trial."

"Correct enough. 'The universe and its follies,' " Mord said. "After several years of encouraging the worst in men, Desmoulins published *Le Vieux Cordelier*, begging for clemency, a turnabout from his fierce demands for blood and more blood. His wish for clemency turned out to be his death sentence—" He stopped himself, shook his head violently, then muttered in Yiddish, " 'Everything that happens is merely working a thin thread of metal in relation to the Infinite.' "

"Who said that?" Jaska asked.

"Rebbe Nachman. When I reminded him that a thin thread of metal can cut to the bone, he said, 'Yes.' "

They walked in silence, until Mord peeled off and played in the woods, the violin solo beautiful in its anguish.

There were no brigand attacks. Marauding revolutionary veterans had been left behind, and the locals might have been dissuaded from attempting a career change as highway robbers by the increasing numbers of soldiers riding back and forth along the road.

At first the trio ignored these, merely walking to the side when they heard the rumble of horse hooves or the tramp of boots. But one morning a party of young toughs in faded Jäger uniforms rode by, their gilding tarnished, but they made up for it in attitude. "Who are you?! Where are you going?"

Jaska said, "We are musicians, going to Vienna to study." He pointed to Mord's violin case, as his clarinet case was in his haversack.

"Musicians?" the youngest one scoffed. From the fluffiness of his mustache, he couldn't have been over eighteen. "Too cowardly to put on a uniform?"

"He's walking with a stick," another pointed out. "Cripple."

The leader was a stout guy with corn silk hair and a heavy scar on his left cheek—either a dueling scar or from battle. He squinted at Jaska, then said, "You seen some fighting, musician?"

"I was at Warsaw in ninety four," Jaska replied with heavy irony.

The second one whistled, and the leader said appreciatively, "That was some hot work. Those damned Poles can fight." He was about to turn away, when he hitched, and slewed around again to scowl at Mord. "That one a Jew? A Jew, carrying a pistol?"

Jaska said, "He's my servant. And this one is my apprentice." He indicated Aurélie.

The soldiers ignored her and eyed Mord, whose hand tightened on the sword hilt, his eyes narrowed to slits. He was probably only trying to bring them into focus, but he looked really dangerous. The young soldier actually backed his horse away, and the leader slid his hand to his pistol belt.

Jaska's fingers tightened on his stick, his thumb pressing. I heard a faint snap. It was a sword stick!

Mord glanced his way, then said, "I am a Pole."

The second one said, "You better get rid of that beard, fellow. Someone might take you for a Jew and string you up for bearing arms."

The young soldier with the fluffy moustache seemed to regret having backed off. Now he had to make up for it. "My father says, if in doubt, shove some bacon down their throats and take a stick to their backs. If they yell *Oy! Oy! Oy!*, you know it's a Jew instead of a man."

"Let's be off," the leader said impatiently.

Fluffy Mustache guffawed, echoed by the second guy as the leader raised a genial hand. They rode on by.

Mord glared after them, a vein ticking in his forehead.

"Animals. They do not think," Jaska said wearily, as Aurélie glared after the vanishing soldiers.

Mord began walking. Jaska picked up in the book where he'd left off.

After that, when they heard the jingle of many horse harnesses, they drew off the road altogether, and Jaska always chose to stand between Mord and whoever rode by.

In the next large town, they got their usual two rooms, and the next morning, Mord came downstairs clean-shaven once again.

At the others' concerned expressions, he said flatly, "It is just a beard. And I'll not have it be the cause of your murders."

There were no more incidents like that one as they progressed. However, there were other things to think about. For one thing, I was fairly sure that I sensed that deep-freeze chill of vampires, though I never saw any.

What I did see were some of those dark winged beings. They floated over valleys and towns, sometimes crossed the road with dreamy languor. Three of them, the ones I thought of as Fake Jaska, Pewter Hair, and Lady Midnight, were familiar. But they never came close enough to speak, and it wasn't like they'd ever done anything threatening. They were just weird.

THIRTY-ONE

WHEN JASKA, Aurélie, and Mord reached Ulm and stood on the stone ramparts gazing down at the waters of the Danube, Mord said abruptly, "I have a question. But I will ask it when next I play."

Jaska set about finding an inn, one that might cater to musicians. They were directed to a place known for its musical gatherings. In the low-ceilinged common room with its rough-hewn walls, many locals brought instruments and played for one another. The trio performed to enthusiastic applause.

Then Mord launched into one of his own pieces. He played with his eyes closed, his long, taut body swaying and twisting like a young tree in a wind.

And at the end, he addressed the audience in his heavily accented German, "What heard you?"

Aurélie and Jaska burst out in praise, as did the circle of listeners. He thanked them politely, but when the three withdrew a little so that someone else could play, he asked more quietly, in a tone that indicated the question had more than idle importance, "What did you hear?"

"Music," Aurélie said. "But it made me think of things."

"Ah! What was that, Monsieur Baptiste?" Mord seemed to prefer formality as well as her boy's name, though he was still careful that they never touched.

"It made me think of home. My first home, but it was not all happy, for I remembered the pirate attack, and . . . and other things. But good things, too," she added hastily when Mord's brows knit pensively.

"I thought of the good days in Warsaw," Jaska said. "When we gathered with the General at Czartoryski Palace, with the other cadets, and how people would crowd at the windows trying to get a glimpse of him."

"Ah," Mord said sadly. "Then I have failed."

Jaska held out a hand. "How can you say that? I have never heard you play better than you have since your return. Never. And you were always good."

But Mord went silent again. Except for his playing.

They turned their backs on the towering spire of Ulm Minster, untouched by revolution, and descended past the interlocking pattern of slanted roofs, careful on wet cobblestones. Here and there the double-headed eagle marked corbels and mullioned glass; this city belonged to the emperor who would be surrendering to Napoleon within a couple of years.

I didn't tell them that. I wasn't talking at all, as they drew ever eastward. I was watching how Aurélie and Jaska fell into patterns of talk, each turning automatically to the other when they met in the mornings, or when ideas occurred. I didn't know whether to be apprehensive or glad, because I still didn't know if Jaska was the third son of some cadet branch of the Dsarets, sent off to Poland to get rid of him; or whether, no matter who he was, he would be the means to get Aurélie to Dobrenica.

Aurélie gazed in awe at the ranks on ranks of Alpine mountains, still clothed in blue-white snow, until they were swallowed again by the trees and towering buildings with their tripled tiers of oriel windows.

The food had changed again. Aurélie devoured the different kinds of potato dishes and dumplings, many covered thickly with cheese, and the ubiquitous cabbage, here doused with vinegar and a spot of sugar.

In one inn, the stout, friendly innkeeper set down a tankard of foam-topped beer in front of Aurélie, saying, *"Trink, Jüngling!"*—following with a kindly speech about how the boy was too thin, he would fly away on the wind, he must fatten up!

And as Aurélie tasted the beer, the man bent toward Jaska, whose

German was perfect, and said in a voice that was probably supposed to be low but sounded like a rumble of thunder, "He's a dark one, your apprentice. Spanish?"

Aurélie said nothing.

Jaska glanced her way, then said, "Portuguese. A noble father."

"Ah." The innkeeper put a finger in the air. "A second son, perhaps? Or born on the wrong side of the blanket? The important thing is nobility. Rank has its privileges, the world says. Excuses many sins. In everyone's eyes but the church." He laughed then hastily crossed himself.

Aurélie ignored all that and sipped the dark beer. Her expressive face altered to a muted surprise. She liked it. She sipped some more, and as conversation languished—Jaska thoughtful, Mord lost in his inner world—she finished the evening rather owl-eyed.

Later that night, when she was alone in her room, she broached the subject of Mord. "He is very unhappy. Why does he not like what we say about his music?"

"I don't know. He plays better than he ever did. If I had eyes, I'd be crying, sometimes."

"I do weep, a little. I'm so glad that I can finger without looking. Oh, he makes me think of the pure blue sky over Jamaica when there is no storm, and of the roses at Undertree, and the magical symbols on the stone wall that Diana used to touch when we walked past. I think of Mama, and Tante Mimba. Of Diana. Even of James, though I no longer want to marry him. It is more that I miss how, oh, how hopeful we were. But Mord! Did you see, he no longer touches the pork, or any meat. What do you think his reason might be?"

"I think he might be trying to keep the Jewish laws about food."

She said, "Would that and the way that he plays at prayer times, and the fact that we do not move on Sabbath, not mean he's recovered his faith?"

"I don't know what it means. It's not an easy question to answer."

From time to time, as the trio moved from village to walled town, through hills and thick green conifer forests, Mord would ask them, after one of his remarkable, even heart-rending solos, "What did you hear?"

He'd listen intently to their answers, then turn away with an air of silent defeat, and vanish, making it clear he didn't want to talk about it.

Castles were seldom completely out of sight, and the trio avoided them easily enough, for there were always villages or small towns. Spring had finally come. Marsh weed and rushes shot through the brown mud. Brambly shrubs fluffed out in civilizing green, and the deciduous trees tufted with nubs that began to leaf. The wild, fairy-tale landscape of Bavaria and upper Austria closed around them, opening to golden baroque castles and beautiful little hamlets.

They navigated by church bells, echoing through hill and forest. People in the villages were largely friendly as long as they heard German; the trample of the French three years ago was beginning to fade, except in memory. Aurélie loved the onion domes poking up here and there above the rocky hills and treetops.

Between the villages the countryside was rough, always uphill, downhill, the road often running alongside bubbling streams, then plunging them into thick forest, which caused everybody to loosen weapons for quick grabbing. Sometimes they heard the howl of Austrian wolves, which didn't sound any different from French ones. Jaska seemed to lose himself in thought more frequently, which meant fewer book and language conversations.

I wondered if it was his knee until his occasional gazes Aurélie's way made it clear he had something on his mind.

———

They joined up with the Danube again at Linz.

The town was half destroyed, the castle a dramatic ruin as a result of the French cruising through in 1800. Everywhere people were busy rebuilding. I couldn't help thinking, *Don't bother, Napoleon is going to be back through here a couple more times.* One of the worst things about knowing what was to come was the sheer helplessness.

The gossip in inns, and the newspapers shared around, made it clear that everyone was expecting war. For the most part, however, their attitude was, *If he comes back, this time we'll be ready for him.*

I was so glad that our route didn't take us through Austerlitz.

The trio tramped through what remained of Linz's old town, unsuccessfully trying to find lodging. The sky was building toward a spectacular spring storm, and no one wanted to be caught out. Desperate, they were willing to settle for a single room.

One innkeeper said, "Holy Week is a very bad time for travelers. Every bed is taken, twice over! We're sleeping four to a mattress."

Listening to the conversation was a round-faced draper who had just delivered a bolt of cloth. He eyed the three, taking in their travel-worn but fine clothing, and said, "My brother, who runs a stable, sometimes lets his attic during harvest season. It's not fine enough for an archduke, but for students? It's clean and will cost you no more than a room here. You can walk into town for meals."

"Thank you," Jaska said, emulating the south-German accent. "Where will we find him?"

The draper gave directions and admonished Jaska to say that Hansel had sent them. Half an hour later the storm hit, but they were safe and snug as it roared onto the slanted roof over their heads.

Their pose as music students required them to offer some tunes for the household. Their audience, a bunch of cheery faced Austrians, clapped and stamped to the bouncier tunes and listened more quietly to Mord's musical exegesis on the ruined countryside. I could hear it in the fragments of melodies he played, broken apart and shifted to minor keys.

After a sumptuous meal of mainly starches and dairy, as it was too early for any vegetables, the three retired to their attic. They were camping in the same room for the first time since the days of their jaunt down the Seine.

Wool-stuffed pallets had been laid out amid neat stacks of horse and human gear. As he set his haversack down, Mord said again, "What did you hear?"

Jaska said, "I heard a story about war, and how it disrupts life."

Aurélie said, "The broken melodies, yes."

Mord set his violin gently in its battered case. "Perhaps I am learning," he admitted.

"Learning what?" Jaska asked. "I say you play better than ever, but you sigh and look as if you caused the strings to squawk like a chicken. My opinion's worthless?" He put his fist to his chest. "I'm insulted!"

Mord raised his hands, smiling and shaking his head. "Sorry. Sorry."

Aurélie looked sorrowful. "I don't want to tell you what I see, because it always makes you sad."

Mord flushed. "I've been arrogant. Your words humble me, for which I thank you. I see only my failure to successfully tell Rabbi Nachman's stories through music. The Rabbi, may he live in peace, teaches that music is the highest form of *deveikut*, higher than prayer. I do not understand *deveikut*—you could say devotion—anymore. I do not understand prayer. But I understand music. So I thought, maybe I can spread those stories to others through my music." He pressed his hands to his eyes and then startled everybody by lifting his head and saying directly to me, "Do you see the seraphs following us, ghost?"

I'd forgotten he could see me.

I said, without expecting to be heard, "Do you mean by 'seraphs' those beings with the dark wings? I've seen them. Three in particular, one of which spoke to me in Paris."

Mord frowned. "They spoke? The seraphs spoke? Do you see your fellow ghosts as well?"

"Some are clear, and others waver, like light in water," I said.

Aurélie whispered my words to Jaska, who looked surprised.

Mord gave a thoughtful nod. "When you spoke to this seraph. What did it say?"

Totally unused to anyone hearing me except Aurélie, I touched her, and whispered in English, "It was when you were with Bonaparte. Do you want me talking about that?"

She wrinkled her nose. "You didn't tell me."

"There was no time, and the winged creature didn't do anything, just talked."

Mord was gazing at me warily, so I said, "One of the seraphs was there when she was talking to Bonaparte."

"Bonaparte? You had an interview with Bonaparte?" Jaska asked.

Aurélie blushed. "Yes."

"Perhaps the time has come to tell us what your mission is?" Jaska looked troubled.

"But I did," Aurélie exclaimed, hands open. "Madame Bonaparte is sending me to the Sisters of the Piarists, in Vienna."

"You did not tell me what she wants," Jaska went on, "from the smallest and humblest of convents, attached to a small group of teaching brethren. The same brethren, as it happens, who ran the school where General Kosciusko was taught."

"What has that to do with Madame Bonaparte wishing to conceive an heir?" Aurélie asked in surprise. "I told you the mission was personal."

He thought Aurélie was a spy.

It hit me about two heartbeats before it hit Aurélie. Then her hands became fists, and for a second or two I thought she was going to take a swing at him. "*You* thought I was *a spy*?"

Then she turned her face into the crook of her elbow and laughed.

It was Jaska's turn to blush.

Tears glittered along her eyelids as she struggled to get control. "Oh, oh," she said, gasping. "I am almost angry, except . . . How could you think me a spy? What possible motive could I have?"

"What motive does anyone have? It could be ideals, it could be profit, or power," he said. "Your circumstances appear to be both mysterious and strange. And you just admitted to a private interview with Bonaparte."

Aurélie blushed deeply. "That interview was an accident. He—he encountered me when I was leaving Madame Bonaparte, and he made— he mistook—he wanted something I would not give." She looked miserable, facing away.

Jaska's expression cleared. "Ah," he said.

Aurélie looked down, a small, wretchedly embarrassed figure.

"If that's so, it explains the search for you. He's said to be vindictive when crossed. The General attests to that. And everyone's circumstances are strange these days." Jaska's tone was apologetic.

Aurélie looked up at that. "So very, very many lives disrupted, even destroyed by these wars. So many different motives! There's a general whom Madame Josephine says is now very high in Bonaparte's regard. He wants Bonaparte to declare himself king, but this is the very man who accused Madame's first husband of anti-republicanism and caused him to die on the guillotine."

"I think," Jaska said, "we've only to point to Fouché for changing political motivations as circumstances dictate. But we'll acquit you of that, especially if . . . well, if Bonaparte saw fit to add you to the list of wanted spies, without giving any reason."

Aurélie said with dignity, "I am no spy!"

"Because you're haunted by a ghost who seems to get information by mysterious means, I'll admit that this particular convent is known to me, to certain among my own people. They have connections with magic."

Vrajhus, I thought. *He's got to be from Dobrenica.*

Aurélie threw her hands wide. "And that's exactly what Madame seeks, a magical solution to her failure to bear a child. Did you know she was severely wounded at Plombières several years ago, when she went for a cure?"

"I remember that. The physicians published their treatment regimen," Jaska said. "Madame de Staël was reading these. I was in Paris at that time. It was enough to turn the stomach of a ghoul." He seemed to come to a decision and pulled from his haversack a small shaving mirror. This he held up, turning it until he saw me. Which he could do without Aurélie touching the mirror first, a fact that hit her the same moment it hit me.

"You told us before that Napoleon was about to declare war on England. Only Bonaparte would have known that or perhaps a trusted few. Including demons following him to overhear."

"Look," I said. "I can't prove that I'm not a demon. No one can prove a negative. All I can tell you is that my powers are pretty much limited to knowing some facts about what Bonaparte is—" *going to do* "—doing and the ability to talk to Aurélie and now to you. If I had greater powers, I'd waft her to safety right now."

Mord glanced up. "And yet something protects her from the demons drawing near, the shadowed shapes that one perceives at the edge of vision, at a distance. And from the vampires. I heard them from time to time as we traversed the woods. Yet they never came close."

I had completely forgotten about the necklace, worn all this time around Aurélie's ankle, hidden by sturdy socks and her voluminous breeches.

I think she had forgotten it as well. She said uncertainly, "Maybe they sense my duppy and are afraid to come near. It was that way with the fae . . ." She was remembering the necklace *now*. And clammed up.

Okay. If she wasn't going to mention it, I wouldn't either. It was her promise to keep, and I didn't see how the necklace mattered one way or another to the problems of Bonaparte, spies, or secret missions, even if it did ward off vampires and demons.

Jaska glanced to the side, something he did when uncomfortable. "After we reach the Piarist Sisters in Vienna, what do you plan to do?"

Aurélie looked troubled. "I must take the cure back to Madame." She didn't look any too happy about that.

Jaska didn't, either. "Permit me to make one more observation: Whatever Bonaparte's motivation for reporting you as a spy, the fact that you were added to the lists of suspects indicates that Madame Bonaparte did nothing to keep suspicion from you."

Aurélie said in a low voice, "I thought about that after we left Strasbourg. But she's oftentimes so very afraid. She cannot always influence the First Consul. In any case, I made a promise. So I have to keep it."

Jaska said finally, "I don't want to be suspicious of you, Mademoiselle. Especially as it appears that you aren't Bonaparte's creature, or he wouldn't have put you on that list. But there are still mysteries here, and one of them is this ghost."

"Think of me however you must, but Kim is not a demon," Aurélie declared.

Almost at the same moment Mord said, "Citizen René's ghost is not a demon."

Jaska smiled and made a whimsical half-bow to Aurélie. "I shall accept that and be satisfied. My apologies for doubting."

She said in a low voice, "My apologies for keeping secrets that are not mine to reveal."

Jaska made a business of spreading out his greatcoat and placing his haversack just so, to act as pillow. Then he said, "Tomorrow I will arrange for us to take a riverboat the remainder of the way to Vienna."

Mord murmured something about *yichud*, the religious prohibition against opposite sexes, not married to each other, residing together in private. He retired to the far end of the attic. Aurélie curled up, facing away from the guys.

It took a long time for Aurélie to fall asleep. When she woke, Jaska had already gone. He rejoined them at breakfast, which was served at a gigantic table with the rest of the stable family and staff.

After that, they walked down to the riverside, where their boat was readying to cast off. They joined the gaggle of passengers moving up the ramp.

The seats were unsheltered, exposing them to the misting rain. Aurélie sat forward shivering, gazing at the mountains against the ragged sky. Her mouth dropped open when she first glimpsed the monumental stonework of Melk, which I knew contained books going back a thousand years. She gazed up at the picturesque ruin of Dürnstein, where Richard the Lionheart had been kept prisoner above a charming golden baroque village. It was Richard's vast ransom that had paid for the city walls we were about to pass.

But by then it was too dark to see much, so she dozed off until, early in the morning, the riverboat docked outside Vienna. Because of the arrowhead juts of the city walls, Vienna, in the distance, looked like the Castle of an Evil Doomlord.

THIRTY-TWO

VIENNA WAS WHERE I'D MET ALEC. I could see the familiar spire of St. Stephen's poking above those mighty ramparts—which, in my day, had become the Ringstrasse, a wide street circling the inner city. St. Stephen's was the single familiar sight, basically unchanged since the late 1200s.

Once we got closer, the impression of a vast and villainous lair evaporated as the baroque glory of Vienna opened up. The fortified city that had withstood two sieges by the Turkish invaders had been moderated by Emperor Joseph II. His trees were everywhere, giving the lovely pale-stone and golden baroque buildings the sense of a gigantic and secluded palace surrounded by pocket gardens.

The city streets were pretty clean. That, too, was a result of the resolutely enlightened Emperor Joseph II. It was strange to think that this guy had died only thirteen years before. At least he didn't see the horrific excesses of the French Revolution, or what happened to his little sister, Marie Antoinette.

The trio took a coach into the inner city, which was an amazing tangle of narrow streets and palaces, a fantasia of statuary, carvings, ironwork, bow windows, fountains, and pediments rich with images from Greek, Roman, and Christian myth.

Jaska looked around with a kind of alert, subtle tension, then finally said to Aurélie, "I will take you directly to the Piarists, or you will have to wait until Monday, as they will be busy from Maundy Thursday through Easter."

The coach stopped outside a street too narrow to admit passage. The walls were high with no windows. A door was fitted into them, however, with a tiny peephole. Above the door jamb was a bell pull on a chain. Aurélie rang the bell.

The elderly nun who opened the peephole said, "We do not interview during Holy Week. And we only educate the daughters of the poor."

She began to shut the peephole, but Aurélie leaned up and said quickly, "I am sent by Madame Bonaparte. I'm a woman, and I must speak to the prioress." Her French accent was unmistakable.

The door opened, and Jaska said from the coach door, "I'll return for you."

Aurélie cast him a distracted glance then followed the nun inside. She was conducted into a plain, clean hall. Distant voices could be heard—girls' voices praying, rising and falling in unison. Aurélie in a small room furnished with nothing but a couple of benches and a crucifix on the wall.

"It smells of incense here," she whispered to me. "Oh, that takes me back to Saint-Domingue." And she put her hand to her chest, where she had been carrying her mother's letter inside the waistcoat, ever since that night at Saint-Cloud.

An older woman appeared. From her manner she had to be the prioress, though her robes—plain black except for the thin band of her white wimple—were exactly like those of the first nun.

She sat down on the bench next to Aurélie. "You wish to speak to me, my daughter?" Her French was accented and quaint.

Out came Josephine's story, exactly as Aurélie had heard it. "And so," she finished. "What can you give her for a cure? She said she would pay anything. See? I brought these gold coins all the way, minus a small amount as my portion of our travel." Aurélie brought out the small purse and shook its clinking contents.

The prioress bowed her head and was silent for a time, then opened her eyes. "It is true that some of us can, at times, see and hear a little of the world unseen. Our sacristan is one of these. We also know enough to effect cures for some of the ills common to this world, though that is not our primary calling. But I would have to see her directly."

"She is in Paris and does not believe the First Consul would let her come here to consult you."

"Sometimes," the prioress said, "the path we see is difficult to explain, except in terms of sacred image. Are you a daughter of the church?"

Aurélie said, "I was baptized by my grandmother in Saint-Domingue, but I have been part of many traditions."

The prioress was again quiet for a time, then lifted a hand. "Here is what I can tell you in practical terms. The way to Paris lies in shadow. The reason you were sent, a young girl, traveling in dangerous times, instead of a diplomatic query, is the very reason you cannot return."

"But I must return," Aurélie said. I could hear the stress in her voice. "I promised Madame that I would."

"If you do, you will endanger her."

"Madame Josephine? Endangered by my return? How?"

"Your reappearance, even with a verbal message, will occasion exactly the questions your friend wishes to avoid."

"The *mouchards*," Aurélie exclaimed as I said to her, "She's right. You can't go back to Paris." Relief flooded through my invisible self.

"Then I must send her a letter," Aurélie said.

"A letter would meet the same treatment. However, I know of a way to get an answer to her through ecclesiastical channels. One of our order is being sent to Paris to consult with fellow Christians who are re-establishing schools. I can charge this nun with a simple message to your friend that will not endanger either party. If Madame wishes to hear what I have to say, she must find her path to me. She has the means. She must have the will, and perhaps I can do something for her, even if it is only to attempt to give her peace."

Aurélie handed the prioress the remainder of Josephine's gold coins. "I think she'd want you to have these, for your students. Perhaps you could pray for her, until she can come here?"

"We will put the money to good use," the nun said. "And we will dedicate a Mass to her." She made the sign of the cross between them, and said, "Go in peace, my daughter."

Aurélie thanked her politely and walked out. The moment the outer door shut, she leaned against the whitewashed stone wall, her eyes closed.

"Are you all right?" I asked.

"I am giddy," she whispered.

"With relief that you do not have to go back to Paris?"

She opened her eyes. "No. Yes. I'm glad that I needn't return to Paris, but I cannot say I need never again be afraid of Bonaparte, because is he not going to bring war all this way?" She didn't wait for an answer. "Duppy Kim, the conversation with the prioress, I dreamed it. Every word, only it was as if I saw myself through someone else's eyes."

"When did you do that?" My relief vanished like smoke, leaving me kind of creeped out.

"Long ago—very long. So long ago I had forgotten, until she began talking about Madame Bonaparte. I think it might have been when Aunt Kittredge confined me to my room for lying, or right after. None of it made sense, because I did not then know what *eine Priorin*—a prioress— was, or a Piarist, or who Madame Bonaparte was. I had never heard the name 'Bonaparte' when I was twelve. I only knew of her by her previous name, which was Rose Tascher de la Pagerie, and sometimes Madame de Beauharnais."

"Aurélie, I think you are dreaming people's actual lives."

"Yes. I came to that conclusion a fortnight or so ago. Each woman who wore the necklace. But this is different, because it's part of my own life."

"You saw a possible future," I said, trying to be comforting. "Dreams can't harm you, even if some of them don't end that well."

Aurélie's hands pressed flat against the gray stone wall, her eyes wide. "You don't understand. There is one more dream with me in it. Jaska is in it, too. In some place I have never seen."

I kept back a yip of joy. "That can't be bad," I said cautiously.

"But you are also in it. Standing next to me, in your body."

THIRTY-THREE

S HE BROKE OFF AT THE SOUND of horse's hooves and wheels rattling over cobblestones. She looked as scared as I felt. I was in my physical form, in her time? *This cannot be good.*

She fingered her pistol inside the waistcoat as a very fine carriage pulled up, a coat of arms painted on the door. Then I recognized the Dobreni golden twin falcons, each holding sprigs of green, one acanthus and the other amaranth, against a red background.

Aurélie pulled her fingers away from the grip of the pistol when the door opened and Jaska leaped out. "Come inside," he invited. He was still in his travel clothes, his forehead taut with tension.

Aurélie settled onto the bench opposite him and looked around appreciatively. "This is a very fine coach. Where did you find it?"

"It belongs to the legation from my homeland. Dobrenica is a subject of the empire, and my friend Hippolyte is first secretary to the legate. I've taken the liberty of engaging you a hotel room, which we'll go to directly. Feel free to give orders for laundry and to have your coat brushed. Or did you wish to become a female again?"

"I thought of that." Aurélie set her satchel down, dug way to the bottom, and pulled out a tight roll of fabric, which unrolled to disclose one of her pretty little French gowns with the cap sleeves, edged with Grecian patterns.

In Paris this gown was the latest fashion, perfectly tasteful. But a single day's look at people on the streets of Vienna made it plain that here, Paris fashions were out of place. Aurélie regarded the rumpled gown in dismay, then shoved it back into her satchel. "Perhaps I'd better go as I am."

Jaska said, "Yes. There's another aspect that we didn't consider. As a young lady, you'd require a maidservant. Those are easy enough to find, but more difficult would be a suitable *dame de compagnie*."

Aurélie sighed. "*Les convenances.* It's so much easier to be a boy."

"So my sister used to say, when we were small. She used to steal my clothes from time to time, and go out as me. Everyone was properly scandalized when at last she was caught, but I sometimes wondered, what's the harm, really, when she did nothing but what every boy does when he has time on his hands? No one could give me sufficient answer except, *Her reputation will be forever ruined.*" He smiled.

Aurélie smiled back, and I waited impatiently for her to ask more about his family. Her lips parted. But then she gave her head a tiny shake and said, "'Twas the same in England. My cousins and I couldn't understand it either."

Jaska gestured toward the coach window. "I've a suggestion. Vienna is famed for her music, and Hippolyte told me that there is an oratorio being performed tonight by a newcomer named Beethoven. He and a Herr Wölffl are reputed to be the best pianists since Mozart, and he also writes music, they say. There's a new theater out by the market."

Her whole face brightened with anticipation, causing his to brighten as well.

He'd arranged for a room in a hotel not far from St. Stephen's, whose bells echoed carillons down the stone canyons of the streets. The hotel seemed to cater to young, well-born secretaries to ambassadors and legates, and to local imperial officers, couriers, and gentry-class music students.

As servants carried up hot water to the copper tub set in an alcove off the room, she retreated to the window seat and looked down at the busy street below.

I poked her and asked, "Why didn't you ask about his family?"

She blushed. "I thought it would be too forward."

"He looked like he wanted to tell you."

She pulled the mirror up and peered earnestly at me. "I thought so, too. And yet I'm afraid. If he answers such questions readily, will he not want to ask the same sorts of questions from me?"

A servant came into the room to inform 'the young gentleman' that the bath was ready and would he like anything else?

She dismissed him with thanks and retired to the bath. When she emerged, her damp hair fluffed and curled around her neat queue. She dressed in her second-best shirt and waistcoat and breeches. The servant had brushed her coat and borne the rest of her clothes off to a laundry. She looked very young as well as strikingly handsome.

She arrived downstairs to find Jaska waiting in a sober-colored coat, his hair neatly tied back, his cravat plain, no rings or fobs. It was impossible to guess his status, from his clothes—he could have been anything from a prosperous middle class student to a slumming prince.

Here was something new, though. The expression on his face as she appeared, was quick and unguarded. And tender.

But she didn't have the experience to see what I saw. She blushed and wouldn't look at him at all as he opened the door and led the way out.

When they reached the street, she absently smoothed her ruffled curls off her brow and said, "Where is Mord?"

"He left for a place called Eisenstadt, but he'll return." Jaska glanced down the street, then back. Then he electrified me by speaking quickly, as if he'd rehearsed his words: "I hoped you would consider riding with us to visit my homeland."

Aurélie gave a start.

"Sorry," I whispered. "I did not mean to poke you."

Jaska continued, ". . . and I flatter myself by thinking you might like it in spite of its being small and provincial, as the French say. There is always music. It resembles Vienna in that way, though Riev is a very small capital of an equally small kingdom. But—" He switched to Latin. "They understand magic there, and they might be able to help your spirit to return to where she belongs. And Mord is going to rejoin me on the road," he added, as if that offered additional incentive. "He has no home to go to, like you. Though Dobrenica has been subject to the empire for over a hundred years, our laws respecting the Jews are closer to the Polish enlightenment."

If I'd been breathing, I would have held my breath.

But Aurélie didn't hesitate. "Thank you. I would like to see your homeland."

If I'd had a body I would have cried for joy, and grief, and worry, and . . . well, you get the idea. *Okay, that's the first hurdle. Now for his identity . . . and I hope by then I've figured out why and how I'm to save Dobrenica.*

———

"You want me to go to his country?" Aurélie asked later.

I'd made so many mistakes that I'd resolved to start small. If she asked questions, I'd answer only that question. But no information offered beyond. "It has a reputation for its music. And magical studies," I said.

She looked down at her hands for a long time, as if turning ideas over in her mind. Then she changed her coat and neck cloth and brushed her hair again, to prepare for the night's concert.

From the first broody chords of the oratorio, Aurélie was enthralled. All the way back she and Jaska talked about musical theory, and both predicted a great future for Herr Beethoven with all the enthusiasm of a couple in our day who has just discovered a great new band.

Over the next few days, they attended as many musical events as Jaska could locate. He was scrupulously careful, treating her rather like James had, as if she were a fellow student, but betraying by little signs his awareness that she wasn't, in spite of her boy's wear. I don't think she saw them, because she avoided his glance and kept a scrupulous distance, betraying her own growing interest only when his gaze was elsewhere.

Occasionally, Aurélie glimpsed the elusive Hippolyte (de) Vauban, a tall Frenchman with an eye-patch, so homely he was appealing. Or maybe it was his smile, his air of gallantry. He appeared and vanished like a stage magician, supplying the legation coach and tickets. He also looked at her with an interest that made me wonder if Jaska had confided in his old army buddy.

I hoped to get a hint about Jaska's identity from Hippolyte, but he was too circumspect. The only time Aurélie and Jaska got into personal stuff was when the bells tolled at midday on Good Friday, when everything was draped in black. "Do you not wish to attend Mass?" Aurélie asked. "Or are you still an apostate?"

Jaska looked around their café with an air of discomfort. "Mord once said that he was angry at God for the curse of free will. That we had to live in a world that contained Russians like Suvorov and Cossacks who could murder good people like his grandfather and his intended wife. I share that anger, yet a world without God somewhere makes no sense. That is, it implies no meaning when anyone can see there is an order to the stars and in the patterns of small things, to the patterns of colors in the shells of snails. Perhaps, though, I am merely unwilling to live in a world of no meaning."

Aurélie gave a short nod of agreement.

"But I am not ready to confess and to mean it. 'Thou shalt not kill' is one of the Ten Commandments, a mortal sin. I killed in the battle at Praga. I enjoyed it. The first death was a Russian who looked this tall when he came at me." Jaska held his hand up high. "When he was dead at my feet, his face smoothed out, I saw he could not be any older than I was. After that . . . it was easier. If God is there and listens to us, then He knows what lies in my heart. Until I get home . . ." Jaska looked away bleakly. "I have a close relation in the Benedictines. We used to debate. He always had a knack for explaining things," Jaska added, then said with a quick, sideways look, "Mord will only marry within his religion, if he marries at all."

Aurélie spread her hands. "I pity his wife, if he does choose to marry. That is, I'd pity her for having to support his moods, though she would be a very, very lucky woman if he plays music for her."

Jaska listened to that with muted surprise. She tipped her head. "He is a very romantical person. A little like a fire, I have come to see. Very bright, but you do not want to draw too near."

"He is a very loyal friend," Jaska said, his tone reflective, midway between relief and question.

"Very," she agreed. "My cousin Diana is just such a one."

On Easter Sunday, they were out in the streets with the Austrians when St. Stephen's rang the *Pummerin*, the great bell—one of the largest in all of Europe. Its deep, voluminous sound reverberated through stone and wood and bone and muscle. That day, I noticed no winged beings around, though I could not tell you if there was a connection.

The next day Jaska appeared at Aurélie's hotel with a pair of excellent horses, and they departed for Dobrenica.

Alec, I'm coming home, I thought.

THIRTY-FOUR

EISENSTADT WAS NOT THAT FAR from Vienna. Mord was waiting for them on the road that afternoon, looking like something out of a vengeance movie with a killer soundtrack—you know, like *Reservoir Dogs*—with his wild hair, scruffy chin, violin case in one hand, sword, pistol, and cavalry carbine in a holster at his back.

"There are more seraphs following you," he said by way of greeting.

Aurélie slewed around on her horse (she was still a death-grip rider) and I saw . . . nothing.

Mord blinked. "They evaporated. But they were there."

"Let's go," Jaska said, clucking his mount into a trot. "I would rather get to an inn before dark."

We didn't see any more of them as the days wore on, and we gradually moved into increasingly wild countryside.

I was not prepared for the cascade of memories and emotions when I heard the first clickety-clack of waterwheels, hidden in the soft fan-spreads of fern and wild tangles of ancient trees. Dobrenica is basically a large comma-shaped valley surrounded by mountains, whose streams and rivers trickle and splash into countless gorges and vales and hollows, some of which get only the occasional shaft of sunlight during the warm months of the year.

Jaska seemed to expand as we neared his homeland, or maybe the guises of soldier, student, diplomat, and aide de camp all coalesced. He didn't turn gabby or bossy. I don't think Mord would have put up with that—or Aurélie, either. It was more that he seemed to draw on a sense of alertness, even responsibility, which you'd expect when taking people to your home turf. Yet he still didn't talk about his life there.

Then we reached the border.

What would be a rough few hours' drive in my time was now a week of tortuous travel up a very narrow road that too frequently dwindled to the width of an animal path, due to fallen trees or rocks or landslides. Then the road would widen again as it caught up with hidden thoroughfares between concealed villages.

Jaska said one night, as an entire small inn turned out to welcome them, "I sent a message ahead with the legation courier. We should be met along the road here somewhere."

The next morning, as they rode out under the still dripping conifers into a world scrubbed into bright spring colors by a midnight thunderstorm, they heard noise ahead that resolved into many horse hooves. The rumble of male voices was punctuated by the ring and clatter of heavy martial gear.

Mord rammed the book he had been reading into his saddle bag, snatched off his spectacles, then snapped the carbine out in two practiced moves. Jaska put his hand to his sword, and Aurélie whipped from the saddle sheath the pistol that she had not fired since they had reached Linz.

The first of the cavalcade arrived. Pistol and carbine leveled, sword loosened in scabbard.

Then Jaska let out a shout of laughter. "Piotr Andreyevich! I did not expect you so early." Mord and Aurélie holstered their weapons.

The leader was a slim guy of about twenty-five, dressed in the eighteenth-century version of the Vigilzhi uniform; that is, the deep cuffed sleeves and full skirted coat of blue, the cross belt instead of a Sam Browne, a plumed shako instead of a helmet. The front of the shako had the same brass plaque of the Dobreni falcons as the one on the Vigilzhi helmet of modern times.

This particular shako was worn at a rakish angle on wild blond curls that framed a face with the sharp cheekbones and uptilted eyes that hinted at Mongol ancestry. He held up a gloved hand to slow the column following behind him, drew his horse alongside Jaska's, then murmured in Dobreni, "*She* would have it her way."

Jaska whispered in consternation, "You do not mean Irena?"

"Insisted. And as her brother is my commanding officer, and you did not specifically order to the contrary . . ."

Jaska became aware of Aurélie's and Mord's curious looks at either side, and his horse sidled, ears back. "René—Aurélie—Mordechai, this is Captain Piotr Andreyevich Danilov, of the King's Guard," he said in French, then quickly, in Dobreni, "How long do we have?"

"She hadn't left the Golden Chestnut when we departed. We thought we ought to ride ahead as fast as we could." He moved his horse aside as someone left the column and approached. This was a tall, sober-faced young woman with a hint of blond braids under the hood of her riding cloak, diamonds winking at her ears.

"Margit," Jaska exclaimed with unmistakable relief. "I knew I could rely on you. Though I did not mean to put you to this trouble. A trunk would have sufficed."

The hood was thrown back, disclosing a pretty bonnet above a face so much like Jaska's it was instantly clear that not only was this young woman his sister, she was his twin.

She drew her horse alongside Jaska's, laughing and crying both, then leaned out to grab his arm. They kissed, the horses sidled, ears awry (unlike their riders, they did not know one another) and Margit whirled her mount back into line with an expert turn of wrist and knee.

Then she swept a speculative gaze from Aurélie's much battered hat to her mud splashed, worn soled, buckled shoes. With that steady, assessing gaze still on Aurélie's masculine coat and her trousered legs, Margit said in Dobreni, "Irena is not far behind."

"We will have to ride back to Mierz."

"Did you leave suitable clothing in Mierz?" Margit asked, without removing her gaze from Aurélie.

"All we have is what we carry," Jaska said.

"What is the problem?" Mord asked in German.

Aurélie's wide gaze flicked from one to the other, as in the distance, the clopping of hooves heralded new arrivals. Not knowing what was going on, she nipped her pistol from the saddle sheath and held it ready as Margit muttered in Dobreni, "I always fight fair," to her brother, and fumbled at the neck of her cloak. She gathered the fine yards of wool in her arms as she kneed her horse closer to Aurélie, who looked at her with a pucker of apprehension in her brow.

Margit snatched off Aurélie's hat, and then, with a quick flick of her wrists, threw the cloak around Aurélie's shoulders. "Pull it together. Pull the hood forward," she ordered in German.

Aurélie stuffed the pistol in her waistband and pulled the cloak around herself. She tugged the hood over her head about five seconds before another cavalcade of Vigilzhi (or King's Guard, as I guess they were called in 1803) appeared, with another woman in their center. This woman was short, wearing a masculine-looking riding habit that made the most of a very curvy figure and a ramrod-straight back. An enormous diamond glittered in the lace at her high collar, and I bet myself it was loaded with anti-vampire spells. Her black hair, drawn away from an extravagant widow's peak, was pulled up into a dashing riding hat rather like a laced shako with wide scarlet ribbons pulled down to tie under her chin. Wide-set black eyes gazed from below straight brows, in a face pale as porcelain.

"Jaska." Her voice was high and clear. "We could not wait a moment longer. Seven years!" Her clear tones tried, convicted, and sentenced Jaska to a lifetime of guilt. "Seven *years.*"

"Irena Sergeyevna," Jaska said, without answering the prosecutorial query. The black-haired Irena forced her horse between Jaska's and Aurélie's, and he kissed the gloved hand she held out imperiously.

He relinquished her hand and indicated Aurélie. "May I present Lady Aurélie de Mascarenhas, and here is Domnu Mordechai ben Aaron Zusya." And to the two, "Countess Irena Sergeyevna Trasyemova."

Irena had no interest in Mord at that moment. She lifted her brows and made a business of searching the air earnestly behind Aurélie, as if to spot an invisible train of respectability. "Donna Aurélie?"

Again the accusatory tone.

Jaska said, "Alas, Donna Aurélie's maid—" He faltered.

Margit took over without a hitch. "—is down the hill, with a delicate complaint. I shall have to make suitable arrangements, but leave such tedium to me, Irena. Why don't you lead everyone back to the Golden Chestnut? Domnu Balik will require a number for ordering dinner."

Aurélie looked down at her hands in their masculine gloves and let the hood fall over her face. "Where have you come from?" Irena asked of Jaska. "Your mother—"

"I beg your pardon," Jaska interrupted, speaking in German. "But not everyone understands Dobreni. We will continue in a tongue comprehensible to all." And for the next forty-five minutes or so, as they rode up the mountain from where the cavalcades had just come, Jaska spoke steadily, in German, about all the musical events in Vienna. Nobody got a word in edgewise.

We rode past a stone plinth, which I took to be the official border into Dobrenica. Jaska's music lecture ceased when the road widened, and the hard-packed ground gave way to stone flagging. A village of stone houses appeared, their walls cream-colored, the roofs sharply slanted. Window boxes were everywhere, including in the dormer and attic windows, giving the buildings a festive air.

The mounted procession entered a broad plaza of patterned brick. Villagers stopped their wagons, carts, and conversations to stare, the men pulling off hats in salute as the columns passed.

The biggest three buildings in the village were a town hall, a church, and an inn; the latter of two stories beneath a steep patterned roof, its third story with dormer windows—each with its flowery window box—punctuating that roof. The sign suspended from a graceful wrought iron pole depicted a bright yellowish chestnut.

The two cavalcades blended into one and, at a lifted hand from Captain Danilov, rode around the corner in twos toward an enormous stable.

Captain Danilov leaped off his horse and handed Margit down first, and then he moved to Irena. Aurélie, not knowing horse etiquette, began to throw her leg over, but Jaska held up a hand, one side of his mouth quirking into a grin.

Aurélie regarded him in amazement but waited as he got Irena safely out of the way. He then held out his hand to her with an air, and she took that hand with exaggerated politesse and descended from the horse, careful to keep the cloak clutched tightly around herself.

This by-play was observed by Margit, her mouth pursed.

Unfortunately, the cloak's hem settled into a puddle around Aurélie, which she hastily gathered up into both arms. Margit was tall and willowy, probably five nine or ten, an inch or two taller than I am. Aurélie was, I would guess, about five one in heels.

Irena, on the other side of Jaska's horse, saw none of this. She had refused to walk on her own but waited where she was, her arm held out expectantly to Jaska. As he put his hand under her elbow, she addressed Mord. "So you are the one who saved his life? We owe you our gratitude. I will introduce you to . . ."

They passed up the steps and into the inn, Margit and Aurélie following.

"This way," Margit said to Aurélie, and indicated a sweeping slate stair to the right, as the others crossed into a parlor at the left.

Margit led Aurélie to the second floor and down the hall to the end, where a liveried footman opened double doors. Aurélie walked into a beautiful room with deep set window embrasures on either side, revealing the thickness of the walls. The room was plastered in a soft cream color, with Dobreni folk patterns painted all around under the ceiling.

Aurélie slipped off the cloak, gathered its folds together, and then held it out. "I beg pardon for the dust," she said in German.

Margit took the cloak, but dropped it onto a hassock embroidered with huckleberries and thistles. "You do have a pistol," she said. "I thought I saw one."

"Yes."

"Can you use it?" Margit asked, her tone midway between challenge and distrust.

"*Naturellement!* Why should I have such a weapon if I do not know its use?" Aurélie's French accent was strong. "You desire to see my skill?" she asked, and I wondered if she was thinking back to those scornful midshipmen a thousand years ago.

Margit put up her hands as if to stop a bullet, but Aurélie had already turned away. Two quick strides into the window embrasure and she flung open the window. There was a broad kitchen yard below. Adjacent to the yard, the stable, a weathervane on its roof. "See that?" Aurélie asked, indicating the weather vane. "*Peste*, I believe this weapon will throw that far. I had better aim high."

She leveled the pistol and fired. Below, chickens clucked and scattered at the loud report, and a man carrying a basket of cabbages looked up, startled. Otherwise the noise went unnoticed in the tumult resounding from the stable, as the King's Guard went about unsaddling their horses, talking and laughing.

Aurélie pulled her head back. "I was correct, it was almost out of range. But the ball hit it on its fall."

Margit gazed past her at the weather vane, which was lazily spinning, then back at Aurélie. Her expression had smoothed the way Jaska's did as she said, "I obeyed my brother's request, but I am trying to understand why he made such a request."

"Request?" Aurélie repeated.

"You did not know?"

"He told us only that he sent a message ahead. We were to be met, I thought because the road is dangerous. I am used to that. This is why I carry a pistol."

Margit walked a large circle around Aurélie, gazing at her from every angle, as if to penetrate inside her head. "He sent a message to Piotr, asking for a company to meet him on the road, but he included a note to me. The first since he, Mordechai, and Hippolyte de Vauban were taken prisoner in Prussia, seven years ago."

"Prisoners!" Aurélie exclaimed. "He did not tell me that. But all I know of his life is this terrible battle in Warsaw."

"He was taken prisoner after that and conducted to Berlin, where there was a diplomatic exchange over his hostage arrangements. But did he come home when we had paid? He did not. He sent us a letter about Polish reunification and vanished for three years. My mother heard from him next in Sweden. Gustav would not come to Poland's aid, but we could have told him that. No further communication from Jaska except to our mother through our legation in Vienna, until he favored me at last with a note, saying he was bringing his savior of Warsaw and a young lady 'who would require female clothes.'"

"He did not have to do that. I can find myself some clothes," Aurélie said. "I even brought a gown. It was ordered by Madame Bonaparte herself. But it was not right for Vienna."

Margit sat down on a chair. "Madame Bonaparte," she repeated, her tone changing again.

"Where—*malédiction!* My satchel is still upon the horse."

"The servant will have brought it in the back way." Margit rose and crossed to one of the far doors.

Beyond was another large chamber twin to the salon but for the curtained bed adjacent the fireplace. Set below a wardrobe was Aurélie's ragged satchel, which she fell upon with a glad cry. She sat on a footstool, laid her pistol down, opened the satchel, and pulled out her gown. Wrinkled and stained as it was by rain and bits of gunpowder, its stylishness breathed Paris. "It was chosen by Madame Josephine herself."

Margit leaned against a heavy escritoire, arms crossed. "There is much I do not understand here, but it must wait. I owe it to my brother, or more correctly to the years we were close, to do as he asks. You will find a bath waiting through that door over there. All should be in readiness by now. And a small selection of my gowns, what could be put together at a moment's notice by Viorel, who is young, but very discreet. I can see that the shoes will be completely wrong, but that cannot be helped."

"I also have one pair of my indoor shoes, at the very bottom," Aurélie offered.

"Excellent. Go and dress as quickly as you can. I will join the others and make excuses, but dinner will no doubt be served soon, and Irena will be impatient."

"Who is this countess? Why does she come when not expected, or I think, when she is not wanted?"

"Because she has waited seven years for a crown, of course," Margit said with a sardonic smile.

"Pardon me, but a crown?" Aurélie asked. "Whose crown?"

Margit put her head to one side. "*Donnerwetter!* Do you really not know?" She eyed Aurélie with unhidden suspicion.

"Know what?"

"Shall we begin with my brother's full name? That he is Karl-Rudolph Alexander Jaska Dsaret, Crown Prince of Dobrenica."

THIRTY-FIVE

"**H**E IS WHAT?" Aurélie jumped to her feet. "Then you are a princess?"

Margit curtseyed mockingly. "Anna-Maria Elisabetta Margit Dsaret, older than my brother by half an hour, but alas, a mere female. Mother's reward after four females was a son at the last." She raised her hand toward the *salle de bain*. "I believe the French say, *c'est fini, touche cela. Vite!*"

She walked out, leaving me wishing I could grab her—or follow her and hear what she was going to say to Jaska.

Aurélie sat down abruptly on the footstool, the dress forgotten on her lap. She looked anything but gratified. I could practically feel my future unraveling as she said, "Did you hear that? Did you know?" Her brows twitched together as she sprang to the long elegant mirror and slapped it peremptorily. She scowled at me when our fingers touched on the glass. "You *did* know. Did you not? I remember what you said when James and I became betrothed."

"I knew it was a possibility," I said cautiously. "You know the future is not sure until it becomes the present."

Her brow cleared. "The crossroads. Decisions. Yes, I remember. Nanny Hiasinte must have seen this. Is that why she sent you?" She turned away, wringing her hands. "No, that no longer matters. You're here. You saved my life, I am convinced, when I was in Dieppe." She turned back. "If it wasn't for you, I would never have thought to go into that tavern. Did you know then?"

I shook my head, happy to be telling the truth. "I had no idea who was inside that tavern. It was their music that drew my attention."

She let out a deep breath. "Such excellent music. And such excellent company as we traveled." She put her hands to her flushed cheeks. "But a prince? It changes *everything*."

"Why? You would undo your friendship?"

"No!"

"If I knew, back then, who he was, what would you have done if I'd told you?" I asked.

The scowl changed to a questioning look. She threw down the dress and went to the *salle de bain*, where an enormous copper tub waited, full of steaming water. Then she whirled around and faced the mirror. "I cannot answer that," she said as she wrestled out of her male clothes. "I think it would depend on how I was told. Crowns! Do you remember when Bonaparte offered me a crown? I wonder if he was serious. Who gives his mistress a crown?"

"He could give you a crown without the title or the land that usually comes with it," I said.

"Oh, 'crown' in the sense of a necklace or bracelet, the price for one's favors. He has so many treasures from his wars, there must be crowns among them." Aurélie peeled off her stocking and paused. "My necklace. It's been so long on my ankle that I forgot about it. Should I wear it?"

"Perhaps not yet."

She wrinkled her nose. "I'm thinking of finery and crowns because of this news about Jaska. There goes our ease! I wish I didn't know. Our walk, our talks . . . I didn't think about how much each day came to be more interesting than the last. How much I looked forward to talking to him, a fellow musician. We didn't know one another's past, because that didn't matter. So I thought!" She crossed her arms across her chest and gripped her shoulders. "Why didn't he tell me?"

"Because there would go the ease, the comfort," I said.

"*Parbleu!* What should I do?"

"Go on as if you don't know."

"I should lie? Pretend this princess didn't tell me who he is?"

"No. I think you should act like you did before she told you. Don't let his rank get between you."

"But it *is* between us." She turned her back on the bath and picked up her travel-stained shirt. "I think I'd better leave. I could put on my student clothes and vanish back down the trail."

"Why?" I asked, alarm zapping through me. Though part of my motivation was selfish, it was only part. With real conviction, I said, "I think you'd make a perfect princess."

She grimaced. "You've forgotten that I'm not the daughter of a marquis."

I took another risk. "I told you once I got glimpses of your future. What would you say if I told you one of those glimpses was you and Jaska on your honeymoon? Here? In this country?"

She stilled, head lifted. Then shook it. "A possible future, didn't we agree? If he were not a prince, then I could believe it. You know they always marry their own kind."

"They certainly did in the past." Again, ideas cascaded: Alec and our Princess Conversation. The first time we had it, he said, *Surely you know by now that royalty is only a state of mind?*

I said to Aurélie, "One thing you must have learned in Paris is that crowns can be worn by anyone. Usually with an army backing them, but not always." I was thinking of Désirée Clary and her Jean-Baptiste Bernadotte, who would be invited to be Crown Prince of Sweden. The Bernadottes are the ruling family of Sweden to this day. "Rank is an idea, like republicanism. You know that. You talked about it all the way from Strasbourg to Ulm."

"But . . ." Her graceful fingers fluttered from her forehead down her towel-draped person. "This is different."

"Because it's personal. I understand that."

Aurélie gave a short nod. "Here's another question. Do you think this Countess Irena loves Jaska?"

"I am not certain."

"Personal. Do you think he—"

"Cares for you? Oh, yes."

"So, here we are." She retreated to the bath, took the fastest one of her life, and then returned to look at Margit's trunk. Whatever her misgivings about her brother's strange request, the princess had brought exquisite linens for underclothes and chemisettes, and two gowns of embroidered lawn, one for day and one for evening, both high waisted. The third outfit was a riding habit.

There were ribbon sashes, and more ribbons for the hair. Stockings of the finest cotton and two shawls with knotted fringes completed the selection of clothes.

Aurélie dug out her old sewing kit and pulled on one of the gowns. It was a basic tube, flaring out so that the skirt draped over the chemisette. She turned this way and that. The gown was too wide and long, dragging on the floor. She carefully placed her toes on the hem, then picked up several pins, put them in her mouth, pinched the fabric under her arm and at the ribs, and pinned the pinches.

She slipped carefully out of the gown, loaded her needle, then used the place her toe had been to mark the new hem.

As she began whipping up the hem with the speed of all those teenage years of sewing, she finally said, "There's knowing that I'm as good as anyone else, and the facts of my parentage. It's very well to say that I know I'm as good as anyone else, but that won't matter much if everyone else thinks the way Aunt Kittredge did. And you know most people will."

"Do you believe, after you heard General Kosciusko, that *Jaska* would treat you that way if he found out?"

"I don't know," she said finally, as she began stitching the first of the tucks. "Ah, don't speak, Duppy Kim. I must concentrate."

She scowled as she thrust the needle through the cloth.

Gradually her tense brow cleared as she quickly transformed the dress. It was as if she transformed herself with the gown; she'd watched Leroy, Josephine's dressmaker, and had learned the art of drapery. When she slipped the gown on again it had become a different dress. Her posture in it was straight-backed, her chin high. But her gaze was still troubled.

She turned in a slow circle, then came to a decision. She pulled out her tiny sewing scissors and carefully trimmed some of the damp hair around her face. Josephine and her ladies wore theirs short in front. Aurélie fingered the locks, which sprang into what Josephine had called "kiss curls." They were charming on her forehead and cheeks and neck.

I watched, rejoicing at every primp and tuck, for each seemed to bring her closer to the decision to stay and tough it out.

Finally she used one of the cherry-colored ribbons to bind up the rest of her thick, wavy black hair in the Grecian style, which accentuated the beautiful shape of her head and the graceful curve of her throat. She tied the cherry sash high, put on her old slippers, and glanced at herself in the mirror.

"You're a princess," I said.

She laughed, then curtseyed with mocking grace. "I won't retreat. He must send me away. But I won't tell him about my history just yet. I must determine if I'll trust him that much, because he didn't trust me enough to tell me who he was. There might be reasons. I'll wait to hear them."

She swept out.

The others sat in a private dining room, paneled and enameled in white and gold with intricate rococo frieze-work. Their faces were flushed. Aurélie sniffed. From the looks of things, she was taking in the sweet fumes of a double-distilled plum brandy called *tzuica*.

She'd spent a year learning not only the intricacies of court etiquette, but how to move with the blend of balletic grace and allure that was so much a part of Josephine's style. The men stopped talking and stared as she glided into the room.

Seating arrangements mean something in court circles, and there was Mord in the place of honor at Jaska's right. At Jaska's left, his sister. Then Captain Danilov, an empty chair, and Irena, who was on Mord's other side, leaving a spot for Aurélie between the captain and the countess, and opposite Jaska. It was a perfect arrangement, as equal as one could get, and yet not neutral.

Aurélie sat, and Jaska spoke: "It is said that German is the language of empire, but French is still the language of civilization, so we are exhibiting our civilized selves tonight."

It was another perfect touch, because the best French speakers there were Jaska, Mord, and Aurélie.

If Aurélie hadn't been told who Jaska was, I'm sure she would've figured it out fast, for the servants bowed to him whenever they came forward to offer foods or take things away, and everything was prefaced with *Durchlaucht*—"your highness."

I could see Jaska eyeing her covertly, a hint of apprehension in the slight quirk of his brows. He was clearly waiting for the anvil to drop.

But Aurélie gave no sign that anything was different. He led the conversation firmly in safe channels, mostly music, weather, the roads. During a break, the Countess fired her first shot across the bow, asking where Jaska and his mystery guest had met.

Jaska said, "I first became acquainted with Doña Aurélie in Paris. Come, I know Domnu Balik's chief pride is his new fortepiano in the big salon. Would you like to hear some of our music? By the time we reached Vienna, I venture to say that we had become a very fine trio. You shall judge."

When a prince asks if you would like, you say you would like.

And so the rest of the evening was musical. A rough start, as the three hadn't played for a while, but as always, by the end of the first song, they found their rhythm.

Also as usual, the attention gradually shifted to Mord. They finished with a gorgeous adaption of Bach's Flute Sonata in G Minor, the violin counterpoint entirely extemporaneous. Mord spun the melodic line into enchantment.

The company parted around midnight, everyone in a thoughtful mood. When they reached the landing again, Aurélie looked inquiringly at Margit, who pointed and said, "That's your suite." And in a lower voice, "I'll send Viorel. I brought her for you."

"I don't need a maid," Aurélie whispered back.

Margit's brows rose, and she said, "Viorel will pack for you in the morning, then."

Aurélie thanked her, wished her good night, and slipped inside.

She was crossing the outer room, moving from lamp to lamp when a soft knock sounded from outside.

I heard it immediately, and I think she did as well, for she sped to the door. Jaska was there, alone.

"May I come inside? Only for a moment," he said.

Aurélie backed up, her face in shadow, his dimly lit by the one remaining lamp. "I wanted to apologize. I intended to tell you before we reached Riev. I didn't think my sister would come herself when I asked her by note to send clothing."

"They missed you."

"Margit did. I owe her an apology for that, and I'll go to her next. Am I forgiven for my sin against you?"

Aurélie looked at him with a troubled expression. "In the words of my grandmother's priest, it would a sin of omission, not commission. I think I can understand your not telling me who you were. And you are forgiven."

"Thank you," he said, and looked around. If he was waiting for her to disclose her background, he waited in vain. Finally: "You'll be comfortable here?"

Aurélie laughed. "You're asking someone who's slept in horse stalls and on unswept attic floors?"

Jaska gave her a quick smile, a questioning glance, and wished her a good night.

She blew the last lamp out and walked into the bedroom.

The next morning, Aurélie was up early adapting the riding habit. By the time they set out, she had it fitting perfectly.

———

There was little interesting conversation on the ride until the last day. Aurélie was silent, especially as Irena tried to monopolize Jaska by talking to him in Dobreni. Margit hung back, neither aiding nor deflecting Irena's assumption of the place at Jaska's side.

The evening before they descended into the valley of Dobrenica, they spent as guests of a baron whose name was familiar, but I didn't know any of his descendants except by sight. Word had definitely gone on ahead. They arrived not only to a magnificent feast that lasted for hours, but the local choir trooped over and performed a surprisingly good rendition of Praetorius's *"Nun komm der heiden heiland."*

The obsequious attention to Jaska and the bowing and studied professions of delight that he was at last returned safely to his homeland were a pretty good indication of what lay ahead.

Next morning bright and early, Jaska declared that he wanted to reach Riev by nightfall, and so anyone who did not wish to rise early had his leave to depart at a more leisurely time. By sunrise they were all there, Irena looking disgruntled.

Eighteenth century roads being vastly different from 20th century ones (especially as experienced from the back of a horse instead of in a car or train) kept me from recognizing the landscape. Not all the villages had signs, and though a couple of them looked familiar, that could have been because they resembled one another.

I finally got my bearings when the cavalcade rounded a forested bend, topped a rise—and there, on the mountaintops across the broad expanse of the checkerboarded valley, was Tony's castle, silhouetted against the morning sky.

Not Tony's, of course. He wouldn't be born for two centuries.

Aurélie gave a gasp and pointed.

I almost spoke, then Margit said, "That is Mount Dhiavilyi, the duchy von Mecklundburg."

"The castle?" Aurélie asked.

"It's called the Eyrie, as you might expect. 'Eagles' nest.' Fischer von Erlach rebuilt it for them after he finished the royal palace."

Jaska glanced back. "Later this morning we should reach Antonius Summit. From there you can see all six of Dobrenica's highest peaks."

A little before noon the horses plodded the last of the steep road to the Summit under a fast-clouding sky. Irena complained about the rain, ostensibly to Margit but in a loud voice, and when Jaska did not respond, she addressed him directly. "Jaska, we ought to ride down the Paduzal Valley road. Baroness Vezsar would welcome us."

"Irena, I believe we can make it to Riev, but please. If you're more comfortable visiting the baroness, don't feel obliged to ride on." Jaska's voice changed timbre, from politeness to anticipation. "Here we are."

For a timeless moment everyone halted. All around the horizon rose the mountains, majestic and mysterious.

Jaska's voice was husky as he said, "Here to our left, the closest is Mount Tanazca. Above it, at the westmost reach of our border, is Mount Adeliad. You can see Riev on its slope. Our northernmost point is Mount Domitrian, the duchy of the Ysvorods. To the east is Mount Corbesc, and south of that is the highest of all the mountains, said to be the crown, Dsaretsenberg—you hear the German word for mountain in the name?— and south of it, across the valley, is Mount Dhiavilyi, with the Eyrie atop."

Jaska stilled, his manner alert. I looked about, but within my limitations saw and heard nothing extraordinary. Mord also stilled then peered intently down the tree-covered slopes below us.

"Piotr," Jaska called.

Captain Danilov brought his horse alongside Jaska's, his manner also intent. Jaska bent toward him and said in Dobreni, "You and I both know who that must be, and can guess at how many are with him. Can you flank them?"

"I'll take half down into Paduzal. I know the old bandits' path. It should do."

"Go."

Captain Danilov clucked to his horse and rode back down the column, peeling off half his troops. Soon we heard the thunder of hooves rapidly diminishing.

Mord edged up. "Do we need arms?" He glanced toward Aurélie.

Jaska said, "I'd rather avoid the . . . let's call it the appearance of expectation. This is probably going to be a matter of maneuvering. I want to keep it that way if I can."

Margit had stiffened. She turned an ironic eye on her brother. "What about *us*?" She indicated the women.

"He'll know you're with me," Jaska said, and Margit looked away quickly, making me suspect that her twin had missed an important cue.

"He?" Aurélie asked.

I was thinking, *Big surprise. The von Mecklundburgs are trouble now, too.* So imagine my surprise when Margit said in a flat voice, "Unless I'm completely wrong, this will be Benedek Ysvorod, Duke of Domitrian." And another sneaky look Jaska's way.

Oh, yeah. There was a cue, all right.

But Jaska was busy positioning everyone. He motioned the remainder of the guards forward, placing riders at either side of the three women, plus three behind them, and the remainder in pairs, directly behind him, weapons in reach but not brandished.

The only sounds other than the horse hooves were the sough of foliage, the twitter of birds, and the sudden crash of a chamois through the underbrush, briefly visible, tense and graceful as a ballet dancer in the middle of a leap, and then gone downstream as we passed over a mossy old bridge.

Jaska increased the pace and looked around with an intent air that made it clear he was going to try to pick the ground before the inevitable encounter. It wasn't too long before we heard the echoing thud of hooves clattering over a bridge and saw subtle golden smears of dust smudging the forest growth here and there below.

Then they appeared. It looked at first like an army but quickly resolved into nineteen riders: twelve in uniforms of green with silver facings and cuffs, six in servants' liveries—although each carried a cudgel and a long hunting knife—and at their head, a tall, saturnine guy in his early to mid-thirties, dark hair swept back from a high brow, hazel eyes narrowed. He wore elegant hunting clothes and carried a musket, two silver-chased pistols, and a beautiful swept-hilted sword in a saddle sheath. He was a Ysvorod, so I expected to find precursory signs of Alec, but the only resemblance was in the quantity of that flowing dark hair. This duke's, however, was chestnut brown and not the almost-black of Alec's.

He pulled off his chapeau bras and bowed low over his horse's withers, diamonds glinting in his cravat. "I see I am not the first to welcome you home, your highness."

"What's he saying?" Aurélie whispered.

I told her, not bothering to whisper since only Mord could hear me.

She seemed to assume that I'd know Dobreni. I continued to translate as Jaska said, "As you see. Will you join us, Benedek? I would rather not subject the ladies to the rain if I can avoid it."

"It is this very rain that concerns me," was the amused response. "I wish to offer shelter to you and your party. Trapetra Castle is a short distance away. Baron Szontos bids me extend his hospitality to you, and as always," the sardonic voice deepened with amusement, "I am your very obedient servant."

Jaska lifted his head, listening, then said, "And how is the Baron? I am lamentably behind in the news."

"He flourishes, your highness. And exhorts me to extend his welcome to you and your esteemed party. Princess Margit, well met."

Margit gave a stiff nod.

"Countess Irena, what a delightful surprise to find you here."

She flushed as she gave him a haughty nod.

"Who is this lady?"

"Donna Aurélie de Mascarenhas, on tour of Europe. We met over music."

"How very . . . civilized. The gentleman?"

"Domnu Zusya, who preserved my life."

"Then this is the hero! Chevalier de Vauban spoke his praises when the ransom was being raised to free you from the Prussians."

"Behold, he is here in the flesh," Jaska said.

"Permit me to interrupt this interesting conversation with a repeat of the Baron's invitation. We can continue more comfortably at Trapetra Castle. As you mentioned, there are signs of rain. My concern is for the ladies."

"Why are they talking so?" Aurélie whispered under her breath.

"Nobody can move until Jaska does. If they stay with the safety of etiquette, it hides the implied threat. If the duke makes an overt attack, then he's committing *lèse-majesté*. I think he wants to coerce them to this castle under the guise of friendship."

"Why?"

"We will find out."

". . . when your servants catch up," the duke was saying, a smile curling the corners of his mouth, "I can send one of my servants here to guide them to the castle."

"Servants, yes," Jaska said. "Do you always ride with six manservants, Benedek?"

"Regretfully, I must admit that I am a creature of comfort," the duke replied.

I remembered a stray fact that I'd learned from Honoré de Vauban, Hippolyte's descendant and a kind of gentleman archivist: There was once a law that Dobreni nobles could ride around with no more than twelve men-at-arms. Any more was strictly against the law.

For just this reason.

". . . you observe that my servants carry no more than the stout stick and hunting knife permitted the common man traveling the mountain roads," Benedek said politely.

"One wonders why they have need of such things when protected by so many fine men at arms. Or do they question the prowess of said men?" Jaska returned in the same polite voice.

The rain drops were larger, rustling the treetops. Jaska settled back as if prepared to discourse for the rest of the day—then the faint but unmistakable rumble of hoofbeats sounded underneath the soft hiss and patter of rain.

Benedek's expression quirked into a rueful smile. He knew instantly what had happened and, indeed, betrayed no surprise when Captain Danilov and his twelve horsemen appeared directly behind Benedek's gang.

Some of the Ysvorod men at arms betrayed surprise and dismay as their horses were shouldered out of the way. Captain Danilov rode forward, his shako regimentally correct, his manner parade-ground sharp as he politely saluted the duke with a touch of a finger to the brim of the cap. He had just divided the Ysvorod party.

Then a full salute to Jaska, after which he bawled as if a hundred men rode at his back, "Sal-UTE!"

All twenty-four of the King's Guard snapped off formal salutes, underscoring who had the upper hand.

"Permit us," Benedek said with mocking suavity, "to augment your guard of honor."

Jaska inclined his head as if he were in the middle of a ballroom or at a diplomatic affair.

The ladies' hats were now pretty sodden, but no one complained as the horses were once again put in motion.

THIRTY-SIX

T HE RAIN CAME DOWN HARD for about half an hour, then lifted. From the grim way people carried themselves, however, the cold wind wasn't much improvement on the wet.

Rain was intermittent as they rode up and down the hillsides of Mt. Tanazca, the smallest of the mountains. How it hurt me to see again the tumbled hush of the slopes matted with primeval leaves, pine needles, chestnuts, and pinecones, the lancing beams of light dancing from between the canopies of green.

Oh, to be able to breathe that air! To see Alec again, our footsteps crunching as we walked hand in hand over ancient animal paths, he pointing out this site of an old song, that place he and his teenaged companions had run from the Russians after sabotaging a weapons dump. *I am home*, I kept thinking. And yet I was two hundred years distant.

They reached the outskirts of Riev as the sun crowned Mt. Adeliad behind them. Up a steep road, with me taking in as much as I could, and grateful that Aurélie was curious. I didn't dare ask her to turn her head for the same reason I didn't want to mention the future, but I kept thinking, I'm *back*, I'm *here*, Aurélie's here. They are nearly a couple, they don't need me anymore. So where is the danger to Dobrenica?

On the right we passed a familiar half timbered, half stone building— Zorfal! In the future it would be the popular place to go for the twentysomethings and younger, especially the Vigilzhi. Now it was clearly a guardhouse, as men in uniform came and went, the dye-jobs on their blue coats not always matching.

Up the hill, I gazed to the right, over the plateau where the nobles and wealthy now live. And there was Mecklundburg House. And then Ysvorod House! I recognized the roof, though the rest was hidden by a stone fence around which a couple of guards patrolled. In the future, more fine houses would fill in the spaces between those walled semi-palaces, semi-fortresses. There were a lot more trees, almost a wood-land.

When we reached the road leading to Ysvorod House, Benedek urged his horse forward. "With your permission, your highness?" he asked, doffing his sodden hat.

Even with his wet hair hanging like worms around his rain-washed face, he was strikingly handsome. I noticed Margit giving him a narrow look as Jaska lifted a tired hand, then checked the gesture, and with a bow toward Irena, said to Benedek, "*Hertsa'vos—*" the honorific for a duke "—will you do me the honor of escorting Countess Irena in safety to her home?"

It was a polite order. Irena inclined her head. "Good evening," she said. "Will you convey my best to her majesty, and inform her that I shall wait upon her on the morrow?" Last she gave Aurélie a polite nod, which was returned.

Benedek bowed elaborately to Jaska and Margit from the back of his horse. He raised his gauntleted hand, and his followers peeled off, fol-lowing him and Irena. Aurélie gazed after Irena's straight back in the middle of all those guys.

Up St. Katarina Street we rode. There on the left, instead of the Vigil-zhi command center, was a beautiful medieval convent, fruit trees visible above its high wall. On the right, another walled fortress in the grand Renaissance style. This was the Riding School, which would become a library, a smaller Vigilzhi station, and a grand opera house.

A left turn, and there were the buildings that would be the bank and city administration, their fronts on the great square below the palace. Way off to the right was the spire of St. Peter's Cathedral, still dominating the skyline, and beyond, the roof of the temple with its rose window lit from within: the men had to be inside, attending evening prayer.

The cathedral bells began the call to Vespers, echoed within seconds by the bells of the Orthodox church. The sound, the fading light, called to mind Rachmaninoff's *Vespers*; so beautiful, so profoundly evocative of a passing world.

Then we were borne away, the bells fading behind us as the last of the day faded. The animals perked up, smelling the stable, warmth, comfort, and food.

We'd reached the royal palace, gone through its massive gates.

They rode directly to the front entrance, and Jaska, Mord, Aurélie, and Margit dismounted, Jaska covertly observing Aurélie with a revealing glance of worry.

Guards and servants swarmed at a respectful distance, everyone wanting to get a look at the royal prodigal, back after so many years.

The palace was the same architecturally, but so much of the statuary, even the fountains, had been removed or destroyed before I had ever seen it. The elaborate coat of arms over the entry, set in a glory of baroque flourishes, was totally gone in modern times, replaced by a modest, vaguely Greek pediment, reminding me of those scarred buildings back in post-revolutionary Paris.

Immediately outside the carved doors waited a stout, apple-cheeked fellow with a bushy beard and a round furry hat. His face appeared so young the beard seemed incongruous, but as Aurélie got closer, I recognized the adult in that steady gaze. He wore the eighteenth century frock coat that we soon discovered was still the fashion here. I spotted in the beautiful embroidery along facings and cuffs Kabbalistic signs mixed with amaranth and acanthus.

Jaska exclaimed, "Shmuel!"

"I give thanks, Jaska, that you are safely returned!"

Jaska grabbed Shmuel by the shoulders and said in Dobreni, "I give thanks to you for holding things together. Hippolyte told me when I was in Vienna. We will talk as soon as I see my mother." He turned his head. "This is Mordechai ben Aaron Zusya. Will you put him up?"

"You need not ask. It would be my honor. Domnu Zusya will wish to make his bow to her majesty, then bring him to me."

"What exactly is this language?" Aurélie whispered to me. "I hear bits of Latin, but altered, and bits of German."

"It's called Dobreni." I braced for more questions, but she was distracted by Jaska, who led them up the shallow marble stairs. It appeared to be enough that I knew the language: I was a resource, not an object of interest. She had enough to focus on now, with the expectation of meeting Jaska's mother—and a queen.

The plain white plaster walls of the twenty-first century were paneled with beautiful rococo paintings of religious and mythological symbols, in gorgeous pastels, the framing either of white and gold or else magnificent woodworked patterns.

The ground floor was the marble checkerboard so common in palaces of that day. Up the stairs to the state rooms, and here was the lovely furniture that would completely vanish in World War II: shield-backed chairs with embroidered cushions in forest green and gold, drake-footed cabriole legs. Carved cabinetry and more statuary, enormous murals, and tapestries. I only recognized bits here and there—sometimes no more than a brass candle sconce on a wall, which would later be wired to hold a candle-shaped electric light.

Liveried footmen opened doors, and we passed into a woman's world, with rounded rococo furnishings of dusty blue, rose, and gold in a white setting. And there, seated in a pillow-festooned recliner, was a very old lady whose light brown eyes were familiar. Queen Sofia!

"Mother," Jaska said. He bowed, then leaned down to kiss her forehead and blue-veined hands. "I trust you got my messages."

"These are the ones I received," the queen said, laying her hand over a carved box on her little side table. "Since you apparently never stayed long enough in one place for me to answer, I could not discover if one might have gone astray."

"I sent everything through Hippolyte," Jaska said.

The queen smiled. "You were clever to do so. I will venture to promise that anything *he* received most certainly reached me. I am troubled
by what I am hearing out of Vienna."

"It's going to get worse before it gets better," Jaska said, and stepped
back so that Margit could salute her mother. "We will talk about it when
you wish."

"The morning will be sufficient," the queen said and smiled at her
daughter. "Dearest. So you could not wait to meet your brother, but must
ride out willy-nilly to meet him?"

"As you perceive, Mother. Jaska, shall you perform the introductions,
or shall I?"

But the queen forestalled them both. "You must be Mordechai ben
Aaron? Domnu Zusya, I wish I could rise to properly thank the preserver
of my son's life. Some days are better than others. Today I am con-
founded, alas, but pray do not take that amiss."

Mord bowed awkwardly.

Jaska said, "May I present Donna Aurélie de Mascarenhas?"

Aurélie gave the court curtsey that Madame Campan had drilled
into Josephine's ladies.

"Welcome among us, Donna Aurélie," the queen said, and Aurélie
dipped again. "Margit will see you comfortably established, as I gather
her brother has requisitioned her aid." A glance at the riding habit, which
she obviously recognized.

Aurélie colored.

"We shall gather in the morning and discuss events once everyone
has rested, shall we, my dears?"

Two bows, two curtseys, and Jaska and Margit turned away, Mord
following. Only Aurélie backed with little steps, head inclined, hands at
her sides, the way she'd been taught. With her head lowered she couldn't
see the queen's interested look, but I could.

Margit took Aurélie to one of the wings that in the twentieth century
would be used as Soviet head offices for the secret police; then, as the
Soviet empire began breaking up, the desks emptied of agents one by

one, to be stacked with boxes and broken Dictaphones and envelope steamers and PBX equipment, then locked up for a decade and a half. It was in the process of being transformed into a guest wing again when I vanished.

The room Aurélie was given was charming, the cushions and curtains embroidered with roses, cherubs flying above puffy clouds in the ceiling paintings.

Margit said, "Viorel will be here anon. I will have a seamstress up here in the morning, if that suits you."

Aurélie thanked her.

"I will send a tray, if you like. I do not know when we will dine or if. My brother will probably be closeted with at least one minister all evening, once he and our mother have had a private interview. She retires early." Margit held out her hands. "In short, we are not what you are used to in Paris, I suspect."

"That would be a fine thing," Aurélie said. And added, "Though I admired Madame Bonaparte in many ways."

Margit gave that quick smile again, then inclined her head. "Have you any questions?"

"Yes. What happened with this Duke Benedek Ysvorod of Domitrian? Was he going to attack us?"

"No." Margit flushed. "Perhaps he considered it. Perhaps he wanted us to believe he considered it." She took a step toward the door, then turned around and said flatly, "Benedek was the heir until my brother and I were born. He was nearly ten, very much of an age to have been groomed to expectations. Then my mother, at the age of fifty-five, unexpectedly found herself with child. Twins. Including a boy, an heir."

"And so this duke would like to rid the world of Jaska. Do I understand that right?"

Margit put her hand to the door, then once again turned back, as though she'd undergone internal struggle before answering. "I think he was testing Jaska. I will send someone directly."

THIRTY-SEVEN

AURÉLIE WAS ABRUPTLY AWAKENED by a vast roar, as from the throats of a great crowd.

She sat up, eyes wide, then shot out of bed and scrambled for her clothes. A crowd could only mean one thing to a person who had grown up on the detritus of crowd destruction: revolution, riot, chaos.

Teenage Viorel entered while Aurélie was feverishly pulling on the nearest gown. The maid entered with a brisk step and a shy smile, her hands filled with a heavy silver tray.

"Is a mob attacking the palace?" Aurélie asked in French, and at Viorel's uncomprehending look, repeated it in German, adding, "Where is my pistol?"

Viorel gave her a glance of mild surprise. "Attack?" She set the tray on the sideboard and dropped a hasty curtsey. "It is only the city people gathered to welcome the prince. They have been outside the palace and all through the square, since dawn, so he has ridden out to greet them."

Aurélie sank into a chair.

"Here is porridge, new-baked bread and cheese, and an apricot tartlet, as we won't have fresh peaches or apricots for some weeks yet. I was told you do not wish for meat. Is that true, my lady, is there anything else I can bring?"

"This is sufficient," Aurélie said. "Thank you."

Viorel curtseyed again, and left.

"Duppy Kim, I don't know what to do next," Aurélie said. "We talked about this. I trust Jaska, and I think he feels about me the way I do about him. But is that going to put him in a terrible position? If his family thinks the way my aunt does, which is common to many, then the knowledge of my background will force a difficult choice on him."

Wow. Talk about déjà vu! Recollecting my stupid decision to run in order to save Alec from difficult choices, I said, "I suggest you talk to him before going anywhere."

"Yes, I feel I owe him that." She went on seriously, "But comes this thought: Besides trust, there is respect. If he *were* to see me the way my aunt does . . . oh, I do not want to lose my respect for him."

I said with all the power of She Who Made Stupid Choices For (she thought) The Best of Reasons: "I think you've already lost your respect for him if you think he's going to fail you now."

Her scowl deepened, but I was fairly certain she wasn't angry so much as conflicted. She turned her attention to her breakfast, and I shut up.

She was just finishing when there came a knock at the door, and Margit entered.

After her polite greeting, Margit said, "Jaska told us last night about the ghost you have following you."

"She's not a ghost," Aurélie said. "She's a duppy." And forestalling the *She's a what?* that always followed, she added quickly, "Her body is alive somewhere."

"Ah," Margit said, clearly with something else on her mind. "I would like you to speak to someone."

"Someone?" Aurélie repeated.

"A seer."

Aurélie's eyes widened. "Tell me about this seer, pray?"

Margit said slowly, "Elisheva is five years younger than I, but in some ways, she has been old since she could talk. She used to spend more time with ghosts than with other children, they said. There is a fountain not far from the temple, where she insists that the children and animal ghosts play and dance."

Xanpia's fountain! My focus sharpened.

Margit was still talking. "I always liked the idea of child ghosts and animals playing, except not that they were dead. Anyway, her mother was my piano teacher, so Elisheva used to come to my lessons when their father was in *shul*, after her sister began singing lessons. Then, when she turned thirteen or so, she was tested for her abilities and . . . began training."

"I will speak to your seer, and gladly," Aurélie said.

Margit went to the door and opened it. In came a young woman with vivid coloring—flame-bright red hair above a high forehead, a thousand freckles, eyes the light blue of a summer morning. Her gown was made high to the neck and covered her to the wrists, its color a soft gray. The only ornamentation was the embroidery around the neck and wrists of Kabbalistic symbols twined with leaves of hawthorn, laurel, with amaranth blossoms. Fixed at the neck of her gown was a faceted crystal, catching the light with gleams and glitters, but it was scarcely brighter than her hair, which, though worn in a modest bun, did its best to escape in whorls and curls.

"This is Elisheva Barta, Donna Aurélie," Margit said. "I will teach you your first word in our language: *Salfmatta*. These are women who understand Vrajhus."

"Vrajhus?"

"You could call it magic."

"Magic!" Aurélie exclaimed. And then, "Do you have a book? I will teach myself Dobreni while I learn Vrajhus."

Elisheva said, "You can learn our language, but you will find nothing about magic written down." She pulled a prism from a pocket of her gown, and I thought, *At last maybe some answers about the mysterious danger to Dobrenica?*

"Why is nothing written?" Aurélie asked.

"The pursuit of Vrajhus is perilous," Margit said. "Far too many people have been executed by fire, water, or rope—magicians good and bad but mostly ordinary folk who, at most, followed superstition and knew nothing of Vrajhus at all."

"Hundreds and hundreds in the last century alone," Elisheva said. "But also, if nothing is written, then the teacher can test the student at each step along the path. No one with evil in her heart can steal a book not written. Or his heart, for there are also *Salfpatras*. Spirit?" She addressed me, though her attention was on the prism. She could see me, apparently.

"My name is Kim," I said in Dobreni.

"You speak our language."

Elisheva looked from one of us to the other as Margit sighed and said, "I hear nothing and see nothing. But from your faces, it is not the same for you."

"Take my hand," Aurélie said to Margit. "And look in yon mirror. Your brother was able to see Kim that way. At first, mirrors were the only way I could see her."

I said to Elisheva, "Is there a danger to Dobrenica besides the obvious threat from Napoleon? Does it have something to do with the Esplumoir?"

Elisheva looked startled. "How do you know about the Esplumoir?"

Margit said in Dobreni with a doubtful glance at Aurélie's uncomprehending face, "We *never* talk about that."

"We are going to have to," Elisheva retorted. "This spirit introduced it first. And the news that Domnu Zusya brought is deeply troubling to the Grandmothers and Grandfathers. But that must wait." She peered down into her prism, turning it until she caught me again. "Kim-Spirit, I do not know yet if this danger you speak of is the threat that Domnu Zusya spoke of. Let me ask this: Did you become attached to Donna Aurélie by going through an Esplumoir?"

"You say *an*. There are more than one?"

"We are taught that there are three. One high in the mountains between the Far East and the Land of the Hindu, and another on the continent of the New World, in a place where the mountains once breathed fire. And ours. All are in mountains, and some of the stories insist that these mountains all breathed fire at one time."

Dobrenica, the Himalayas, and either Washington, Oregon, or Hawaii, I translated mentally.

"All guarded by people of peace," Elisheva said. She corrected conscientiously, "Or so we try to be."

Though Tony and I had closed one, we never understood what it was we'd found. "What exactly *is* an Esplumoir?" I asked.

"That is the name given to the gate between worlds," Elisheva said.

"So, that is not the same as a portal?"

"Portals take one to other portals, if you have sufficient Vrajhus, or from here into the Nasdrafus. I have never used one, nor has anyone else I know, but I was taught that once you are through a portal, you can use them to go from one place to another."

That tugged at my memory. Someone had mentioned something somewhere, sometime, but I could not remember.

She went on. "Perhaps I ought to stop here. But as you are a spirit, I will tell you what we are told in our early training." She looked around, spotted a pen sharpener on the escritoire, and tried to balance it on the point of her finger. "You see how the handle goes down and the blade goes up? Those are the places between heaven and earth, always shifting. If I were to put a pea on top of this sharpener, it could roll either way, depending upon how the pen sharpener is moving. But this point underneath, here, where it touches my finger and does not move? That is the gate—the Esplumoir."

"And so the Nasdrafus is what?"

"It is the path between portals. It is what you find beyond a portal."

"And what do you find beyond a gate? Nasdrafus, or . . ."

"Nasdrafus *and*," she corrected. "And, and, and. A plentitude of *ands*. The portal is simpler, but a gate reaches realms we know nothing of. All we know is that no one who stepped through the gates ever returned."

While she spoke, Aurélie had gone to the mirror and beckoned. Margit touched her fingertips to Aurélie's hand and peered into the mirror. As soon as Elisheva finished speaking, Margit said, "I see the outline of something. I think. Or is it the light?"

"Light is what my cousin saw," Aurélie said.

Margit let go of Aurélie's hand and walked away. "Yet my brother can see. Is it because he is the heir? Yet Elisheva and the elders are not of royal blood."

"The ability will be in some families, but not everyone is the same," Elisheva said. "You know that my sister Shoshanna does not see. She used to think I told untruths."

"She would," Margit observed.

Elisheva flashed a smile, which she quickly suppressed. "I will not harbor unkind thoughts in my heart about my sister," she said quickly, as if by habit. Then she focused on me. "Spirit, I ask again, how did you become attached to Donna Aurélie? Was it through an Esplumoir?"

"I was brought by a seer in Donna Aurélie's land of origin. But before that, I was warned by a vision of Xanpia that there is danger to Dobrenica."

Both Elisheva and Margit stilled when I said *Xanpia*. It was good to be back in Dobrenica—it was a relief to be instantly believed—but the goodness and relief lasted about a nanosecond, because far stronger was their evident tension.

"I will have to consult the Elders," Elisheva said. "This goes beyond my learning. But before I do, I must ask. Did you tell Domnu Zusya that seraphs spoke to you?"

"Yes. One did."

Elisheva whispered some words in Hebrew and touched the crystal at her neck, then said, "Demons do not speak in this world, or not that I have heard. Another thing that Domnu Zusya told us: He can sometimes hear demons, like a vast wind. He says that all across the western horizon they are gathering and facing east."

"How reliable is he?" Margit asked. "I know he's the savior of my brother. I've been hearing that for all these years, as Jaska apparently preferred his company to being home. But a brute on the battlefield does not necessarily make a good mage, or a good man."

"I've been asked to listen as they question him," Elisheva said. "The Eldest sent a message down from Mount Dhiavilyi a week ago, saying that he saw someone, or something, of great power. He saw it as a light, shaped like a crown, coming toward us. He told someone the same day you met his highness, your brother, that this crown of power had crossed the border into Dobrenica." She glanced at the window. "The Eldest does not know if it be thing, spell, or person . . . and that reminds me. I must be at Ridotski House at noon, and it is half an hour's walk."

"There's no hurry," Margit said. "I gave the order for the gig."

"It's a kind thought, but to trouble a horse when I have two good legs?" Elisheva curtseyed.

"I believe we should all go to Ridotski House," Margit said, with a meaningful glance Aurélie's way. "If you're willing, Donna Aurélie."

Aurélie dropped a little curtsey, graceful and dignified.

"Then let us go. I will give orders for wraps to be brought."

The two started out, then Aurélie said, "A moment—I will catch up—the ribbon is loose on my shoe."

The moment the other two were out of sight Aurélie bent, pulling aside the hem of her gown. But instead of retying her shoe, she checked to make certain the necklace was as flat as she could make it beneath her stocking as she whispered in English, "Until I know I can trust them, I do not want anyone seeing the necklace. It should stay well hidden now. What were they talking about?"

"A *Salfpatra*, the one they call the Eldest, saw something or someone powerful coming with us, and they don't know if it's the same danger that Mord apparently sees."

"Is the powerful thing you?" Aurélie asked. "Except that you have no powers!"

"That's what we're going to find out."

She hastened after the others and caught up at the grand marble stairway.

The gig was not a simple open carriage the size of a cart, pulled by a single horse, like the one Aurélie and Cassandra had driven. This was a stylish affair rather like en elegant sleigh with wheels, pulled by a team and driven by a liveried fellow complete to powdered wig, with another riding behind in order to open the low door and let down the two steps.

The conversation was desultory—about a concert the week before.

The cobbled streets were clean swept, and citizens with their carts and tools dressed in eighteenth-century clothes, with medieval-looking smocks and caps.

Ridotski House had an impressive garden on either side. I was used to the broad sweep for cars that circled up to the entrance; instead, the front of the house was more a garden edged by roses at either side of a narrow lane.

The house from the outside looked pretty much the same, but inside, it was very different. There were still Dobreni folk patterns painted under the ceiling, but they were actually embellished sayings in calligraphic Hebrew.

The furniture was beautiful carved wood in Renaissance styles. I wondered if it had all come straight from Italy, as it had that Florentine flavor.

Gathered were a small group of older folk: two nuns, a monk in a white cassock, a bearded man wearing a furry cap, and the familiar cherubic face of Shmuel Ridotski.

The *Salfmattas* and *Salfpatras* looked in muted surprise at Aurélie until Margit said, "I desired Donna Aurélie to attend, as she is a concerned party."

The Princess Had Spoken. You could hear it in her tone, if not in the actual words. No one demurred.

They settled in a circle, the format I'd experienced in my day. Though no one had told me, I now recognized that no one was foremost and no one least.

Seated inside the circle was Mord, almost unrecognizable. Someone had taken him in hand. His long, tangled hair was confined neatly behind him, for the Jews of Dobrenica did not wear the *payot*, the long side-locks, with hair short in back. His coat was new, though severely plain. Not for him, apparently, the woven charms. His beard had begun to grow, giving him that ancient prophet look, and the rest of him was neat. He also had one of the small furry hats on his head.

On the other side of the room stood a drop-dead gorgeous girl. She was dressed in subdued colors, like Elisheva, but if anything the gray linen gown with its subtle embroidery served to draw attention to her amazing red-gold hair and perfect oval face. Her pose was modest, head down, hands together, but she peered under her long lashes, taking everyone in. Most of all Mord.

Elisheva went straight to her. "What are you doing here, Shoshanna?" she whispered.

Shoshanna gave a smug simper. "Singing the blessing."

Soon after Shmuel signaled for her to begin, and the circle bowed heads—some crossing themselves, others not—Shoshanna began to sing. Her voice was pure and sweet and beautiful, but if it was aimed at Mord (and from the subtle way Margit and Elisheva and even Aurélie watched her, it was) she may as well have croaked like a bullfrog. He never once glanced her way.

Could have told you that guy was a waste of time, I was thinking as the song ended.

Shoshanna was thanked and sent to the sidelines, and the meeting got under way.

I was worried about Aurélie being grilled—and about the necklace—but very swiftly the session took a startling turn. I suspect Aurélie could have danced around waving the necklace and no one would have noticed.

The initial question came from the old monk in white. He spoke in Latin, and Mord answered shortly in Latin. Two, three of the adults spoke to him, and his answers were succinct.

Unfortunately, my Latin is beginner-level and only reading. I picked out a word here and there—*spiritus* being the most frequent—and Nasdrafus, but there were subtle signs that Mord's trenchant view of the universe disturbed some.

Then Elisheva stepped up behind Shmuel and spoke. Not in Latin, though it was clear she understood it. She spoke in Hebrew. I think she was quoting something, either the Talmud or spiritual debates; that is, Halachic debates based on the Mishna. Beka had been telling me about these things not a month before I vanished.

At any rate, Mord looked up, clearly startled.

He answered slowly, and Elisheva responded.

Back and forth they went. By the end of their exchange he faced her, intent, his hands gripping his knees.

Five, six quick exchanges, and she stepped back.

Mord lifted a hand half toward her, almost a gesture of appeal. Then he dropped his hand and his pale, sharp-boned cheeks reddened. He spoke in German, his attitude completely more open, reflective instead of trenchant, even careful. That signaled the rest of the group to begin asking their questions. Mord answered politely, but no matter who asked the question, he glanced toward Elisheva to see how she reacted.

"What just happened?" Aurélie breathed.

I almost said, *If we were watching a film, I'd say he just fell in love.* "Mord is experiencing severe attitude readjustment," I responded.

Aurélie smothered a soft laugh.

No use reporting any of the rest of the conversation. Mord recounted everything that had happened on the journey, from the seraphs to the howlings, from forests to the flights of demons that only Mord could see in the distant skies. It was all news to the *Salfmattas* and *Salfpatras*, who indicated they needed time to process.

The meeting was just breaking up when servants opened the door, and Jaska walked in, which caused a general rise and bow.

Jaska was dressed like a prince in a brocade coat with turned back cuffs and wide skirts in the pre-Revolutionary style. His knee breeches were satin, his high heeled shoes buckled, though he certainly did not need the added height. But high heels turned a leg nicely, which explained why they were lingering in fashion. He walked with his sword cane still.

He gave Margit a considering gaze. "If you're finished with Lady Aurélie, I came to give her a ride back."

Margit said, in a voice meant for his ears alone, "She needs to closet herself with a seamstress." There was question in her tone.

Jaska whispered back, "It was necessary to come away without her wardrobe. Minister Fouché sent agents to arrest her."

"Ah," Margit said on a long note, invisible question marks in the air all around.

Jaska turned to Aurélie. "You've that Paris gown still, do you not? Margit can tell your maid to take measurements from it. Come!"

Jaska led the way out.

Before I lost sight of the room, I glimpsed Mord's steady gaze tracking Elisheva as she and Margit were absorbed into the group of old folks. Shoshanna was left on the sidelines, pouting.

Then Jaska escorted Aurélie to the front door where an equerry waited with an open carriage and a pair of matched grays to draw it.

"I can drive," Jaska said, dismissing the waiting footman.

Aurélie was handed up, then he took his place beside her, clucked to the well-mannered pair, and they rolled toward the palace again.

He didn't launch into a biography, but bits of his life emerged as he pointed out places he remembered. The king had died in a riding accident when Jaska and Margit were very young. Their older sisters had either married or were about to when the twins were born, so the twins pretty much had the palace to themselves. The queen was Regent, and the government held in trust for Jaska by her and the Grand Council.

He'd been tutored in the palace and attended the Riding School most afternoons, beginning at age ten. In his teens he was invited by his Polish grandmother to be finished at their military school in Warsaw. That was when he met General Kosciusko.

The great triumphal arch was not yet on the other side of the cathedral. That would happen in 1813.

They began to round Xanpia's fountain, which was exactly as it is now, including the ghostly animals and creatures dancing around it. I watched the statue of Xanpia, beaming thoughts at her. *Are we okay? Any hints on the danger part? When can I get home?*

The statue remained exactly that: a statue.

Aurélie looked at the fountain, the high shooting water catching light in the sun. She smiled at the people who were there to get water and to chat. Xanpia's fountain seemed to be the local Internet café.

Jaska's anecdotes got more disjointed as he interrupted himself to return nods to those who bowed and curtseyed. "I thought this would be over after I went out this morning," he admitted as he turned up a narrow street of leaning, half-timbered houses.

Aurélie cast a troubled glance at those smiling, curious faces as Jaska drove the horses up to the ridge on the north edge of the city, just below the graveyard. On the bluffs, the conical shapes of beehives poked up. There was almost no traffic here.

"Now that we are alone," he said, "I have some questions for you."

"Yes? I should like to learn some words in Dobreni," she said. "It is terrible not to understand, especially when people speak before one's face."

"I beg pardon for that."

"It happens." She gripped her fingers tightly, and I saw Jaska glance down at her hands as she said, "Your questions?"

She was looking not at him but at the wildflowers in the park, where one day would be a row of early Victorian houses. The Dominican monastery was not far off, its garden stretching upslope to the left.

"I'm certain you heard," Jaska began, "that Mord thinks we were shadowed by demons as we traveled."

"I heard that."

"He also said you were protected against them. Can you tell me how?"

Aurélie looked unhappy.

He pointed to Prinz Karl-Rafael Street, which bisected the city below. It was newly cobblestoned, with a fine gutter down the center.

He said in a light voice that did not quite hide the hurt, "New drainage, as you see. Riev doesn't stink, though it is near summer. The streets are clean due to our Minister of the Interior, my old friend Shmuel Ridotski. Night soil used to be carried off only on the south side of the city, where the palaces are. But now the people at Market End have a confederation. They gather it and sell it to the farmers. Every morning, the carts go down the alleys. These carts have many different names that would give you an amusing lesson in our language."

"Jaska, my protection is a secret thing," Aurélie said. "My Nanny

Hiasinte said it was important to keep it secret. And it brings me many dreams from the past, from when others had this thing. Whenever one of them broke confidence, terrible things happened. I've seen it in the dreams, and I believe these dreams are true."

Jaska fell silent as they drew even with the temple. Its square was filled with flowers. People went about shopping, the Jews identifiable in their sober colors with fine embroidery, wives scarved, men going to the temple wearing their small, round hats, the Dobreni version of the *kolpik*.

He said finally, "I can understand, then, why you don't trust me."

"I do trust you," she responded quickly. "But I made a promise."

"I honor that," he said, "and you for telling me. From this street and below is the market section of the city. It's still somewhat problematical, though from city records, it's improved vastly over the past two centuries. It seems to be a problem inherent in cities: the more they're made pleasing and comfortable, the more people wish to live in them. And the more people, the more difficult it is to make them comfortable again."

He talked on like that for a time, then said, "Is your spirit, your duppy, still with you?"

"Duppy Kim?" Aurélie asked the air.

I touched them both. "I'm here."

He stilled, then said, "I don't know if I'll ever become accustomed to that." He went on talking about the city, and I looked longingly at familiar buildings, pocket parks, gargoyles, and young trees that would in my day be gigantic. It was a while before I figured out that when Jaska said "accustomed," he didn't mean to my touch but to the fact that I was perforce listening to what should have been a private conversation.

In other words, *I* was now the thing in the way of the two of them getting together.

Xanpia, are you listening?

No answer.

THIRTY-EIGHT

W HEN WE GOT BACK TO THE PALACE, as soon as she was
alone, Aurélie hit the mirror so she could see me. "This guest
chamber, it's not a servant's room."

"No."

"I expected to have such, as I did in Paris. And on that ride, those
people, they looked at me as they bowed to him."

"So? They're curious about their prince being back. He went away a
teenager and returned a man. They're probably going to be talking about
an official coronation soon, as he came of age while he was gone."

She made a gesture as if pushing aside the matter of coronations.
"They'll ask who I am."

"Yes."

"They'll ask why he takes me out in his cabriolet."

"Yes. You mean he has little privacy? Kings don't get a lot of privacy.
They can close doors, but the people outside of them talk about what
might be going on inside."

"I hate that."

"Think of it as a balance," I said. "You know what can happen to
kings if enough people don't like what they're doing. And you know what
kings can do to people on a whim if they have that much power."

"The Place de la Revolution, either way." She rubbed her arms.

There was a knock, and Viorel was back with a small army of seamstresses. They had indeed taken her French dress, but that opened a new set of questions. Should they use this new fashion, was it a morning gown or evening, what did the French wear for this occasion or that?

I blurred out.

As always, a change in situation snapped me back, in this case when a summons came: The queen had invited Donna Aurélie to an early dinner. They would gather in the Rose chamber when the clocks struck the hour.

"What do I wear?" Aurélie exclaimed as soon as the footman was gone. "I cannot wear this same gown. But the only one finished is . . ." She sped into the next room, where gowns lay with bolts of fabric. These were basic, requiring lace and ribbon embellishments. The seamstresses had taken away chosen fabrics to put together more elaborate gowns, complete to embroidery.

Aurélie took up a plain white muslin gown and then shook out a length of shimmering green gauze that was to be made into an under dress. She pulled it over her head and let both ends flutter to the floor. "Yes," she said. "I learned this from Madame Josephine."

She hunted among the trims, and located gold edging. With quick snips, measures, and a few stitches, she made a simple headband to fit around her head, holding the gauze in place like a draped headscarf. Then she looped the ends of the gauze up and fastened them to the gold wrist bands she had made. The green draped in graceful loops from her head down her sides to her wrists, evoking that lovely Grecian look again.

"It's perfect," I said.

The clock rang then. She twitched her kiss curls below the edge of the green so they clustered charmingly around her face, and walked out, the gauze billowing.

Jaska was waiting at the end of the marble landing, his demeanor changing when he saw her. Oh yeah, he was smitten. And now that he was home, he was way less guarded about showing it. "May I compliment you on your appearance?" He smiled.

"If I may compliment you on yours," she returned with a laughing glance, then sobered. "Am I to start bowing to you now? Saying 'Durchlaucht' with every sentence?"

"Don't," he said quickly. Then caught himself and sighed. "In public, where we are observed, yes."

"Duppy Kim was right."

"In what regard?" he asked as they started down the hall toward the queen's rooms.

"That you have a very public private life."

He gave a crack of laughter and then lowered his voice, going on in English. I wondered if English had ever been spoken in those halls as he said, "One of the reasons I went to Poland was to get away from the people who had planned out my life, right down to my marriage."

"The Countess Irena?" Aurélie asked.

"Yes. We never got along as children. She and my sister squabbled every time they saw one another. But the Duke of Trasyemova wanted a royal grandson and because he commands the Guard, my mother, as regent, placated him by promising to consider it, though she maintained she would make no decisions about either of us until we reached the age of understanding. Between that and the Ysvorods' bitterness about my birth—" He stopped. "What did Fielding say in *Tom Jones*? 'By thunder!' That sounds foolish. The German is better, *Donnerwetter!* German swearing is altogether preferable. *Teufelsblut!* I'm beginning to sound bitter all on my own."

A few paces more, and the footmen sprang to open the doors to the queen's receiving antechamber.

Aurélie gave her court curtsey as Jaska bowed to his mother. Margit came forward to greet them, and I saw Aurélie watching. Margit did not bow to her brother, but inclined her head to him as she greeted him, and a slight nod for Aurélie.

The queen rose. She was dressed in a *robe d'anglaise*, which I already knew was her favorite style. It was strange to think that I dressed in a copy of one of her gowns for a masquerade ball in this very palace, two centuries farther up the timeline. This gown was peach and silver, with green ribbons. She held out her arm to Jaska, who took it with his free hand, leaving Margit to walk beside Aurélie into the adjoining chamber.

The table was set for four. At least that many servants came and went as fine porcelain and real gold implements were brought out. Aurélie was served some kind of a pie thing that appeared to be baked cheese, with layers of hot-house tomatoes, onion, and some type of herb that looked like shredded basil.

"This dish," the queen said to her in slow German, "was introduced to us through the Chevalier de Vauban. It was actually in the form of a soup, comprised of those browned onions, with the cheese atop. He said it was the food of the people, though I cannot imagine that nobles didn't also partake. It is delicious, I find."

Aurélie took a cautious bite and agreed.

"Excellent. My cook has been experimenting with the basic form, as you see. We have relied on that particular dish during the Lenten season. My son." The queen turned her head. "I hear that young Elisheva finds your friend Mordechai rude, irreverent, and nearly uncivilized."

"And he found her altogether astonishing," Margit said. "He was almost affronted to discover that her scholarship is superlative. I don't understand."

"You would have to know the Jewish traditions of Poland, perhaps," Jaska said. "Some of the customs of our Jews diverge from those of the Polish Jews."

"I thought Mordechai Zusya followed the strictures of the Baal Shem Tov," the queen said. "Rabbi Avramesçu has disclosed that much in a report to me."

"He does, and yet not altogether. You know how traditions say that the Jews wrote to Maimonides after Dobrenica rejoined the world five-hundred years ago?"

"Yes. Tell me something I do not know."

"And it happened again a couple of centuries ago, when they wrote to the Ari-Hakadosh and were taught that the scattered sparks of the Divine Light must be regathered—"

"The *tikkun olam*, which is doing the great work of fixing the world's peace, which aligned the Jews even more closely with Dobrenica. Son—"

"Bear with me! One more: When Rabbi Yosef Ridotski came back from studying with the Ari-Hakadosh, he had learned that teaching women to study Talmud and other holy texts was to gather those sparks of knowledge and do holy work."

"His three holy daughters, before he had a son," Margit said.

"And that's where we diverged. In Poland, Jewish women are not part of the study of sacred texts," Jaska said. "In some circles they're not even supposed to make music, because it's not considered modest. So here's Mordechai, questioned by a girl several years younger than he, who can return a quotation—three—to every disparaging, angry remark he makes about the absurdity and evil of the world. I gather that Mord was undone."

The queen gave a lady-like sniff, and flickered her beringed fingers as if brushing the subject of Mord aside. "So what were *you* doing while being rude, irreverent, and uncivilized, these past few years? I have your letters, which were remarkable for what you did not tell me," the queen said. "Except that you were still alive," she added quickly. "And I understand about fearing that they would be opened, but there is surely no fear now. Here we are at dinner, completely free of Russian, Prussian, Imperial, or French spies."

Jaska looked down at his hands. I felt sorry for him—I could have told them all that he and Mord seemed to be poster boys for PTSD but that concept was a couple centuries away.

"I believed that duty and honor obliged me to help determine what Bonaparte was doing with the Poles," Jaska said finally. "But it became plain that no agreement is to be found there. Many believe him sincere and will fight for him willingly, because he is undoubtedly a great commander. As for his promises for Poland? General Kosciusko does not believe them. Neither do I."

"We will discuss Bonaparte anon. And before that?"

"Mord and I were dispatched by Prince Poniatowski to learn the semaphore system if we could, with an idea to establishing it in Poland."

"And?" the queen asked as she signaled to the waiting footman to pour more watered wine for the ladies, and wine for Jaska.

"Line of sight, sun, problems with lanterns and weather—there are many drawbacks," Jaska said, using a piece of bread and a pointing finger to demonstrate each problem. "Above all, the Poles would need the kind of control over people and countryside that Bonaparte is busy establishing."

The queen set her fork down, her frown formidable. "Bonaparte supports Polish freedom, does he not?"

Jaska looked away. "He says what the Poles wish to hear. He says what everyone wants to hear. But he does what he wants."

"Which is?"

Jaska indicated Aurélie. "Her ghost told us that Bonaparte would declare war on England a week or so before he did it. She also said that his next battle will not be north into England, in spite of this war. It'll be east, into the empire."

The queen had picked up her fork again, but she dropped it to make a warding gesture. "Poland fallen, and the empire soon engaged with the French. It will be worse than it was a few years ago."

"Yes," Jaska said. "From what I heard at the legation, we won't be able to look to Sweden for aid."

"My sister does not write well of Gustav," the queen said, nodding in agreement. "He's violently opposed to Bonaparte and insists that he, Gustav, must lead any efforts against him."

"It was a mistake to ask Gustav for help. And to offer my services, after having been trained under Kosciusko."

"Oh, Jaska, I'm certain Gustav regarded you as a foreigner, and with distrust," the queen said. "He talks wildly about how he would've fought the Russians in seventeen ninety-four and won if only this, if only that. No matter. The situation in Sweden is not as dire as our own. *We* need peace all the more, if we're not to be overrun from either direction."

Her emphasis on the word *peace* caused him to still, and I knew exactly what she was talking about: the Blessing. Supposedly, it would magically close off those roads into the valley.

Of course. The Blessing. I'd forgotten all about it. Well, I'd never believed it was real.

Xanpia, if the Blessing really works, why do you need me? Or was that a roundabout way of saying that though vampires walk, and magic exists, and seraphs fly around Paris, the Blessing is really only symbolic?

As always, no answer.

The queen had been watching Aurélie, whose table manners were neat and graceful. She signaled for the next course to be brought in, each dish on heavy silver platters, then said, "I fear we are boring our guest with our chatter of international politics."

"It was a frequent topic in Paris," Aurélie said as the footman took away her old plate and set down a new one with a layered pastry. "I am accustomed, your majesty."

"Did Bonaparte ever talk to you?" the queen asked as she dug her fork into her pastry. "From what I hear, he talks and it is the part of all in earshot to listen, your majesty."

Aurélie flashed her quick, crooked smile. "*Vraiment!* He'd never ask our opinions. Our part was to listen, and to cheer when he made a pronouncement."

"I feel sympathy for Madame Bonaparte," the queen said lightly. "Hers cannot have been an easy life, either before he seized power or now."

Jaska said, "Madame Bonaparte sent Donna Aurélie to the Piarist Sisters in Vienna for a magical solution to her problem of begetting an heir."

The queen's eyes closed briefly. "That poor woman. How very desperate she must be, to send a young girl in secret. We will leave her problems, though, as we are not asked to solve them. Come! Tell me about this mysterious ghost of yours who can predict Bonaparte's next war, but cannot help his wife?"

Jaska said, "Perhaps we ought to postpone these questions until after the meal, whence we can confront a mirror. It's much easier to talk to this ghost when she can be seen."

"*I* cannot see her," Margit said.

"I probably won't either," the queen stated cheerfully, and saluted them with her watered wine. "Never have seen one."

But you, as a ghost, will seek me out in Vienna, I thought.

"I am far more interested in discovering how to avoid the threat to Dobrenica that seems poised in all directions. Ghost? What say you?"

Maybe this was the danger after all.

I began to speak, Aurélie repeating my words: "You know from the seers that predicting the future is problematical." When she agreed, I said, "Then you will understand when I put my statements in the form of conditions. If I am correct, next March, Bonaparte will have the Duc d'Enghien arrested and shot."

"Condé's son!" the queen stated. "He works hard to raise the royalists' standard. He is said to be determined."

"If that happens, then look to Bonaparte to declare himself emperor," I said.

"Emperor! Not king, but emperor," the queen repeated. She set down her fork. "And so the war to the east. For an emperor must have an empire. France is not enough. How far will he go, then?"

"If all these things come to pass," I said, "then look for him to push all the way to Russia."

That hit them all hard. Dobrenica was squarely in the way though not on the main roads from east to west. But armies were notorious for not sticking to roads, especially when they needed to forage. And when you had armies of hundreds of thousands of men and horses, that forage basically meant sacking every town, village, farm, and dovecote within raiding distance. And they all knew it. They had grown up hearing their grandparents' horror stories, told them by *their* grandparents during the Thirty Years' War.

"This is terrible," the queen said. "This is terrible. Yes, I hear what your ghost says about conditions, Donna Aurélie, but the wise would take that as a serious threat. Son, you know what must be done. But we will say no more about that now."

"With respect," Jaska said, "I will make this suggestion: that we recall our legation from Vienna. We are small. The Emperor will take little notice. All his attention will be westward."

"I agree. We must get you crowned and on the proper day. At least we have until September, but we would be unwise to dally. We shall together summon the Grand Council tomorrow and fête them afterward, in honor of your safe return." She looked at her empty plate, and without glancing at the others to see if they were done, she rose. "If we are finished, we shall go downstairs. Minister Ridotski was going to bring your Domnu Zusya to us, that we may hear this music my daughter praised so extravagantly. Donna Aurélie, I trust you will favor us with your talents?"

Mord gave Aurélie a brief bow when he saw her, and Jaska a brief smile, but he seemed preoccupied until they began to play. Then it was like always, the three separate voices threaded together until Mord, eyes closed, took off into his amazing flights. There was a different quality to his extemporaneous solos, a tender, searching, questioning sense.

Margit kept wiping her eyes, and the queen sat as if carved in stone, her chin in her hand. She was so still the diamond on her hand glimmered only with its own gathered light.

When Aurélie looked up, it was to discover that the audience had increased slightly. The queen's household music master, an elderly gent, had joined them. With him sat Shmuel Ridotski and a young woman in a pearl gray gown. She also wore a beautiful patterned scarf in shades of blue from cobalt to midnight, with golden threads woven in the amaranth pattern. This scarf draped over her head and down her back. She had to be Ridotski's wife.

On the wife's other side sat Elisheva, arms crossed, head slightly to one side. The Ridotski pair were silent. When the concert was done, the music master's attitude toward Mord was respectful bordering on awestruck, and the queen's voice rang with sincerity when she praised the trio. But she kept looking back at Mord as if a hopping robin had entered her music chamber and metamorphosed into a phoenix.

"We must do this again. Soon," the queen declared.

Mord bowed, his gaze straying beyond the queen to Elisheva. As the others stood in a group, talking, he looked down at his hands as though surprised to discover them attached to his wrists.

*   *   *

When we were alone, Aurélie said, "What was the queen talking about? Twice she said that Jaska must do something, and she made reference to September, but she didn't say what. I think she didn't want me hearing it."

"Think of it like your necklace, a secret kept because of vows and long habit. Its magic will only work, protecting the borders, if everyone in Dobrenica is living in peace with one another."

"But this Duke Benedek has not a peaceful demeanor."

"No."

"And Irena was very angry when Jaska sent her home with the duke."

"Yes."

"So if I were not here . . . ?"

"I don't think anything would be different," I said quickly. "Living in peace with one another means acceptance. It doesn't mean everyone has to be great friends."

She sighed. "You want me to stay," she observed, "and I want to. I think. Ah, I'm so confused. But Kim, that dream I told you, where I saw you and me side by side? It was not in this place."

THIRTY-NINE

I WAS GLOOMY WHEN AURÉLIE WENT TO SLEEP, and the gloom
was still there when she woke. Viorel brought breakfast, after which
the army of seamstresses hauled in a ton of clothes. While Aurélie was in
the midst of a personalized retail blowout, a note was delivered.

She read it with surprise, then said, "There's to be some sort of party for
someone who is getting married. Princess Margit begs me to play for them."

That sounded friendly enough. Aurélie spent the morning practicing, since she was not accompanying anyone, and the hours flew by un-
interrupted. At noon, she bathed, put on one of her new day dresses, and
carried her music case out into the hall. She asked the footman to take
her to Queen Karolina's *salle*—by my time it would have long lost that
name—where she found Margit with a lot of other ladies between sixteen and thirty.

The first sign of trouble was the way Margit introduced her after taking her to a beautiful piano and ordering a servant to set a branch of
candles near so Aurélie could see her music. The rest of the women were
gathered at a long table next to a bank of windows looking out over the
terrace and beyond that the garden.

When Aurélie had set up her music, Margit said, "Donna Aurélie de
Mascarenhas, the musician from Paris, will entertain us now." Then she
sat down at the table and resumed eating and drinking. And talking.

I think it hit us both at the same time that Aurélie was back in lady-in-waiting status. I could see her mental shrug. This was what she had done for Josephine.

The windows were open to let in the balmy spring air. Some ladies talked, others listened as Aurélie began her performance. At first, she played softly, as she and her fellow musicians had done when providing background music in Paris. But gradually she became more involved, the volume rising when the music required it and softening naturally. At the end of one of her fae songs, a couple of people applauded lightly.

Then Irena called out, "Play something by Haydn. He is my favorite."

"Oh, Mozart," someone else said. "I love Mozart."

"It is Gabrielle's day. She must choose," Margit said, and everyone called out, *Mozart, Mozart.*

Aurélie began to play Mozart's Piano Concerto no. 3, and the party went right on. Except for Gabrielle, a slight young lady in a lacy gown of different shades of yellow that complemented her auburn hair. She slipped from her place and came up to the piano, her head swaying back and forth as the treble rippled up and down, her forefinger tapping in time to the dancing rhythm.

At the end she gave Aurélie a sunny smile. "Oh, thank you. That was truly good. *How* I tried to master that and never did."

"Now it's time for Haydn," Irena called.

Gabrielle glanced her way, tucked a curl back, then flitted restlessly to the window, reminding me of a butterfly as Aurélie began Haydn's Sonata in C.

"Gabrielle?" someone called. "You should hear what Burinka said to the baroness . . ."

Gabrielle fluttered back to the table, obviously distracted by the romantic, moody music.

At the end, Irena said, "Margit, get her to play Haydn."

Aurélie flushed. The message was loud and clear: Irena and Margit had undercut the interloper socially with one effective stroke. A lady-in-waiting was a fancy word for servant, and these snotty women were treating her like one.

Aurélie plunged into Beethoven's Serenade in D Major, which she and Jaska had bought in Vienna. Mord had begun practicing it the first night out of Eisenstadt. It was not written for piano, but Aurélie adapted the violin and cello parts, the melodic line evocative of trumpet flourishes.

As before, the party paid little attention—until, through the open windows, sounded the flute accompaniment, sweet and clear.

One by one the party people became aware of the flute. Then they realized it was not in the room.

Gabrielle flitted to the window to peer out.

Her jaw dropped, and she made a hasty curtsey. The others flocked to the window, peacocks in pastels. Aurélie had known within three notes that Jaska was playing, and brought her hands down on the keys, sending those flourishes ringing.

At the end, the ladies clapped wildly, but he apparently vanished inside, for they all bent forward, a couple of them almost falling out the window as they tried to track him. They walked back to their seats, sat down, talking in Dobreni, mostly wondering what oddness his highness was up to—must be a joke—then the door opened, and there was Jaska, dressed elegantly in his silks, flute in hand.

The ladies shot to their feet to curtsey. "Go on talking," he invited. "Gabrielle, in your honor."

Gabrielle turned scarlet with pleasure as Jaska lifted his flute to his lips. He started one of their French airs, and Aurélie began the accompaniment. After playing it through three countries, she had no need of the written music.

Gabrielle listened with eyes closed, and the others perforce in silence. You don't talk while a prince is playing.

Jaska thus made them sit quietly through six long pieces, and at the end he said, "We will compose an air for your wedding gift, Gabrielle. Come, Aurélie, let's begin." He held out his arm.

"My music."

"Leave it," Jaska said. "Margit can have it sent to your room later."

Aurélie placed her fingertips lightly on the crook of his arm, the warm brown of her skin contrasting with the ice blue of his satin. Was it the first time they had touched? It was the first significant touch. A quick look made it clear they were both aware of it.

Jaska bowed to the guest of honor, nodded to the rest, and as they curtseyed, he led Aurélie out of the room.

When they reached the hall, she lifted her hand. "I'm not quite certain what happened in there, but I thank you for the duet."

"In war, I would call it maneuvering," Jaska said. "I don't know what the women call it. Perhaps my manners leave something to be desired. I learned all the outward forms of etiquette before I left for Poland but only practiced in Warsaw. Since then," he cast her a rueful glance, "my closest companions for the longest time were only lice."

"And Mord."

"Who falls short of the ideal as a dance partner." When she laughed, he said more seriously, "The Eldest, who has the greatest Sight, is very old. He lives in a village on Mount Dhiavilyi. Fritzl von Mecklundburg, my sister's son—but we've always thought of one another as cousins, being the same age—he will invite you to Gabrielle's wedding, which will take place at the Eyrie at the week's end. We can visit the Eldest quietly during the merrymaking."

"But surely people would notice and ask questions if we leave."

Jaska laughed. "Wait until you see the Eyrie. You'll understand. It's like a fortified city, only everyone lives under four connected roofs, instead of numerous separate ones, the servants tucked away in corners with their own warren of halls that no one else sees. Everyone says the first duke who built it was a madman, and once you try to find your way around in there, you'll agree." He leaned against one of the deep inset windows and began describing the Eyrie, while outside, a series of pretty little pony carts lined up along the garden path below one of the side doors.

Jaska glanced out, interrupted himself, and said, "Margit's bride party has ended. That means it's later than I thought. I must get to the Riding School and review a parade."

"Will you have to do those weekly, now?" she asked as he started away.

He turned around, laughing, his expression tender. The sunlight slanting under approaching clouds caught his eyes, turning the light brown to topaz. I heard Aurélie's breath catch as he said, "Weekly! Bonaparte did that, didn't he? I'd forgotten. Proof that the man is mad. What could be more boring? I should know, I've ridden in enough of them." He kissed his hand to her and strode away.

Alone, Aurélie went out to explore the garden with a quick glance skyward. "How horrid, to watch a military parade in the rain," she began, addressing me as she passed under an arched trellis laden with roses of three different shades.

"Talking to your ghost?" Margit appeared from the other side of the trellis.

Aurélie paused then curtseyed silently. Her manner was grave, the gesture so formal.

"She's a duppy, not a ghost," Aurélie said. "Your highness."

The clouds were boiling up fast, big splatters of rain began falling. One hit Margit on the cheek and Aurélie on the hand. The two turned instinctively toward the gazebo nearby, as the palace was a ways downslope.

"A duppy. What kind of word is that, 'duppy'?"

"I think you could call it Creole, as the language we used was made up of parts of many languages. That's my understanding of Creole, a whole made up of parts."

"It sounds heathen," Margit stated.

Aurélie did not answer.

"Do you really practice heathen ways?"

Aurélie stepped up into the gazebo, followed by Margit. She said, "My practices, such as they are, are mine, your highness. I hope you'll pardon the liberty I take in observing that they can be of no interest to anyone else."

"Speak plainly, please. As for no interest, that will no longer be true if you—if you stay." Margit stood in the middle of the gazebo, arms crossed.

Thanks to Madame Campan, Aurélie knew the etiquette of royalty.

One did not sit down in the presence of a princess without invitation, though all eight sides of the gazebo sported unoccupied benches. So she walked along the perimeter, looking out as the rain began to fall in earnest, a silvery sheet.

When she looked back, she said, "What is it that you find objectionable, since you know nothing of me? Was it my wearing breeches?"

"If I said it was, I suppose Jaska will be the first one to claim I'm a hypocrite, as I used to steal his clothing when we were small. I did not want the constraints of a princess. I wanted a boy's freedom."

"So did I," Aurélie said. "When I first met them, I took great care not to reveal myself to Jaska or Mord. The second trip, the masquerade was a matter of necessity."

Margit looked away, Jaska's same gesture when uncomfortable or disturbed, as Aurélie walked around and around the perimeter, looking out at the rain obscuring the garden. Far away, over the Dsaret mountain, lightning flashed, and on the other side of the garden, perceptible as silver etched against the slanting gray rain, ethereal figures danced.

When the long rumble of thunder died away, Margit said, "Jaska is angry with me. I'll have to make my peace with him, but I'm angry with him for returning all these years late and bringing what we might be forgiven for assuming was . . ."

"Was what, your highness?"

Margit grimaced slightly. "One of *those* females."

"Those what?"

Margit made a gesture. "I scarcely like to say. Adventuress, perhaps."

"Are they not women, too?" Aurélie asked and passed her hands over her eyes as the wind shifted direction, blowing a draft of rain into the gazebo. "Perhaps my once being so very close to starvation renders my morals suspect, but the only difference I see between a woman who sells herself for an hour in order to get enough to eat and one who sells herself for a crown is the amount of material wealth handed over for the transaction."

Margit was silent, then said slowly, "Sometimes the woman who is sold for a crown—I use your words, though I don't think I would put it that way—has little choice in the matter."

"Do you think the starving woman has more choice?"

"I think—oh, I don't know what a starving woman faces."

"She faces the very real possibility that the drunken lout offering her a *livre* or two for an hour might, after she completes her part of the transaction, beat her senseless instead of paying. No one will help her. They'll say, 'She's getting what she deserves.' Though there were two in the immoral act."

"You think the woman forced against her will to marry because she carries a great dowry or her marriage secures political gain between two men—do you think she gets a better opportunity if she sits down to a poisoned meat pie or is thrust from behind to tumble down the castle stairs, once the dowry changes hands?"

Aurélie started to pace in the other direction, an abrupt alteration that shifted my perspective. And there, outlined against the climbing roses, stood Pewter Hair the seraph, smiling directly at me as Aurélie said, "I condition only for a different word. Something merciful, perhaps? That doesn't condemn those forced between terrible choices? But I've yet to learn of such words in any of the languages I've studied."

"I've no answer to make to that, but only an observation to offer. Here in Dobrenica, there are poor people, but no one starves. The churches and the temples see to that. My mother once said that there is a kind of competition among the religions, but as it benefits all, why interfere? Those who are poor are so for many reasons, just as there are also women who sell themselves here, though they do so not because they starve."

Aurélie lifted a shoulder. "And so there are in other places. I met one younger than I am who intrigued Bonaparte. I also met women who, once they secured a husband, took as many lovers as they liked. I ask again, why is it that nothing is said about the male's part in any of these transactions? Why should men keep the moral advantage, just because they have the stronger arm?"

"Because they make the laws." Margit spread her hands.

"And women's social laws? The ones unwritten in any law book, but in force all the time? What of those?" Aurélie asked. She lifted her hands.

"Perhaps it's too large a question. When I was twelve, my Nanny Hiasinte made me promise never to sell myself, and I kept that promise. Out of ignorance when I was starving, for I didn't know then how desperate women earn money. Now, I wouldn't sell myself for any crown. And I was offered one, by Bonaparte himself."

She whirled around and ran out into the rain, leaving Margit standing alone in the gazebo.

Aurélie reached the palace drenched to the skin and shivering. When she got upstairs, she asked Viorel if she could have a bath. The maid took one look and dashed off to fetch her fellows to make a hot bath and fetch something warm to drink.

They hadn't lit the fires, as the day had started so nice. Viorel took care of that. Aurélie sat on the hearth shivering and staring into the fire until the bath was ready. When she had warmed up in the steaming water, she let out an extravagant sigh then said, "Kim, I don't think I can stay here."

Chill gripped me, though I can't tell you how. "You're going to surrender to Margit's pettiness?"

"Won't everyone say what she said?"

"You don't know that."

"This queen—"

"May surprise you."

Aurélie frowned at the window. "It hurts, the things she said. She despises me."

"I think some of that is her natural demeanor. But a lot of it is because she's angry with her brother. She can't strike out at him, so she's striking at you instead."

Aurélie ran to the mirror and looked into my face. "Angry with Jaska, yes. So she said. Because he was gone? But for such an important reason, having such dreadful experiences!"

"They are twins, and he left her here. I know and *she* knows she would never be permitted to go with him to war, but feelings are often illogical. And then, to make matters worse, he didn't communicate with her. He still doesn't." How to explain post traumatic stress disorder? "His experiences were so terrible he can't talk about them to anyone who didn't share them, and so there's a gulf between brother and sister."

"That grieves me," she said. "One thing I can do: avoid their mother. I feel certain she, too, thinks of me as an *adventuress*."

When she had dressed again, the rain had cleared up, and afternoon light slanted in.

Viorel came back to say, "Donna Aurélie, I am bid by Her Majesty the Queen to request that you honor her with your company on the ride to Mount Dhiavilyi tomorrow morning."

As soon as Viorel left, Aurélie leaned against the mirror and whispered, "It seems the last blow. Duppy Kim, I think it better if I leave now."

"If you do, you'll never see Jaska again," I said, my last-ditch argument. "Royal invitations are commands, and to leave when a queen invites you. . . . You know this. It would be perceived as the worst sort of insult."

Her chin came up. "Very well. But if she insults me directly, I will jump out of the carriage, and I don't care what they say or think."

FORTY

AURÉLIE ATE WITH THE ROYAL FAMILY that night. The conversation, led by the queen, was about music. The twins were largely silent; Margit subdued, and Jaska distracted.

Afterward, at the queen's invitation, they walked down to the private theater, where a concert had been arranged. A small chamber group and five singers. The only piece I recognized was something by Scarlatti, otherwise the choral pieces were Russian, complex, and interesting.

After that everyone parted, the queen admonishing them to rise betimes. What in my time was a few hours' drive would take two days.

Viorel had Aurélie all packed up by the time she woke. There was nothing to do but eat breakfast and get ready.

Aurélie walked out in her new traveling cloak and halted when she caught sight of the coach and six waiting in the morning chill, people's and horses' breath steaming, collars turned up. A company of impeccably dressed King's Guard also waited, plumes on their helmets. The queen emerged, walking with stately dignity, a sturdy footman at either side.

As she took the first step into the carriage, the queen paused, looked around, saw Aurélie, and beckoned.

Aurélie made her curtsey then skimmed down the broad terrace steps and climbed into the carriage, where she took up the backward seat, cramming herself into the corner in expectation of being joined by an entourage of royal servants.

But when the servants got the queen settled nicely in the middle of the seat opposite, they backed out again. The queen leaned toward the door and said, "Depart."

Trumpets blared, and horse hooves clattered as the guards at either side began moving. A lurch of the carriage, and there Aurélie was, alone with the queen.

Except for me.

"We can speak at leisure without interruption or interference," the queen said.

Aurélie bit her lip as she bowed from her seat. "I am honored, your majesty."

"What do you think of the city?" The queen indicated the cathedral sliding by on one side and its park on the other.

"Very fine, your majesty."

"And our weather? I understand you took a walk in our garden yesterday and ended up drenched."

"I should have been more watchful, your majesty." Aurélie glanced out at Prinz Karl-Rafael Street, along which Dobreni of every type had gathered. They were waving hats or handkerchiefs and cheering.

The queen smiled broadly out one window and then the other, until the houses got older and smaller and more scattered, and finally the road turned sharply to avoid the swamp where the city's branch of the river dumped into the main flow. In the future, the sewage treatment plan was here and the high road planted with hedgerows to hide the swamp.

The horses picked up the pace. They were heading down into the broad plain of the valley with its many farms.

The queen sat back. "Your answers are properly demure but reflect my words back at me. This gives me no portrait of you. Did you learn that from Bonaparte's lady?"

"From my aunt, your majesty."

"Your aunt. We will leave that for the time being. My daughter tells me you are a heathen. Is that so?"

"Heathen, your majesty," Aurélie repeated. "Who claims to be heathen? I understand it to mean evil, or rather, to worship evil things, which I do not. The Great Creole includes all religions that look to the goodness of *le bon Dieu*." She slipped from her careful German to the French of the islands.

"Let me ask this, then. First, the circumstances. I was born and raised as a Lutheran. To marry the man I wanted—king of a land so tiny my parents had to summon a cartographer from the university to find out where it lay—I first had to become a Roman Catholic. If the renowned Bourbon, Henri IV, could do so, could I do less? And I try to be a good Catholic, but in my heart of hearts I still think like a Lutheran. So does that make me a woman who sells herself?"

Aurélie colored deeply. "Did you feel you had sold yourself?" She seemed unsettled enough to have forgotten the honorific.

Nor did the queen remind her. "I never did. Here is my second point. Do I feel that it is the only true church, as I attest when we repeat the Credo? Again, in my heart of hearts, I adhere to the Lutheran understanding of 'apostolic' that includes all forms of Christianity. It seems that you have an even wider interpretation of the sacred mysteries, am I to understand that?"

"It is so," Aurélie stated. And added quickly, "Your majesty."

The queen smiled. "You must remember that I am the one who sent her son off to learn war with a Missal in one pocket and Leibniz in the other."

Aurélie regarded the queen solemnly. "I confess I am puzzled to know how I am to understand that, your majesty."

"Perhaps I am hinting that you are not the only one to be misjudged on too little evidence."

"My apologies, your majesty."

"Accepted, and in my turn, I apologize for, ah, the difficulties any of us might have added to your attempt to understand your place among us. We cannot help the sense of impending doom that Bonaparte, but . . .

no, I promised not to speak for anyone else. Anything you tell me is for my ears alone, child, but in your turn, you are about to hear a secret that you must promise to keep."

"I promise, your majesty."

"Very well. Dobrenica, as you have noticed, is small. We could so easily be slaughtered like far too many villages, polities, towns, and, of late, an entire kingdom, carved up between Russia, Prussia, and Austria."

She paused, as the carriage swayed and jolted over a bridge. Then she went on. "We have a protection by Vrajhus that sometimes removes us from the notice of the outer world. It has persisted for as much as several generations, though usually at least one. But the Vrajhus is contingent on the Dobreni's living in harmony with one another. What that means now is that my son, before he can be crowned on September 2nd, which is the traditional date, must bring about peace between the noble families, the guilds, and the crown. This is usually easiest with the people, as long as we keep covenant with them. Not as easy with the nobles, who are customarily bred to expect privilege and frequently harbor the ambition to accrue more."

"Many feel that is the natural law," Aurélie said.

"Divine right of kings? I was brought up to believe implicitly in the privileges of blood. But privilege ought to bring with it superior minds and morals, ought it not?"

Aurélie said, "I think so."

"When Martin Luther translated the Bible for us, we could see right there that nothing whatsoever was said in the Gospels about the divine right of kings, and I've met too many of them to believe them chosen by God rather than the accident of birth. That was before all these revolutions, when kings and the *noblesse* could die as miserably as the meanest serf. In England, I am told, the king is completely mad and does not govern at all. And my cousin Gustav in Sweden . . ." She shook her head.

"I have no opinion on the matters of kings, your majesty," Aurélie said.

"Of course you do, but you've been well trained not to speak it before anyone who might take exception. So let us not talk about kings. Let us talk about you."

"I am of no interest, your majesty."

"That is the first lie you've told me," the queen declared. "I was favorably impressed until this moment. You did not utter the pious-sounding inanities you might be forgiven for thinking I wanted to hear, when I asked if you are heathen. But the arrogance of informing me what I may or may not be interested in!" The queen mocked.

Aurélie flushed. "I did not expect to be of interest to . . . that is, I know nothing about . . ."

"My son," said the queen, "walked quite painfully from France to Vienna, when he could have summoned a carriage and servitors. Should have, some will say. All because he seems to have found you of interest."

"I am not a spy," Aurélie stated. "I don't know anything of interest to kings, or emperors. And I wouldn't spy for Bonaparte even if I did know any state secrets."

"I will accept that you are no spy. But you are still a mystery, Donna Aurélie."

Aurélie flushed and looked out the window at a thatched-roof farmhouse and a girl herding cows with a switch. Then out the other window, where a donkey and a man ploughed up the ground, and dust rose in their wake. Beyond, washing fluttered in the rising breeze that rocked the carriage.

Aurélie stiffened her shoulders. There was a hint of challenge in her voice—lower and rougher than usual, the French accent pronounced— as she said, "The truth about me is that I am not Donna Aurélie. That is, my name is Aurélie, but 'de Mascarenhas' was added by my mother, along with a dowry, in hopes of getting me a good life in England. When my aunt discovered that my father was an escaped slave, and my mother a privateer captain, she abandoned me the moment we reached France, so her friends in England would not be tainted by knowledge of the truth. And she kept the dowry."

The queen sat back. "A privateer captain?"

"Yes, your majesty."

"Your *mother* is a privateer captain?"

"Yes, your majesty."

"I admit I would like very much to meet this lady. Is she French?"

"Half. Her father was connected to the English aunt I mentioned."

The queen put her hands on her knees. "For the first time in twenty-five years, I am making this long journey without the least sense of boredom. Tell me everything, child. You pledged to keep the secret of our Blessing. In turn, I pledge to keep your secret."

Out it all came, in a torrent. All of it. Even the necklace. Aurélie pulled up her stocking to reveal the bulge, and when the queen bent forward to examine it, Aurélie rolled down the stocking.

The gold flashed, impossibly ancient, with its nine different gems augmented by three lesser ones, the diamond glinting coolly in the afternoon light slanting in.

"That is quite the most unusual thing I have ever seen. The irony is, such things are looted every day by armies crossing this way and that, and yet, if you were to wear that tomorrow at the ball my son-in-law will give for Gabrielle, it would be deemed as visual evidence of your lofty pedigree."

Aurélie could not hide her surprise.

The queen smiled wryly. "You did not mishear. As far as I am concerned, you are the daughter of a most noble and puissant Portuguese duke. Portugal might as well be your islands, or even the moon, for none of us are ever likely to travel that far. Especially if we manage to invoke Vrajhus in the Blessing."

"I thank you for your forbearance, your majesty."

"You are welcome, though part of my motivation is entirely self-interest. Or . . . but I said I would speak for no one else. However. There are plenty among us for whom names and rank carry their own magic, and I would never gainsay that, as such things bind us closer to our responsibilities toward others. You have seen in Paris what happens when all the rules are thrown over."

"I comprehend."

"Yonder is the last hill. We should be seeing Baron Elias's castle tow-
ers soon, and that means our posting inn is not far beyond. Tomorrow I
will return to diplomatic duty in my efforts to bolster my son's prestige.
But I desire you to remember what he must achieve if we are to survive
what must come."

FORTY-ONE

THEY REACHED THE INN shortly after the late afternoon light was abruptly snuffed by the curve of the first ridge of Mt. Dhiavilyi. Day ended early, deep in the Dobreni valleys; the shadows merged so swiftly I was not certain if I was seeing those shadow beings, the ones Mord had called seraphs, or just the shifting of vanishing sunbeams.

The inn yard was crammed with fine carriages. All of Dobreni polite society was on its way to the Eyrie for Gabrielle's wedding.

The inn itself was an enormous, rambling building with massive stone fireplaces in every room. Aurélie, as part of the queen's party, had a room to herself. Viorel was already there, busy laying out evening clothes. A hot bath waited.

The dinner was a crowded affair. Aurélie was introduced all around, including to some of the women who had been at Margit's bridal party for Gabrielle. Irena responded with a stiff curtsey. Jaska announced that, as soon as the Ridotski party arrived, there would be entertainment in the inn's large salon, and any who had thought to bring musical instruments were welcome to play after he and Donna Aurélie and Domnu Zusya began the evening.

Out came a couple of harps, lugged along in the servants' coaches with the trunks, plus a variety of winds and strings. During the chaos of people fetching (or ordering servants to bring) their instruments, finish-

ing dinner, grouping and regrouping, Jaska kept watch on the door until
it opened and a new crowd of people entered. Among them I recognized
Shmuel Ridotski, Mord, and Elisheva. The Jewish folk had obviously
dined elsewhere and were now ready to join the entertainment.

Jaska had made it clear that the original trio was to kick things off.
But where was Mord?

Margit appeared out of the crowd, gave a polite, unsmiling nod to
Aurélie, then said low-voiced, "If you are going to begin the playing, you
and Donna Aurélie will have to perform as duet. There seems to be a
problem with Domnu Zusya."

"Where?" Jaska asked, looking around for Mord.

Margit pointed to one of the chambers off the main room where
extra wraps and such had been left.

Jaska cast Aurélie a glance of appeal, and the two threaded their way
through to the side chamber, where they found Mord at the window,
Elisheva beside him, arms crossed.

The pair were talking in Hebrew—maybe arguing, except there was
no rancor in their voices, none of the sharpness of anger. Back and forth,
quick as a tennis match, then she retorted something that made him huff
a laugh. I couldn't remember having heard him laugh out loud. He was
devastatingly attractive when he laughed, his whole being radiating the
humor, but quick as a flash of lightning, it illuminated then vanished.

He said something. She turned away, her hand coming up to hide
her face as she hiccoughed on a giggle. Then she saw Jaska and Aurélie,
and the crowd of curious faces behind.

She marched over and shut the door behind Jaska, Margit, and Aurélie without a word of apology to those behind, then whirled around,
her brown skirt flaring to reveal the tops of her shoes. "Tell him," she
began in Dobreni, and then, with a quick, concerned look at Aurélie, she
began again in German. "Your highness, I beg of you. Tell him that he
hears the *sound* of sacred words but not the *sense*."

"There is no sense," he muttered. "I promised Rebbe Nachman that
I would obey the letter of the law, for he promised that I'd rediscover the
spirit. But the spirit is a void, each person hearing a different thing. Not

only when I play his teaching stories. Even when I relate them, in his own words."

Elisheva clapped her hands together in frustration. "But you're not listening to the heart behind the words your listeners use. Yes, everyone interprets the music into different words, just as one part of the story speaks to them more, but don't you see it, the kinship here?" She pressed her fists below her collarbones. "Here." Up to her forehead. "That is how we build the *tikkun olam*, one heart, one mind at a time. Together." She flung her hands wide. "All the shards of light gathered back to one great candle. Remember the tale of the Baal Shem Tov, may his memory be blessed, and the sheep? Do the sheep know words? *Tell* him."

"He won't listen to me," Jaska said, smiling ruefully. "Except to argue with. And much I've valued those arguments. We sharpened our wits on one another for many leagues that otherwise would have been tedious, but has he ever been convinced by anything I've said? No."

"Am I being arrogant again?" Mord asked earnestly. "It is not arrogance inside my mind. I want to achieve rightness, I want to know it again, I want the peace I knew when young."

"You know that music binds, it does not divide," Jaska said. "We saw that time and again. Perhaps that is the beginning of peace?"

"I can begin there." Mord turned away from the window. "Yes. So shall it be, then. Mademoiselle Aurélie, where is your music? Jaska, your flute?"

Because the three were so practiced together, they set a high bar. Elisheva's sister Shoshanna, who swanned about like a princess, sang with a voice that would shame nightingales. The sardonic Benedek had a smooth baritone. The brittle Irena played with passion on her harp, accompanied by her brother Mikhail, whose eye was on someone far back in the room as he sang. I didn't pick up the significance of that until later.

They kept it going until midnight, then parted to recruit against the long ride up the mountain on the morrow.

When Aurélie woke, Viorel brought some strong eastern coffee and a pastry, then told her that everyone would be wearing their spring clothes.

"We always celebrate the first of May, but as that's Sunday, the day of the wedding, it's going to start early," she explained.

"What does that mean?" Aurélie asked.

"You will ride in wagons. They are open if the sky stays clear, and have canopies if it doesn't," Viorel said.

And so it was. The queen stayed in her carriage, but everyone else climbed into wagons that had been festooned with evergreen boughs and flowers.

The first and most decorated wagon was for Jaska, Margit, and the "Duke de Mascarenhas's daughter from France." Sturdy horses in teams of four and six worked to pull the wagons up the mountain, with fresh pairs waiting at certain villages on the way.

Up and up past moss-antlered oaks, the shrouded depths marked by pale beech like stilled lightning. Ivy looped in festoons, catching the greeny light, and everywhere, everywhere, water trickled, dripped, gurgled, and rushed, water-weed trailing like mermaids' hair. Protected in the mysterious ravines were the villages, out of the reach of arctic winds and angry storms, their thick roofs testament to the cold that was an inescapable part of winter, punctuated here and there by onion-domed steeples, for this was the heart of Orthodox territory.

Again and again I thought I glimpsed among the sheltering trees shadowy winged beings that were not seraphs, but I couldn't be certain. Since they'd never been any kind of threat, I didn't worry about them.

Villagers came out to welcome the parade. This procession was, for them, rare and heavy-duty entertainment. They wore their embroidered plain-spun blues and browns, girls crowned with wreaths of scarlet begonias and pure white rosebuds. As the horses were changed, they brought out refreshments—foaming beer, the last of winter's cider, and zhoumnyar, the distilled liquor that has a mule's kick. It was served in tiny cups decorated with flowers; a wise idea or the guests would have arrived at the Eyrie totally snockered.

At first the royal wagon was mostly silent as they jolted up the road under deep spring green branches, past fragrant flowering shrubs. Jaska tried to cover over by talking about the evening's concert—how much everyone loved Mord's playing, favorite songs, where they originated, the difference in lyrics depending on the region. "Even here, we get variations, mountain to mountain. Small as Dobrenica is, there are many who have not been a day's walk from their villages in their entire lives."

"There are many of us who have not been outside of Dobrenica, small as it is," Margit retorted.

That silenced Jaska. Aurélie looked down at the wildflowers growing along the side of the road.

Margit addressed her. "You're thinking that I'm provincial, Donna Aurélie."

Aurélie looked up. "I'm thinking that I would've traded with you if I could, except I wouldn't wish . . . ah, certain days on anyone else."

Margit stirred uncomfortably, her fingers twitching unconsciously at the blossoms festooned at the wagon's side. Petals fluttered down to the road unheeded. "My mother seems to think you're perfect."

Aurélie replied gravely, "Her majesty is forbearing."

"And I'm not? No, Jaska, don't speak," Margit said. "I see that I'm arguing." She glanced away then back at Aurélie. "Our mother pointed out that you didn't remonstrate with me. She said I took your words as a reproach because I'm in need of such, and that puts me doubly in the wrong. I hate being in the wrong when I feel wronged."

"It's understandable. We all do," Aurélie said.

"Shall we begin anew?" Margit asked.

Aurélie spread her skirt, rose a little, and tried to curtsey. Its grace was ruined by potholes, but the intent was there as she said, "Your highness, permit me to introduce myself as Donna Aurélie de Mascarenhas . . ." She stopped there, a revealing glance Jaska's way making her thoughts pretty clear: She still hadn't told him her history. And from the way he was acting (like nothing had changed) it was evident that the queen had kept her word.

The two began a halting conversation, feeling their way toward some sort of understanding. The actual words were trivial—mostly about music, lessons, how disappointing it was to discover one couldn't sing, favorites. But the reach for understanding was apparent, even if they were not instantly best friends.

So the mood lightened considerably as the Eyrie began to appear between cracks in the peaks ahead. The first few times it was hailed by the group in what sounded like time-honored fashion.

Those hails lessened as the glimpses widened into longer views, blocked by fewer ridges and forested peaks. The afternoon shadows began to coalesce into twilight.

At the last horse stop, lanterns were brought to each wagon, one forward and one aft. When they arrived, the Eyrie was lit with a zillion twinkling lights. Lanterns and candles don't have the reach of mega-wattage electricity, but the effect was even more startling, especially seen from below. The place looked like the capital of fairyland.

Up close it was just as wonderful. In modern times there were a series of tumble-down garages, considerably the worse for wear after decades of occupiers' misuses. But here were well-kept stables, marked off by a row of hedges that the locals had decorated with fairy lamps of various spring colors. The resultant path to the main doors (which I had never been through) looked like a stairway to heaven.

Up we streamed, everyone in a party mood. There were enough servants to form a small army. The King's Guard didn't look any too worried, though there was only a company of them. From what I saw, although as they stayed more or less in parade-ground order until the queen had been saluted with trumpets and helped inside, more than half were giving surreptitious winks and flicks of the fingers to friends and relatives.

Here was the black and white marble checkerboard floor that I vividly remembered from a sword battle I would have two centuries into the future . . . I hoped.

Greeting the queen with deep bows and curtseys were the duke and his wife, Princess Maria, Gabrielle's parents. The duke was a fair-haired middle-aged guy who didn't look the least like the von Mecklundburgs I knew. His wife looked like a gray-haired version of Margit, only stouter. Next to her, in a row, stood her three children: the heir, tall and square-jawed with a winsome smile, Count Karl-Friedrich, whom everyone called Fritzl; Father Marcus, a Benedictine; Gabrielle, looking like a fairy princess all in white gauze and lace; and next to her, a short, muscular guy with curly dark hair who turned out to be her betrothed, Baron Ilya Carolos.

Once we'd passed the reception line, the queen was helped, with great tenderness, to a vast state guest room to recover from the journey.

Aurélie's suite of three rooms was not far. About four doors down from it was the suite through whose window I'd once jumped while trying to escape the horde of bad guys chasing me. Aurélie opened the French windows of her outer chamber and stepped out onto the marble balcony. She peered into the garden below. "Observe those statues," she said. "They look so real in the moonlight."

Viorel said in a low, thrilling voice, "Those are vampires, turned forever to stone by the daylight."

"Vampires!" Aurélie exclaimed, drawing back as if the statues could pop into life again.

"There was a terrible attack during my grandmother's day," Margit said from the doorway of the adjoining chamber. "Riev was under siege by the *Inimasang*, the Dobreni word for vampires. You will find that every house has its hawthorn wreaths during winter, roses during summer, and crystal charms the year through. That reminds me, you'll need protections. But didn't Domnu Zusya say you have one?"

"I do," Aurélie said.

"That's as well, though no one has seen any *Inimasang* for years. But people relate the strangest rumors about this mountain. Come, Jaska says they're gathering for dinner, and no one can eat a bite until we're there. We'll have dancing after it's done. What are the popular dances in Paris? The gavotte, I am certain, and the minuet?"

"The waltz—" Aurélie began as she started out with Margit.

"What is that?"

"You dance in pairs, twirling." Aurélie held up her arms and danced lightly across the bedroom, turning on her toes.

"Pairs of what?"

"A man and a woman," Aurélie said, looking surprised.

"Touching?" Margit *tsk*ed. "That is impossible."

"Then there is the quadrille."

"That is a pattern for horses. Do people prance around like horses?"

"It is very complicated, and popular, I assure you. It is again danced in pairs."

"Our court dances are done in pairs, but the folk prefer to separate men's dances from women's. The May dances especially. Weapons have been forbidden in the men's dances for generations. They sometimes use fans, but the women still dance with flowers." Margit added, "I do so like to watch a man who can dance well, or is that outré in Paris?"

"Oh, no," Aurélie said with feeling. "The officers are all dressed up, and everybody is watching them, I assure you. And they are watching the ladies."

"Officers? It's all officers?"

"That's all I ever saw at the Tuileries and Saint-Cloud, with a few diplomatic exceptions."

FORTY-TWO

THERE WAS A LITTLE DANCING AFTER DINNER, but most people, in preparation for tomorrow's wedding, were resting up in expectation of a long day and night following.

When she returned to her room, Aurélie found Viorel proudly laying out the just-finished ball gown. For extremely formal affairs, the fashions in Dobrenica were closer to late eighteenth century tastes than the skimpy, low cut Parisian fashions. The skirts were full, the waist slightly raised and sashed, the skirt a swooped polonaise that revealed an underskirt of silver tissue. The bodice and overdress were white, embroidered all over with green leaves and tiny crimson clusters of berries, the neck and sleeves edged with silver lace and spring green ribbon.

The headdress to go with it was a wreath of silk flowers, and crimson ribbon hanging down the back. It looked terrific against her black curls.

Viorel stood by, smiling expectantly, then flushed with pleasure when Aurélie heaped her with praise, going over every detail. They did a last fitting, the maid twitched and pinched here and there, then the gown was swept off for finishing touches, as Aurélie went to bed. I think she was asleep in less than a minute.

Her life experience—with the Kittredges, travel, lady-in-waiting—so far had made her an early riser. She'd bathed and was about to take her coffee and pastry out onto the balcony when there was a soft knock at her door.

Viorel ran to it, then turned around eyes wide. "It's his highness," she said, turning back and curtseying hastily.

At Aurélie's gesture, Viorel let Jaska into the outer chamber, and he joined Aurélie out on the balcony. "I thought you might also be up early," he said.

"Shall I call for more coffee or pastry?" Aurélie asked.

"I ate. Thank you." He stared down into the garden.

"I'm trying to pretend that the vampire statues are carvings," she said.

"That one *is* a carving," Jaska replied. "See? No vampire's going to pose with a lyre as the sun rises."

Aurélie stood on tiptoe to peer over, and I could see the neo-Roman mythological figure below. Probably Orpheus. "Oh," she said. "Now I feel foolish."

"The rest of the garden really is full of stone vampires," Jaska said. "A few of them from my grandmother's day. There was a conflict with them in seventeen twenty-two."

Aurélie shuddered.

"But it's daylight now, and even after the sun goes down, it's unlikely any vampires roaming free would disturb a gathering this size, especially with everyone wearing charms, and in a castle full of weapons ready to hand." His smile became one of inquiry. "My mother sought me out to say how much she enjoyed the journey."

He sounded pleasant, his eyes kindly, but even though she was only eighteen, she had become attuned to him. I could see that she sensed his question by the way it mirrored in her troubled glance.

She had been playing with the porcelain coffee cup, turning it around and around so that the gilding on the lip glinted in the morning sun rising over the distant mountains of Russia. Then she set it down with a *ching* of decisiveness. "I think the time has come to tell you something," she said, and watched him carefully.

The issue was trust. They both knew it, I could see it so plainly. But she had to be free to speak. He was trying hard not to put any pressure on her.

She said, "I thought I'd wait until we visit the Eldest and get answers to our questions."

"Before you can speak to me?" he asked, leaning a little forward, one hand resting on the table.

"I don't have a question so much as a confession," she said, her brow puckered. "I'm not ashamed of who I am, but I'm not who you think. My birth is . . . not noble."

His expression eased, and he leaned back. "Is that all?"

"'Is that all'?" she repeated. "What is 'all'? That I have no claim to de Mascarenhas as a name? That in fact, I do not rightly know what my name is?"

"That was disclosed by Fouché's secretaries before I brought you that letter from Jamaica," Jaska said. "An English secretary at one of the island offices traded the information for something Fouché needed: According to them, your mother's people are gentry folk from somewhere in the southern part of England, and *her* mother was a French émigré as a result of the Gallican heresy. Your father was a privateer, and it was said born a slave, though slavery was afterward abolished in Saint-Domingue. No one understood whether Bonaparte's orders were to reinstitute it or not, but in any case, the last I heard he was losing his battle there anyway, and I have to say, I rejoiced to hear that a large number of the few Poles to escape death had joined the side of the defenders."

Aurélie gazed at him in astonishment. "You knew?"

He opened his hands. "Can you forgive me for knowing?"

Aurélie blinked away tears. "I was so afraid . . . how you might react."

"Do you trust me so little?" he asked whimsically, but his eyes were sad.

"No! Yes!" She clasped her hands tightly and set her chin on them. "Oh, I'm not making sense. It's just that it *mattered* so much. More than anything. I don't know quite how it happened, but so it is. And I could not *bear* the idea that you would be disgusted, and tell me to go back to Paris, or . . ."

"Or abandon you, as apparently your English relations did?" Jaska added. "Last night, when my mother discovered that I already knew, she told me that she thinks the Dsarets will be better for the blood of a privateer captain and a seer."

She gave an unsteady laugh.

He went on. "I can't blame you for not telling me, as I'd kept my own secret for quite a while. I kept thinking I ought to tell you, but then I'd tell myself to wait, that you deserved a true courtship. The truth is, those days of walking and talking so freely, just Jaska and René, two musicians, became so precious to me that I would willingly have walked to Moscow, if only nothing else were at stake."

"I don't want a courtship," she murmured, low and fervent, "if it means talking nothings in a stuffy ballroom, constrained by strict etiquette. Oh, how I loved our days of travel!"

"How I love *you*," he said, so softly it was barely above a whisper.

She looked from his eyes to his hands as he stretched them both out to her. "I love you, too, oh, much! I did not see it at first, but when we were in Vienna, I knew it then."

His sudden smile transformed his face, making him seem younger. "Will you marry me, Aurélie?"

Their hands met, touched, fingers entwined. Jaska began to pull her toward him—and then halted. "She *is* there, isn't she?"

"Duppy Kim?" Aurélie asked, blinking.

"I am *very* sorry," I said with heartfelt sorrow. "If I could shut my eyes, I would."

"I don't care," Aurélie said and flung herself into Jaska's arms.

He gave a laugh as unsteady as hers and closed his arms around her. As they fit themselves together with the awkward tenderness of a first kiss, sorrow and joy swooped through me. Though I could not measure time, it seemed forever since I had felt Alec's arms, and I thought, *Am I done yet, Xanpia?*

No. Because I was still there.

I tried not to see as they whispered and cuddled, and time mercifully blurred. I found them leaning side by side on the balcony, arms twined around one another. His hand ruffled through her curls as he said, "There is much we can say when we can be truly alone. I look forward to it. Less of a pleasure is the task facing me. Us." He lifted her hand and traced his fingers over her palm. "It might be too soon, but you know what threats we face. My mother said she explained the Blessing. Aurélie, are you ready for the burdens that come with a crown? If this is too soon to speak of it, I understand."

"I want to marry you," she said quickly. "I have known since Vienna that every day with you in it would be a good one, and every day with you away would have to be endured. These other things," she gave a little shrug, "the palace and the crowns . . . I have an understanding now of how Madame Bonaparte must feel."

He lifted his brows in mock affront. "You find me similar to Bonaparte?"

She chuckled. "You don't make people stand around for hours while you talk and talk and talk."

"I probably will, some day." He shook his head. "You'll have to put me on my guard, because no one ever tells a king he's boring. As for the other matter, once we're married, no one will remember de Mascarenhas, a name no Dobreni can pronounce. Aurélie Dsaret, how beautiful that sounds!"

"Except that few can say my given name, either," she replied, laughing.

"Can you become accustomed to Aurelia Dsaret?"

"It doesn't sound like me, but what does? Now I understand what Nanny Hiasinte was telling me about names. I am me, whatever others call me. *Bon!* Aurelia Dsaret I shall be. It is pretty and sounds like what a proper princess ought to have as a name."

He lifted her hand and kissed it, then gently let it go as he got to his feet. "There is much to be done if we're to bring everyone peacefully together by September. I've seven years of absence to make up for. Oh, how good it feels to know that you'll be with me! But speaking of burdens, there are people waiting. I had better go."

She walked him to her outer door. He kissed her hand then left.

When the door was shut, she pressed her hand against her cheek, then walked to the mirror. "I know what I must do," she told me. "Try to make his task easier."

The von Mecklundburgs had arranged several entertainments. Some locals did dance exhibitions. There was shooting and riding in the practice yard beyond the stable, and in the middle of this, the good weather ended at last. As clouds began sailing in from the west, most of the women went inside where parlor games were played, like Hunt the Slipper and various guessing games.

Aurélie played along, but she seemed increasingly distracted, and when people began to go upstairs to rest or spend quiet time before getting ready for the ball, she retreated to her room. She found it lit with a fire on the grate. The temperature was already dropping, judging by the way she plucked up a heavy shawl.

She stared at the white and gold escritoire set between the windows, then went to the mirror. "What do you think of this idea? I've been forming it all day. As the future bride of a crown prince I'll write Aunt Kittredge, and tell her that if she doesn't give my dowry to Diana I'll take it up with Parliament through the diplomats. How does that sound? I know it won't come to that, because she worries so about what others might think."

"Excellent idea," I said heartily.

"And I'll write to Diana. I won't tell her about the dowry. Let it be a surprise, if my aunt complies. I'll only tell her that I'd very much like some of those English roses from the garden. She'll know the ones I mean. I loved those roses! And if I'm to write as a future princess, my aunt will assuredly not dare to destroy my letter, do you think?"

She got right to work, grinning from time to time as she underscored words. On the outside of the papers she wrote their names above *Undertree, in Hampshire, England*, then folded the letters with a flourish. But the escritoire did not have seals. She pulled tiny drawers out one by one to find them all empty.

She dropped the folded letters onto the desk and moved to the armoire on the other side of the room, but just as she opened the door

Viorel knocked to let her know the bath was ready, and she had her majesty's hairdresser waiting.

Aurélie bustled off to get ready for the ball. When she was done, she paused to admire herself in the long framed mirror. When Viorel ran out to do something, Aurélie pulled up her foot, rolled down her stocking, and removed the necklace.

She clasped it on and stood back to admire the effect. The gold glinted in a graceful arc, accentuating the equally graceful line of her neck. The stones picked up the colors in the embroidery and in the flowers of her wreath. She truly looked like a princess.

As she walked out, I thought, one down—they're pledged—one to go, the danger thing. But the Blessing would take care of that, right? After speeding through the years from 1795 to 1803, I could hang on a few more months, right?

Alec, here I come.

FORTY-THREE

VIOREL REAPPEARED. Her mouth dropped open when she saw the necklace. I could see from the way she stared at it that she badly wanted to ask where it came from. "I am to tell you they are gathering on the landing, Donna Aurélie."

The queen was already seated in the gigantic ballroom, in the place of honor. Jaska and Margit awaited Aurélie, he in silver-gray brocade with rose and gold accents, and Margit in white, with crimson and gold touches. "One on each arm," Jaska said, crooking his elbows. "And if my knee objects to these stairs, I expect you two to keep me from pitching down."

A fanfare pealed out. Liveried guards alternated with King's Guard at intervals, bracing to attention.

The three descended the stairs, Aurélie's whole being alight with joy, her bearing regal yet softened by the style she'd learned from Josephine.

A minuet opened the ball, Jaska and Aurélie in the lead, Margit with Fritzl behind, and the bride and groom after. Then Jaska retired from dancing, murmuring with regret that he could not hop the gavotte.

That signaled open season on Aurélie and Margit. After dancing the gavotte with Gabrielle's baron, Aurélie found herself confronted for the country dance by the formidable Mikhail Trasyemova, dark-browed and black-haired, his skin only a shade or two lighter than Aurélie's.

He scowled the entire time, not speaking a word. Aurélie maintained the silence, her expression somber when the end came at last, and they performed the bow and curtsey.

A rumble of tambourines, the wail of woodwinds, and a distinctively Russian melody spun a bunch of guys out onto the floor, dancing on their toes, whirling and kicking.

Aurélie glanced across the ballroom to where Jaska stood in a small knot of people, talking animatedly. She began to make her way around the perimeter, trying to step behind those watching the dancers. She'd progressed about ten feet when she found herself face to face with the Countess Irena.

Aurélie made a slight curtsey, the set of her shoulders ready for a duel. But it turned out battle was not on Irena's mind.

"Did my brother speak to you when you danced?" Irena asked, her cheeks flushed, her chin high.

"He said nothing at all, Countess," Aurélie said.

"*Donnerwetter!* So simple a thing." And as Aurélie waited politely, Irena fidgeted with her painted fan, then said, "It seems that the queen herself negotiated your marriage with Jaska. Or, you negotiated it with her, and if so, I commend your skills."

Aurélie made another slight curtsey.

"I must beg your forgiveness, I see. I do. I misunderstood what was before my eyes. You arrived with the barest vestige of a respectable entourage, but I didn't know you were ahead of French pursuit. Jaska might've told me," Irena said darkly. "But he was ever such. The last time I saw him, it was in this very ballroom. I was turned sixteen, and my father wished us to cement the betrothal. Jaska had only to speak the words, and what did he do? He bored on the entire night about the differences between the *uhlans* and the winged hussars, their tactics upon the battlefield, and how such was useless in our mountains."

Aurélie put her hand to her mouth, but it was too late.

"You laugh," Irena stated, her brows raised. "Do you find that interesting? Is that how you attached him, with such talk?"

"No, not at all," Aurélie said, valiantly trying to subdue her mirth. It betrayed her only in an added huskiness to her voice.

Irena flung a curl back from her neck in a grand gesture. "It is an impossible subject. He never talked of anything but war when he was a boy, either that or he nattered with Marcus von Mecklundburg and Shmuel Ridotski about philosophy, every bit as boring. Very well! It's done, and I profess to be well rid of him. But there's so much talk of how Domnu Zusya, the angel of the battlefield and of the violin, refuses a barony. Why should not the Chevalier Hippolyte de Vauban be so fortunate? That is what I ask. It is a simple enough thing."

Aurélie blinked in surprise at the introduction of Hippolyte from out of the blue.

Irena was scowling at her hands, which gave Aurélie a second or two to recover. She said, "Am I to understand, Countess, that you have formed an attachment to the Chevalier? So gallant a man," she added, and Irena bridled with such pleasure, that the question was answered before she spoke a word.

"You don't know, then?" Irena seemed amazed, as if everyone in the country was aware of her love life. Maybe they were. "My father expects my brother or me to marry one of the Dsarets. At least, it cannot be both. There is a law against brothers and sisters of the same family marrying here, though I don't know what obtains in France."

"So . . . your brother is to marry Princess Margit?"

"That's what Father wants. He and the king spoke of it when Father served as one of the sponsors at Jaska's baptism. But neither Mikhail nor Margit want to marry the other, and so there was also the possibility of Jaska coming back, in which case Father regarded me as honor bound."

"Does your brother have someone in mind?"

Irena scowled again. "Of course, and she's impossible. A beautiful face, and no birth. But he is the heir! *He* can do what he wants. If Father cuts him off for a year, at the birth of a grandson he welcomes him back. But I? I'm told I must marry at least a baron, if I fail to become a princess."

"And if the Chevalier became a baron?"

"That's what Mikhail was to ask you. A favor for a bride, so simple a thing for Jaska to agree to! But I see he failed me. Tchah!"

Aurélie said, "I promise I'll speak to Jaska about Chevalier de Vauban. He's a very . . ." I could see her hesitating at the word *handsome* because that, de Vauban was emphatically not, even if he'd had both eyes and no hideous scar on one side of his face. ". . . charming gallant."

The two parted with mutual curtseys, then Aurélie made her way through the watchers. She observed the observers, coming back most often to the princess.

"Who is Margit watching, Kim?" Aurélie breathed.

Floating as I did somewhat above Aurélie's shoulder, I could see Margit on the other side of the ballroom. She had her lasers locked on . . .

"Benedek Ysvorod," I said.

Aurélie betrayed astonishment, then tipped her head inquiringly. "Is he watching her back?"

"No. Oh, yes. Yes, he is. But he's at the other end of the ballroom. Is there some political trouble there?"

Aurélie's expression was thoughtful as she made her way around the ballroom, pausing to nod or curtsey when others saluted her.

Jaska was in conversation with a couple of graybeards and a gloriously dressed guy in purple brocade—all three wore gold chains on their shoulders. Jaska broke off what he was saying then excused himself right and left.

He leaned heavily on his cane. After his, "How are you doing?" which Aurélie asked him right back, he said: "It's the standing. I can walk all day. I can even dance, if there isn't much jumping. But standing? And they all want to stand."

"You can't get them to sit?"

"I'm not holding court," he said apologetically. "I'm fine. That necklace is quite striking. I don't remember ever seeing it. Or did I, once? In Paris? Yes. It was the first time I saw you as a young lady."

She whispered in English, "It's my protection. I hid it on my ankle."

"I'm amazed I never noticed that," he observed.

She shrugged. "Nobody ever saw it."

Instinct prompted her to dart her fingers to her collarbones in a defensive check, though this was Dobrenica, and she was safe.

Wait. Was that a shadow, or the curve of a wing beyond the cluster of women watching the dancers? I looked the other way, as far as I could. Was the shadow in the alcove deeper than normal beyond that group over there? The alcove was at the edge of my vision. Well, if the seraphs, or the shadow wing things, had come to the Eyrie, what matter? They seemed to like hanging around, but they didn't do anything beyond that.

The piece ended. The orchestra in the galley began the introduction to a new country dance as some left the floor and others took their places in the forming line. Aurélie turned, giving me a wider view. The extra deep shadow seemed to have been only a trick of the eye. Relief!

"Jaska, I wish to ask a favor," Aurélie said.

"A favor, is it?" he responded as they began to stroll. "I'm already offering you the smallest kingdom I know of. Do you desire me to conquer France?"

She chuckled, then said earnestly, "It's for Irena, not for me. If you'd consider making the Chevalier de Vauban into a baron. Can you do that?"

He glanced down at her, tenderness in his smile. "I was already planning that as one of my first actions when I'm crowned. I put the notion before Hippolyte in Vienna, knowing his republican dedication. He's reconciled. He said that if restoring the *de* before his name magically reestablished his bona fides, then who was he to deny others the absurdity of giving greater value to his words as a baron than as a citizen? He agreed to accept as long as he could continue to despise all human hierarchies."

Aurélie grinned. "Including you as king?"

"I believe that's what he meant when he exclaimed, '*Scélérat!* Remember this, I have seen you naked, and your backside is made exactly like mine.'"

They laughed, then Jaska said, "Shmuel is also going to become a baron. The empire forbade the admission of Jews to the privileged ranks until Emperor Joseph changed some of the punitive laws. Did you know Shmuel's father was killed on a diplomatic mission to Russia? I'll have to drop a word about Hippolyte in Irena's ear. I wonder why she didn't ask me during that interminable ride that she spent glaring at my back, when we arrived in Dobrenica."

"Perhaps that was her intent when she rode to meet you. Then she saw me."

"I should have foreseen that," he said ruefully. "I planned badly. Here, let's step into this little room. I do need to sit for a moment and rest my knee."

She'd taken his arm. They turned into a small antechamber with a side table, a bench, an old framed mirror, and a door on the other side that probably led to a garderobe.

Jaska sank down on the bench next to the mirror and stretched out his bad leg. "Much better." He glanced toward the door, which they did not close—not before they were properly married. He lowered his voice and continued in English. "The biggest problem before me is Benedek and Margit. I think I told you that our oldest sister wouldn't marry any-one below a prince, and so they her found one in Russia. She in turn tried to arrange a suit for Margit with one of her husband's connections. The Empress Catherine favored this suit, as she needed the wealth of our mines for her wars. My mother didn't dare to refuse Catherine outright. But neither was she going to give away the Dsaret mines as Margit's dowry. She protracted negotiations, trusting a solution would present itself. Then Catherine died. Paul had no interest in us, with vast tracts of new land to play with."

"Yet Margit is still unmarried."

"Now the problem is the other nobles who want Margit to marry Mikhail Trasyemova only because they *don't* want her to marry Benedek Ysvorod. The Duke of Trasyemova wants a royal grandchild, and the rest of them don't want to see the Ysvorods gain power—they were kings for a long time. The last Ysvorod king is reviled in our history as our worst. That was centuries ago, but memory is long in Dobrenica."

"Can you help her?"

"Not until I'm king. If I'd died, Benedek would've been my heir. If I marry and have no sons, he will be my heir. Many resist this prospect."

"There can be no reigning queens?" she asked.

He gave his head a shake. "No. Though my mother has been queen regnant in all but name—she's a regent, and a good one—for twenty-five years. But now that I'm home, everyone clamors for me to claim the crown." He took her hands. "A prospect I resisted mightily but am swiftly becoming reconciled to." He kissed her hands and pulled her into a quick kiss, then they drew apart, both sending self-conscious glances at the open door.

She let go his hands and ran hers up her arms. "The next thing is to find this Eldest."

"We'll do that Monday, when everyone else is traveling back down the mountain."

Aurélie agreed, and rubbed her arms again. "Why is it so cold in here?"

"There you are." Mord walked in with Elisheva at his side. She was dressed in leaf green with embroidery in shades of wheat, gold, and yellow. Mord wore new clothes, though as before his black coat was free of embroidery charms. "Jaska, did you know that this castle is filled with seraphs?"

Elisheva clapped her hands, her eyes flashing wide when she saw the necklace. "Where did you get that?" She thrust her hand into a hidden pocket of her gown and pulled out her prism.

"It is my protection," Aurélie said.

"That's it," Elisheva whispered. "*That's* what they saw." She turned an astonished gaze to Mord, then Jaska, then Aurélie again. Then Elisheva took a step closer and recited in a melodic chant as she pointed to each of the necklace gems:

There is the stone of Reuben Odem that protects families
Shimon Pitda that protects animals,
Levi Bareket that protects children,
Yehuda Nofech that gives the power to overcome evil intent,
Yisschar Saphir that heals and protects vision,
Zevulon Yahalom that protects the sleeper and guides dreams on the
    righteous path,

Gad Leshem that grants true sight,
Dan Shevo that protects the home,
Naftali Ahlamah that prevents sudden death,
Asher Tashish that protects the growing things,
Yosef Shoam that protects the seasons, and
Binyamin Yashfeh that wards the evil blood drinkers.

Aurélie touched the necklace. "My Nanny named the stones differently, and she didn't have words for these three lesser stones."

Elisheva said, "It is *very* ancient, this protection." She turned her head, addressing Jaska. "I'm convinced that the crown of power wasn't you, your highness, nor yet Domnu Zusya, nor even the spirit that follows Donna Aurélie, as we once thought. This necklace is the crown of power that the seers saw coming east."

"How do you know that, Elisheva?" Jaska asked.

"I *see* it." Her hands lifted. "Its light in the Nasdrafus is nearly blinding."

"And it has also drawn the seraphs." Mord lifted his head.

Aurélie turned to look, and there they were, reflecting in the mirror. Jaska's hand tightened on his sword cane.

"Be not afraid," Pewter Hair said. "Call me Uriel."

"Call me Raguel," said Fake Jaska.

"Call me Jeremiel," said Lady Midnight, who up close lost the female semblance. Such beauty had no gender, the long midnight-black hair shrouded a slender, androgynous form.

"Angels?" Elisheva whispered, her face so blanched the only color was the stippling of her freckles. It was difficult to see the seraph's wings in the mists surrounding them.

"Was it not you," Raguel turned my way, "who said that one cannot prove a negative? Permit us to prove our good will with gifts."

Aurélie had been fingering her necklace. She yanked her hand down, closing her fingers over Jaska's on the hilt of the sword cane.

"A gift of knowledge," the soft voice went on as the beautiful face smiled at Aurélie. "You wish to be sundered from the spirit enslaved to you." Aurélie recoiled, her breath catching on the word *enslaved*. "You already know you can touch hands within the mirror. Take her hand," he said to me. "Pull her within."

Jaska, Aurélie, and Mord looked totally confused. They could only see the reflection of me, and they clearly thought I somehow lived in the mirror. Only Elisheva had her eyes closed, her lips moving as she breathed a prayer.

But that command also confused me, because I saw the seraphs—if that's what they were—in the mirror, but I didn't see myself with them.

"Within where?" I asked, and then it hit me. "The Nasdrafus? Is that how I'm to get free again?" I didn't trust them enough to mention Xanpia, the Blessing, or even Dobrenica in danger.

"Yes. There, you will be two again. And then you have only to go back as two."

"Don't do it," Elisheva said urgently. "You are not prepared for the Nasdrafus. *I* am not prepared. Everything is different there, even death."

"You will not die, for you will be under our protection," Jeremiel declared. She (or he) had a voice like wind chimes.

Aurélie looked up at Jaska then back at the seraphs. "My guardian has completed her task. It is time for her to return to her own home." She had spent all these years touching my hand in the mirror. Now she reached, intending to grip my hand—

There was a dizzying sensation and my awareness smeared as if I'd fallen into jello as she put a foot over the frame.

Jaska's face blanched. "You are vanishing. I won't lose you."

He grabbed her hand, as Elisheva cried, "No, do not—do not—"

She reached out to pull them back. Mord glanced at Elisheva's anxious face, then lunged forward to grip Jaska's hand. Whatever happened, he was determined yet again to protect his friend if he could.

Elisheva gritted her teeth and took hold of Mord's coat tail.

They were all through.

They stared at me as I gazed down at myself.

"How did that happen?" I asked, delighted to see my rumpled blouse with the Dobreni embroidery, my long blue skirt, my sandals.

Aurélie was staring at me. "This is what I dreamed. This moment."
She looked from one of us to the next, blinking as if fighting dizziness.

"Okay. Let's get out of here," I said, thinking, *Alec, I'm coming home!*

We were in the reverse image of the little antechamber, which disoriented me. I whirled around, and there was the mirror.

But instead of reflecting us, it had gone dark.

FORTY-FOUR

"WHAT'S THE MEANING OF *OKAY*?" Aurélie asked me in a whisper as we looked around room. The seraphs had vanished. I blinked rapidly against the light, which brightened steadily to incandescence.

I was too distracted to answer. I stepped uncertainly toward the mirror, then Elisheva darted between me and it.

"Do *not* touch it," Elisheva commanded, glancing over her shoulder in horror at the mirror. The brilliant glow bleached her skin, making her freckles stand out and her blue eyes startlingly pale.

"Why?"

"It is cursed. In the Nasdrafus, a lightless mirror sends you to eternal darkness."

"While I don't believe in hell," I muttered, backing away, "I am *not* testing that theory."

Elisheva wasn't listening. She gazed at Aurélie. I whirled around and discovered the source of the bright light. The stones in that necklace were glowing like lasers.

"Stop it," Elisheva whispered, waving her hands. "Hide it. Do you not see? *That* is what drew the demons. Here in the Nasdrafus, it has even greater power. It is going to draw all manner of magical things."

Aurélie fumbled at the clasp. The light vanished like a switch had been turned as she bent and once again clasped it onto her ankle. "I don't understand how—"

"Uh, oh," I said.

Through the doorway shot the Ugly Squad. You name the monster, it seemed to be there. Green, blotchy gray, scaled, bulbous eyes or red lizard ones, snake-tongues, hulking orcish things in leather armor that looked grown on, skinny, warped bodies . . . they all one thing in common: weapons.

With a screeching and gobbling and grunting, they began to advance, waving maces, scimitars, cleavers.

I kicked the bench into their way, halting their advance. Jaska took Aurélie's arm and dashed through the servants' door into a narrow hall, followed by Elisheva and me, Mord last. He pulled the door shut behind him and turned the antique lock. The uglies whammed into the door, pounding, bellowing, and gibbering. *Somebody gave them a couple extra doses of ugly instead of brains*, I thought as I sprinted after Jaska through another door. It felt so good to run again. I stretched my legs out into a leap. Nothing hurt, no weakness. Awesome!

We burst back into the main hallways. I ran past the others, desperately looking for some of the mounted weapons the von Mecklundburgs had decorating the walls.

There they were! Some were so cold to the touch they numbed my hands, and I snatched my fingers away. Finally I found a swept-hilted rapier that gleamed with a faint bluish cast to it. It came away from the wall freely. I swung it, smiling. It fit my hand as if designed for me.

A bit farther along, Aurélie found a shorter rapier, seconds before uglies closed in from both sides. Jaska dashed in, his sword humming.

The air filled with the clash and ring of metal, grunts of effort, the stamp and hiss of feet on the floor. Aurélie fought with difficulty, enduring the handicaps of a ball gown. I sympathized thoroughly. Her fluttering ribbons and filmy draperies got in the way at every turn.

Mord was the first to skewer one. The ugly imploded with a sharp *pop!* like a branch breaking, and then disappeared.

Fighting at Mord's side, protecting his useless arm, Jaska burst three in quick succession. Surprise made me falter for a split second. A skinny ugly with a generous collection of warts got past my guard. Its sword glanced off my shoulder, sending a shock through me, kind of like electrical static and a hit with an ice cube at the same time. Where I'd been hit, numbness followed.

Now I was pissed.

My years of fencing had been competitive, with safety fully in mind at all times. Twice I'd been in real fights, once against mercenaries in this very castle. I'd gone for wounding, not killing. The second fight was against vampires, and that time I didn't care how or where my blade struck, because the vamps were already dead.

In my mental taxonomy, the uglies categorized themselves with vamps, as things instead of people, so my only reaction was triumph when I popped two of them in succession. As sensation painfully (pins and needles to the max) returned to my shoulder, I looked around.

Mord nailed the last one, then sank against the wall, his face blanched. He must have taken a bunch of hits. Jaska pointed at the servants' door, almost invisible in the plaster wall.

"That way."

Elisheva sprang to open it. We shot through, Jaska last. He slammed the door on a fresh supply of uglies and scanned the hall.

No King's Guard in sight. From a long distance came the sound of violins and flutes and merrymaking, heedless of the fighting.

The five of us made our way down the hall, poking our heads into rooms as we sought mirrors. We found three, and every one of them was blackened.

"I hear the demons coming," Mord gasped, his voice hoarse. "Uncountable, a vast stirring of wings."

"How do you hear what I cannot?" Elisheva asked.

Mord opened his eyes, his face a mask of pain. "How can I see the pattern of the birds shifting in and out of the world as they fly about in the air?" He sank back.

"He's not recovering. There were too many blows." Elisheva turned to Aurélie. "You can heal him quickly."

"How?"

"Try touching this stone. It appears to be an early type of our healing stones." She pointed at one of the gleaming gems in Aurélie's necklace. "Repeat these words, and see him whole and healed in your mind."

It took a couple of tries, but when Aurélie succeeded, we saw a flash of glittery gold light around Mord.

He straightened up, his coloring normal. "Thank you," he said to them both.

"We must find a portal," Elisheva said. "We can go to another place where the mirrors have not been enchanted."

"Enchanted," Aurélie repeated. "But this looks like the von Mecklundburg castle. I hear the music."

"The Nasdrafus doesn't take us out of the world entirely, it makes manifest the unseen," Elisheva said over her shoulder. "I'll find the nearest portal." She pulled out her prism and held it up to her face as she ran. "This way," she said, pointing.

"How do you use portals?" I asked.

"I haven't actually seen it done," Elisheva said. "But they taught us to see the place you want to go, and you step through and find yourself there. But you must be familiar with your destination."

Jaska trotted near, running without a limp. "Is this the way you want to go? We're nearly at the doors to the top of the fountain terrace."

I remembered that terrace from the turn of the year, when Tony tried to make the blood pact with vampires. Only they didn't show up because they were all down in Riev.

My neck prickled at the memory. If I felt *any* sense of refrigerator cold, I was going to run like a rabbit.

I followed Jaska, swinging my sword from hand to hand and glorying in being able to move again, to turn my head and look wherever I wanted. And no ill effects! Even my hair hanging down to the back of my skirt wasn't matted up after my long snooze and then swordplay.

We burst out of the doors and ran up the long curving marble stair to the secluded garden behind the Sky Suite, where the ducal family lived. In the center of the garden stood the huge, shallow, marble fountain that reminded me of a Greek kylix.

Elisheva slowed, turning in a circle as she gazed into her prism. "Somewhere here is a portal."

The light was strange, with an aqueous quality of shifting color, and directly overhead, between the thousands of leaves, discs of liquid sunlight shimmered.

"Was it not evening?" Aurélie asked.

I'd forgotten the time. Jaska and Mord looked around, and then from the door and over the wall at the sides boiled a bazillion uglies, screeching and gobbling.

The four of us with swords took up defensive stances and met them head on. It felt great to be back in action! Mord laid into them, sword humming. He was so fast that he cleared a swath around Elisheva, who cried, "Your necklace, is it a religious symbol?"

"No—yes—I don't know how to answer that," Aurélie gasped, and hopped out of the way of a cleaver the size of Texas. She poked at the ugly's short, bowed leg, but all it did was stumble. I reached over and popped it.

Elisheva persisted. "Is it bound up with your faith?"

"It's from my Nanny." Aurélie threw Elisheva a distracted glance. "It is said that the cross wards evil. Should I have a cross, or—"

"Only if it has power for you, otherwise it is a piece of wood or metal," Elisheva said. "If your necklace—"

She didn't get past that. The fountain itself was the portal. From the air over its lip poured a fresh set of uglies, who homed straight for Elisheva.

Mord shouted something and attacked with fury, Jaska at his side. I waled in from the other side, but there were too many of them. The uglies poked and pricked Elisheva with their weapons. She stiffened, head arched back in anguish. From her hands flew the prism in a sparkling parabola, and a tiny golden thing.

She fell. The uglies swarmed, grabbing her arms and legs. The high screeching gibber was not nonsense, its patterns were too regular: My

Latin wasn't all that great, but I made out, *They said bring her to the garden, our garden in Lutetium!*

And they were gone. All of them. With Elisheva.

Two objects hit the ground. The prism smashed into tiny shards, but the golden thing bounced. I swooped down and caught it up in my hand. Beka Ridotski had one—it was a Kemah, a golden amulet. There were nine fields, with tiny Hebrew letters and words engraved on each.

Mord appeared next to me, and stretched out his palm. I glanced up. He was much taller than I—maybe Alec's height—his face tight with misery. The moody music genius had fallen hard, in no more than two days, for the fierce *Salfmatta*-in-training.

And now she was gone. Maybe dead.

I dropped the little golden amulet into his hand, then Mord turned an angry look Aurélie's way.

She faced him steadily. "I cannot kill."

"Those things are demon-spawn. Evil."

"They are living," Aurélie said. "I won't take away a life. I tried to stop them the way I did before, attacking their legs or arms, but they took no notice." Her voice went husky with unshed tears.

"They carried Elisheva off. Alive or dead, we must find her," Mord said, poking with his sword in an effort to locate the portal.

"Paris," Aurélie said, her black eyes reflecting the weird light as she looked from one of us to the other. "They took her to Paris. I heard them say it, didn't you? What does it mean, to put her in a garden?"

Nothing good, I was afraid to say.

"The portal," Mord said. "How do we get into it?" He slashed the sword through the air next to the fountain.

For *once* I knew what to do! "I can't get us to Paris, but I think I know who can," I said quickly as telltale gibbering sounded from somewhere below the wall. "More uglies on the way!" I said to Jaska. Then to Aurélie: "Your Piarist Sisters. They know about Vrajhus, right?"

"But how do we get to Vienna?"

"Elisheva said you can only go to familiar places. Well, I am familiar with Vienna, and I am almost certain I saw a portal there, once. Take hands!"

Jaska grabbed Aurélie and Mord, and I grabbed Aurélie, casting my mind back to the day after I first met Alec, to that weird door I'd seen for only a moment in Vienna, in the Crypt of the Emperors.

"Follow me," I shouted, focusing on the faint sheen of light directly in front of the fountain. I started toward the fountain as if I was going to bump into it, but once again felt that falling-into-jello sensation.

FORTY-FIVE

WE STUMBLED INTO DARKNESS. Our eyes adjusted to dim, flickering light that resolved into a reddish glow.

"We are in hell," Aurélie whispered.

"No," I said. "That is, I am reasonably sure that this is the *Kaisergruft*, the emperors' crypt under the *Kapuzinerkirche*, the Church of the Capuchin Friars. If I'm right, we're behind the grave of Countess Fuchs-Mollard. This way."

We emerged from the narrow inset past Emperor Joseph's plain sarcophagus into the wider area where Maria Theresia and her emperor gazed in stone effigy at one another. The weak reddish light turned out to be votive candles.

We seemed to be alone in the crypt. No uglies, no monk attendants either. We emerged in the New Market section of Vienna's inner city, but it was not my Vienna. I turned to Jaska, pointing my sword at the street. "Lead on."

"The legation," Jaska said. "Hippolyte is surely still here. We can equip ourselves with funds, which we can use to get necessary supplies." He flicked his hand over his silken clothes and smiled at Aurélie, gorgeous but wildly out of place walking on the street in the daylight, wearing a ball gown. Not to mention the sword.

"What means 'okay'?" Aurélie asked again, looking up into my face.

It was so strange to be walking beside her instead of bobbing help-lessly behind or in front of her, always facing her. I could look away! "It's an idiom for assent," I said as I scanned the passers-by.

Aurélie stated in a sunny voice, "You will have to tell me more about where you come from. But if you don't mind, later? I am so distracted here. For the first time, I'm seeing ghosts." She smiled up at Jaska, and he smiled back at her.

It was great to see great-Gramma and Gramps hooked up at last, but that private, tender, shared smile hit me like one of those cold rapiers, right in the heart. I'd thought I was one step from being done, and here we were, once again, far from Dobrenica.

Okay, pay attention or you really *won't* get back, I told myself, and looked around. I expected to see people in early nineteenth-century clothes, but I didn't expect to see them shimmer. Not all did. There were bunches of them in the fashions of older times who didn't shimmer.

"We have to be still in the Nasdrafus," I muttered, eyeing a couple of guys riding by, their hats low, swords at their sides. Both turned in their saddles to stare at us. Mord gazed back with his best mad-prophet ex-pression.

From a side street came a foursome of swaggering tough guys in musketeer bucket boots, billowing trousers, and swashbuckling wide-skirted coats decorated with yards of ribbon, their hair (or wigs) long and curly.

The pair Mord was busy glaring at leaped off their horses and at-tacked the four bigwigs. We backed away except for Mord, who as-sessed rapidly and decided to fight in aid of the outnumbered two, though they'd started the brawl. Swords flashed, and all four swash-bucklers fell groaning in the street. The two winners rammed their swords back in their sheaths with the *hoo, lookit me!* manner of a high five, failed to acknowledge Mord with so much as a nod, then mounted up and rode on.

From buildings all around servants emerged, moving with the same odd, drifting slowness of the seraphs. But these had no wings. They bent over the fallen, shrouding them. Was there a kind of shadowy mist blurring the air between the crouched and the recumbent figures? I took a step nearer in an effort to see, though my nerves tingled with warning.

But then the servants, or helpers, straightened and backed away, and the four rose, straightened themselves out, picked up their weapons, and moved somewhat aimlessly down a narrow side street. They shook their heads as they went, and swung their arms.

So we couldn't be killed as long as we were in the Nasdrafus, was that it? Awesome! No wonder there were no after-effects from my being gone so long.

"Elisheva must be alive," I said, looking at the others. From their expressions, it was clear that the same idea had occurred to all of us.

"Legation is this way," Jaska said.

He'd lost the sheath to his cane back in the von Mecklundburg castle. He leaned on the point as he began to walk, probably from habit as his limp was completely gone. Aurélie paced at his side, but Mord lingered, his head up.

"What's that music?" he murmured.

I didn't hear anything but street noise. Jaska, Aurélie, and I looked around. No music. That was odd. Well, everything was odd.

The New Market district wasn't far from the narrow street off which the legation was located. People came and went into the building, which was typically baroque, above the door a winsome gargoyle staring at us.

As I looked up at that stone face, the deep-carved eyes sparked, and a forked tongue flickered out from between the sharp teeth.

I jumped back, and when everyone stared at me, I pointed up with my sword. "Did you see that?"

Of course the gargoyle was now totally still.

"Wait below," Jaska said. "It will be easier than having to explain." He shot a covert glance at Aurélie's gown and my outfit, and ran upstairs.

We stepped inside the building, standing to either side of the door. The floor was a pattern of mosaic tiles, the walls supplied with homely pegs for coats. In the future, those would be mail slots.

I looked out into the street, wary of uglies or other nasties. All the passersby were slightly odd in one way or another; that is, they looked like highwaymen from some romance, like soldiers of the late 1700s. Some of the women tripped along in full ball gowns, others in more ordinary clothes, but I spotted one woman wearing a brace of pistols, high boots, and a frilly shirt, her hair tumbled down her back. Her hat reminded me of musketeer hats, and at her side, on a baldric, she wore a bell-hilted rapier. She swaggered along, definitely looking for a fight.

Mord stood with his eyes shut, his head slightly tilted. "That music," he murmured.

Jaska ran downstairs. "I was not visible to them. Nobody in the legation office could see me," Jaska reported. "And they . . ." He paused. "The edges of their clothing shone with a faint light. "

"They shimmered," I said. "Like the people dressed in—" I was about to say *early nineteenth century clothing*, but altered that to "—everyday clothing. I think they are the ghosts, here in the Nasdrafus, unlike the rest of us."

"Yes! And so, in the world on the other side of the portal, we would be ghosts to them," Aurélie said. "If they can see ghosts," she added as an old woman carrying a basket of market goods under a checkered cloth passed within a pace of us. Her edges shimmered. Surely she would have noticed someone in a ball gown, but she walked along, her gaze passing right through us.

Mord said, "Hippolyte would see you, surely. He saw ghosts, remember? That was why he joined the Freemasons."

"But he's not here. We can try at his lodging or push on to the Piarists."

"They might not see us, either," Aurélie said.

"How about the one the prioress mentioned? The sacristan who had visions in her dreams?" I asked.

Mord was now staring at the mosaic, which was laid out in squares about a yard wide and long, the tiles six-pointed, fitted in patterns of threes, their colors a soft golden, cream, and sky blue. He turned to Jaska. "Is that the same pattern that was here when we visited this place, before I left for Eisenstadt?"

Jaska looked down. "How strange." He glanced around. "Everything else is the same, but the floor should be the check pattern, white and black marble squares alternating. Not this mosaic. What can that mean?"

"Is it Freemason work?" Mord asked.

Jaska looked surprised, then shook his head. "Weren't they outlawed when Franz came to the throne as emperor the year before last?"

"Perhaps marble slabs were laid over the mosaic," I suggested, "but we don't know what it means, to be seeing this instead of the marble."

Jaska looked up. "It reminds us that we must not expect things here to be the way we have experienced them. We'd better get to the Piarists."

We all agreed. "Should we hire a coach to get there faster?" Aurélie asked.

"We have no funds," Jaska reminded her. "And I have misgivings about drawing any more notice than we can help. Slow as it is, I suggest we walk."

We kept up a brisk pace, Jaska striding along freely. When we reached the bridge, we looked around in all directions. No uglies.

We started over the bridge. Seen from this vantage, the city looked subtly different. I tried a slower scan. The palace was the same, except for some of the side buildings that seemed to have an after-image, or a shadow twin. I made out ghostly forms—the famous dancing white horses called Lipizzaners. Real or not, they pranced proudly, silky manes drifting, tails flashing, their riders dressed in Imperial uniform.

I turned toward where the Rathaus tower should stick up, knowing that it was gothic-Victorian and had been built in the 1880s. A faint shadow bisected the horizon, perceptible if I gazed straight at it, but invisible if I shifted my attention away a fraction.

Okay, that made (sort of) sense. People and buildings existed in different states, different times.

We descended the bridge on the other side and were surrounded by buildings again. Here and there echoed the clashes and shouts of fighting, but suppressing that noise was music, coming from various sides. The sky had darkened overhead, but golden light poured out from windows and doors. In and out through those doors, couples and groups strolled. In the more shadowy darkness, silent individuals lurked about or darted here and there.

We reached the quiet alley that ended at the Piarist convent. Knocking got no response. We looked at one another, then I figured, Why not? And tried the door.

It opened to my touch.

Aurélie and I walked in. Even in the Nasdrafus, the guys were not about to enter a nunnery. They stayed outside.

The place was quiet, light gleaming here and there in lamps. Nobody was awake. I walked right up to a sleeping nun in her little cell. Touching her made my hand feel numb, and all she did was stir in her sleep.

"There's a ghost," Aurélie whispered—though we could have danced the Funky Chicken while whooping like banshees for all the notice the nuns would have given us.

I turned around, and there in the doorway to the cell stood an elderly nun in her habit. We could see the lintel through her.

"I am dream-walking," she said in German, her tone declarative. I suspected the statement was more for her than for us.

"I was here a fortnight or so ago," Aurélie said. "I asked about magic. For Madame Bonaparte. But now we need to ask on our own behalf."

"We will not disturb the rest of Sister Bernard," the ghostly nun whispered, finger to her lips, as behind me the sleeping nun stirred restlessly.

Aurélie and I followed the ghost from the cells to an inner chamber with a single candle flickering.

"What do you seek?" the nun asked.

"Demons took away one of us," Aurélie said. The nun had crossed herself at the word *demon*. "Her name is Elisheva Barta, and it happened in Dobrenica a short time ago."

"Time is not reliable in the realm of dreams," the nun murmured.

"It was a short time ago for us," Aurélie said politely. "We want to find her as quick as we can. They said something about putting her in a garden in Lutetium."

The nun said, "Do you have any connection with her?"

"Connection?" I asked.

"Any connection. It could be by blood, by bond, by a personal object of significance."

Aurélie looked nonplussed, so I said, "She dropped an amulet. One of us has it."

"Then you will be able to use that to find her," the nun said. "Follow the connection."

"How?"

"The same way you brought yourselves here," she replied.

It can't be that easy, I thought.

The nun was thinking along a parallel path, or else ghosts could hear others' thoughts, because she said, "The demons will try to hide her. But faith and love will always defeat them."

"How?" I asked, remembering far too many historical instances where faith and love had not defeated evil.

The nun turned my way. "You walk in the dream realm, where strength is measured differently, as is time."

"How do we get to Paris, Sister?" Aurélie asked.

"You must use the portal." She began to fade.

"Which portal? We only know of the two that brought us here."

"The oldest," the nun said, looking surprised. "In the bell tower at Nôtre Dame de Paris, on Île de la Cité," she said in the *but everybody knows that* tone.

"I've been there," Aurélie and I said at the same time. I laughed and said, "I remember when Hortense took you there."

The nun vanished, so we left.

Out in the alley, we found the guys waiting. "Back to the portal," I said. "We're on our way to Paris. The portal we need is at Nôtre Dame. But how we're going to find this garden of theirs is anyone's guess."

"We must search where the demons are thickest," said Mord.

Oh, great.

Well, at least the uglies went *pop* and not *squish*, I thought as I swung my sword.

As we passed an inn, music came from its open doors and windows.

Visible in the huge windows were silhouettes of couples hopping and twirling as they wove the geometric patterns of the dance.

"I hear it again," Mord said, and then in a different voice, "That is Mozart." It was clear from his distant gaze that he didn't mean the mazurka being played in the tavern we were passing.

"Which composition?"

"None that I know."

That got three variations on "Huh?" which Mord ignored. As we crossed the bridge, he walked faster. From all around came at least five separate kinds of music, punctuated by the occasion snap of a pistol report, or the clang of steel. Shouts and bellows. Closer, in the dark-shrouded corners, intimate laughter from couples.

But I heard no Mozart, or anything close.

Mord made a beeline for St. Stephen's cathedral. Light poured from the open doors and the clerestory windows, the stained glass luminous with color. Inside, a thirty-something guy in a 1780s powder-dusted wig conducted an enormous orchestra, spread in both directions through both transepts. Blocking the view of the church altar was a choir that looked five hundred strong, singing at tremendous volume, complicated melodic lines.

Mord stopped in the middle of the nave. "That *is* Mozart," he said. "And he is conducting."

Jaska stared, then looked back. "How do you know? Mozart died when we were boys."

Mord said, "I tell you, that's Mozart." He listened raptly.

All around us the audience listened raptly.

The music reminded me a little of *The Magic Flute*, which was Mozart's last opera, but it also carried the gravitas of his unfinished Requiem.

For a time we stood while the music built, weaving complicated chains of melody around us. That's the only way I can describe it, not being a musician. Back in college, I'd taken music appreciation. The professor had talked about how Mozart had worked secret Freemason symbols into his music. I couldn't hear them, but the idea had stayed with me, because the memory was back, and there I was in class, sitting at my desk, pencil tapping in time as I listened for something I wasn't sophisticated enough to discern.

The memories came, vivid and nearly real: college, music, dance. I was so absorbed that Aurélie's touch made me jump. "We're forgetting Elisheva," she said.

"Elisheva," Mord repeated, and horror constricted his features.

He whirled and plunged out, but he could not help a longing glance back.

"This way," Jaska said, leading us into the New Market sections again.

Aurélie walked next to me, holding up her skirts with both hands. "It was like the fae," she said. "You all were . . ."

"Enchanted?" I said, chill tightening my neck. "Did you hear her?" I spoke up. "That was some kind of enchantment, back there."

"If so, it must be an advantageous one," Mord stated. "I intend to return, if I can. But you are right to remind us of Elisheva."

Aurélie seemed uneasy as we walked faster, again Mord in the lead, as if he had to escape the music's spell. Maybe he did.

We reached the Graben street to find it full of uglies fighting locals. I ran forward, sword ready. The guys kept pace at either side. We began spreading out as a clump of uglies took down a guy with a scimitar. The man fell full length, the sword clanging on the cobblestones. The uglies howled and turned to attack someone else as more of those silent, tidy servants came out of the deep-set doorways. Sometimes they tended the person right on the street, but a few of the fallen were borne away.

That's when the uglies saw us.

Mord took point, his sword whirling. Jaska and I fought at either side of him, taking on the scatterers.

We made it all the way to the crypt, but as soon as we got inside, an ambush party rushed us. We tried to fight our way past—we were in sight of Maria Theresia's sarcophagus—but there were too many, the light too dim, and we were forced back outside again, foot by foot. None of us wanted to end up taken away to wherever the fallen went, even if it wasn't death in the sense that we understood it.

The fight spilled back into the street. I switched hands. From the sidewalks shouts of encouragement rose as people streamed from cafes and theaters, restaurants and other emporia. Most joined the battle, some preferred to cheer from the sidewalks.

"Heroes!"

"Kill them all—they've made it impossible to go about at night!"

More people poured out, and the street filled with mass fighting until every ugly had been popped.

That left the Viennese smiling in triumph at one another. A few paces away, the woman in the swashbuckler costume sheathed her sword with a flourish. She saw my glance, doffed her hat and bowed. I bowed back, flourishing my hand as if it held an invisible plumed hat. When I clapped my pretend hat back on my head, she laughed.

Aurélie blinked back tears. "She looks like my mother," she whispered.

I gazed back in surprise. The woman didn't look like my memory of Anne, except for the blond hair. For one thing, she was at least ten years younger than Anne had been in 1795.

"Come celebrate!" someone called.

"No charge for the heroes," a restaurant owner declared, to general cheering.

Mord shook his head. "We have to go."

The smiles vanished from the faces. Quick as lightning the crowd's mood changed. "What, too good for the likes of us?"

"Got a better offer?"

"Their majesties are expected at the Hofburg!"

A threat would have caused the two guys, at least, to ready for action. But an accusation of anti-egalitarianism hit us all.

"A glass, thank you," Jaska said. "But then we have someone else to rescue."

The crowd sent up a cheer at that and closed around us. We ended up in a Heuriger, a wine tavern, with beautiful Egyptian-themed décor, and a light, crisp, local white wine was poured for all. Before I drank mine, I stared into the depths of the cup, trying to recall if anyone had said that eating or drinking was dangerous in the Nasdrafus. Not that I remembered. Fairy food and drink, yes, but then everything with them was fake.

This wine smelled like wine, and Jaska was already toasting and then drinking. Aurélie followed with an air of *whatever happens to you will happen to me.* Mord raised his glass, and sipped—or pretended to, I wasn't sure.

Then out came baskets and wrapped packages of food to be shared around, and people gathered expectantly as musicians muscled through the crowd.

I tried a sip. The flavor of wine burst along my tongue, but when I swallowed there was a sense of the liquid vanishing like vapor somewhere inside me. Excellent. I didn't want to be soused in case another batch of uglies trundled up, swords a-waving.

We drank our wine, not feeling it in the least. The innkeeper kept pouring it out, everyone's mood happy and generous as they clinked glasses and drank to heroes.

Bouncy, catchy *Volkslieder* were the order of the day, branching out into other types of folk music. When a Gypsy tune was offered, the woman with the pistols, who reminded Aurélie of her mother, moved out on the floor and began dancing a kind of sailor's hornpipe/clog dance, causing everyone to start clapping.

And so it went around, people expected to play or to sing or to dance in turn. A very fine harpsichord was disclosed, upon which Aurélie played; instruments were shared, Jaska picking up a Pandean pipe. When eyes turned my way, I didn't want to say that I'd never learned an instrument, so I moved out to dance, and discovered that though I hadn't done any ballet for a long while, my skills were, if anything, better than ever.

It was exhilarating! Without much effort, I turned a series of twenty fouettés, with double-pirouettes every fourth, causing the crowd to roar its approval and clap in time. I finished without being breathless, took a bow to a storm of applause, and as my hair swung down to my skirts in a waterfall, free of the slightest tangle, I thought, *I could do this forever.*

I definitely wanted another turn and waited eagerly as the songs came and went, working around the circle.

"That was wonderful," Aurélie said to me as a shift in the crowd put us side by side. "I didn't know you were a dancer."

"You didn't know me with a body!"

She laughed, then looked up expectantly when it was Mord's turn. The fiddle that had passed from hand to hand came to him. As he touched the strings lightly and tuned them, he said, "Let us play the Beethoven."

They began the Serenade in D Major, with Aurélie adapting the harpsichord to the viola part. For the first few pages, that is. They were playing from memory, but as yet they had not learned it the way they knew the repertoire from their travels.

When Jaska faltered on a note, then repeated a phrase, Mord shut his eyes. He'd been pacing them, gathering his strength, or his thoughts. His eyes closed, and the music took off, rapid as a kestrel, soaring high and remote. The battered fiddle was again a violin, reaching for spiritual union, or as Mord would say, *davening* in *nigun*.

The entire room fell silent, eyes focused beyond the tall man swaying before them, his expression exalted. Then, one by one, they slowly sank down onto benches and barrels, stools, even the floor, and their eyes closed.

When Mord drew out the last poignantly sweet note and lifted the bow from the violin, everyone was asleep but us.

He slowly lowered violin and bow, looking around in bemusement.

"What did you do?" Jaska whispered.

"Evening prayers. I sought to bring them to contemplate the divine, um, mysteries," Mord said softly, setting the violin noiselessly on the counter. "I did not think it would succeed." He wiped his hair back, and blinked. "We should leave before they stir."

We picked our way among the recumbent figures, halting when we reached the door. Someone was waiting, a man of medium height, wearing a long satin coat of gray, turned back cuffs, a wig . . . it was Mozart. Or someone who looked like Mozart.

"If you come play for me, I will write you a symphony," he said to Mord.

Mord stopped just outside the doorway. We could see from his expression the intense inner conflict. He looked up sharply. "There is someone in need of rescue."

"Did you write down what you did to that composition?" Mozart asked. "Those embellishments—" He went off into highly abstruse commentary.

For a time Mord answered, and they talked rapidly back and forth, one or the other sometimes sawing the air or humming snatches of melody.

"Have you heard my concerti for Haydn?" Mozart finally asked, humming a main theme. "I mention them only as proof that I can write for others. I have been making further experiments with polyphony and with glass harmonica, binding charms from the Craft—you know the Craft?—through the form of *opera seria*, for I have come to the conclusion that opera should not belong exclusively to the Italians! Come, pick up your instrument, for I have need of your skill to play these pages I have written out. But as yet I've no one, *no one*, who can play with the skill I require."

"I cannot," Mord said, after a painful pause. And then, more forcefully, "I must go. Now."

Mozart put out a hand. "Is it love? You go for *amore*?" He gave the word the Italian pronunciation.

Mord reddened slightly, but gave a short nod.

"Ah." Mozart kissed his hand to Mord and waved it airily. "Go! Find your beloved. Then you will return, yes? If you work for *amore*, then you are one of *us*. I have an instrument for you," he added in a low voice. "It is the finest ever made. By one of the Craft, every piece of wood charmed . . ."

"I promise to return," Mord said. "After I am successful."

Mozart threw his hands wide. "I shall count the moments until I have you back, and with my music before you."

Now that we were outside, urgency returned. I could see it in everyone's face. I gripped my sword, ready for a new batch of uglies, but this time nothing got in the way of our reaching the crypt. We ran inside, stopping when we reached the portal beyond Countess Fuchs-Mollard's sarcophagus.

"Think of the bell tower at Nôtre Dame de Paris," I said.

There was that brief soggy sense of pressure, almost of suffocation, and then we were through.

FORTY-SIX

—————— ·⁂· ——————

BACK IN PARIS. The noises were the same. I sniffed, bracing for the famous stench, but at the same time realized I had yet to eat anything, nor did I feel the need. And the wine I'd drunk in Vienna had no effect.

So here we were in Paris, even farther from Dobrenica than before. *Not so far by portal*, I reminded myself.

We emerged from the bell tower and found ourselves in the cathedral as the great bourdon bell Emmanuel rang once, the sound shivering through the air.

Before the altar stood a choir of children dressed in white robes, singing Palestrina's "Kyrie." The slow fading of the bell's tone, the sweet young voices echoing, resonated through bones and spirit. *Nothing here is what it seems . . .* The music had intent, I knew it, but could not discern what. I could not even tell if those children were ghosts.

We stepped outside the massive doors. Mord began to speak, his hands closed around Elisheva's amulet. He halted when he saw the three seraphs standing outside the cathedral awaiting us: Uriel, Raguel, and the beautiful Jeremiel, who spoke in that voice like wind chimes, "You are in good time!"

"We seek the demons' garden," Jaska said.

"It is here." Uriel extended a long hand, indicating the Place de Grève on the other side of the river. We could see a series of tall maples in full summer leaf. There must have been hundreds of them.

We stared, for none of us had seen a forest of maple in that spot. Moving among the trees, almost invisible in the slanting ochre rays of the sinking sun, uglies hopped, slithered, lumbered, as they carried little pails to the trees, inserted taps, and let clear liquid drain.

"It is going to take time to determine which is the person you seek, and then to accomplish the transformation," Raguel said kindly, indicating the glorious late-afternoon light, lurid with high clouds against which thousands of tiny birds flew in streams.

An ugly sidling along nearby raised a weapon and charged. We put hands to weapons, but Jeremiel lifted a hand, palm toward the ugly, whose face corrugated in fear a second before the thing went pop. "The demons fear us," Jeremiel said. "We can walk among them without harm, and find your companion."

Mord held the amulet tightly. "I think we can find her."

"Will you know how to transform her?" Uriel asked.

Mord looked our way. No one answered.

Raguel murmured, "It would be our delight to restore her to you. Give us a few hours, and then you will be free to regain your world."

Jeremiel said, "Once you go through the portal to your world, you cannot return here. Or to be more correct, you could, but nothing is ever the same." And to Mord, "Is there not something dear to your heart that you could do while you wait?"

Uriel said, "I expect we shall find her by the time the bells ring at *None*. If not before."

Mord looked down at his hands, then at the trees. He was taut with uncertainty—responsibility—and a new love of three days, against music, the passion of his life, and a musician he admired.

"Go," Uriel urged with infinite kindness. "Be back by nightfall. Surely it will take no longer than that."

"Listen for the bells."

"It is so short a distance."

Mord dipped his head in a nod, said to us, "I'll be back at nightfall. Come for me. You know where, if she's found sooner."

"I promise," Jaska said.

"You have the entirety of Paris before you, and a short time to enjoy its attractions," Uriel said to Jaska and Aurélie. And to me: "Tonight is the premier of the ballet *Cyrano de Bergerac*."

"Ballet?" I repeated, startled. Wasn't that ballet mounted just a few years before I first visited Europe?

"A new ballet, by Jean-Georges Noverre," Jeremiel said, smiling. "Very innovative. He has forbidden the traditional mask. The new ballet is based upon the life of the famous duelist and writer. If you leave at once, you should be able to arrive in time."

A ballet! And one I'd never heard of.

"Shall we walk together?" Jaska asked. And to the three, "Thank you for your help."

"It is our pleasure," Raguel said.

"We will return at nightfall," I said, trying to establish a firm boundary. I knew as soon as the words were out that I sounded officious, but I was uneasy. On the surface, everything made as much sense as one could get in the Nasdrafus, but I walked with that shoulder-blade sense that I was missing something. The solution seemed too easy, but maybe that was because I didn't trust those seraphs. Was that because the solution really *was* too easy, or because I was a skeptic about the existence of angels, with that heavy theological overlay?

I glanced back a couple of times, but all I saw was the cathedral glowing in the slanting rays of late afternoon, the seraphs silhouetted against the golden sun sinking toward the horizon.

We started over the bridge. Little boats floated along the Seine, people talking and laughing as they floated along, gold-lit by pretty paper lanterns. Nowhere was there any sign of war. The buildings were in good repair, the air was warm, the streets even clean. Set in the trees along the quay against nightfall were more of those delicate lanterns, each with a tiny candle inside its oiled paper shape.

One last glance at that weird forest of maples, now a distant mat of green, and we were out of sight. Jaska and Aurélie walked together, talking softly. I wondered if this sense that something was missing had to do with not bobbing along behind her for the first time. I noticed Aurélie glancing back once or twice, her lower lip caught in her teeth, but her fingers gripped Jaska's. She looked up, and they both smiled.

We headed into the city, avoiding by mutual and unspoken consent the entire Tuileries area, then turned toward the rue de la Loi. Everybody seemed to be out enjoying the summer weather. We walked at a brisk pace, no one tired. Jaska did not limp at all, as he and Aurélie talked softly. No one paid the least attention to them in their Dobreni ball dress.

When we reached the huge square on which the theater stood, we saw a young guy with a shock of blond hair; he ran about accosting people. He soon came to us, desperate, repeating the same words, "Anyone know ballet? Anyone know ballet?"

"I do," I said, taken by surprise. Then blushed.

But the guy turned my way with relief. "You do? Oh, I am so grateful. Come! We will pay anything—we are desperate for a substitute!"

I found myself drawn away.

"We will meet you back at the cathedral at nine," Jaska called, smiling.

They could hardly wait to get rid of me. And who could blame them? Intrigued by the impossible situation, I followed the young man as he gave me a disjointed explanation: Their premier danseuse slipped and fell—being tended to, but cannot go on—the understudy is away in the country, out of reach, and a full house—

It was like dreams I'd had back when I performed, except that there was no sense of worry or anxiety that I did not know the choreography, had never set foot on the stage, knew no one in the company. The dance I'd done at the Heuriger had energized me, so I thought, why not follow this as far as it goes? I can always say no, and I have time to kill until the bells ring at nine.

The guy turned earnest blue eyes my way as we rushed to a side door and into a narrow backstage. Oh, being backstage again! Flats being shifted this way and that, actors all over—in this case the comedians who would mime some of the story—dancers warming up in a cleared space.

They crowded around when we appeared. "I found someone for Roxane!"

Roxane? But she's the lead!

"What can you do?" asked a stern older man. Was it possibly Noverre? He rattled off a string of ballet terms. All familiar, even elementary. Ballet had developed a great deal since he revamped the stultified seventeenth century forms.

Adrenaline spiked as I kicked off my sandals, moved out into the center of the floor, and whipped out the combination he'd asked for. Because I was barefoot I danced half-toe, but at the end I stiffened my toes and lifted *en pointe* in an attitude, holding it for a few seconds. My toes seemed, if anything, to have been strengthened by my long separation from my body.

Gratified by the gasps of the watchers, I came down in a dancer's bow.

A young girl watched intently from the side; she shimmered, unnoticed by the others. I wondered if she could possibly be one of the Gosselin sisters—who had done so much for the female in ballet—here in ghost form. As I watched her, the other dancers marveled and clapped for me, their admiration gratifying.

"Will you dance for us?" the ballet master asked.

"I'd love to," I admitted. "However I don't know your steps."

"But you are magnificent!" His hands lifted expressively. "If you know the story . . ."

"I do."

"Then you must interpret freely. Embellish! Fly!"

"What about *pas de deux*?" I asked, trying to remember when the formal structure of the duet was instituted.

"Balthazar will talk you through it," he said, motioning forward a man in musketeer costume. "He dances Cyrano."

"Hurry, hurry," the dancers said, taking their places on the stage. Beyond the curtain, the orchestra had already begun the overture.

I took my place where Noverre indicated, heart beating fast, nerves controlled down to fingertips and toes. As the curtain rose, revealing the enormous sea of faces below the magnificent chandeliers, I thought, wait, wait, costume?

But it was too late. The music had begun and an expectant hush fell over the crowd.

And so I danced on the stage of the principal theater of Paris, in the Nasdrafus, two hundred years before my birth.

I can't begin to describe the exhilaration, especially as my body responded as it never had before. My leaps soared, but I came down as light as ash. My pirouettes never wobbled, and as for choreography, muscle memory provided the well-drilled dances of my past, which I strung together as befitted the story. The more I remembered, the better I danced, exhilaration streaming off me in sparks.

I had never been ballerina grade; I'd had the right body and could move well, but I hadn't the dedication it takes to turn good into great. And it takes dedication, except in very rare instances. Ballet can eat your entire life, rehearsals and lessons and warm-ups and practice every single day, for long hours. When I got to college and discovered many of my fellow dancers ignorant of anything outside of dance, I'd lost the desire to dance professionally. I loved my books and languages too much. So dance was relegated to recreational, and I took my place back in the chorus.

Well, today I was a star. As I floated and twirled across the stage, the audience gasped—cheered—oohed. Balthazar, who partnered me, whispered a few commands, but *pas de deux* were in their infancy at that time, so it was easy to follow and to embellish.

Too soon it was over, and to thunderous applause. I stood alone, glorying in the powerful thrill of audience love, my entire body humming with energy. Until now, my dancing had been for fun, the applause nothing more than the expected polite acknowledgement of the group's effort. Standing ovations were always for someone else.

This time it was for me. As the volume of sound shook the air, the glory of popular adulation battered me, more powerful and sweet than any magic. I understood for the first time why dancers gave themselves to their art ten, twelve, eighteen hours a day. Why commanders raised their banners, why people reached for crowns.

I knew through bone and muscle and nerve what Napoleon craved. I could *never* get enough of it.

We took many bows, and then the triumphant dancers bore me off through the back exits into the street, under an indigo sky still purple in the west. We sailed into a café with a cleared floor where they shed the after-performance excitement by dancing for one another, as musicians from the orchestra played.

No one was more eager than I for a reprise of our brilliant success. The dancers crowded around, begging me to dance for them, so I moved out to perform another solo. They hailed it with delight, even more fervor than the theater audience, the accolade of artists. They pressed me to stay, to join them. "We are talking of remounting *Children of Prometheus*—will you dance the premier role?"

I was poised to shout *YES!* I can't describe how much I longed to say it, to surrender to that life, but poised as I was to surrender to the joy of art, I was aware of myself still listening for the bells of *None*, and with that, the memory of Elisheva. Aurélie. Alec, and my own time.

Though it hurt worse than the uglies' swords, I said, "I have another life that I need to get to."

"An artiste must follow her heart." Noverre threw up his hands. "Then celebrate while we may! Come!"

And so we moved from place to place, different music, all kinds of dance. Everywhere I went, I danced to great admiration and applause, and I was good. I never tired, my balance was impeccable, which drove me to greater efforts. I sought to test my limits, leaping higher, tighter turns, complicated steps that had defeated me in the world I'd grown up in.

The old sense of competition woke up, squashed years ago when I discovered that ensemble work was fun, that competition made me anxious and took all the joy out of dance. I was like a sixteen-year-old again, I craved more applause, to be the best ever. My training was better than anything the dancers of 1800 had. Women were not yet on toe. This was the era just before the romantic, when male dancers would reach the peak of balletic development, and the men demonstrated it by the strength and skill of their aerials, their turns, their kicks. But I could leap and turn nearly as high.

Gradually my intent altered as I sought a partner who was as good as I was—who could give me the challenge I wanted—who I could defeat, all in dance. When I walked out of a café (I checked, but the sun was still a finger above the horizon) and craved the duel of tango, I was not surprised to find a bistro across the street.

I walked into the hazy air of cigarette smoke. Sloe-eyed women in cloche hats and peek-a-boo marcelled haircuts moved languidly about in flapper dresses, fringes swinging.

The shift in time was a jolt, but I dismissed it, intent on my challenge. If time had a curious pocket here, well, this was the Nasdrafus, right?

On a small stage, as jazz musicians wailed in a lightless corner, a man and woman prowled around one another, the man shirtless, wearing only trousers and low boots, the woman in a thin shift cut up to the hip, fishnet stockings, high heels.

Thrump! He made a leap, landed behind her, took her arm, and snapped her into him so hard I thought her neck would crack. She leaned out, and with a sharp, deliberate twitch of her hips drove her spiked heel down onto his foot. She kicked high with the other as he recoiled, jaw lifted. He groped, but she evaded his reach and swung her arm down with enough force to bring him to his knees. He leaped up and twisted out of her grip, then took her hand and spun her into him to lock hard, nose to nose, hip to hip.

And so began what was once called an apache dance, brutally sexy, then just brutal, as he pulled her around by the hair, and she slugged him with a roundhouse that sounded like a butcher's whack on a hambone. His response was to pull her into a lift, but as she arched her back for a kick, he threw her down and though she twisted lithely like a cat, gravity failed her and she hit the floor with a neck-shattering crack. And lay there, eyes staring emptily as the audience booed and catcalled.

Those smooth servants oozed out, tenderly carrying her limp form off the stage as the guy cruised around, daring anyone to come forward. The woman in the shift appeared, blinking and wiping her hair back, looking around as if trying to find someone or something.

I buzzed with energy. *I could take that guy. My fencing training—blocks—and no one dies, right?*

I took one step, then another, and stepped up onto the stage.

The audience clapped mockingly, calling out sarcastic endearments, insults, challenges.

From the noise came one familiar voice: "Kim?"

I turned—and stared directly into my own face.

Only it wasn't my face. The sulky lower lip, the short hair shingled, dyed platinum blonde . . .

"Ruli?"

FORTY-SEVEN

"**K**IM? What are *you* doing here?"

"Ruli." A horrible thought hit me. "This *is* a time pocket? Right? Did I somehow get shot into modern times?"

"What?" she responded, and then, "Kim, there is no time in the Nasdrafus. Or rather, time is whatever you—or whoever you are following—wants. What are you doing here?"

"I'm trying to . . . where to start?" Questions multiplied so rapidly I didn't know which to voice first. "Easiest first. How did you find me?"

"I wasn't looking for you," Ruli said, with an uncharacteristic ironic twist to her crooked mouth, reminding me very much of her brother Tony. "But in the Nasdrafus, affinity, connection . . ." She lifted a shoulder. "One begins to see how everything is connected in some way. I was looking for entertainment, nothing in mind, and so I found you. Apache dancing?" Her sardonic glance definitely brought Tony to mind.

"I didn't start out that way," I said. "I was just dancing and more dancing, and I wanted to push the limits . . ." I stopped, aware that the challenge, the lure, the *insanity*—was gone. Ignoring the hot-eyed guy who'd come right up behind me, the insinuating jazz, the disappointed, scoffing audience, I jumped off the stage.

A couple of big, menacing guys stepped toward me, led by a cold-eyed woman with long nails. Ruli murmured, "Allow me."

She bared her fangs. They backpedaled with less dignity than haste and returned to their shadowy little tables as the jazz band started up again behind us.

"Whoa," I croaked, as we walked out into the street. "First time I ever enjoyed seeing the flash of vamp teeth."

"I truly enjoy that," Ruli said, and that was definitely Tony's smile. "The demons don't like us stealing their prey, but they can't do anything about us *here*." She didn't explain what she meant by *here*, but went right on. "The last time I walked through my old house, you'd not shown up for some meeting with Cerisette, and she was hoping you'd changed your mind and run out on Alec. Someone else said you were ill. What's happened?"

"It's too long to go into," I said, then what she said hit me with sickening force. "You mean time *has* passed? Oh no! How long? I've got to get back!"

"Relax. You'd been missing a day or two, and I just told you: Time does what you want here. Talking to me is going to make no difference. What *are* you doing here?"

"I came to this Paris with some others to rescue one of us. We were told she'd be fine by the strike of nine . . ." The anvil finally clonked me on the head. "They said to meet them when the bells ring *None*. The bells aren't going to ring, is that it? We've been scammed?"

Ruli took a hit from her cigarette in its long holder. The cherry-red end glowed and faded. She let out a stream of smoke (which I didn't smell) and said, "I can answer that better if you tell me who *they* is."

What would that have to do with telling time? *Nothing is as it seems.*

I put up three fingers. "Seraphs, three. Named Uriel, Raguel, and Jeremiel."

"Seraphs?" Ruli repeated. "Aren't those the names of angels?"

"Angels? There really *are* angels? Seraphs seems less . . ." I searched for a word and shrugged, "Biblical? But even then, I just don't believe they're angels, however they call themselves, or even if they have smoky sets of wings."

"There are seraphs in the Bible, too. Kim, what's going on?"

I gave her the fastest rundown in history. Not always in order, and skipping huge wads, but she listened all the way through and then said, "I'd be skeptical, too. If they said *call me* something, it could be they wanted you to believe they were angels."

"So you think they're something else? Like what?"

She shrugged. "Demons."

"Those beautiful creatures? I thought the uglies were the demons."

"Demons can look like anything and will claim to be angels. Some say they *were* angels once. Everyone says two things about angels: They are made of light, and they don't lie, even by indirection. So, for instance, a real angel—if there are any, and I haven't met any—would never claim to be a demon."

"I'm pretty sure they even said that the uglies were the demons. *Demon-spawn.* You know, the gargoyle creatures. They go *pop* if you stab them. They carried Elisheva away!"

"That's because they must execute the will of the demons, even to die. And die again and again, until they . . ." She lifted a shoulder, "disappear, a piece at a time. As does everyone who comes here and gives the demons life."

"Life?"

"I'd better show you. It won't take long." She led the way across a square and down an alley to a picturesque street of what in Paris had been grand houses, with sculpture all around doors and windows. The fleur-de-lis was prominent, and coats of arms. We walked inside an open one with light spilling out, and the civilized resonance of violins and violas and winds in a restrained minuet. The marble hall opened onto a magnificent ballroom filled with guests as quiet servants in black livery moved about, carrying trays and candles. No one paid us the least heed as couples with snowy white wigs promenaded down the center of the room, the women in panniered gowns polonaised with lace and ribbons, the men in fitted silken suits, tight in the body and legs, the coats with skirts that accommodated their small-swords, their high-heeled shoes glittering with diamond buckles.

We passed arched openings into little anterooms. A couple canoodled in one. The woman was wearing a mask. "The mask means that her identity is officially not known. Probably she's sneaked away from her husband," Ruli said. "There will be a demon, dressed as a servant, to bring them whatever they need, while feeding off them."

"Sucking their blood?"

"Call it the energy of their relishing illicit lust. Angry lust."

"So they feed off sex."

"It's not the sex so much as the man's intent to steal from some other man, and the woman's intent to cheat this other man. Anger and violence—destruction in all forms, that's what they feed on. The two will get a little weaker, the demon a little stronger." She glanced at me, and laughed when she saw the horror in my face. "It's a teacup. War gives them a river."

In a gallery at the end of the hall, a couple of men dueled with rapiers. "Ah! Here you go," Ruli said. "Watch."

Before we'd taken two steps, one of the duelists stabbed his opponent through the heart. He fell, and servants flowed out of the gloom of the corners to tend him. The creepy thing was, they seemed to bring the darkness with them. The gallery was lit by chandeliers on stands, so the lighting was uneven on the gigantic paintings of posed noblemen and generals astride rearing horses. But the shadows above were not as obscure as those between the kneeling servants and the fallen.

"Those servants are demons?"

"Yes."

"And they're feeding instead of healing that guy?"

"That's difficult to define, here. Both, I guess you'd say. It's not healing in the sense you understand it. The man will shortly be back on his feet, but he'll be a little slower, a little weaker, a little unsteady."

"Do the victims know?"

"They might. Some do, some don't. They find their way here by various means. Or find themselves here. Ignorance," she added with that mocking smile, "is no excuse."

"So the Nasdrafus is all about creatures that feed on others?"

"This part is," she said. "Where you have come."

This was so disturbing, my mind couldn't grapple and reached for a side issue. "They can't see us?"

"Not now. You were willing to follow me, and I chose to keep us invisible."

"Wait. I don't get it. You wish things, or will things?"

"Watch."

She didn't do anything but suddenly the winner of the duel and his seconds looked up. Their expressions changed from surprise to a smarmy interest.

"What are you doing in my house?"

"Women? Of the streets, perhaps?"

Ruli smiled at me. The men blinked, then turned back to talking among themselves as Ruli said, "Now I want us invisible."

I tried. *See me*, I commanded mentally, and sure enough, one man pointed with his rapier. "There's one of 'em again!"

Don't see me, I shouted mentally.

"*Sangdieu*, de Châtelet! You're seeing phantasms."

Ruli lifted her shoulder in a shrug, and sent a stream of smoke in the direction of the bewigged aristocrats. "Let's go."

We walked out. The clues were fitting together into a puzzle of horror.

"The uglies are controlled by demons, and demons lie, and they are like vampires who vacuum up life energy. Oh, hell. That forest of maples."

"A convenience, masking the truth with acceptable symbol."

"So she's being drained of blood?"

"Not blood, Kim. Think beyond the purely physical. You know that is not your physical body, it's your memory of your body, *n'est-ce pas?*"

I fingered my perfect hair, still not the least tangled after all that wild dancing. Nor was I sweaty. "Oh."

"None of us go near the demon grounds. The Place de Grève has belonged to them for centuries."

A sudden thought. "Do demons fly?"

"They can, in the form they often take."

"Would they seem to stream across the sky, to one who can see them?"

"They can," she said.

The clues inexorably locked together. "So, if great numbers—thousands—are flying somewhere, where are they going?"

"To the slaughter, of course," she said. "As I said. They are drawn to death, the more violent the better. Then they can proliferate."

"So in Aurélie's time, those shadows I saw around Fouché and Napoleon?"

Ruli tapped her cigarette on an iron railing topped with fleur-de-lis, and watched snowy ash drift into the garden to vanish among perfect flowers, not a petal withered, not a leaf grown old. "First at the trough are the strongest and most dangerous," she said. "I am surprised you survived that."

Aurélie's necklace had protected her, even as it drew them. I saw it now, but I didn't explain that. I was too sickened by a realization I could not escape. "What have we done?"

"You have not done anything," she said. "From what you've told me."

"That's just it. While we've been having fun, Elisheva is . . . I don't get it, how fun could be evil. It seems a cheat. If the demons had threatened us, come at us with weapons, we'd know the rules. We could fight back."

"Violence is best. Destruction next. They get little from what we were taught as the seven sins. Worst of all for them are the emotions at the polar opposite of destruction." Ruli took another hit off her cigarette. "Did you ever read *The Adventures of Pinocchio*?"

"Collodi's book? Yes, I struggled through it when I tried taking Italian my second year in college. Oh. This aspect of the Nasdrafus is like Toyland, is that it? Except here the donkey ears are more insidious and interior? I've got to find the others." I faced Ruli, urgency poising me to run. "Thank you."

She gazed back at me, her eyes so like mine, yet so different. "Remember your promise to me," she whispered, and was gone.

Promise—yes. I'd promised if she ever turned evil, I would push her into the sunlight. With a great sense of relief I let her go.

Remembering what Ruli had said about time (*time does what you*

want here) and place (*in the Nasdrafus, affinity, connection . . .*), before I
took a step I shut my eyes, willing myself to see Aurélie.

And there she was, not far away. Then I began to run. Wish and will,
I repeated to myself, willing the shadows to recede. Where had I left my
sword? Back at the theater, blocks away.

They're gonna send uglies after me. I tried to halt the thought. I didn't
want to end up willing them to come after me because I dreaded not
being able to fight them.

"Think about Aurélie, think about Aurélie," I muttered as I darted
around the strolling crowd.

Paris had become the ideal Paris, though some buildings were blurry
and others clear. But my eyes were drawn to rows of pretty trees filled
with twinkling lights, the clean sweep of the quay along the quiet Seine,
the lovely arch of the bridges. I had to look away from intriguing
glimpses—the carving of a king on a bridge, a cute little café with stained
glass windows, the sounds of ballet music through the open doors of a
little theater—and keep Aurélie firmly in mind, because the lure was
there to take just a look. Just a moment.

I found the two sitting in a tiny booth at a cozy café near a lovely
fountain of the Three Graces. Aurélie and Jaska had their arms wrapped
around one another, every line of their bodies expressing tenderness,
affection, passion. For the first time, they were alone without the invisible ears of Yours T.

The sight triggered off my sorrow and longing for Alec. Not only for
his arms around me but for the broken conversation we'd barely begun.

They looked up, shocked at my abrupt appearance.

"We've been had," I said, and at their incomprehension: "The demons are killing Elisheva a drop at a time while we wait."

Aurélie jumped up. "Where?"

"They?" Jaska asked.

"Demons. Come," I said and explained as we went.

"A vampire? You got the truth from a *vampire*?" Jaska asked, halting.

"Let's test the truth of her words," I said. "It's still not sunset yet, the
sun above the city roofs. Right?"

They assented, Jaska warily, Aurélie with a troubled expression.

"Let's each will it to be nightfall." And when nothing happened, "*Expect* to see it. No. *See* it. The sun is gone. There are stars overhead." I pointed at the sky.

And there they were, twinkling peacefully. My heart chilled as Aurélie gasped, her eyes filling with tears.

"We have done evil," she whispered. "In wanting to be alone, just the two of us."

"Oh, no, you haven't." I waved my arms. "No, *that* was natural. It was good. The mistake, which you made without being aware, was in accepting the manipulation of time." I thought of Las Vegas casinos, always well lit, no clocks, no windows, the addition of oxygen to keep you feeling fresh and frisky as you empty your wallet. But there was no explaining that! "You were together, at last able to talk things out without me perched on Aurélie's shoulder. And it's pretty here, and the bells never rang."

"It was temptation," Jaska said, looking distraught. "Don't say we didn't know. We didn't ask, didn't want to know."

I could see guilt in both their faces, and shame. "There are the trees," he said, brandishing his sword. "I hope the demons come out. I'll find out if they bleed or not."

Aurélie caught his wrist in her hands. "No. No more killing."

"They will send the demon-spawn against us," Jaska said. "What good do we do if we are overcome and carried away into darkness?"

She shook her head. "I felt it was wrong to walk away from the Place de Greve. Now I *know* it was wrong. I feel even more strongly it is wrong to take any life."

"They want you doing that," I said. "They like violence."

"But those things are vile," Jaska said. "Evil and ugly."

Aurélie looked down. "The last time I heard these words, or words very like—*black devils, ugly, they don't know better, they need the whip to make them work*—it was said about *us*." She laid her hand over her heart.

Jaska flushed to the ears.

"We all made that mistake about the demon-spawn," I said. "And I am sorry for my part, but there's the forest of maples, though I wonder how much of what those seraphs told us is true. But yes, we do have to check," I said hastily as both began to speak. "However. Without the amulet, which Mord has, how will we find her? I'm trying to see her, but I don't know her, really—no affinity—it's not working."

Aurélie had been scowling at the forest of maples. "All I see is trees."

"And so it is with me. We have to fetch Mord back," Jaska said in a low, determined voice. His face was tight in that stricken, sickened expression of someone who understands too late how badly they've stepped in it.

Ruli had said that anger and violence fed the demons, but I was still ready to kick the first one I saw. Guilt, regret, betrayal. Three emotions I really hate.

"Think ourselves at the cathedral. Don't give 'em the chance," I said.

Guilt might have driven us, but suddenly we stepped off the bridge, and there was Nôtre Dame, from which drifted the rise and fall of plainchant, the Latin soothing and melodic as it promised forgiveness and redemption.

Not five hundred yards from the church entry, there were the hordes, squealing, hopping, lumbering, weapons waving in the lurid red and purple light.

Jaska gripped his sword, but Aurélie put out her hand. "Wait." Her forehead was taut with tension, her lips compressed. She began to glow with that blue-silver light: the necklace.

"Go free," she said in French, and in stumbling Latin, "*Animas vestras sunt liber, ire in libertatem.*"

Your souls are free, go in freedom.

Red eyes, green-glowing, yellow, snake-pupiled and black, lidless and bulging, the demon-spawn gazed at her, then some scampered and scuttled off into the darkness, squealing and howling in triumph. Others waved weapons and advanced menacingly, maybe confused, but definitely angry.

Jaska gripped his sword, stepping in front of Aurélie. Wrong it might be, but he was going to defend his lady.

"Did you expect gratitude?" came Uriel's beautiful voice. "Command gives them purpose."

Aurélie did not answer, nor did she need saving. The light intensified to an eye-watering radiance, and the uglies and the fake angels stayed well back of it as we slowly walked to the cathedral. The presence of the necklace might have drawn the demons to us, but they could do nothing to it, or to any of us in proximity to it.

We reached the steps. We reached the narthex, then the nave. The plainchant enfolded us, and Aurélie staggered then straightened. Jaska and I each took one of her hands. "It's nothing, I was dizzy," she said, her deep voice huskier with strain.

We hustled into the bell tower, through the jello, and back into the emperors' crypt in Vienna.

Aurélie lit the way with the necklace, throwing back the shadows to reveal the baroque glory of Maria Theresia's and her emperor's sarcophagi.

Aurélie and Jaska paused, staring at the sarcophagi, and I knew what was hitting them: the reminder of Time. The *memento mori*, a young couple (one royal, the other about to be) gazing at the remains of another royal couple, aware of their youth and beauty, so fleeting.

"We could stay," Aurélie whispered.

Jaska shook his head. Just once. For him, there was no choice: He would go back to the uncertain world, where he was maimed in one leg, where he would grow old and die, because that's where his responsibilities lay.

Aurélie gazed up at him. She didn't say anything, but I saw the way her fingers tightened on his.

They'd made their choice, and so had I. Like there had ever really been a choice, in spite of the craziness of my dancing, of the stage.

All the more reason to appreciate every moment we get with one another, I thought, the longing to see Alec so strong I felt it in bones and nerves.

"As fast as we can," Jaska said in Dobreni.

Aurélie might not have known the words, but she understood the intent.

———

Mord was shocked to see us.

That's the word—shocked. Like he'd forgotten our existence. All the way to the St. Stephen's Cathedral, Aurélie whispered to herself, depending on Jaska to guide her as she concentrated on willing demons to stay away. But when they walked into the profound sensorium of that music, they froze in equal shock.

Music had been the solace for all three for most of their lives. Complex and compelling harmony filled the enormous space. You could listen to that forever, I thought, giddy with elation.

As Mozart directed his orchestra and choir, I could see the effort Jaska expended not to get lost in the song. He took Mord aside and filled him in. I could see the impact as each point hit Mord, and I mean hit. His fingers tightened on the sword he wore at his side, his breath hitching as if he was stabbed by an invisible knife: demons, time, Elisheva left to suffer, and *we have to get out of here as fast as possible.*

I'd been dreading Mozart's turning into a demon and threatening us, or trying something worse, but in a way, the torture was more exquisite, as Mord stood there divided between his lifelong love, music, and his new love.

Mozart said sadly, "Another unfinished composition?"

Mord said, "We have been tempted by the seraphs." His voice flattened. "And we are lost."

"No you are not," Mozart retorted. "You're only lost when you surrender will. Here—I have a gift. It may help you."

He dashed into the transept and returned with a violin. "Take this, and go quickly." He pressed it into Mord's hands.

Chords soared in a glorious crescendo around us as we retreated, and this time, we heard the music all the way back to the crypt, only losing it to silence when we stepped back into Nôtre Dame.

Paris was silent and empty when we emerged, shrouded in starless night. Aurélie still had the necklace light cranked to the max, but beyond its nimbus pressed cold, malevolent threat. When we neared the horrible forest, it blinked into another reality: still human figures, young and old, some looking like corpses freshly dug up, others near death, many marked by rivulets of blood, like cracks in sculpture. Each still, gazes fixed on hopelessness and darkness.

Mord held the amulet gripped in one hand, the violin in the other. He began walking toward the victims, searching each face intently as he passed.

Aurélie gave a muffled cry and darted around him, one hand clutching her necklace, the other outstretched, fingers distended. She ran from tree to tree like someone demented as Jaska followed in her wake. Light bloomed on every person she touched with the necklace. Of course she wasn't going to leave anyone behind, though many of the people she touched crumpled to the ground, apparently lifeless. Others staggered, some shying away when Jaska or I tried to help them. Most vanished like smoke.

Nobody tried to stop Aurélie. That necklace was too powerful.

She found Elisheva.

Mord was there to catch Elisheva when she started to fall. He crushed her in his arms, his head bent as he whispered endearments. I gripped my nails in my palms, afraid she was dead. But her eyelashes fluttered, and she gazed up into his face.

"I'm sorry," he said, over and over. "I'm sorry."

"I had faith you would come," she whispered.

"Let's—" I began, *go* unspoken.

An army of gargoyles, trolls, scaly things, snake-fiends, you name it, encircled us. Leading them were the three seraphs, who I mentally termed *the fake angels*, as beautiful as ever.

FORTY-EIGHT

———⟡———

THE PEWTER-HAIRED ONE SAID, "Your power is not strong enough."

Elisheva touched Aurélie. "They want you to use the necklace's power to attack them."

"I know," Aurélie said, without shifting her steady gaze from the three demons. "That is, I don't know everything about this necklace that there is to know. But I've seen in dreams what it can do," she whispered as the silvery light expanded to touch the slowly advancing hordes of nightmare figures: she was trying to free their souls.

Either her magic did not work, or else they embraced their evil, because there was no visible effect outside of the cold glitter of reflected light in those malicious eyes. One goblin creature licked his chops, drool hanging down in a long strand.

Jaska gripped the sword. Mord gravely held the amulet out to Elisheva, who accepted it with a voiceless word of thanks. She stirred, standing on her own, and he moved away from her, courteous and somber. Then his hand closed around the hilt of his sword, a finger at a time.

For a measureless interval we stood there, waiting to be attacked, as the demons probably anticipated the mayhem to come.

"No," Aurélie said, laying a finger on Jaska's wrist. "No."

He dropped the point of his sword, looking at her in silent grief. Her hand stole into his free hand, her intention plain: If death was nigh, they'd face it together. But she couldn't take lives, even in defeat.

I wavered, wondering if I was going to have to be the one to cross that line, because I was *not* going tamely, I would *not* let evil win without fighting back. Even if fighting was what the demons wanted, I craved justice, and there was none in standing by to watch Aurélie and Jaska, Mordechai and Elisheva, hashed to bits for the entertainment of these worse-than-bloodsuckers.

Then Mord stretched out his hand, which was gripped white-knuckled on the sword. He dropped the weapon to the ground. Mozart's violin had been tucked up under his armpit. He took hold of it now, bow and instrument, which he swung into position. He touched the bow to the strings and closed his eyes. One long, liquid note spooled through the tension, pure and clean and simple as water—and as compelling. With infinite absorption, and a touch as delicate as a butterfly, he began to play. Rabbi Nachman had taught him that storytelling rests on the distinction between sleep and waking, death and life, good and evil, light and lightlessness. The world cries out with longing for good, and music is one of the ways to get it there—and the Rabbi had sung a *nigun* to demonstrate.

It had taken time for Mord to internalize Rabbi Nachman's wisdom, but he had it now. From all directions, faster than wind, Mord drew bits of light: from the city's candles, from the hearths, the torches, from the stars beyond the gathered clouds overhead, and he fashioned the light into song. Storytelling through music was his conduit to the healing of the world, the restoration of the shards of light scattered through the universe.

Before the feet of the menacing army sprang tongues of flame, small at first, but growing larger as light gathered in streamers, coalescing in a great wheel overhead.

The violin no longer spoke alone. Voices joined, at first in whispers, then in songs—I heard the children of Nôtre Dame—and then instruments added one by one.

We heard Mozart's mighty choirs, all the way from Vienna.

Those who walked through this part of the Nasdrafus striving against the tide of violence gave their strength to Mord, forming their own army of harmony until the music broke the limits of sound and spread to the horizon, the music of the spheres, beyond beauty and beyond anguish, but partaking of both. We are finite vessels and cannot hold that much glory without burning up, but even so I exerted mind, heart, and spirit to hold the glory.

But it slipped away, because one thing we cannot control is time.

I don't know when the demons vanished. I only knew that we reached Nôtre Dame and Mord was still playing, though the violin glowed, runnels of flame blue along the bow, the joins of the instrument incandescent.

We reached the bell tower. We reached the portal . . . and we fell out of the *Nasdrafus*, into the real world through the mirror we'd first gone through, back into that small antechamber just off the ballroom in the von Mecklundburg castle. Aurélie and Jaska laughed unsteadily with relief. Mord looked more like a mad prophet than ever as he flexed his hands, in which the magic violin, Mozart's gift, had burned to ash. Then he gently helped Elisheva, who nearly collapsed as they stepped away from thin air onto the terrace next to the kylix fountain. They were at the Eyrie, and all four looked my way.

I was still in their time. Not where I'd hoped to be.

FORTY-NINE

———————※———————

A
T FIRST, the terrace looked the same as it had when we left, but we
perceived subtle differences: some seemed taller, and the colors
were not the fresh light green of spring, but the crackling deep greens
and lemon yellows of late summer.

"We've missed weeks. Maybe months," Jaska said, straightening up.
The stiff way he moved, the pain he tried to hide, made it clear that his
bad knee was the same as it had been before. His face was drawn, the
planes shadowed by faint lines.

"We might have been gone longer," Elisheva said.

"How do you know that?" Mord asked as he helped her to her feet.

She ducked her head. "I made a vow not to talk about what they said
to me when I was prisoned in that place, for that would be to give their
words added power." She wiped her hands down her dress—her rumpled, grimy dress. Now that they were in the real world, they all showed
the effects of time.

Elisheva turned her bruised, tired eyes to me as she wiped absently
at grime on her face. "You are still a ghost."

"Yes," I said, trying to hide the sharpness of disappointment. "Then
there's still something to be done. Maybe the Blessing and their marriage
will free me?"

Elisheva's eyelids flickered. Then she straightened her shoulders. "I'll not hazard a guess at this moment." But she knew something.

I didn't press her, as she seemed barely able to hold it together. The other three looked tired, but she looked beyond exhausted. I could almost feel her effort to marshal the last of her strength as she said, "The mirrors will still be dangerous, but I was taught that there's a portal at Angel Xanpia's Fountain. Shall we try it? We know how to use portals now, and the necklace should provide the Vrajhus to make the transfer possible."

"What will happen if the Vrajhus fails?" Aurélie asked. "Will we go back to that terrible place?"

"I think only that we must beg a ride down the mountainside to Angel Xanpia's Fountain," Elisheva said.

They took hands. I took hold of Aurélie's shoulder—I don't know if she felt my grip, as I could see her ruined gown through my shimmery fingers. The transfer was too quick. It felt more like we'd been shoved by an invisible hand. We fell into the water of Xanpia's Fountain, the four of them getting thoroughly soaked.

Being invisible, I didn't get wet. I gazed up at the smiling face of the stone statue, hoping that Xanpia would come forward and tell me that I was nearly done, but nothing happened.

It was dawn, the sun crowning Dsaret mountain. Very few people were about. The only one who noticed the sudden appearance of four persons splashing in the fountain was an old man driving a couple of cows toward Prinz Karl-Rafael Street. He did a double-take, his bearded face expressing astonishment as the four sloshed over the low rim of the fountain, Mord helping Jaska. I was shocked to see gray strands in Mord's hair at his temples, and faint lines around Jaska's eyes. Both Elisheva and Aurélie looked subtly different, the contours of their faces planed somewhat of the roundness of youth. There were silvery strands among the red in Elisheva's hair. All four had aged.

They wrung their clothes out as best they could and started up the street toward the great square, shedding water at every step. Aurélie's once-beautiful ball gown was a spectacular mess, the once-pretty green ribbons trailing like seaweed.

About a block and a half later a patrol of King's Guard trotted up. Cue astonishment: "The king?"

"The king!"

Their profound shock would have been funny except for the consternation that was so clear in those wide eyes and open mouths. Their consternation was reflected in Jaska as he breathed, "The *king*?"

Half the patrol was sent galloping, and the other half closed protectively around Jaska, though there was no attacker. Maybe they were trying to keep him from vanishing again.

The reason became clear when we reached the palace a short time later, and Margit came flying out, heedless of her dignity. Her face was careworn, her silk gown was the gray of half-mourning. "Jaska," she cried, and we could see faint lines at the corners of her eyes, same as her brother's. "Jaska, you are back!"

She flung herself into his arms. "Ten years," she cried. "Jaska, it's been ten *years*."

"I think . . . I can explain," Elisheva said faintly.

"Let us get her inside." Mord's voice was urgent.

"Please forgive me," Jaska said to his sister, who motioned hovering servants to help Mord with Elisheva. Despite her efforts, she was tottering. "We were striving beyond our knowledge," Jaska said, "almost beyond our strength. But we did finally prevail."

A crowd was fast forming. Jaska turned around and raised his voice. "I am home. This time, for good."

A cheer went up, tentative at first then gathering force.

"Come inside," Margit murmured, as a new figure appeared in the door to the palace—Benedek Ysvorod, hair gray at the temples, otherwise looking fit and aware. Kingly.

His brows lifted, then he bowed. If there was an air of mockery— yeah, Jaska saw it, all right—nothing was said out loud as I followed them into the palace. Behind us, the King's Guard began clearing everyone away.

"Mother?" Jaska asked.

Margit stopped and took his hands. "She died two years ago."

He winced, his head bowing.

They continued on into one of the state rooms, and she shut the door, then stood with her back to it. "She believed to the end that you were in the Nasdrafus, that you were doing something about this terrible situation."

"What situation?" Jaska asked.

But Margit swept on. "You vanished so suddenly the night before Gabrielle's wedding. No trace. We let the word spread that you had gone to the Nasdrafus on our behalf, because oh, Jaska, Aurélie, it was just as you predicted." She turned to Aurélie. "d'Enghien assassinated, Bonaparte declaring himself emperor. And then he marched against the empire, and in the Year Nine, against *Russia*. France against Russia. All Europe was a battlefield. The campaign was disastrous even for Bonaparte, who until then could not be beaten. So we had the fear of reprisal when they retreated, marauding where they could to stay alive."

"So Dobrenica escaped?"

"Only because their road lay to the north. But he is back, and the goal is Dresden—and beyond. So much of Europe lies in ruins. And it seems we are about to join them." She paused as Jaska took a quick step, and stumbled. "Jaska, what happened?"

"Nothing. It's only my knee. I forgot about it. . . . Never mind that, I must know everything. I must make amends." The stress was shifting from her to him.

"Here," she said in a practical tone. "Permit us to first get you fed and rested. Though things are dire, you all look travel worn. Ten years! I will tell you everything."

"I am to understand that Benedek has not been crowned, then?"

Margit colored. "I said I'd marry him, but not . . . He understood. Jaska, he's been my mainstay. He offered the dukes and the Grand Council five years after Mother died, at which time we would have to declare you dead. And they accepted because everyone feels, especially in these times, that we must have a king."

"Is Hippolyte safe?"

"Oh, he returned long ago. The year you left, as you commanded. And our legation was closed before the French invaded Vienna. He's been wonderful—he's our main source of information. Has contacts everywhere, and Irena stayed true, but the duke won't permit them to marry. You know why."

"Hippolyte shall be declared a baron the day we're crowned," Jaska promised, holding tightly to Aurélie's hand. "I'd make him a duke if we had another mountain." He turned his head. "Mordechai, I wish you would reconsider. A barony is all I have to give you, and it would never repay my debt."

Mord had been whispering to Elisheva, who was reclining in a deep chair, the needs of the moment transcending royal protocol. He lifted his head at that. "I cannot accept." And at Jaska's weary disappointment, he said, "I am honored. Deeply. But I am wary of secular rank. I believe my father was right that such things draw attention to us, and attention is never good for Jews in a Christian world."

"Not here," Jaska protested, clearly distraught. "Not in Dobrenica."

Elisheva struggled to sit upright. "That must wait."

Everyone fell silent and gathered around her chair. She gripped Mord's hand tightly, as if to draw strength as she struggled to lift her voice. "Their plan was this: to keep you ensorcelled until Napoleon and his wars reached Dobrenica. In the resulting slaughter, they would gain enough power to take the Esplumoir, the gate between worlds. Remember: there are only three on all the earth, and one is here. It has been their goal all along."

She turned to look my way, then dropped her gaze. Uh-oh.

"But the demons have not won yet," Margit declared and smiled thinly at her brother. "If the cheer I heard today is indicative, we might have our true peace at last. If so, on September 2nd, we shall be able to evoke the Blessing. We can be rid of the demons altogether!"

Elisheva shook her head minutely, but the others didn't notice because Mord took them all by surprise. "After what we just experienced, I can trust it is possible. But . . . if we are closed from the world, how does the Messiah find us if he comes?"

Aurélie whispered to Jaska, "And if we are closed away forever, that means I will never again see my family?"

Elisheva drew a deep breath and turned her grave gaze upward to meet Mord's. "Mordechai, our rabbi, may he be forever blessed, can answer your question. Our rabbinical father wrote many centuries ago to the Ari-Hakadosh, the most holy, who said, that surely, when the Messiah comes, he will have the power to bring us all together, wherever we have scattered."

"Then my only wish, besides to marry you, Elisheva *bashert*—" Mord turned from her to Jaska, "—is to start a music school. With music, I know where I am in the world."

Elisheva flicked a glance at Aurélie. "Nothing on Earth is forever. The enchantment of the Blessing breaks when any of us break the peace, or cross the border into the outer world. If Bonaparte ceases to be a threat, well, then we shall re-engage with the world."

"And you can bring your family here, Aurélie," Jaska said to her. "And welcome."

She clasped her hands with joy, as Elisheva closed her eyes again.

Margit said across Elisheva to Aurélie, "Those letters, do you remember writing them? Of course you do, if it was only days ago for you. I sent the letters off. I think it was two or three years after that, one summer, we received via the Swedish legation a trunk of rose slips sent by your cousin, a Mrs. Charles Kittredge. We could not lay them by, of course, and not knowing what you wished done, we divided them to see where they would grow best. My share I planted myself, out there by the gazebo as a reminder of, oh, many things. I think you understand me?"

"I do," Aurélie said. "And I thank you."

"Then this very year, she sent another letter, along with a book. The book is in English, so we do not know if is fiction or philosophy, but Hippolyte translated the formidable title, *Pride and Prejudice*. We have it laid by." She shook her head. "But all that can wait. Is it the Blessing, then, that we need?"

Elisheva had been resting her head against the back of the chair while this conversation was going on.

Jaska said to her, "Forgive me, Elisheva. I know you need rest, and I believe a room is in preparation for you right now. But I must understand: Can we wait until September? Must we wait until September? Will the Blessing protect the kingdom from these demons? It troubles me, when you mention the Esplumoir."

Elisheva opened her eyes again, and once again struggled to sit up. "We know that the demons feed upon the violence and desolation of war. It will strengthen them. I fear that, because they know we are now in our world, they will use whatever influence they can to bring the war to us the sooner, because their goal is to take control of the Esplumoir."

"Why?" Aurélie asked. "It sounds like it's another portal."

Jaska shook his head, and Margit said, "The *Salfmattas* guard the Esplumoir, so that balance is maintained between all the spheres. The worlds. It is better to close it to all than surrender it to those with evil intent. If the demons do not take control of it, the Esplumoir will eventually restore itself."

"Then we must close it," Jaska said.

I thought Elisheva had looked bad before. She blanched as if the vamps had teleported all her blood. Her lips moved. Mord and Aurélie both bent to hear her, then Aurélie looked up, her eyes huge.

"Human *sacrifice?*" she whispered.

FIFTY

"RUMOR." Elisheva's voice was a thread. "The demons declared that it will only close if someone living walks into it, and we know they never return. I don't know if it's true. Or half-true. I don't know enough. We must talk to the Elders!"

Mord knelt down at her side, sending a quick, unhappy frown up at the others, but before he could speak, Margit stepped between Elisheva's chair and everybody else. "But you won't. If the world is to end tonight, then so be it. We've lived with the threat of Napoleon's demonic intent these ten years and more. Another night won't make a difference, but I'm afraid any more talk, and it'll be the end for Elisheva." When the others made murmurs of agreement, she said, "Everyone is to rest, and no more speech."

Jaska began to protest.

Margit took his hands. "Just this once, let me be queen. You can barely stand. Go and rest, Jaska. I shall send an equerry to the Clares. Before this night is done, I intend to consult with Sister Mathilde. If she knows nothing, then we'll make a journey to the Eldest. Nothing will be decided before morning."

They began to disperse, Aurélie walking between Margit and Jaska toward her old room—away from me.

Away from me.

I was not bound to her.

And so, because I didn't need to bother with eating, drinking, or catching my breath, I thought, why don't I go to the Esplumoir on my own? Who was to stop me? Yeah, going by foot to Dsaret mountain seemed a long trek, but it wasn't like my feet could hurt. I just needed someone to open the door.

I followed the equerry who carried the message to the nun Margit wished to consult. As soon as he got the door open, I started to run.

I don't know how long it took me. Time was so strange, so untrustworthy. It might have been that night, or a couple of days later. The last time I'd come that way was on a sleigh in winter, two centuries forward, but enough of the biggest landmarks tugged at memory to guide me, and so I arrived at last, late at night, on the cliff that I remembered so well.

It was different. Wider. A standing stone had been erected directly below the cliff. It was a shrine to St. Xanpia, with religious symbols belonging to the three main faiths of Dobrenica, side by side, carved into the stone in medieval lettering. The shrine glowed in moonlight.

I looked around the peaceful valley, feeling disconnected, unreal. Ghostly.

That thought was sufficiently disturbing to send me the last few steps toward the cave. As I passed through the mossy crevasse, I wondered what I was doing there. What could I possibly learn?

I had no idea, except for the fact that the Blessing, if it even worked, was not going to be enough. There was something else needed, something to close the Esplumoir . . . and I knew who had closed the Esplumoir a century and a half later: Grandfather Armandros.

I also knew how.

That was the memory driving me across the kingdom.

I walked into the cave, feeling for Vrajhus—for any sign of strangeness, or rather, extra strangeness, as my existence at that moment was (I'd thought) at maximum weird.

I'd gone maybe ten paces into the cave when I was startled by a jolt like a three-point quake on the Richter scale, followed by a flash of light. Then the beating red of fire.

I whirled around, ran to the entrance, then skidded back instinctively, though I had no body to catch fire. The peaceful forested hillside and shrine I'd just seen had transformed to an inferno. I watched debris rain down around the ruined shape of a crashed plane as fireballs roiled upward. The air shivered with heat waves.

"Damn."

I jumped. Next to me stood a man in a shabby German general issue field uniform, with Lancer's tabs on the shoulders, a cigarette hanging from his lips. "My wits seemed to have been blasted to bits with the hillside"

"Armandros?" I yelped. My grandfather was the one who had closed the Esplumoir in the last days of World War II. He'd sacrificed his own life by crashing a plane directly into this mountain, obliterating the cave entrance.

Where we stood now.

He saluted with two fingers, a casual, mocking gesture. "In the flesh. *Am* I in the flesh? I sighted on the damn shrine. They said it glowed in the dark. Didn't believe a word of it. Until I saw the winged devils." He took a drag on the cigarette, pointed downward at what was probably supposed to be the cockpit floor, and went on conversationally, "Cut the dive brakes before I took 'er up. Rammed the dive stick back. Shut the flaps. And when she rolled, I lit this fag so I wouldn't see the shrine heading for my head. Then all I saw were stars." He grinned. "And now you."

"You closed the Esplumoir," I said.

His smile vanished. "Couldn't undo what I'd done to the country by taking Lily away and setting everyone at one another's throats. But by all the devils in hell I could stop Maritza from letting 'em in through here." He jerked his chin over his shoulder at the dark interior of the cave, the flames reflecting in his eyes.

"Maritza?"

"Stone mason's girl. Rescued me after I blew up a Boche ammo dump, and the patrol shot out the tires on my motorcycle. I went over a cliff. She picked up the pieces. Sewed me back together." His grin was slanting and wicked. "Had a hankering to be a duchess. Or better."

Maritza was the mother of that psychopath Jerzy, I thought, shivering.

"She thought I was too drunk to see 'em but I saw. I could stomach her consorting with the vampires. Our family has a pact with 'em. Did you know that? Of course you do, you're one of us, I can see it in your crooked mouth." He shook his head as he looked at the inferno blazing a few steps beyond us, the burning bits of foliage and wood and metal raining all around us. "I couldn't let her hand over the damn gate to those winged devils—either them or the Russians." His expression changed to question. "I've seen you before. Which one are you?"

I looked out at that inferno, trying to frame an answer, but when I decided on the truth—why not? It wasn't like talking to a ghost would change the timeline—I looked back, and he was gone.

"Kim."

I turned, and there was the inferno again.

No, it wasn't an inferno, it was the steady light of morning, revealing the peaceful valley. The shrine was silhouetted in the cave mouth. Slanting beams of light revealed several figures, Aurélie in the lead, looking solemn and determined. Behind her came a group of people, still in shadow.

"Elisheva said you would come here," Aurélie addressed me. "Sister Mathilde has been explaining things to me."

"The gate has to close against the demons," I said. "They're going to try to take it. Somebody has to close it. And if a life has to be given up, it had better be mine. You have a life here." *You have a place in history, and I don't.* If I'd had a body, I would have had clammy hands and a dry mouth. The physical sensations were not there, only the sorrow, as I said, "This is why I'm here. Was all along. Apparently it's my task."

"No, it is mine," she said, but on a note of question, and I suspected she'd been arguing with the others.

"It's not," I said. "I saw your happy ending. You can't change the future, or it will ruin how many lives?"

She was fingering the necklace. "It's this," she said. "It's not the spending of a life, it's the necklace that has the power to close the Esplumoir."

"What?"

Her smile was sad. "The *Salfmattas* say only that whoever bears it into the Esplumoir will not return. It was given to me, and so mine is the responsibility."

She lifted her graceful hand toward the others. "They've tried to argue, but I know what's right, and mine is the honor, and the task. Faith and good will and Vrajhus, those three will shut out the demons." She jerked around, her shoulders tight, as tears slipped down her cheeks. "Elisheva, you said there is a song that must be sung?"

"Wait," I said, my nerves flashing hot and then cold as the last puzzle piece fell into place. "It all might be true, except for one thing. You would never sell the necklace, or let evil beings take it, but you can give it to someone, just like Nanny Hiasinte did. Aurélie, give the necklace to me. And I will walk into the Esplumoir and close it off. Then your duty is to marry and make the Blessing happen, to keep out Napoleon's soldiers."

She paused, head to one side, and again I saw the tears she had been trying to hide. At her shoulder stood Jaska. He drew in a sharp breath, his pained expression turning to hope. Holding his hand was Margit, looking sorrowful.

Aurélie waited, her pulse beating in her throat.

"Nanny Hiasinte did say I would bear it. Maybe that's now. We both have our duties," I said. "And you and I know we can touch, even if no one else can touch me."

She said, "You would do this for me?"

"For you, for Jaska. For Dobrenica." *For our future, though I don't know if I'm in it.* "Hey, what's the worst that can happen?" I tried for a joking tone. "Go and be happy."

She drew her sleeve across her eyes then slowly held out the necklace. For the last time my fingers touched hers, and the golden chain transferred to my hands and dangled there.

Quickly Elisheva began to sing "Xanpia's Wreath." She didn't have her sister's beautiful voice, but joy infused the words anyway, because Aurélie was not walking into the unknown in order to shut the Esplumoir.

Margit, Mord, Jaska, and several people I didn't know joined hands one by one and began to sing.

I stepped deeper into the cave, which glimmered with a tracery of glowing light. With Alec's image in my mind, I said softly, "This is for Dobrenica, Alec. If anyone will understand, it would be you."

I took a giant step.

FIFTY-ONE

AND I CAME OUT ON A HILLSIDE that overlooked the entire valley of Dobrenica, my hands empty. The necklace had vanished. Immediately below me lay the city of Riev.

The *modern* city of Riev. There were all the buildings Alec had showed me on my first visit.

And I was still a ghost.

I whirled around, and there behind me was the ancient mosaic dating back to Roman times. Behind it, the Romanesque church.

"Is it not beautiful?"

I turned. Xanpia perched on a rock overlooking the city in the early light, her light brown braids untidy. She still wore her bulky knit top and a skirt embroidered with flowers and leaves. "Well done," she said, smiling. "*Well* done!"

"But I'm not me," I said. "Was that it, then? I'm a ghost?"

"You walked in the spirit realm." She smiled. "It was the only way that wouldn't cost someone dear. You are free, now. You'll find yourself as soon as you walk again through the painted door."

"I'll be in my body again?"

"Yes."

"Aging and everything?" I had a horrid thought. "Am I ten years older?"

"No. Because you were only in spirit form, your body was beyond reach of the demons."

Up I jumped. "Then I am outta here." Running so lightly that I did not disturb any of the summer grasses, I skimmed down the pathway that the young girls would walk, or had walked, on August 15th, for centuries, and I skirted the back of the palace.

There was the gazebo, surrounded by a wild, high hedge of rambling roses. Beyond that, past the Vigilzhi annex, to the main gates, standing open.

The square. There was the fading hammer and sickle.

The triumphal arch of 1813—whose purpose I now knew: It was built by Jaska, and I knew why.

The Renaissance buildings . . .

The painted door.

I reached with trembling hands for that painted latch. Music beckoned, a familiar melody that I loved. I plunged into the glare-bright doorway.

My chest felt as if an elephant had stepped on it. I gave a gasp, sucking in air. I coughed and opened sticky eyes, and the first thing I saw was Alec's beloved face, so worn, so tired, but as our eyes met, his lips parted, and he gave a wordless cry and crushed me in his arms.

FIFTY-TWO

GRADUALLY I BECAME AWARE that there were people in the room. A kid with a shock of messy dark hair put his flute down and beamed at me.

"Misha?" I said from Alec's arms.

I discovered I was not strong enough to sit up on my own. But that was okay. Alec could hold me, oh yes.

Alec wiped his eyes with his free hand. "Misha offered to come play for you. He picked all your favorites. In fact, several of the students from the temple school have been coming in rotation to play for you, all sworn to secrecy. But it was 'Aurelia's Air' that just now did the trick. I didn't know you knew that piece."

"I didn't," I said, "until recently. Aurélie wrote that when she was about thirteen, and they played it—*Mom?*"

My mother dropped down on her knees beside my bed. "Kimli, darling," she said. "They wouldn't let me up here. They didn't want me seeing you stretched out like a stoned vamp. What the hell happened?"

"Water first. Please? How long has it been?"

Alec peered into my face. "It was a month ago. Natalie and Beka found you lying on the ground near those old buildings off Roskvit Square, near the painted door. When you didn't show up for lunch they came to me, then went out to reconstruct your path. By the time we got you back here, you'd nearly turned to stone, and Beka said there was Vrajhus involved. Nat agreed. Said that your state was a medical impossibility, therefore we should back off from medically invasive cures. Kim, you breathed maybe once an hour." He said in a low voice, "Three nights ago that slowed to once a day." He thumbed a strand of hair off my cheek. "We kept it a secret, but we've traded off watching over you."

"I saw you," I said. "And I called to you." It took all my strength to say that much, especially since he crushed me in another hug. It felt wonderful.

"I heard you," he murmured into my hair. "I thought I was going mad."

Everyone gave way before my grandmother, who leaned down to kiss my forehead. "Aurelia Kim. It is good to see you awake." To the others. "Perhaps, in addition to the water she asked for, a meal?"

A couple hours later, after I'd got some bread and soup into me, and about a gallon of water, we began the catch-up process. Alec told me that they'd gone right ahead with the wedding plans, as a way to fend off curiosity. "We told them you had caught a violent cold."

"What is the date, anyway?" I asked.

"August 13th," he said.

"Then I'm in time for the March of the Innocents. Good."

He said with concern, "Don't you think you'd better take it easy?"

"I've *been* taking it easy. Too easy. I want to be there, Alec. I know we're not worrying about the Blessing anymore. It's important for other reasons. I can't even explain them to myself yet. It just is."

"Then you'll be there," he said, "if I have to carry you myself."

But I rapidly regained strength. I hadn't been in a coma, in which muscles waste and organs shut down.

I hadn't aged, either. My physical self could not be harmed by those demons, even if they'd tried to lure my spirit to stay and dance forever. I had been enchanted into a state not unlike stone. When I found that out, I ventured a joke about how they could have set me up in a garden with the vamps, but nobody found it funny.

It's eerie, how mutable time can seem. Here I'd been away for nearly twenty years, sort of—about ten years of Aurélie's life and then ten years in the Nasdrafus, and it felt like a weekend marathon of movie watching. But for the people who loved me, in my time, it had seemed an eternity, even though only a month had passed. They'd had the tough time, not me. I dropped the feeble attempts at humor.

That first night, Alec and I sat up until dawn, mostly me talking. He didn't want to leave. I think he was afraid I'd wink out a second time.

The next day, Beka Ridotski showed up, and I had to go through it all again. But this time it was easier. I didn't go into the personal side the way I had with Alec. I kept it to the magical, with side-trips into history.

She liked hearing about her greats-grandfather Shmuel, and she leaned forward with interest when I told her I'd met Elisheva. It turns out that she's famous among the *Salfmattas*—she and Mordechai both. He's known for having established the temple music school the way it is now, making it top notch in spite of Dobrenica being so small. And what few know is that magical charms are taught along with the music.

I ended with, "And so, at least, the timeline is preserved, because all they knew of me was that I was a ghost. They thought I was English, because there was no record of me in Dobrenica's history."

"Actually," Beka said, "that's not true."

My turn to be surprised. "You're kidding! You mean I went to all that trouble to preserve the timeline for nothing?"

"Not quite." Beka grinned, her light brown eyes narrowed with sardonic humor. "The ghost named Kim who closed the Esplumoir is a legend among the *Salfmattas*, a well-known, extremely well kept secret. Your sudden appearance, your name, your ability to see the past worried people quite a bit. We didn't know what it meant, you see: the young *English* ghost named Kim." Her smile faded. "Over New Year's, when you told me about your visions, I figured it might be you, though no one could explain the English connection, since no one in your family had ever been to England until you went for your first visit. I was afraid it meant you would not survive the year, because how else would you become a ghost? But I didn't dare tell you that. It would be horrible, especially if we were wrong."

"That definitely would have been horrible," I said feelingly. "And that convinces me more than anything that I was right not to tell Aurélie who I was, or what I knew about her life. But I am really glad I didn't know when she dies."

"She lived a good life. They both did. Their three daughters married into the Ysvorods, the Trasyemovas, and the von Mecklundburgs respectively. It was the son of the eldest daughter who brought the crown back to the Ysvorods, and in turn their grandson who was Alexander IV."

"Did Mord and Elisheva have kids?"

"Oh, yes. Three. Their sons both moved away from Dobrenica. One died as a revolutionary in one of the eighteen forty-eight uprisings, the other went on to a career in Vienna, playing for the royal orchestra. Their daughter took over the school."

"Did Aurélie's family ever show up?"

"No, and now I understand some odd context." Beka smiled. "They wrote many letters back and forth. Burned by the Soviets when the archive went up in flames, but someone somewhere had copied out portions of them, and that is what we have. Anyway, her mother kept putting off the visit, then finally admitted she couldn't stick going anywhere away from the sea, especially corseted. I remember debate in my royal history class about what that might have meant."

"It meant she couldn't stand corsets," I said, laughing.

Beka flashed a smile. "The last letter made it clear that they were settled in San Francisco, having established a trading enterprise. They were bringing in gold miners when the letters ceased."

"Okay, here's my last question. If the *Salfmattas* knew that I, as a ghost, closed the Esplumoir back then, why were we struggling so hard over New Year's find out what and where it was?"

Her nose wrinkled in a quick grimace. "Remember that I told you knowledge was passed verbally to novices one at a time, according to internal standards? The knowledge about the Esplumoir, which had not been opened for all those generations, was only known to the Elders. The oldest was a victim of the Gestapo fairly early on. You know that the Nazis were secretly seeking information about magic in any form."

"Yes, that's generally known. There are even TV shows about the Nazis and their crackpot theories about supernatural powers."

"I have been told that real mages often saw to it that false facts were passed to them, to keep them haring off down the paths of superstition and futility and bypassing real power, because their intent was evil from the beginning. But anyway, we Dobreni lost a lot of knowledge, and so we were trying to reconstruct it all last year. I suspect that Aurélie's necklace lies somewhere inside that mountain."

"Or it's caught somewhere in the Nasdrafus."

"I think some of the present Elders hope that *their* Elders are somewhere in the Nasdrafus, but that is not known. Grandmother Ziglieri, whom you have met, said her Elders feared demons were working on the Esplumoir to open it again, while the war raged all around. We didn't know that Jerzy von Mecklundburg's mother, Maritza the Stone mason's daughter, was the one helping them by gleaning what information she could get. Your encounter with Duke Armandros has cleared up some mysteries. He must've overheard her, or maybe she even bragged to him, not realizing that she would stir his latent loyalties."

"I wonder if we'll ever see him again," I said.

"You," Beka said, getting to her feet. "Not we. You are the one who sees ghosts."

"I hope I *was* the one to see ghosts," I corrected. "I am ready for a nice, boring, ghost-free and Vrajhus-free life now."

I said that, but it wasn't really true. What I wanted was no more surprises, magical or ghostly. When I got out of the car on the 15th, on the top of the mountain near the Roman church, shivering in my white gown, I did have ghosts in mind, but my experiment was one of intent.

August is usually a beautiful month in Dobrenica. Seldom hot, and that only for a few hours in the day. If there is rain, it's generally an afternoon thunderstorm, well-behaved enough to roll over the mountains by sunset, leaving a clean-washed sky.

The morning was chilly but promised warmth when the sun came up behind us. There I found a dozen or so girls and young women waiting, some in elaborate white dresses that they had made themselves or that had been handed down for generations. Everyone had a wreath of white flowers on her head.

The March of the Innocents was usually brides-to-be but could be any young woman at a milestone: someone going into a religious vocation, or these days, who had been promoted from journeyman to full-fledged artisan in her chosen career. There was no equivalent for the guys, as in the past, public parades of any kind had been a male thing, excepting only nobles and royalty on their way to festivals. There was only this one exception for the females.

My white gown had been bought the day before, the wreath made from flowers plucked in the Ysvorod garden by Madam Emilio, the household steward. The important object was the braided candle in my hand. Soul candles, Beka had told me, were a Jewish custom that had been adopted long ago by Dobrenica at large. A soul candle was three wicks braided during a lovely ritual, adapted to be distinctly Dobreni.

The eastern sky blued gently, blanketing the stars one by one. The blue had turned peach when the girls began to sing "Xanpia's Wreath."

Beka had told me that I, as the soon-to-be-princess, would be expected to light my candle first and touch the flame to the next girl's. So I did, meeting the smiling face of someone I didn't know. Her singing voice was pretty (as mine isn't), and strong enough to keep everybody around her on the right pitch.

From one to the next multiplied the flames, casting a glow over smiling faces, and then we started down the mountain path. The wildflowers, trees, and shrubs were in full bloom. There was the plateau where Alec and I had spent the night before I fled back to Los Angeles.

I waited until my walking rhythm was well established, and then it was time for my experiment. For some reason I existed in liminal space, so I meant to learn how to control it. I reached back a couple of centuries, to this very morning . . .

And there they were.

For Aurélie and Elisheva, Margit and Irena, it was a foggy morning. Their candles were much bigger than ours, and they walked arm in arm, their gowns silken, tied high in Empire style. They were not singing "Xanpia's Wreath" but a round that blended perfectly—a Jewish hymn, something Russian, and something in Latin. I wondered if Mord had found the music and made it match like that.

Aurélie walked with her face lifted, full of joy.

And then they were gone, and I was back, nearly stumbling over a rock. I hopped just in time, my candle flickering and splattering wax down my front. Ow.

It was full morning when we reached the palace garden, and a short while later the square, where families waited. Some separated off to go to church, basilica, or temple, others to be fêted at family breakfasts.

My breakfast was at the palace, with my parents, Gran, Alec, and soon-to-be-King Milo, Alec's father, whose health was frail these days. Also present were all the cousins: tall, stylish Phaedra Danilov and her brother, descendants of Captain Danilov of the King's Guard; Honoré de Vauban, baron, whose new house was nearly finished. I wondered how much he knew about his one-eyed diplomat forebear. Oh yes, he was an archivist. He'd know if anyone did.

The von Mecklundburgs were all there. Tony lounged in the background while watching me narrow-eyed, as though trying to figure out the mystery. Even Cerisette was there. She was blond again, perfectly turned out in the latest French fashion.

Her only comment was, "I trust you are well enough to favor me with a long overdue consultation. Unless you want your wedding to be a surprise?"

"I'll be there tomorrow," I said.

Tony cornered me at the end of breakfast, when everyone was talking to everyone else. "Cold feet?" he asked, one brow aslant.

I looked into his tilted black eyes, throwbacks to Aurélie's beautiful family. I don't know what he saw in my expression, but his altered to inquiry, and I said, "I saw Ruli."

That he did not expect. "And?"

"She was in Paris. I think she likes her new state. She seemed more self-assured."

He whistled softly. "You ran away to Paris?"

"I was sent there," I said. "No choice. And it was not the Paris you are accustomed to."

"I don't know whether to be relieved or terrified. About my sister, I mean."

"Both, I expect," I said, grinning.

After that, things became a whirl of activity: fittings, inspections, shifting belongings, tastings with Mom presiding. Everybody wanted to talk, and I rejoiced in all the details of daily life, from brushing snarls out of my hair (my ordinary hair, that needed some serious conditioning) to smelling wet grass after a rain. Even tired feet made me happy, because I was me again, and any time I wanted a hug and kiss, I could find Alec, and he dropped everything to offer them.

So I woke up on my wedding day, glad to find myself in my body, and in my time.

The problem with a perfect wedding is that superlatives seem to cancel one another out. The intensity of bliss was so poignant it was almost painful when I walked into the cathedral on my father's arm, his wild hair actually combed, and his usual aging-hippie clothes replaced by a tailored tux. "Look like Cary Grant, don't I?" he muttered out of the side of his mouth as we started down the aisle, which was decorated with flowers from the palace garden.

"Better," I whispered back. "A better Cary Grant. With a beard."

Alec looked fantastic in his elegant suit with the vaguely Edwardian line. My gown was a copy of my great-grandmother's, taken from her portrait: lace over silk, with white pearls embroidered at the neck and tight sleeves.

Memory comes in shards after that: Alec's tight grip on my hands, as if to keep me anchored; Gran wiping her eyes; Tony flashed his challenging grin from the first pew. Tania, wearing sea green velvet, in the first row with her younger sister Teresa and her best friend Miriam. Those teenage girls had been a great help to me, and I'd insisted they sit up front. Next to Tania was Natalie Miller, giving me a private thumbs up when our eyes met.

Then the choir began one of the songs that Mord had adapted, and flash! I saw the past. They were all there, not just Jaska and Aurélie kneeling at the altar side by side, but faint and shimmering Queen Sofia, who was the first ghost I had ever seen. She seemed to be looking right at me, her smile benevolent.

But I did not want to slip into the past. I blinked, willed them back into their time, and I was safely restored to mine.

After the wedding came the coronation part. It was a simple ceremony, involving hereditary crowns for Milo, Alec, Gran, and me, worn only for the duration of the ceremony. We each had vows to make, echoed back by the nobles, the Council, and then representatives of various professional guilds. The vows were much the same as they had been for many years. Probably Jaska had said the same words. Though monarchy was officially re-established after all those years of occupation, the agreement by the citizenry was an active thing, not passive: it was a conspiracy to invent the fiction of nobility, with all its constraints and obligations as well as the perks.

And then it was done.

We exited following King Milo, who walked with straight back, his hand tight on his cane, Gran at his side. Alec had gone in as Statthalter, but walked out as Crown Prince, arm in arm with me in my newly minted Princess Aurelia persona.

We stopped in a side room and shed the crowns, which would go back to live in their vault until the next special occasion.

Then came the parade. Mom and Tony had gotten the Bugatti cleaned up and running, and there it was, second in line, a dashingly handsome car. You could only call it archeo-modern, as it was so old-fashioned it was cool.

Milo and Gran led the parade in the huge car I thought of as the Kingmobile, a '36 Mercedes-Benz Special Roadster. We drove in a circle along Riev's four biggest streets, which had been decorated with flowers of every hue by the citizens. People flung flowers into our open car until Alec and I sat in a sweet-smelling moat of blossoms. At various streets, representatives of guilds—mostly little kids in their very best clothes—presented us with symbolic gifts, and we gave them symbolic bags of coins, the speeches pretty much the same over and over, but at least they were short.

We started off from the cathedral going south, so we did not reach Xanpia's Fountain until near the end of our loop. It was then, with the light just so, and the angle one I seldom took, that I happened to glance up at the statue itself. Usually I paid attention to the ghost shapes of animals and figures dancing in and out of liminal space around the fountain. Now it was Xanpia who drew my attention, though she didn't do anything unnerving. The stone was just that, a carved smiling face, the lines blurred by ten centuries.

"What is it?" Alec asked, instantly concerned. I hadn't been aware until that moment how intently he'd been observing me, and it struck me again that my long absence had been much harder on him than on me.

"Xanpia seemed really nice, but I hope I never meet her again."

He reached for my hand. Our fingers laced, and tightened.

When we got back to the palace we changed out of our wedding clothes for the reception for the Five Families and the Council, after which everybody took a break to change into their evening clothes for the grand ball.

It came off brilliantly. The weather was perfect. I couldn't help remembering the last time I'd danced on that marble floor, and of course Tony had to tease me about it. I made sure (from a distance) that Cerisette, looking impossibly elegant in her favorite Balenciaga, got the compliments she deserved for masterminding the entire day. At least we could work professionally, I thought, which was a step in the right direction. When she arrived home after the ball, she'd find my thanks in the form of a trip for two to Paris, a stay in her favorite hotel, the Renaissance Paris Vendôme, and tickets to what Phaedra said were her favorite places.

Alec and I danced together six times.

"Not too shabby," Nat said to us during one of those dances, as she and her current sweetheart twirled by.

I looked across the crowded ballroom, where everyone seemed to be having a good time, to the cluster of teen girls in their new finery. A weed of a boy who couldn't have been more than seventeen, obviously in his first tux, was tentatively approaching the girls, his huskier best bud at his shoulder. From the way the girls were whispering and poking at red-haired Miriam, she seemed to be embarking on the deep waters of a first dance.

Then we spun away.

An hour or so before dawn everybody started for home. This palace was now to be my home, Milo and Gran taking over Ysvorod House. The restoration work wasn't completely done upstairs in the palace, but that was okay, because we wouldn't be there.

I thought about Aurélie and Jaska on their way up to Sedania, the Dsaret hunting lodge back in those days, for their honeymoon.

I had no idea where we were going. This was Alec's surprise for me. We changed one more time and then climbed into his new Daimler, suitcases already in the back. Alec slid into the driver's seat and I next to him. I looked at him. He looked at me.

Next thing I knew we were in each other's arms. For a while it seemed like we weren't going to get out of the driveway, but eventually we pried ourselves apart, and he started driving. "You're going to like this," he said, grinning.

"As long it doesn't involve ghosts, powerful artifacts, portals, or duels, I'm easy."

"Maybe a duel. But only one."

"Oh, well, I can handle that. Did you remember to pack swords, or is it dueling pistols?"

"Trunk is an arsenal. You can take your pick."

It was going to take a while to extricate my thoughts from the past. "The truth is, I kind of liked popping demons. I totally agree with what Aurélie said, and I'm glad she freed them, even if they didn't seem to know what to do with freedom. But . . . the cause seemed so right, and fighting them was fun. Does that make me a bad person?"

Alec said, "It means you are human, with all that implies, good and bad. I have to confess that when you told me about it, my strongest reaction was the wish that I could have been fighting demons at your side."

"Oh, I love that image."

"Fighting demons?" He cast me an amused glance.

"No! Us. Side by side."